Lucy Smoke

BADDIES

Wicked Dark Heathens

"It is only in love and murder that we still remain sincere."

—Friedrich Dürrenmatt

PROLOGUE
RYLIE

"Give in," he whispers.

"Said the spider to the fly," I reply.

The deep, reverberating chuckle that leaves him rumbles against my back and I have to hold my breath to resist the urge to flip over and face him. Why does he affect me this way? Why does he drive me to absolute insanity with just the sound of his voice? "Oh, Riot Girl, you're not a fly. You're so much more than that."

"If I'm so much more, then why am I here?" I ask seriously. "Tangled up in your web like any other girl."

"Because you're smart," he says. "You know a predator when you see one, and you know when that predator wants to eat you in the most delicious way."

My eyes slide shut as his hand delves down and tugs my shirt up. Warm, rough, masculine fingers slip into my panties and spear through my wetness. He groans against my ear. "Maybe you know far more than you'd like me to think," he says. "Definitely more than you're willing to admit. What I wouldn't give to hear you say it..."

Is that what he wants? For me to say it. I never have. Not once. I don't know if I can.

My lips part and I arch as he flicks my clit, and then rubs that little bundle of nerves in a circle—slow and then fast. My hips lift to meet his movements and I follow him, chasing the feelings he elicits in me. I can't stop. He's like a fucking addiction I can't stop myself from wanting. Sparks flicker to life behind my closed eyelids. Warm breaths escape my mouth in soft pants. It's never felt like this before. Like I'm poised on the edge of a cliff about to dive into an abyss. I've certainly never wanted it the way I want him.

"That's it, Riot Girl," he says, his mouth trailing alongside my jaw as he brushes my hair back with his free hand. "Ride my hand. Get my fingers soaking wet. Give me a taste of this sweet pussy."

My head thrashes against his shoulder and the bed. "I can't," I say, panting. "I can't." This is wrong. *He's* wrong—so fucking wrong for me. I shouldn't want this. No, I think. That's just my fear talking. Abel isn't wrong. He's ... everything that's right. The only right thing that I've ever let myself have.

"You can," he urges me, and suddenly, his fingers aren't just on my clit, they're pushing even further down—dipping inside as his thumb takes over the task of driving me insane. His thick fingers push into my core, spearing me, and the rumble of a groan in his chest vibrates through me as he finds out just how wet I really am. I was never like this before, but with him, with Abel, I'm starting to realize that it doesn't matter what I've done before. He's wrecked everything in his path to get to me, completely destroyed my barriers and rebuilt them, sealing himself inside along with me.

Even if this doesn't last, for as long as I live, there will be a piece of Abel Frazier buried deep within my soul.

1

RYLIE

OBSESSION IS DANGEROUS. I know that better than most people. Daniel Dickerson is the perfect example of what happens when a man becomes too obsessed with something, with some*one*. Yet, still, I don't regret it. No matter how much his mother still believes that I'm a lying whore and there's no possible way her precious son could do the things that I claimed he did to a little girl, especially one as scrawny and ugly as me. No matter how my name has been dragged through the mud, and how many times I've been called everything under the sun. Liar. Wicked little girl. Jezebel. Whore. Slut.

The names only got worse as I got older. No matter where I go, the stories follow. The only place I've ever managed to find any sort of salvation is right here in Eastpoint. Now that salvation is being threatened, not only by my past but my obsession with the worst man I could've fucking chosen. My hand skates towards the bag at the end of my desk and the plastic crinkles as I reach inside only to come up with nothing but salty crumbs.

"Fuck." I'm out of chips. My stomach rumbles in protest. Skittles. God, I need some skittles. Or hell, I could go for

Twizzlers too. Maybe a Monster or a Mountain Dew. I wonder what would happen if I just chugged both—one right after the other. On one hand, it'll probably wake me the fuck up. On the other, it could also kill me. Death, however, feels preferable to this half-awake, foggy purgatory that I've been stuck in.

Scrunching my nose and leaning forward, I set my elbows on the edge of my desk and hang my head in my hands. *What the fuck am I doing?* I think. I know what I need to do. I need to just give in. I need to ask the Eastpoint heirs for help, and if they're unwilling, then I need to just disappear.

It's not the best option, but I know I can do it. I've planned for this moment; when I recognized that my world would get rocked once again. I just never expected it to happen so soon.

My cell goes off, and for a brief moment—in that space between the ping hitting my ears and when I reach for it—I think maybe he knows. Maybe *he's* the one contacting me. Neither of us has said much in the last few weeks. Avalon's been staying over at the Carter Estate, practically forced into a life of sedentariness, and I've been going over more. Every time I go, it's always as if he's leaving. Sometimes, he goes with Braxton, and sometimes it's just him by himself. Gone. Cut off. Distant from the others. The desire to know his thoughts is a fucking stupid craving in my veins. I shouldn't care, but curiosity holds me captive. Enough that I even went to his stupid father's funeral. I don't have the mental energy to ask myself why because that'll just lead to places in my twisted soul that I'm not willing to traverse right now.

When I finally flick open the lock on my phone screen, I realize that all of my thoughts were for nothing because it's not even him. It's Ava. She must be impatient, though, because I don't even have a second to read the message she sent before my screen lights up with her face and name as her call comes through. With a sigh, I swipe the green button and put the phone to my ear.

"What?" In my short nineteen years, I've learned the easiest way to distract someone is with a bad attitude. Anxiety can be easily covered with irritation.

"Whoa," she whistles into the receiver. "What crawled up your ass and died?"

I roll my eyes. "Nothing," I lie. The truth is my past has come back to haunt me and soon enough I'll be the one at death's door if I don't figure something out. "You called for a reason. What is it? If it's about that thing you asked me for, I still haven't gotten any hits on the chick we're looking for. It's like she's a ghost or something." This time when my annoyance comes through, it's real. I've never had such a difficult time finding someone, and the fact that it was Avalon that asked me for this favor and in the six weeks since she asked, I still haven't come up with any new information irks me to no end.

"I'm not calling about that." She blows out a breath. I know that breath. It's the death-sentence breath. Well, not really, but it feels like that. Those little sighs of hers are really more preludes to requests I know I'm not going to like. At least it's a request, though, and not a demand. Demands from her come in the form of knives pressed against your throat, fists in your face, or the threat of broken fingers—and I really need the use of my fingers if I'm gonna find this Micki chick she's looking for.

"Then what are you calling about?" I prompt when she doesn't immediately say it. Hesitation is unlike her.

"A favor..." she hedges. "But I know you're not going to like it and you're probably going to say no, so I'm trying to figure out a way to ask *nicely*." I can hear the wrinkle of disgust in that last word. Bitch.

Repressing a laugh but unable to contain the amusement in my tone, I lean back in my chair and stretch my ill-used muscles, pushing my chair until the front two legs pop off the floor and I'm left balancing on the back ones. "Ahhh, how the tables have turned, Mrs. Carter," I tease. "What does the Queen of Eastpoint need from a peon like me?"

"Fuck you," is her immediate reply and that's the last of my restraint. A laugh bursts out of my lips unbidden. "I'm not even fucking married yet," she mutters that last bit as if it's the most unwelcome event of her life, but I know better. She's just a stubborn bitch who hates anything that reflects the status quo.

With a shake of my head, I let my chair thump back to the floor and get serious. "What's the favor?"

"You're gonna say no," she says.

"Do I have that option?" I ask.

She snorts. "You always have the option."

"Alright," I reply. "I'll rephrase. Do I have the option to say no and keep breathing?"

Silence. I curse internally. That, too, is an answer, and not one that I necessarily want.

"Well," I continue, "holding back on me doesn't make this go any faster. Ask your favor and I'll decide if death is worth saying no."

"I need you to come stay at Dean's for a few days."

I frown. "Why?"

She huffs out a breath. "We're going to visit his mother in California and while we're there, his dad set him up to see a sports physical therapist to check him out before football season starts. We want to make sure his injury is healing up properly before they start throwing shit at him."

"Kaaay..." I wait for the punchline, but there doesn't seem to be one. "That still doesn't explain why I need to stay at his house? Don't Braxton and Abel live with you guys?"

"Yeah, that's um ... the other part of it," she says. "Since it's the week before school starts, Brax took off last night. He said he'd be back in a few days, so it's just Abel here, and he's..." She doesn't need to say it. Thanks to my newfound obsession, I know exactly what she's about to say. "I just want to make sure

6

someone is keeping an eye on him," she says. "Dean and I both do. He's been a little off since the fire and ... you know."

"Yeah," I say. "I know." But of all the people in the world she would ask me to fuckboy-sit, why did it have to be him?

I scrub a hand down my face. There's no way I can say no. One, because she's not really asking. And two, because I owe my fucking life to the Eastpoint heirs. Everything I have is an extension of them. My laptop, my dorm room, my bed. Shit, even the clothes on my back are thanks to them. Then again, it's not like I haven't earned my keep. All the background checks they want on their program recruits, I get. Any dirty information they want on business, school, sports, or just rivals in general, I procure. For the Sick Boys, and now Avalon, I'm like a one-stop-shop hacker department store.

"I know you two have got your ... whatever it is you two have going on..." She drifts off and her voice wavers. There's really not a name for the animosity between Abel and me. If only that night hadn't happened, maybe we might've been friends—or not friends, but quiet, distant acquaintances. Unfortunately, there's no taking back past mistakes and there's certainly no erasing the thing he awoke inside of me. As many times as I've punished my body with people in the past, none of them ever made me truly *want* it. None of them ever made me *feel*. Not like *him*.

"Fine," I say. "I'll do it."

"You will?" Even Ava can't disguise the shock in her tone.

"Yeah, I wasn't really looking forward to meeting my new roommate anyway," I say. "And it's move-in weekend for programees. It might be good to get out and avoid the oncoming wave."

Ava is quiet for a moment and then, "I don't think you'll have to worry about that, but I appreciate the help, seriously. Dean was ready to tell his dad to fuck off—but I'd rather be sure that he's good to go before he starts running after balls and shit."

I snort. "Have you ever actually seen a football game?" I ask.

"*Nope.*"

"Well, it's a little bit more than running after a ball," I tell her. "It's more like throwing a ball and running for the guy that catches it."

She hums. "Cool," she says and then adds, "I don't really care." Yeah, I could've seen that coming. The only thing she cares about is Dean and the other Sick Boys. As much as I like and respect her, I know I'm not a real friend in her eyes. I'm someone useful. That's okay, though. As long as I'm useful, the Sick Boys will have to keep me around, and as long as my abilities can do something for them, they'll have to keep me protected.

This is a good thing, I tell myself. While everyone is out of town, maybe I can convince Abel to give me some extra security. If I need to, I can use my savings to do something. All I know is that I can't let things just sit. Though it's only been days since I got the email about Daniel's release from prison, I need to act fast. I need to make sure my tracks have been erased and if all else fails, maybe I'll just disappear.

"Rylie?" I blink and refocus on the voice against my ear.

"I'm sorry," I say. "Got distracted, what did you say?"

"I told you we're leaving the day after tomorrow. When can you be here?"

"The day after tomorrow?" I look at the top right-hand corner of my computer screen. It's already half past eleven at night. "I can be there before you guys leave. Tomorrow? You're just going for a couple of days, right?"

"Yeah, we should be back before classes start," she replies. "You won't really need to do anything, but Abel's been going to weird parties lately. We just want to make sure he doesn't fuck

8

someone up too bad while we're gone. All you need to do is make sure he doesn't choke on vomit or set the house on fire. Whatever happens, you've got Brax and Dean's numbers for emergencies as well as mine."

"I don't know how the hell you think I'll be able to stop him if he gets into a serious brawl or something," I say. "But I'll try."

"I think you've got more power over him than you're willing to admit, Ry," Ava says, and then in a more subdued tone, as if she's speaking more to herself than me, she adds, "more than he is either."

That can't be right, though. As far as I know, Abel hates my guts. Or at the very least, he thinks I'm little more than an annoyance. The only real reason I've been considering going to him is because, despite his playboy facade, Abel seems the most reasonable—rather, he *was* the most reasonable ... before his father's death. Now I'm not sure what to think of this new, unhinged Abel. If Ava's worried, then maybe I should be too.

Avalon and I finish up with the details for tomorrow. I glance back over the collection I've acquired since the majority of my shit burned up almost two months ago when some asshole set the Havers dorm on fire. It's a good thing I've never had anything that was worth much. The one thing I couldn't live without—my original laptop—is the one thing that actually made it out with me unscathed. The rest of this shit is stuff I've gotten from local secondhand and thrift shops.

By the time I finish shooting the shit with Ava and hang up, the clock on my computer screen reads closer to midnight. I could go for a few more hours if I really needed to, but I haven't had an energy drink since early evening and the caffeine crash is already hitting. Without another thought, I close my computer, turn out the light and crawl beneath the sheets of my twin bed, hoping against hope that I won't have the same nightmare that seems to plague me.

The second I shut my eyes, that hope dies a fiery death.

2

RYLIE

6 YEARS OLD...

He's back. I can hear him just outside the room I share with Nadia and Marie. They're both asleep in the bunk beds on the other side of the room. But when he comes in, he won't go for their beds. He'll come for mine. He always comes for mine.

In a way, I hate them—Nadia and Marie. I know I shouldn't. It's not their fault. But just once, just one time ... I wish it wasn't me. I wish it was anyone *but* me.

My fingers slip between the sheets and the pillow beneath my head and my hand finds the weapon I've hidden away there. I don't know why I close my eyes. It's not like that will stop him. Maybe I do it because if I close my eyes and pretend I'm sleeping, Daniel will just keep walking. It's never happened before, but I hope more than anything in the world—more than having ice cream for dinner or another hour of playtime—that tonight won't be the night that I kill him. That when he stops and lingers in front of my bedroom door, that's all he'll do. Linger. Then he'll walk away.

I just can't take it anymore. It hurts when he touches me

and I don't want to hurt anymore. My fingers squeeze against the mattress, wrapping more firmly around the plastic shaft in my grip. My weapon is nothing more than a broken pen. I removed the little white piece inside that holds all of the ink, but the plastic is left jagged—sharp enough to make someone bleed if I need it to. Sharp enough to make them stop doing the horrible things that they do.

But hopes aren't wishes to be granted, and even if they were, no one is around to hear mine.

The door squeaks lightly as it pushes open and Daniel enters. I squeeze my eyes shut tighter until even the soft illumination from Nadia's princess nightlight doesn't reach me. Then, when nothing happens—when I hear no more movement—I chance a peek.

My eyes soften, and I open one to see that closing them hadn't stopped the light from Nadia's princess night light—it's not on at all. Both of my eyes blow wide open and I start panting as the darkness encroaches. Nothing. There's nothing there. It's pitch black. He's never turned off the nightlight before. My chest squeezes tight.

I didn't think it could get any worse, but this—sitting in the darkness, *knowing* he's there—is just that. *Worse.*

Something settles against the end of my bed—a firm hand. It touches my ankle and then smooths upward. Nadia and Marie are deep sleepers—they won't wake up even if I cry. Because Mrs. Tammy always gives them their sleeping meds that the doctor gave them. Wherever they were before here, it must have been bad for doctors to have given them sleeping meds. But here is bad too. They just don't know. They just don't see it. But I do. I *feel* it every night.

It's hard to see in the darkness of the room, but from the window, there's a small sliver of moonlight as well as the dull illumination of the street lights outside that allow me to make out shadows and shapes. Daniel's hand edges ever higher and higher until he reaches the top of the blanket and pulls it down. I freeze, my whole body going stiff as his hand dips under the covers and retraces its last steps. From my ankles, all the way up my legs until he's pushing up my nightgown.

"Please don't," I whisper. Don't make me do this. Don't hurt me. Don't make me hurt you.

"I knew it," he whispers back. "You were awake. What were you doing, little Rylie? Did you think that I wouldn't wake you?"

I ignore his question. "I don't want to tonight," I say. "I fell on the playground and my knee hurts." Just put him off, I tell myself. Put him off for tonight and then tomorrow ... tomorrow I can go to the teacher when I get to school. Mrs. Tammy doesn't believe me—Daniel's her son after all. And why would a sixteen-year-old want to do this with a little girl? But he does. He does, and I can't stand it anymore.

"You hurt your knee?" Daniel pulls the covers down to the bottom of the bed, and I scrunch up, bringing my legs beneath me in an automatic effort to protect myself. I whimper as he takes my ankles in his grip and yanks my legs back down. "Do you want me to kiss it better?"

My head lifts and I glance over to Nadia and Marie's bunk beds, but as expected, neither of them wake at the sound of his voice. Daniel leans over and his lips brush against my bruised knee. "Stop," I beg. "Please stop."

"You know I can't do that, little Rylie," he says. "I came for our special time. We haven't had special time all week."

"I don't want special time," I tell him. "It hurts."

"Oh, you know it doesn't hurt for long. You know you like it eventually."

I don't. I really don't. As Daniel's hands slide further beneath my night shirt, I bite down hard on my lip. A tear escapes and trails down my cheek, rolling until it hits my upper lip and I taste salt. He's not going to stop, I realize. I sniff hard as his fingers grasp the top of my underwear and start to tug them down.

"If you don't st-stop," I stutter. "I'll m-make you."

Daniel chuckles, the sound sinister to me because I know he doesn't take me seriously. What can a little girl do? "No, you won't," he replies. "You like it when I touch you."

"I told you I don't."

"Then why do you shiver when I press my fingers right ... here..." I release a half-scream and scramble back, my skull hitting the headboard of the twin-sized bed when his hand touches me *there*. He's done it before, and he's done other things—things that make me cry. Things that make me wince when I sit down because I'm so sore the next day. I hate those things.

"Stop!" I scream.

Daniel's free hand whips out of the covers and slams over my mouth. His gaze snaps to the bunk beds, but Nadia and Marie slumber on. When he turns his head and his dark, brown eyes clash with mine once more, they're angry. His fingers pinch against my cheeks. The broken pen stabs at the inside of my palm underneath my pillow.

"What have I told you about getting too loud?" he hisses. "I know you like it. Stop lying and stop trying to make me mad. Do you want to get in trouble, Rylie?"

Another tear slides down my cheek, a testament to my weakness. I shake my head, but he doesn't let go of my face. Maybe if he's too mad, he won't be in the mood. Maybe he'll just leave. My hand never leaves the broken pen, though, almost as if I know that'll never happen. Once Daniel wants something, he'll do whatever it takes to get it.

"No, of course you don't want to get in trouble." His voice turns softer as his fingers loosen their hold and he strokes my face, wiping away the tears I've shed. "There, there, sweetheart.

I know how you can make it up to me." His thumb slides across my mouth and dips in. "I know what we can do to make you quiet."

I'm gonna vomit. I feel it churning in my gut. The bile. The disgust. The hate. The pain. It all rolls around inside of me. More tears fall. I can't do this. I can't take it anymore. I want to kill him. I want to make it all stop.

"D-Danny..." I try again, one last time. Am I too hopeful? Maybe. I just don't understand why he keeps doing this to me, why it's always only me and no one else. "Please, I don't want—"

"Shhhh." He puts a finger over my lips, silencing me. Chills chase down my spine as he leans closer. His tongue comes out and scrapes up the side of my face, licking away the remains of my tears. Tonight's dinner threatens to come spewing up. "Open your mouth, Rylie. Open your mouth and say you're sorry for getting loud with me. Then we can have special time, and I can make you feel good."

"*No.*" It's only one word. A single syllable. Yet, I feel it with every fiber of my being. I do not want this. Daniel's hands grow harder, bruising.

"I don't like it when you tell me no, Rylie," he growls.

I don't care. I squirm in his grip. "Let go of me." I can't do it. I don't care anymore. I don't care about getting in trouble. I don't care if Mrs. Tammy kicks me out or if people will find out that I'm a bad girl, that I'm torn and dirty. I'd rather die...

"Rylie!" he snaps. Daniel clamps down on my shoulders, and I just lose it. I scream. I scream and I scream and I rear back, my hand sliding out from under the pillow. I lift my arm and I bring it down right on this thigh. The plastic snaps, but I'm close enough to his groin—to the hard thing dangling between his legs that I hit it with my knuckles. He grunts and curses as he falls over the side of the bed.

I continue to scream and then finally, doors begin opening

somewhere in the house. Feet running. "You little bitch," Daniel wheezes as he cups himself between his legs. There's a tear in his shorts, blood oozes down the side of his leg beneath the hem. *Good*, I think. I hope it hurts. I hope he feels even a little bit of the pain he's given me.

On the bunk beds across the room, Nadia's head finally pops up, her eyes bleary as she scrubs at one with her tiny fist. "Why are you yelling?" she mumbles.

I start to sob, big fat tears rolling down my cheeks. They're gonna know. They're gonna see. I grab the sheets on the bed and drag them up over my body and even though my clothes are still on, I feel naked. I feel exposed. Disgusting.

The door to the bedroom slams open and Mrs. Tammy and Christine—one of the older girls who lives in the home—both run in. They stop when they see Daniel on the floor and me sobbing in my bed.

"Oh, Daniel!" Mrs. Tammy falls to her knees, reaching for her son. I curl up into a ball and wait for the pain to start. She's going to hit me. She's going to yell at me. I don't care. I'll take the pain. I'll take a spanking or a belt or a mouth washing. Anything but what Danny gives me.

"Rylie?" Christine moves around Mrs. Tammy and Daniel and reaches for me. I hide beneath the covers. My hands reach automatically to hold the hem of my nightshirt down as Christine slips onto the side of the bed and lightly tugs at the blanket over me. "Rylie, what happened?"

I don't say—I can't. I just continue to cry. I cry until I feel my eyes burn with the effort and I can't breathe. The sobs choke inside my chest, making me heave with great effort. I can hear Christine talking. Her voice remains soft and gentle, but the words don't reach my ears. What I do know is that as the minutes pass, I become more and more aware of things happening around me. There's the sound of little feet padding over the floor, Daniel's voice growing farther away—

but no less angry—and the bedroom door opening and closing.

Finally, Christine pulls the covers off of my head and crawls up towards the headboard. "Rylie, sweetheart..." Her hand smooths over my hair, pulling away the pieces that are soaked with my tears and stuck to my cheeks. Christine is nice. She's the oldest, older than Daniel even. Maybe...

Christine freezes when she lifts her hand away and without thinking, I flinch. Daniel doesn't usually hit me—if I keep quiet, if I just lay back and take it, he can even be nice. But he has before and tonight's the first time I ever truly fought him.

"Rylie." This time when she speaks her voice is more firm, though she keeps it quiet and low. "Can you tell me now, what happened tonight?"

I hiccup out a breath and shake my head. Do I dare? What will happen if I do?

Her eyes soften. "You're not in trouble, Rylie," she says. "I just want to help."

"W-what if Mrs. Tammy kicks me out?" I gasp as I stutter through my question. It's as if I'm inhaling the thinnest air. It's not doing anything for me. I can't breathe.

"Is that what you're scared of?" she asks, moving up closer, but when I stiffen she stops.

Is that what I'm scared of? I think. *No.* Being kicked out might be better for me. Anything to get away from *him.* I shake my head sharply. What I'm most scared of is Daniel. Even if I leave, I'm terrified he won't ever let me go. That he'll keep hurting me again and again until he swallows me whole.

"Rylie?"

I look up at Christine when she says my name. She's frowning. She's probably never experienced anything like this. I don't know if she'll understand, but if I don't say something now then Daniel will cover it up. He'll lie—he'll expect me to lie, but I'm tired of lying. I'm tired of pretending.

So, in that dark, small room with too many beds in such a cramped space, with my chest growing tighter and tighter with each breath, I decide that it's time to tell the truth. Even if that truth is something better left in the back of a dark closet, never to be seen or heard—just like me. I'm tired of the dark and I'm ready to be free.

3

ABEL

Present Day...

"I DON'T NEED A FUCKING BABYSITTER," I grit out. Even as I speak the words, I know the shades over my eyes aren't helping shit. I can hardly remember the party I went to the night before or how the hell I got home. All I know is that this hangover is killer and the sunlight pouring in through the french glass doors at the back of the kitchen feels like acid on my aching, UV ray protected eyeballs.

"Yeah, well, maybe prove it next time by answering my fucking calls," Dean replies as he shuffles towards the fridge and pops it open to retrieve the pitcher of orange juice.

"I was drunk," I say. "I don't even remember getting home."

"Abel," he snaps, slapping the damn pitcher down on the counter so that it cracks against the marble and makes the headache pounding against my temples even worse. "It's that kinda fucking shit that concerns me, and it's the reason Ava wanted to call Rylie."

"What can the little program girl do?" I sneer. "It's not like she's got the authority to order me around. I can just leave her ass here if I want."

"Yeah?" Dean reaches for the cabinet and lets it slam open. Asshole. He's totally doing this on purpose. "Well, maybe I'll give her the authority to do something then."

I stiffen at the implication of his words. "What the fuck is that supposed to mean?" I demand, leaning forward over the counter.

Anger boils in my blood, shooting up to my already foggy head. My hands ball into fists. No. *Chill the fuck out,* I tell myself. He's just fucking worried.

Dean pours himself a glass and then reaches up for two more, proving me right. He wouldn't be pouring me a glass of orange juice if he was angry enough to give some goth little fucking nobody the authority to tell me what the fuck to do. "Dude, I don't know what the hell is going on with you, but it's not like Viks can come over to cover your ass. Just do us all a favor and maybe stay in for the weekend. You've partied enough for the entire year by now, and Avalon's—"

I roll my neck back on my shoulders and sigh. "Avalon is a girl," I interrupt him. "No matter that she doesn't act like it, you"—I point at him with an irritated scowl—"are corrupting her. Hell, you're practically domesticating her." Without warning, out of the corner of my eye, I spot a shoe come flying out of nowhere, and it smacks me squarely upside the head. "Ow! Jesus, what the fuck?" I look down as the sneaker hits the floor. A few seconds later, Avalon comes striding into the kitchen sans one shoe. She glares at me as she approaches Dean and leans into him when he bends down to press a kiss to the top of her head before handing her a glass of OJ. Something inside me flips and tightens.

I'm happy for Dean and Avalon. If any-fucking-body on this planet deserves to find their soulmate, they do. *I just wish*

... I shake my head, cutting off that thought. I wish for the fucking impossible.

Slowly, Avalon turns back around and glares at me over the rim of her glass. "What the fuck did you say about me and domestication, Frontman?" she challenges.

I retrieve her shoe and hold it up. "I did say practically," I point out. "Not completely. Case in point—your obvious aversion to footwear."

She rolls her eyes and takes a sip of her juice before returning it to the counter and stalking over to me. Her fingers close around the sneaker in my grasp and when I hold on at her first tug, she rears back and punches me in the stomach. "Oh fuck!" I double over as my fingers release the shoe. "Goddamn, girl, you're a violent little thing in the morning. You do know I still have a hangover, right? I thought you loved me."

Avalon walks back to where she was and turns, propping her ass against the counter and lower cabinets as she tugs her sneaker back on. She glares my way. "I do," she says in response as she finishes retying and tightening the laces. "Which is why I'm telling you to knock this shit off. I don't know what's going on in your head since thing number two kicked it"—I almost snort at the way she refers to my father's death, but manage to hold it in. Barely.—"but getting drunk and fucking around ain't the way to deal with it. Your hangover is your own damn fault. You know I don't give a fuck who you bang or what you do, but if you keep going at the rate you're at, you're gonna burn through Eastpoint, and then what? You'll still feel as crappy as you do now. Just take a few days off, for fuck's sake. It's not like it'll kill you."

It's just like Avalon to get right to the heart of the matter. It's unnerving how she sees through people, even me. Instead of commenting, however, I put my all into irritating her. "Avaaaaaaaaa," I whine. "You don't know what it's like to be a man. I *need* pussy."

Her cute face scrunches up and she scowls. "I'll buy you a fucking cat," she says.

I grin her way. "Make it hairless," I say.

"Fine," she agrees, crossing her arms over her chest.

"I want it to have a bow."

Dean's eyes go back and forth between us. "Anything else, your highness?" She deadpans.

"Well..." I pull out my phone. "Now that you mention it. I actually have this list here—"

"Rylie's coming and she's staying for three days," Avalon cuts me off, ruining the joke.

I frown and drop my phone onto the island countertop with a clattering noise. "That's unnecessary."

She arches a brow. "I say it's not."

"And since when have you been the fucking authority, Ava?" I shoot back. "You don't know shit. Just leave me the fuck alone and I promise to be a good little boy for three fucking days. Like I was telling your keeper here"—Dean growls at that, but I can't quite bring myself to give a fuck right now—"I don't need a fucking babysitter."

"Then maybe you should stop acting like a fucking baby and tell someone what the fuck is up with you," Ava says. "Talk to Viks."

"Like you are?" I shoot back.

Her eyes go hard. "Maybe I am," she says coolly.

I blink. She's lying. She's gotta be. Of the four of us, Ava is the least likely to actually seek help for the psychological bullshit she's gotta be dealing with. But, in the back of my mind, I have to wonder ... what if she's not?

"I don't want her here," I say instead of acknowledging Ava's comment.

"Too fucking bad," Ava replies.

My jaw clenches and unclenches as I work not to lose the tightly held control I have on my anger. This is Avalon we're

21

talking about. Not only is she a fucking chick—and I don't fucking hit chicks—she's like my sister. When thirty seconds turns into a minute and one minute turns into two and then more, Ava sighs and glances back at Dean. They don't have to speak actual words to have a conversation, and I find that more painful than I thought I would.

Why? Maybe because I want it. I want what they have. Watching Dean and Avalon together just reminds me how fucking empty my soul is. They're like two halves of a whole and I'm just a sad sack of shit trying to mimic what they share every night with a different unremarkable girl.

4

RYLIE

I STARE at the passing greenery as it flies by outside of the car window before glancing over to the driver of the vehicle. "Did you really need to give me a ride?" I ask as Avalon turns past a pair of double columns and slides through a dark metal gate. "I could've taken the bus."

"The bus doesn't stop anywhere near here," she replies. "And yes—I needed to make sure you'd actually show up."

That's fair. If it had been anyone else asking, I might've taken the opportunity to run. But I know Avalon, and I don't doubt she'd track my ass down, beat it, and then make me fulfill my promise. Just doing it in the first place will save me a lot of pain later.

My overnight bag sits next to my feet. She presses the gas and the front of the SUV turns around the side of the massive mansion she's been living in for the last few months. She stops in front of the garage, hits a button above the visor, and waits for the door on the very end to rise before she ambles inside.

"There are only a few rules," she starts as she shuts off the vehicle and retrieves the keys.

"Thought you were a 'I make the rules' kind of girl," I say as

I unbuckle my seat belt, grab my bag, and slide it over my shoulder.

"I am," she agrees with a grin. "They're my rules too." I roll my eyes and hop out of the car as she does the same, rounding the front and leading me towards the door. "No one comes here," she says. "Ever. Family only. So, don't invite people over. You can eat whatever you find in the kitchen. Use any of the common rooms. Don't go snooping in the guys' spaces."

"Wasn't planning on it," I mutter as I trail her into what has to be one of the biggest foyers I've ever seen in my life—and I've been to a few of my clients' parties before. The majority of the students at Eastpoint come from the top one-percenters, but this is far beyond even them. "Does Abel know why I'm here?" I ask.

Ava stops at the mouth of the hallway and looks back. "Yeah," she says. "He knows."

Great. Then this should be fun.

"You didn't lie and tell him there was something wrong with my room?" I ask. "You probably should have."

"We don't lie to each other," Ava says with a shrug. "He's been a little wild lately and we're all worried. He'll be good this weekend." I give her a doubtful look, and she shrugs. "As good as he can be," she amends smartly.

"I'm literally just here for emergencies," I remind her. "You know I don't have any power or authority over him and I'm not big enough to physically stop him if he gets into any trouble."

"No, but having someone he needs to look after in his space will do most of the work anyway," Ava points out. "The guys aren't super comfortable with outsiders in their space. Even if you're not snooping, I don't think he'll wander too far if you're here, and at least with you around, he won't be able to lie to us."

"I thought you said you didn't lie to each other," I say.

Ava pushes her tongue into her cheek and tilts her head. "Okay poor choice of words, we don't lie to each other, but ...

we don't always tell each other *everything*. You"—she points at me—"are just here to act as a recording device he can't turn off. If he leaves, go with him. If he won't take you, follow him."

I spread my arms out. "I don't know if it's escaped your notice, Ava, I'm not exactly dripping with mobility here."

She rolls her eyes. "Take one of the cars." She flicks her hand back towards the now closed garage door.

My eyes widen. "Um ... I thought you said not to go through their stuff?"

Ava sighs and turns back to fully face me. "Rylie," she says, crossing her arms over her chest, "don't overthink this."

"Yeah, that's easier said than done," I remind her, reaching up to clutch at the strap of my bag. Cold air washes over the back of my neck and I shiver. My eyes bounce from her to the ceiling arching over my head, to the artwork on the walls, to the staircase, and back again. "I feel like a freaking stray you just brought in and one fuck up will see me right back at the pound or out on the street. You do realize these guys control my scholarship, right? You might be an Eastpoint Heir now, but there's no hidden billionaire parent in my past."

Ava drops her arms and moves closer, reaching up and grasping both of my shoulders in her hands, drawing my attention solely back to her. "Hey," she says calmly, "take a deep breath." I suck one in and nearly cough as I try to release it. "It's going to be fine," she repeats. "You're just here to watch and report. If you don't think you can stop him, don't. Abel is a big boy. Just being here should be enough incentive. It's just for the weekend. Three days tops. Eat what's in the kitchen. Work on your laptop. Check in when I call. That's it." She dips her head and gray blue eyes stare back at me. "Think you can handle that?"

If it were anyone else, there would be no question. But this is Abel Frazier we're talking about. Ever since that strange night at Kellen Crawford's party a few months ago, things have been different. He's been different, and if I'm being honest with myself, so have I. Now isn't the time to think about how he made me feel, though. It's not the time to focus on the sudden changes in my body. I need to just do this, find the chick that Ava's been looking for, and find a way to make sure I've covered my tracks lest Daniel Dickerson comes looking for me. Just the reminder of that monster in my mind makes me feel an old creeping sickness swirl around in my gut.

I nod in response and Ava releases a breath I hadn't realized she was holding. "Good," she says, pulling her hands back with a grimace. "Because I'm actually—"

"Look out!" I nearly scream as a masculine voice calls from somewhere up above and a bag comes flying over the balcony above us and lands a few feet behind where we're standing. We look up and I see Dean Carter's face peering down. "Oh, good, you're back."

"Packing up a little early, aren't you?" I comment, looking down at the gym bag now resting a few feet away with a sneaking suspicion that there was another reason for Avalon to pick me up tonight rather than let me come in the morning.

"Yeah..." My head lifts at Ava's drifting tone and my eyes narrow. "About that," she starts.

"You're still leaving tomorrow, right?" I demand, cutting a glance up the hallway. If they're not, does that mean *he's* already here? Another bag comes flying over the railing but this time I don't even glance as it makes a loud thumping noise just a few extra feet from the first one. It mimics the panicked thudding of my heart racing in my chest. "*Right?*" I repeat almost begging Ava to tell me I'm wrong.

Ava sighs. "Dean got an earlier appointment with the doctor," she says, confirming my fears. "We're gonna fly out tonight instead so we don't miss it in case something happens."

"So, you're leaving," I say. "*Right now?*" I wince at how high-pitched my voice comes out on those last two words.

Dean stops at the base of the stairs, another backpack slung over one shoulder. Ava takes one look at me and then turns to him. "Can you take these out with you? I'll be out in a sec."

He eyes me as he stops in front of her and I have to turn my face away as he bends down and takes her mouth in a carnal kiss. Even without looking, I can practically feel the heat radiating off of the two of them. It's several seconds later when he releases her and I hear him finally walking away. I don't know why he felt the need to kiss her when they're literally going to be separated for a few minutes, not like it's going to be weeks or even months.

Ava is good, I'll give her that. She must sense the storm swirling inside of me and my need to let it out, but she also knows my stance on the Sick Boys and keeping my distance. She waits until Dean bends over and retrieves the bags he dropped over the edge and hefts them up his arms before disappearing into the garage, shutting the door behind him as he goes, before she speaks.

"Alright," she says as she moves down the hallway, knowing I'll follow. "Come on, let's get the basics out of the way and then you can freak."

"Too late," I mutter. I'm already fucking freaking.

I don't know why it makes any difference—whether they leave tonight or tomorrow, the result is going to be the same. Me. Alone. With Abel Frazier. Almost as if thinking his name conjures up some of that unspoken, strange craving within me, a chill chases down my spine. I thought I had another night to get used to this place. Another night *not alone*. A low itchy feeling begins at the base of my neck and moves upward, spreading out across my scalp and then down around my throat. It feels like invisible hands covered in poison ivy are strangling me.

We stop in the mouth of what looks like a grand kitchen and living room area. "Eat whatever you want out of there."

She points towards the kitchen. "Feel free to use the internet, password's on the router in the living room, and watch anything you want." She motions towards the living room and keeps moving.

My feet shuffle along as I trail her. "When were you going to tell me that you were leaving early?" I demand, growing increasingly frustrated, especially as she appears not at all inclined to explain herself and instead is just playing almost absentee hostess.

"When you got here," she answers casually.

"Why—"

"No parties are held here, so no worries on that front," she cuts me off as she leads me towards a back staircase that's slightly tucked out of the way around the corner of the far side of the kitchen.

"Is he here?" I ask.

"Abel?" Ava heads up and I shift my hip out, dragging my bag up higher, wincing at the ache in my shoulder. I should've packed lighter. Less equipment maybe.

"No, the Pillsbury Doughboy," I snap, and two seconds later, I nearly slam my front into Ava's back as she stops at the top of the stairs.

"Pillsbury Doughboy?"

Oh, God. No. Please. He can't be that cruel. Not to me. I peek around Ava's frame and realize that God's a motherfucker because he can be, in fact, that fucking cruel. Standing just outside of what looks like a bathroom is the monstrous sex god of Eastpoint himself. And very much *not* a Pillsbury Doughboy.

My mouth dries as my eyes slip down to the towel wrapped low around his hips, shifting as he strides across the hall to another door and then pauses, turning back and crossing his arms as he props himself against the frame there. His wet hair is slicked back away from his face, highlighting the sharp contours

28

of his bone structure, and though I try not to, I can't help looking down ... down ... and down some more to the perfect outline of his abs and the notches of his hips. Has he modeled before? He totally should. Women across the world would fall all over whatever product he represents. Hell, this explains why every fucking straight pussy from Eastpoint to St. Augustine wants Abel Frazier.

"Frontman." Ava's tone is a warning.

Abel grins. "I'm not gonna do anything to the little mouse, Princess," he says. "Not yet anyway."

"Not at all," she tells him. "She's just here in case something happens."

"You mean in case I lose my shit, right?"

I watch him, curious. I did wonder how he would feel about the others siccing a lowly programee like me on him as extra security, but his face doesn't reveal any irritation. In fact, he meets my gaze almost with challenge.

I know I should duck my head, tuck my face down, and avoid his notice. Be the mouse he just claimed I was, but since that night at the Crawford party, I find it hard not to watch him. Not to meet those electric ice blue eyes of his. He's always so cocky. So sure of himself. That night, though, there'd been a different side of him that I'm not sure anyone else had ever seen. An unhinged side.

"We're only going to be gone for a few days," Ava says on a sigh. "I'm showing her to her room and then gonna have a quick chat and then I gotta go—Dean's waiting."

My gaze finds a droplet of water and zeroes in on it as it slides down the center of his chest before hitting the top of his abs. "Why don't you go ahead, Ava?" I hear Abel's suggestion a split second before it registers and my head jerks back up in horror.

Avalon, for her part, looks hesitant. *Yes!* There's no way she'll leave me here now. She'll refuse him because, of course, she's not stupid. There's no doubt in my mind that Abel has something in mind to get me to leave and if it wasn't *him*, I wouldn't have thought twice about sprinting my happy ass right the fuck on out of this murder mansion. Ava's smart. She'll decline and then show me to whatever closet they plan to stick me in for the weekend. I'll lock the door, wait for Abel to go to bed, and then I'll set up some cameras. My plan comes back to me full force. I won't even have to see him in person this weekend. I can just watch him through these cheap security cams I express ordered when she made it clear that there was no refusing this favor of hers. Yes, that's exactly what I'll do.

My shoulders droop as I relax, nodding, ready to agree as Ava opens her mouth. "If you're sure..."

That's right, dick for brains, just go back into your room and —wait, what? Shocked, I don't even have a chance to gasp out a stunned protest because the next thing I know, Ava is turning and moving me out of the way, slipping past me and back down the stairs.

"Good luck," she calls back. "Call me if there's an emergency."

I whirl on her, but she's already disappeared down the stairs and around the corner. Slowly, in small, hesitant increments—like I'm trying not to startle a savage beast—I turn back to face the man watching me with a cold look. Oh the grin is still there. The smirk that says he has me right where the fuck he wants me is planted firmly in place.

Though most people can't see beyond that, I can. And I know, for certain, that he's not as relaxed as he's trying to portray. He's pissed.

5

ABEL

RYLIE MOORE. Hacker. Foster kid. Program chick. There is nothing significant nor important about her ... and yet ... for the last two months, I haven't been able to get it up without thinking of a bratty mouth with lavender hair and fuck me hazel eyes. And now, here she stands before me—the ball and chain given to me by those I trust the most.

Unlike most people, Rylie seems to sense the anger inside of me. Despite the mask of amused indifference I have plastered on my face, she shifts on her feet, looking like a scared rabbit. Still, she doesn't turn and run. That speaks volumes. I flip towards the room.

"Come on," I order, stepping inside, knowing she'll follow. After all, where the fuck else is she gonna go?

I wait, though, until I hear the shuffle of her feet as she slides towards my open doorway. When I know she's stepped just inside the room, with my back turned to her, I drop the towel I've got wrapped around my hips. Her sharp inhale is enough to turn my amusement from a facade into something real.

"What the fuck are you doing?" she gasps and I know

without having to look back that she's staring at my ass. *Good*. If I have to crave that skinny little body masked under dark eyeliner and baggy clothes, then she should feel the same for mine. Tit for tat and all that shit.

"I'm getting dressed," I reply casually as I reach for the top of my dresser drawers and pull out a pair of jeans, sliding into them without looking back.

"Why did you call me in here if you were gonna"—she pauses, hesitating as if she can't find the words she wants to use —"do that," she finally finishes.

I pivot back to her as I finish buttoning up, sans underwear. and finally see that she gathered enough of her meager bravery to remain facing me, even if her eyes are turned towards the floor and her cheeks are stained red. "Because I fucking can," I reply.

That must piss her off because her head lifts and her eyes flash with irritation as she meets mine. And what do you know —the little hacker girl goes from being a confusing interest that I don't fucking understand to a fiery being, ready to flay me alive. I smile her way and plant my hands on my hips. I want to dare her to do whatever it is she's thinking. I'm sure it'll be far more entertaining than this party I'm about to go to. But she disappoints me. She doesn't say anything, instead, letting the electric silence that lingers between us go on for so long that my lips finally twitch downward and I give up and head for the closet.

Without looking her way again, I pull out a t-shirt and slip it on, pulling it down to meet the top of my jeans.

"What are you doing?" she asks, her tone less curious and more suspicious.

"We've been over this, Riot Girl," I say. "I'm getting dressed."

"You don't need to get dressed like that for a night in," she responds immediately and what do you know, I'm right back to amused as I glance at her out of the corner of my eye.

"Whoever said I was staying in?" I reply.

Her jaw drops and the color that stains her cheeks now is more rage than embarrassment. "Ava said—"

I snap the closet doors shut, cutting her off. "Ava says a lot of useless shit," I say through gritted teeth. If I'm going to let this girl sleep in my house—in touching distance ... in *fucking* distance and not do shit to her—I need an outlet. I can either lay her out and devour her or I can pop a couple of pills and get drunk. The second option is far easier and less messy.

"I don't want to go to a party," Rylie says, distracting me from my thoughts.

I turn fully to face her and cross my arms over my chest. "Who said you were invited?" I prompt.

As if she's fed up with my taunts, the little program girl drops her bag and, though she does it slowly as if what's inside is precious cargo, my brows raise when I hear the distinct thump it makes as it lands on the floor. What the hell did she put in that thing?

"Listen," she snaps. "I don't want to be here anymore than you want me here. I promised Avalon that I'd make sure you were good. *Please* don't make this fucking difficult." It's that 'please' that gets me. The way she says it, so full of venom and anger that's barely repressed.

I'm in front of her in a split second. "And who the fuck do you think you are?" I demand, backing her up as her pretty hazel eyes, flecked with different colors from green to brown, widen and shoot up to my face. "Talking to me like you have some sort of authority, huh? Pretty ballsy of you, Riot Girl." Pretty fucking danger inducing because it's also that reluctant courage of hers that gets me hard.

Rylie jerks back, away from me, and nearly falls as she stumbles over her heels. Lucky for her, though, I'm a fast bastard. I catch her around the waist, turn and shove her up against the wall at the entrance of my room.

I've had women of every shape and size, sucking me down their throats, moaning as they came all over my mouth, my fingers, and my cock. This would be the first time I had a chick like Rylie, though. She's fucking tiny—thin, pale, dark circles under her eyes both the painted and sleepless nights kind. Her hair is like a fluttering hazy cloud around her face, long, darker at the roots, and faded down from there.

I expect her to shove me back—not that she really has the strength to do so, but if she did I'd let her go. I'd release her from my cage if she resisted.

Maybe.

Surprisingly, though, she doesn't.

"Riot Girl?" she repeats, sounding almost breathless and a little confused.

I chuckle, low in my throat, and sink down into her, letting her feel the length of my cock against her belly. "You've shown that you're a little more than a scared mouse lately," I say. "So I think a new nickname benefits you. Unless you'd prefer I call you Miss Prude."

She stiffens at the reminder of what I'd called her one of the past times I tried to apologize for what happened two months ago and her eyes flash with something violent. I like that. I like the fighter in her. It turns me on. Maybe that's why I provoke her.

"So, which is it?" I press. "Are you my Riot Girl or Miss Prude?"

Her hands press against my chest. "I'm not *your* anything," she says through clenched teeth.

Oh, I beg to fucking differ. Before this weekend is over and Dean and Brax and Ava return, I want to very much make this girl mine. I want to bury myself into her sweet pussy and then burrow under her skin the way she's done to mine. Every fuck

I've had over the last two months—since that night at the Crawford party—has been with her image in mind and maybe … just maybe … fucking her will fix my current obsession with her. Because nothing else makes sense.

She doesn't fight me as I circle my hips, shifting and making sure she feels just what she fucking does to me. No, instead, she inhales again, her chest rising with the breath she takes and her mouth opens—white teeth flashing as she sinks them into her plump lower lip. I want to know what she tastes like. I wanted it that night and I want it now. It was only her denial that had stopped me.

Even as high and drunk as I was—as fucking horny as the drugs had made me—I'm not the fucking type of guy to take a girl against her will. But … for Rylie … if I don't get over this fascination with her soon … I'm afraid that I may just do more than a little convincing. If she doesn't fight me with her body, then her words mean nothing.

Almost as if she senses my thoughts, Rylie's perfect pink lips part and she speaks, her voice low and cold if a bit trembly. "Get. Off. Of. Me."

I sigh and dip down, my chin resting at the top of her head. "You're a fucking tease, you know that, Riot Girl?"

She moves against me, jerking, and I have to pull away as her knee comes up when she tries to drive it into my groin. Instead of being offended, though, I can't help the laugh that barks out. My hand lands on her head, rubbing against her scalp even when she reaches up to slap me away.

"I'm no such thing," she says.

I shake my head. "You have no fucking clue, do you?" The question is said rather thoughtlessly and her brows draw down in confusion. I turn away, pulling my hand away and staring at it for a brief moment, trying to understand why I felt such strange things when my skin met hers, but now it's gone and all of the irritation that's been sliding through my bones for the last few months returns full force. I clench my fingers into a fist and take a step further away from her.

"Abel—"

"If you want to go to the fucking party," I snap, cutting her off, "be downstairs in five. If you're not there, I'm leaving your ass and you'll have to figure out how to keep your promise to Avalon without me."

With that, I gently push her to the side, step out of the room, and head for the end of the hall, every step away from her another blade under my skin, bleeding me dry and making the darkness slither ever closer to my heart.

6

RYLIE

Iᴛ's uncomfortable sitting next to a man like Abel Frazier and knowing you'll never measure up. His standards are too high for mere mortals like me, and yet, for a split second, I almost fell for it. I almost truly believed that he looked at me and wanted me. That he, of all people, held desire for *me*, the program chick he and his friends use as their own personal IT guru. The truth is, the only thing I attract are monsters.

If someone like Abel Frazier were to want me ... what would that make him?

"You're quiet," he says, startling me out of my thoughts. "What are you thinking?"

I glance at him and realize that his gaze is focused on my face. "I'm thinking you should pay attention to the road," I snap, gesturing to the front of the vehicle as we speed straight down the highway. The dash reads eighty miles per hour and only ever inches up. As if he enjoys the catch in my breath when I realize he has my entire life in the palm of his hand, his foot presses down harder on the gas and the dial moves higher. He could decide to end it right here—jerk that wheel and suddenly I won't need to worry about Daniel anymore. I won't have to worry about anything because I'll be dead.

I've never desired that. I'm not, nor have I ever been, suicidal. Sure, I've looked in the mirror and seen nothing but ugliness, but even ugliness deserves a chance to live, doesn't it?

"Worried?" Abel sounds amused.

"I'd just like to get to this stupid party in one piece," I mutter.

As if he knows my very thoughts and finds them amusing, Abel returns his attention to the road with a smirk. "Don't worry, Riot Girl, I'm not going to crash my baby." He strokes the steering wheel almost lovingly and when I look at his face once more, there's a softness to it.

I'm not a fool to not know the reason behind it. When I first arrived at Eastpoint, I'd done all of my research on the Eastpoint heirs. And though Abel was known for picking cherries and breaking hearts with the callousness that befits a man of his station, I know why he loves this car the way he's never loved another person—at least not anyone that wasn't Braxton Smalls and Dean Carter ... and I suppose, Avalon now too. Because this car was from his mom. It's a well-known fact that before Avalon came along, the only other woman the Sick Boys respected was Josephine Frazier. It doesn't take a hacker to figure out why.

My chest tightens at the reminder. How easily Ava slipped past everyone's defenses. How quickly she adjusted to life here at Eastpoint and then not only dominated it but overcame the three of them. It hadn't been that much of a shock if I'm being honest—when I found out who she really was. It was almost as if this place had been waiting for her, their queen, when all I've ever managed to do was stay in the shadows.

I sit back against the seat and turn to look out the window. Minutes later, the Mustang veers towards the off ramp and we're off the highway, heading towards a neighborhood I've been to more than a few times. Disgust and resolve crawl up my throat as mansions pass by on my right and left. They're all the same in my eyes.

Somehow, though, the single exception is the one that Abel turns the Mustang into. I sit up straighter and whirl my eyes to his face. Though he doesn't look, I know he's aware of my irritation. "What the fuck are we doing here?" I demand.

"What?" he replies, casting me a disinterested look. "You don't like being reminded of old times?"

"The Crawfords moved out," I state. "There shouldn't be anyone living here." But even as I say the words, it's obvious I've missed something. The last I checked—two months ago when I nearly lost myself to Abel Frazier for the first and, I'm still hoping, the only time—they hadn't rebuilt their fortune enough to be able to afford their once luxurious home.

His lips twitch as he parks, pulling the Mustang's front wheels through half of the yard as he maneuvers the vehicle in such a way that no one can box him in later. "Let's just say the Crawfords are a very important family and their business will be rising once again in the near future. Once they have, they'll repay their debt a hundred-fold." He shuts off the car and it clicks in my mind.

"You bought it..." I don't know how and I don't know why, but the fact that he doesn't deny the words that slip from my lips only means it's true. "Why?"

"Having people fear you is good," Abel states as he stares through the windshield at the people collecting on the front lawn—girls in their inappropriate club dresses and bikinis with see through cover ups that do nothing to conceal their lush curves, and the guys lusting after them with drinks in hand. "But that's Brax and Dean's gig. Fear. Mine is something entirely different." He turns to me and fixes me with that icy blue gaze of his. "People don't generally learn to fear me until it's too late. By then, I've already got them in the palm of my hand and they can't move without one of my strings attached to their ankles."

All of the breath in my body leaves me in a single instant. I'd never considered ... I mean Abel is and always has been a part of the Sick Boys crew, but he's always been the easygoing one in my mind. Not a fighter like Braxton. Not a killer like Dean. But the lover that balanced them out. Now, however, I'm seeing a whole new side to him.

He draws people in with his good looks and they don't realize that it's all window dressing. The pretty colors and the beauty is merely a mask to hide a man willing to crush his opponents without them ever seeing him coming. A shiver chases down my spine as I stare back at the profile of his face. The sharp jawline, the deep-set eyes, and dark lashes that contrast against his skin and the near white blonde hair at the top of his head.

"Come on," he says a moment later, popping his door open as he steps out. "I need a fucking drink."

He's not the only one. I open my own door and step out, watching as he pockets his keys and strides up the front slope of what was once a pristine and flawless green lawn.

Abel doesn't even look back to see if I'll follow, and for some reason, that irritates me. Hell, everything about him irritates me. Him and those stupid Sick Boys. To them, I'm nothing but an employee. Someone they can call for information, and I think I'm finally starting to realize that I have a little bit more power than they realize.

But even as I think that, I notice several of my classmates—dicks and chicks alike—staring at me. I know what they're thinking. *What the hell is a program girl doing at an Eastpoint party?* And perhaps, pre-Avalon, I would've ducked my head and scrambled after Abel like the little mouse he once referred to me as. Now, though? Now, I lift a hand and flip them all the bird before I storm towards the front of the Crawford mansion for the second time in two months. Only this time, instead of racing away from Abel Frazier, I'm hunting him.

2 months ago...

I HATE THESE STUPID PARTIES. I'VE NEVER BEEN MUCH OF A partier, but this is where I get most of my clients outside of the Sick Boys, and it's honestly the best place to meet them for an exchange. There are so many people and they're all inebriated in some form or another; no one is paying me any attention. I'm the only one who's sober. The red solo cup of beer I hold clutched in my hand is nothing more than a prop to make me look like I'm fitting in. As much as someone like me can anyway.

It would be funny if it wasn't so pathetic. I know what I seem like—an ugly duckling cloaked in black in a sea of swans dressed head to toe in expensive brand names and diamonds.

Absently, I nibble on the rim of the plastic cup, trying to look like I'm drinking. Acid touches my tongue, a bare taste of the bitter liquid inside. Then I see it—my target is on the move. Or rather, my latest client.

Normally, I don't need to track a client down for payment, but in this instance, it's necessary. After what I found out about Kellen Crawford, I know that the piece of shit never intended to pay me for my services. Hell, I'm stunned he can even keep up the facade of wealth when his family is practically destitute. Within the week, his parents will be moving out of their two-million-dollar home in the wealthiest zip code of Eastpoint and relocating because not only has Crawford's father lost most of their fortune—through various poor decisions and lawsuits—but Kellen and his mother have squandered what was left of

41

their savings trying to keep up the appearance that everything is fine.

Everything is *not* fine.

My hands practically shake with rage, so much so that the cup in my grip trembles with the movement and beer sloshes over the side. *Fuck it,* I think, setting the cup down. It's now or never.

I cut through the crowd at the back of the estate lawn and trail my target as he sways and stumbles towards the house. The same house that will no longer be his next week. *What the fuck is wrong with him?* I mean, seriously. With my skills, I know what kind of savings he and his mother had. They could've lived comfortably for a couple of years at least if they hadn't played pretend.

That's all anyone at Eastpoint does, though. Prevaricate and pretend. If I'm being honest, I'm no different.

Keeping my head down, I duck around a group of giggling girls as they try to impress a couple of the guys from the football team by taking shots from each other's chests. I make it all the way to the back door of the two-story house at the edge of the estate that Kellen Crawford uses as a party and crash pad like that, with my head tucked down and my shoulders drawn in, trying to avoid catching anyone's attention.

I catch the side of the sliding glass door and push it out, slipping inside. The interior of the house is a far different crowd than the exterior. Everyone outside is loud and boisterous—on the cusp of becoming too trashed to remember tomorrow. Everyone inside is already there. The biggest difference, though, is their types of inebriation.

The inside of the house is filled with low moans and the scent of weed in the air. I recognize the scent immediately and a craving starts low in my gut. I could seriously use something relaxing right now. It's too bad that it's work time.

The top of Kellen's dark head catches my attention as he

heads into a room across from the kitchen. I pad across the cold tiled floor, following him. Just as I hit the open doorway, I open my mouth to call after him when I'm grabbed from the side and yanked further inside.

Hard fingers dig into my waist and lift me easily enough. A small yelp escapes as my back hits the wall and then he's there —Kellen Crawford. His gaze is foggy and unfocused, but when he looks at me I know he recognizes me.

"The fuck do you want, Moore?" he hisses, using my last name in the same way that I often use his.

Panic arches up my throat, squeezing tight. Blinking back the haze of hysteria that descends, I shove my hands against his chest, pushing him slightly back. "Let. Go." I grit the words out through my teeth, shoving as much venom as I can into my tone to let him know that I mean fucking business.

Kellen gives me a slow, lazy blink and then tilts his head to the side—like a predator that can't quite understand why its prey is resisting. "You came after me," he points out. "You think I haven't caught you following me all night? What? Are you in love with me or something, Moore? A scrawny little bitch like you thinks she has a chance with me?"

I grimace in disgust. Not in a million years. "I've been following you because you owe me money, you dickshit!" I snap, slapping his chest again when he refuses to let me down. My legs dangle, toes barely touching the floor. Shit, I hate being short. He's not even holding me up that far, but no matter how much I struggle against him, there's really no competition. He's at least twice my weight too.

Kellen snorts and finally—thankfully—drops me. My feet hit the floor and the second he takes a step back, I finally feel like I can breathe. I reach up and touch my neckline, making sure it's at least past my collarbone before I slide along the wall, back towards the door.

"So?" I say. "Are you going to pay me or what?"

43

Kellen shakes his head. "Get the fuck out of here, bitch," he snaps, turning towards the main part of what I realize is a spare bedroom. I slide my eyes to the side, noting there's a golden glow beneath what I assume is an ensuite bathroom, but before it can fully sink in, his words hit my ears.

I scowl, my hands clenching into fists at my side. "You fucking owe me, Crawford," I growl. "It's a couple hundred. I know you have it. So, just fucking pay up and I'll be out of your fucking hair."

"Or what?" Kellen turns back to me, his eyes darkening as he advances. My eyes widen. Before I can move out of the way, his fists slam into the wall above my head and he boxes me in. "You threatening me, Moore? What are you gonna fucking do to me?" He takes a step back, spreading his arms wide. "I'm fucking better than you. You have nothing. You *are* nothing."

A coldness descends over me. It's not the first time I've heard those words, and it's almost like him speaking them has hit a switch inside of me. "Give me the two hundred you fucking owe me, Kellen," I snap, "or I'll tell all your little friends out there that by this time next week, you'll be destitute."

He stiffens and his arms fall back to his sides. And wouldn't you know it, his expression changes. The color that had previously infused his cheeks—likely from any number of alcohols or drugs he'd taken earlier—drains away completely. "W-what the fuck does that mean?" he stutters.

I roll my eyes and then straighten my back, taking a step towards him. "You think you're the only one who requests my services?" I ask him, lowering my voice. If he thought I was threatening him before, he has no fucking clue. I may be physically weak, but in this—dealings of information and secrets—I'm the queen. Everyone always forgets. They think with enough money and connections and power, they become above it all. No one is above reproach. I make sure of that.

"I'm a broker, Crawford," I remind him. "A hacker.

44

Information is what I deal in. I know everything. Every single hidden, disgusting secret you and your mother have tried to hide. You're fucking broke. Or at least, you're well on your way to it." His eyes scan away, but there's no running from the truth.

"You don't know what you're talking about," he spits, but he doesn't sound as confident as he did before. Sweat collects at the top of his brow and on his upper lip.

"Actually," I say, stepping closer, until I'm standing right in front of him, within touching distance. "I do."

He scoffs and turns away, taking another step back—the predator becoming the prey as he feels the walls of the truth closing in on him. He's been trying to put it off—the fact that he's falling, descending into the depths of monetary despair for a while now—but it's too late. It's happening. I could be kinder. I could tell him it's not the end of the world, but for men like him—entitled, rich pricks that have only been able to rely on the golden spoon they were born with their entire life—it is. It's the end of the life he knows and understands. And knowing how he and his family have treated their employees—how they've already fucked their long-term maids and butlers and everyone else that have taken care of them for the past twenty years out of their retirements because they've been trying to keep up the façade—has dried up any and all sympathy I might have felt.

"The information you gave us was supposed to fucking help!" he snaps. "It didn't. It was worthless. That company still—"

"I don't care," I cut him off, crossing my arms over my chest and shaking my head. "I don't guarantee shit. I get the information. You choose how you use it."

"I'm not paying you for bad information," he spits.

"It wasn't bad information," I snap. "It was accurate. It's not my fault that you and your family fucked up."

Kellen's head spins towards me, and I drop my arms as his

nostrils flare and he advances on me. "You're enjoying this, aren't you?" he growls. I gasp as my back hits the wall and I turn, reaching for the door, but he catches it with the flat of his palm and slams it closed, cutting off my means of escape. My heart rate leaps. Sweat begins to collect at the back of my neck. "You want me to fail."

"I don't give a shit if you fail," I snap, jerking my chin up despite the riot of emotions ricocheting through me. Fear. Dread. Anger. Frustration. "What happens to you doesn't matter to me." It's honest. To people like Kellen Crawford, their lives are the center of the universe. In reality, though, they're just as small and insignificant as I am.

"You fucking *bitch*." Kellen pulls a fist back and punches the wall beside my head. I freeze as his knuckles shove past the drywall and little fragments slap the side of my face, a white dust falling over my shoulder.

My lips part. I don't know what I'm going to say, but I know I've made a mistake. I let my negative emotions lead my fucking mouth when I should've been thinking of a way to de-escalate the situation. Before I can figure a way out, Kellen's body over mine disappears. I blink at the giant open space that's now before me as a flash of blond breezes in front of me and then a startlingly familiar face appears.

Oh no. Correction. Oh. *Fuck.* No. Not him. Anyone but him, I beg the universe. But the universe either has a warped sense of humor or it's completely ignorant to my pleas because it is, in fact, *him.*

Abel *fucking* Frazier—with his hand wrapped around Kellen Crawford's throat as he shoves him against a separate wall. "A-Abel?" Kellen stutters out, proving that I'm not the only one shocked by his sudden appearance.

"The fuck you think you're doing?" Abel demands, his voice low.

"I-I was j-just—"

Abel's fist clenches down harder on Kellen's throat, cutting him off. "I don't give a shit what you were fucking just..." His tone drifts off and I frown as he sways a bit on his feet.

"Abel." My head slowly turns and I spot a chick in the doorway of the ensuite bathroom, her body wrapped in a towel, wet hair hanging over one side of her face as she props her hip against the frame, frowning into the room.

Realization clicks. The golden glow under the door—the fact that Abel's here now. *Did he hear ... everything?* I wonder, turning back to the two of them as Abel leans away from Kellen's quickly reddening face and cuts a look at me out of the corner of his eye. It's only when I fully take in his appearance that true shock comes over me. My jaw drops open as my eyes descend.

"What are you doing?" I half shriek, turning into the wall at my back, fist hole and all because Abel Frazier isn't just standing there, holding a man by the throat. He's fucking doing it *buck ass naked.*

But Abel doesn't answer me. His next words aren't for me at all; they're for Kellen. "If you ever put your fucking hands on her again"—I grow still at the low threat in his tone and peek over my shoulder—"If you ever call her a fucking bitch..." Confusion pours through me. Is he ... angry? "I'll fucking end you, do you understand?"

Kellen nods quickly, his hands scrambling at his throat. It's easy to forget Abel when he's with the others—Braxton and Dean. He's the playboy. The guy girls flock to when they don't feel like dealing with the dangerous ones. He doesn't exude this level of animosity usually. Right now, however, he looks every bit the sick, twisted fucker he and the others are known to be. What I don't get, though, is why he's acting like this ... for me.

"Abel, come on..." the girl in the doorway whines. She cocks out her hip, letting her towel dip and open revealing the expanse of skin from her thigh all the way up to the side of her boob. I turn her way with a scowl, but her eyes are on Abel's broad, naked back. It's like I don't even exist.

That is how it should be. My invisibility is what's normal in the Eastpoint world. A thought occurs and I realize that perhaps Abel isn't actually defending me. What if he's just irritated that we disturbed his hookup? I turn to the side, sliding towards the door.

"Don't even think about it." At the sound of Abel's voice, my fingers freeze as they close over the handle of the door.

Abel releases Kellen, and he falls to the floor, coughing and clutching at his bruised throat. He glares down at him and a curl of disgust turns the corner of Abel's mouth. Please don't turn around, I practically beg him silently. It's hard enough to stare at his back and know that he's completely bare in the front. Not that he seems to even fucking notice.

Most guys wouldn't be too comfortable standing in front of another man with his junk hanging out, but Abel doesn't even blink as he ignores my internal pleas and turns back to the room. My gaze shoots to the ceiling as I release the door handle and plaster my whole body back against where Kellen punched a hole in the wall.

"Get out," Abel growls.

I practically dive for the door. I don't even care why he's flipping hot and cold, I just want out of here right now and away from him. My heart's pounding in my ears, screaming at me to run because it knows the truth. Abel Frazier is a dangerous man. Someone up top must fucking hate my guts, though, or maybe they want to see me squirm like a worm on a hook because the next words out of Abel's mouth make me repress a whimper of almost pain.

"Not you, program girl."

Fuck. Me. Sideways. My feet stutter to a stop, an invisible chain wrapping itself around my legs and keeping them pinned to the floor.

Kellen gets up and rushes to the door, practically shoving me out of the way in his path to freedom. I don't even blame him. I'd do the same thing. The girl in the doorway to the bathroom sighs.

"I'm not doing a threesome, Abel," she snaps before turning her attention to me with irritation. "And certainly not with a white trash reject." I bite my lip to keep from saying shit but return her glare with a dull look. That only seems to offend her more. "What are you looking at, bit—"

"The fuck are you still doing here?" Abel demands, cutting her off. My eyes widen as I peek at her face. Her jaw goes slack with disbelief. "Didn't you fucking hear me, cunt?" Abel swings her way and clenches his fists. With slow, cold words, he repeats himself. "I said. Get. Out."

The girl jerks herself up and stares at him for a moment. Something sizzles through the air—an electric current that makes the small baby hairs on the back of my neck and along my arms stand on end. Stumbling from the bathroom—wet hair, towel, and all—the chick practically sprints from the room. I blink in shock as the door slams behind her and I'm left *alone* with him.

Silence descends, practically screaming through my ears as all I can hear is the rapid beat of my heart and the quiet madness that has entered the room. Despite Abel's earlier words, I inch towards the door.

Before I can even touch the handle again, though, his head tilts up and back. Cool, unfocused ice blue eyes level on me.

I frown. "Are you ... high?" I ask.

Abel snorts but proves my suspicion correct when he turns fully towards me and stumbles a bit. I press my back into the wall even harder as he approaches. He doesn't answer though until he's standing right in front of me and one arm lands on the wall above my head—but not in the same way that Kellen's had.

No, that arm is there to hold him up. He looks like he could fall over at any moment.

"Abel." I can't help the bitter irritation that creeps into my tone. I blame Avalon. Before her, I kept my thoughts to myself, kept my head down, and remained invisible unless needed. But there's something about her big, brass balls that make me want to own a pair of my own. If lady balls were contagious—Avalon is the one that gave them to me. "Answer my question: are you high?"

His head drops forward, so low that it almost touches mine. The mop of blond at the top of his head flops to one side as he looks at me through slitted eyelids. "Maybe," he hedges.

I sniff, but I don't scent weed. From the places I've lived— I'd know that smell anywhere no matter what kind. "What did you take?"

He blinks, long and slow. "Can't 'member," he says. His chest presses closer and I gasp as his cold, wet skin comes in contact with mine. When I try to move out to the side, his other hand falls and catches my waist, stopping me. "Where you goin'?"

His voice makes my skin grow hot as trembles cascade down my spine and my eyes squeeze shut. What is *wrong* with me tonight? Something shuffles against me. My eyes pop back open. *Is he—*

"What are you doing?" I half shriek as he drops down even further and moves up against me until the whole of his body is pressed to my front and fuck me, but he's still naked and I'm ten seconds from freaking the fuck out.

"Tired," he mumbles against me. "Horny."

My eyes widen as I feel his hips shift and the long, hard ridge of something I never ever expected to feel from him nudges my lower belly. I roll my eyes up towards the ceiling. I've never been one for prayers. They've never helped me before, but right now, I could use the extra help. After a second, however, and no magical meteor comes rocketing down from space to knock out the man that's plastered to me like a starfish on a rock, I realize it's completely up to me to figure a way out of this mess.

I suck in a breath and blow it out. Why Abel would send his bed partner away and make me stay when he claims he's horny is beyond me, but I am not going to be the one who helps him with his—rather *large*—problem.

I have one major, unbreakable rule when it comes to Eastpoint, and that is: don't fuck with the Sick Boys. Until Avalon, I've been pretty fucking good at that rule. I don't mix business with pleasure, and I'm not going to start now.

"Abel." If he notices the coolness in my tone, he doesn't react. Instead, he settles even more firmly against me, all of that smooth, sinewy skin of his sliding across mine. He's hot—more than hot, he's like a freaking space heater. It feels like fire on my flesh. And strangely ... I don't hate it.

"Abel, come on..." I try again, pushing my arms beneath his and trying to urge him back. If I can just get him to the bed behind him, maybe I can convince him to go to sleep so I can sneak out.

He groans against me, turning his cheek one way and then the other as he nuzzles against my shoulder. My heart nearly leaps up my throat when his lips brush against my neck and his warm breath puffs over the skin there. Somewhere deep down within my body there's an unfamiliar stirring. A type of emotion that I thought I'd buried deep or erased completely resurfaces and flares back to life.

I tighten my thighs. *No. Not here, not now, and certainly not with* him.

Without thinking, I reach beneath Abel's arms and latch onto him as much as I can. Though he's less massive than the other Sick Boys, he's still wide enough that I can't quite wrap my arms completely around his broad shoulders. Once I've locked on, I shove away from the wall, catapulting the two of us back towards the bed sitting in the center of the room.

Abel grunts with what I expect is surprise as he stumbles backwards and then falls, landing on the bed. Gasping for breath, I scramble up to my hands and knees and just as I'm about to launch off of both him and the bed, his arms are around my middle and he swings us both until I'm suddenly under him, his shadow blocking out the light from the bathroom as he comes down over of me.

"Rylie ... Moore..." My name leaves his lips, and I find myself staring up into a face that's perfectly cut. Leonardo Da Vinci would find it impossibly difficult to see any flaws within Abel Frazier's looks. Me, on the other hand, well, I'm not really too fond of good looks. Within beauty, there always lies something more sinister. "What the fuck are you hiding, hmmm?"

I blink, the question that pops out of his mouth confusing me. "Hiding?" I repeat.

He nods, his eyelids lowering until only a small sliver of blue can be seen alongside his blown pupils.

"I'm not hiding anything," I say quickly.

He snickers. "What a pretty liar." My throat squeezes as his unfocused gaze lands on my face. Abel's hand drifts up and his fingers trace the side of my cheek, his thumb curving over the corner of my mouth. Something wicked inside of me tells me to lick it, but that would be ... wrong for all sorts of reasons. "You and I both know the truth," he says.

I stiffen. "The truth?" I narrow my eyes on him, wondering ... he can't know. I made sure to bury everything.

"Your file was way too clean, program girl," he says. "No ... Riot Girl. 'Cause ya know Riot Girls wreck worlds and all..." He's not making any sense.

"I don't know what you're talking about," I say. "But you're not feeling well. You need to get off of me."

"No."

My eyebrows shoot up. *"Excuse me?"*

Abel's hips sink down into me and there's that ... *large* problem again. "I said no," he replies. "I like it here. Right ... fucking ... here." His hands move down to my hips and adjust me to his liking and shockingly enough, there's no disgust in me. Instead, there's an unusual heat. A fire boiling deep within as I feel the pressure. I can feel my brows practically shoot up my face because that is not fucking normal for me. "You're so soft," he whispers, dipping his head, distracting me from the shock of his body against mine.

I swallow around a suddenly dry throat. "You're high."

He hums in the back of his throat, the sound reverberating through his chest and against mine, making me catch my breath. This isn't right. This is so very wrong. Abel Frazier isn't interested in me. He's never even spared me a second glance until ... no, this is about Ava, I think. It has to be. Her presence has brought their attention down on me and not in a good way. I push my hands against his chest and keep them there until he lifts up, tilting his head to the side as if he can't quite understand why I'm not falling into his arms.

"Get. Off. Of. Me." I grit the words out through my teeth, fighting my own instincts which I've never had to do before. My body usually understands when there's a danger. It doesn't go soft like this. It doesn't tingle at the feel of a man's flesh against mine. Tears spring to my eyes. I don't understand why I'm reacting this way, but I don't like it.

"Rylie..."

"No!" I turn my face away when Abel reaches up to cup my cheek. He's going to kiss me. Me! No. I can't. I just want him off. I can't fucking breathe because ... because if he tries again, I just might let him. And that's all sorts of fucked up, especially knowing he's not in his right mind.

"Just..."

"I said no, Abel." My voice grows rough, like something's clogged my throat. It's getting harder and harder to fight against him, but I force myself to squeeze out my next words. "Either you let me go or this is rape."

He freezes at that last word, and almost as if it's the sudden off switch to his arousal, he practically leaps away from me. Instead of instant relief, however, my muscles tighten and almost cry out at the loss. I ignore them.

I look up in time to see Abel backing away from me until his spine slams into the wall. He looks horrified—guess he's not quite as shitty of a guy as I thought he might be. I wasn't even sure mentioning the R-word would do anything, but right now, he looks like he might puke.

My palms land on the mattress and push up. "Are you—" Abel's head ducks down and he growls something unintelligible. "What did you—"

"Get the fuck out, right now, Rylie," he snaps, a bit louder.

He doesn't sound like he did with the girl from before, he sounds well and truly angry—like a furious demon barely suppressed has found its home inside his chest and is speaking through him. A beat passes, and I realize that this is it. This is my moment. I wanted him off; I got him off. If I have any hope of running, now is my chance.

I slide off of the bed and head for the door, circling him and keeping as far from him as possible. My eyes watch him warily, afraid he might change his mind at the last possible moment, but he never does. In fact, Abel Frazier's body could have been carved from stone from how still he holds himself. I grasp the handle to the door and step out, turning and letting it shut behind me. As soon as the latch clicks, a roar sounds from within and there's a crashing noise. I jump and jerk back, away from the wood.

Another crash echoes from inside the room as well as a few curses. It sounds as if he's tearing the place apart. I take a step back and another and another until I'm halfway down the hall. Yet that doesn't seem to lessen the effect the noises coming from inside the room has on me.

Finally, I decide to say fuck it. I turn and take off running. I don't know what Abel needs now, but I know it's not me. It'll never be someone like me.

That reminder, though, makes my chest ache, and I can't quite figure out why.

7

RYLIE

PRESENT DAY...

Everything in the Crawford house has returned to the way it was. It's almost as if time has turned back and what happened all those weeks ago is being set up to be replayed again. Only this time, I'm here chasing after a different prick.

The heat in the house is likely exacerbated by the number of people that have crammed into it. Though it was already big, it feels like more than half of the school is here and they're backing up every wall and hallway. Despite that I detest people touching me, I drag off my black jacket and quickly tie it around my waist and then slip off one of the many ties around my wrist and throw my hair up into a messy bun. I'll never be like the rich girls of Eastpoint, and I never want to be. Whether he likes me or not—whether Abel wants me or not—I'm just who I've always been: a girl from the wrong side of the tracks with trauma engraved on her soul.

It takes me longer than I'd like to track Abel down, but when I do find him, I'm not surprised that he's already moved on to another girl for the evening. I step out onto the back patio, leaving the sliding glass door open and move across the stone tiles and around the pool. I look to where he's set up his throne—sans the other two kings—with a drink already in hand and a tan chick with platinum blonde hair and a gold bikini that looks two sizes too small already practically in his lap.

"What took you so long, Riot Girl?" Abel calls over to me. *Dick,* I think, as every person in the vicinity turns their head directly towards me.

Fire ants crawl across my skin. Not for real, but it sure does fucking feel like it. I hate this attention and the bastard knows it. He grins my way and then downs whatever drink he's holding, chucking it behind him as his hands reach down to grip the ass of the chick riding his crotch.

A spark of something I've never felt before hits me square in the chest. Anger maybe? It must be because there's no fucking way it can be jealousy. I glance to where the bottle he just chucked gets picked up by one of the guys milling about behind him and then another is popped open and placed directly next to him. Servants catering to their master. What utter bullshit.

"Just making sure you're not going off the rails," I snap out, drawing Abel's attention once more, as well as his ire. His cold blue eyes flash and his fingers dig into the fleshy part of gold bikini's ass as he jerks her up harder against him in retaliation.

The girl knows what she's doing apparently, because she throws her head back, blonde hair flying, and lets out the loudest moan I've ever heard in my life as if she's close to coming already and he hasn't even stuck it in. It's the kind of moan I've only ever heard from pornos. Maybe I could recommend a career path for her.

"What's a program chick doing here, Abel?" one of the guys behind him asks.

I stiffen but keep my mouth shut. I want to see what his excuse is going to be. The second he casts a smug grin my way, however, and opens his mouth, I know I've made a fucking mistake.

"She's a present from Avalon," Abel says with a smirk. The freaking liar. "She's my bitch for the weekend. So have a seat, boys, whatever you want—Rylie will get it for you." Abel looks my way once more, his smile spreading. "She'll take real good care of ya."

"Are you serious?" I deadpan as I stare at Abel.

He grins right back. "Dead serious, sweetheart."

I glare back at him, gritting my teeth, but all he does is lean back. "You wanna stay?" he asks. "Why don't you grab some drinks?" Oh, this motherfucker. He's not saying it aloud, but I know what he's saying—this is nothing more than a threat. I'm only here because Avalon asked me to be, but he's not happy about it. So, what is he doing? Dangling the promise I made her over my head. He'll let me tag along and do my job, but he's not going to treat me like I deserve to be here. Because to him, I'm little more than a servant.

"We've got an errand girl? That's fucking awesome," someone says. Several of the guys seated around the patio table turn their attention my way. "In that case, program girl, why don't you run on inside and grab me another six pack. We're running low over here."

Another guy laughs, drawing my attention, and as soon as my eyes are on him, he leans back in his seat, sliding a hand down his front until he's gripping the front of his swim trunks with a full hand. "I know something else you can take care of, sweetheart."

Vomit threatens to shoot up my esophagus, but I don't get a chance to say anything before a loud squeal interrupts.

"Oh, I want a margarita!" Gold bikini yells, forgetting her role for a brief moment as she turns to me and casts a bored look of holier than thou energy my way. "And I want it on the rocks," she says. "I want crushed ice, though, none of those cubes." She waves her perfectly manicured hand at me as if I'm dismissed.

I turn my gaze to Abel, but his eyes are already elsewhere—specifically on the guy who made me want to upchuck my dinner. And instead of amused, he appears flat out furious. Why? I wonder. He's the one who told them I'd take care of them. I slowly let out an annoyed breath, turn, and head back towards the house.

I'll get their fucking drinks. Maybe if Abel gets drunk enough, he won't be able to get it up for gold bikini and I can pour him back into the Mustang and drive him home. Then, I'll take the opportunity to set up my damn cameras. Maybe I'll find something to spike his fucking drink while I'm at it. Dickhead. Maybe double doses of Viagra—you know what they say about erections lasting more than four hours. I grin evilly. I wonder if he'll enjoy the needles in the emergency room later. It would serve him right.

I stomp past the girls giggling with football players and the guys acting like their money makes them top shit and head in through the backdoor, hanging a left towards the kitchen. Minutes later, I'm back out in the sweltering heat of the backyard and crushing bodies as people dance to the music blaring out through the invisible surround sound speakers.

I shove a box of the first type of beer I saw in the fridge at the first guy who looks my way and surprise, sur-fucking-prise, gold bikini has invited a new friend to the party. Her friend is another carbon copy of herself except this one is wearing neon green. Lovely. At least she's been removed from Abel's lap and is instead sitting on one side of him as her friend occupies the other, and as I take a look around, I note that crotch-grabber is mysteriously gone. Good riddance.

"Here's your margarita," I snap, shoving it against her massive chest before turning to Abel.

"Can you please—"

59

"Oh my God!" Before I can finish speaking, gold bikini is up and out of her seat shoving the cup holding her margarita in my face. "What the fuck did I say about my ice cubes! I didn't want these ones!"

Hold it together, Rylie, I urge myself as I feel my eyes slide shut. I suck in a breath and let it back out before I reopen them.

"If you don't like what I gave you," I say slowly. "Go make it yourself." Her painted pink lips part in shock as she gapes at me. I flip back to Abel. "Now, as I was saying, can you please—"

"Abel said you're our bitch for the night," gold bikini snaps, this time cutting me off with a point as she slams the cup against my chest with force. The string of my control frays. "So, do what I fucking said, and go make my margarita right."

Her hand remains against my chest and though her skin isn't touching mine, just knowing that there's nothing but the thin layer of my t-shirt that separates us has my mind hazing over. I can actually feel the warmth of her skin and I. Fucking. Hate. It.

"Get your hand off of me," I say quietly.

"I'm sorry, I can't hear you." The chick pulls her hand away and then brings it back against my chest as she speaks. "Go. Make. It. Right." Each word is a poke to my sternum.

My control snaps. I tip my head back and smile, reaching up and taking the cup from her. It must make her think she's won because she smiles brightly and steps back towards her seat. I'm not about to let her go, though. Without missing a beat, I lift the arm with her margarita still in my grasp and tip the cup over. The second she feels the cold alcohol and juice mixture hit her head, she squeals in shock, as I let the remainder of the drink pour down her face—ruining what has to be at least a full case of makeup painted on her face—and even over her airbag-like tits.

With black mascara running down her cheeks—because, yeah, this girl never planned to get wet in that fucking outfit—

and the sticky liquid ruining her otherwise supermodel worthy look, she looks like what she really is. A cheap whore in expensive fabric.

"What the fuck is wrong with you!" The pitch of her scream has every head in the vicinity turning towards us. Maybe I should care that all eyes are on me. Maybe I should give a living fuck that everyone is watching this bimbo's fucking meltdown as she screams in the goth chick's face. But for the first time in my fucking life, I don't. I just ... don't give a fuck.

My gaze travels from her margarita-soaked face as she spits vile and venom my way, curses flying from her lips to the man seated like a king behind her. He didn't defend her the same way he didn't defend me because to him, girls like us—rich or poor—don't matter. Well, fuck him too. He arches a brow when he meets my gaze, and I return my attention to gold bikini girl.

"—washed up, too fucking stupid to live, brainless—"

"Shut up!" I scream, startling her.

She blinks at me before turning to Abel and her friend. "Do you hear the way she's talking to me, Abel? Aren't you gonna do anything?"

Oh, sweetheart, I think. He's not gonna help you. Abel isn't the type of guy to help anyone but his own fucking self.

And just as I'd expect, he merely grins and leans back in his seat, crossing his arms behind his neck. "Nah, I think you two girls have got it," he says. "But if you want to fist fight, might I suggest waiting a bit. I'm sure we've got some Jell-O around here. We can probs rig up a ring for you two, right, Dash?" He glances to the side and one of the guys laughs, giving him a thumbs up. Abel's gaze finds me again. "I think you're good to go, Jess, but Rylie is probably gonna have to throw down in her underwear."

"Ugh, you are such a pig!" Gold bikini—apparently 'Jess'—huffs before whirling back to me.

"Yet, just ten minutes ago you were moaning and riding his

crotch for all to see," I comment. "Guess you're into bestiality, huh?"

I don't see the slap coming, but to be honest, I should've expected it. What I didn't expect was to hit her back. Yet, the second the sound of her palm hitting my face rings through my ears, I feel myself moving back, and instead of slapping her, I straight up punch her in the mouth. The feel of her teeth cutting into my knuckles as she takes the hit full force is something I thought I'd forgotten growing up, but apparently not because it feels like coming home.

The screech she lets out as she hits the ground echoes off the tiles and the siding of the house. I touch my hand to my cheek and then slowly look down at her. "Just an FYI," I snap as she starts to cry, "No one in this fucking world gives a shit how you take your goddamn margaritas." With that, I look up at Abel and straighten my back. "And you—you can go fuck yourself. I'll find my own ride home. Have fun getting drunk and eating diseased pussy." I hold both fists up, flip them over, and then direct my middle fingers to the sky, holding them for the moment, letting the insult sink in before I back away, turn, and leave.

Avalon asks for too fucking much. I should not have agreed to this.

8

ABEL

I LET HER GO. She's angry, and I've never seen it before. *Rylie Moore losing her cool?* God fucking damn, is it hot. I suspect not many people ever have. I can't help the direction of my eyes as she stomps away, right down to her ass. She's small everywhere. Petite. Scrawny. But there—her ass—that's where she's at least got some decent weight.

Does it make me an asshole to watch it sway as she walks away? Yeah, probably. Do I give a shit? Not even a single one. In fact, it's my right to watch an ass like that. Most girls when they're as small as she is are flat all around, nothing more than sticks with pretty faces. But Rylie ... no matter how little she is, I have a feeling that's an ass that'll never deflate. I really wanna know what it'd be like to fuck it. To bury myself in her pretty little pussy from behind, cup the globes in my hands, and pound her into a mattress, a wall, wherever the fuck I can convince her to drop trou and bend over.

"Abel?" The sound of the chick at my side calling my name snaps me out of my x-rated thoughts. I have little doubt that if Rylie was privy to them, she wouldn't be walking away so freely. After that little outburst of hers, I have the distinct feeling she'd probably try to tear me a new asshole. I'm almost tempted to tell her how good she fucking looks from behind just to see her reaction. Don't know why, but I like them. Every single one. When she ducks her head and tries to retain her composure. When she blushes and starts to stutter. When her hazel eyes flash with warning and anger. I want all of them for myself. "Abel." Bianca whines my name for a second time, making the smile that I hadn't even realized I'd started to make drop into a scowl. I wait to respond, though, until Rylie is out of earshot.

The second she's gone, though, storming around the side of the Crawford estate mansion that I now own, I point to the girl remaining at my side and then to her friend. "Get her out of here," I order.

Bianca bats her dark lashes and her hand touches my chest. "But I thought we were gonna have some fun tonight?" she says. The annoying whine in her voice is enough to have me gripping her wrist and shoving it away.

"I don't give a fuck what you thought," I say blandly.

"A-Abel?" It's clear I've shocked her. I'm rarely this rough with chicks, but she's irritating me and she whispered something really fucking annoying in my ear about Rylie as she was dumping Jessica's drink on her head. Real annoying and real fucking insulting.

"Girl, you're either deaf or fucking stupid," I snap when she reaches for me again. "Maybe you should stop popping the fucking pills that are making you look like an anorexic bitch," I say, repeating the same exact words she'd used to define Rylie. "'Cause it's obviously affecting your intelligence." I lean back and laugh. "Then again, we both know you aren't by my side because you're smart." Not like Rylie is. A fucking genius under the thumb of the heirs of Eastpoint, she is.

Bianca gasps, but I'm not in the mood to soothe her fucking wounded ego. The second I decided to bring Rylie to this thing, I knew I wasn't going to fuck anyone here. "Get your fucking friend out of here," I grit between my teeth. "Or I'll have my boys toss you both in the pool and then out on your ass."

Her eyes widen and she's out of her seat like a rocket. As if to save face, she sneers at me. "You're an asshole, Abel Frazier," she huffs as she bends down and scoops one of her friend's arms over her shoulder and then leads her away.

"Yeah, sweetheart, an asshole just ten seconds ago you were whining at and begging to fuck you," I say it loud enough for everyone nearby to hear, and several guys chuckle, lifting their solo cups and beers to the sky as they nod their heads.

Bianca's face flames red and she tries to hurry her friend. "Come on," she says. "Let's get an ice pack."

A good fucking friend she is, I think sardonically. She didn't even try to back up the girl when she faced off with Rylie. Then again, maybe she thought she didn't need to. Rylie looks as breakable as a piece of fragile glass with all her pale skin and dark circles under her eyes. I could see the tightly held control in her snap, though, when Jess began touching her chest. Girl doesn't like to be touched, and fuck me, but that only makes me want to touch her myself.

"Go give Rylie a ride," I snap to the guy closest to me. Luckily, it's Dash. He'll do right and take care of her, even if he doesn't particularly want to. He's always been reliable like that.

"I'll take her to the dorms and text you when I'm on my way back," he says, getting up.

"No." I stop him. "She goes back to the Carter estate."

His eyes practically bulge out of his head, but other than a brief pause and that look of astonishment, he doesn't say anything else as he moves away from the table, cutting through the crowd on his path to follow the girl I can't seem to stop fucking thinking about.

I'd follow her myself, and say fuck it to the rest of this party, but there's just one more thing I gotta do. I point to one of my teammates. "Bring Javi back," I state.

"Didn't you send him away?" Yeah, after that shit he said and pulled with Rylie? That fucker doesn't deserve to look at her, but now that she's gone...

I smile and I know it's not nice. "Tell him I wanna talk," I say.

I lean back in my seat as the guy nods and moves to do my bidding. The muscles in my forearm clench and unclench as I fist my hands and then release them. Javi comes ambling back, a bright smile on his face.

"Yo, Abel!" He lifts a hand in greeting as he slides back through the crowd. I bite down, baring my teeth as I sit forward and then stand up and descend from the lifted patio. "What's up? I thought you were—"

The stupid motherfucker doesn't get to finish his sentence because in the next second my fist is flying through the air and straight into his face. His nose crunches under my knuckles and the drink in his hand goes flying, spraying sour smelling liquid all over the tiles. A girl screams in surprise as some of it lands on her, but I don't care. I'm no longer paying attention to anything around me because the full breadth of my focus is on the man in front of me and then under me as he falls to the fucking pavement like the pussy he is.

I rear back and slam my fist into his face again. "What the fuck!" Javi's cry is full of blood and pain as he turns his cheek and spits out a wad of red. I rise to my feet, standing above him and glare down at the piece of shit beneath me. "What did I do?" he moans, cupping his hand over his bloodied and bruised face. Feeling cruel, I lift my foot and land it right on his fucking crotch, and just as I expected, he starts screaming like a bitch. "Ahhh! No! Stop!" Javi's fingers grip my foot, trying to lift it up and away, but I don't fucking move. "What are you guys doing? Get him off of me!"

No one moves. No one so much as attempts to help the pissant on the ground. Instead, they all stare. Hard. Fearful. As if they, too, could be next. For Dean or Brax to do something like this would be considered normal. But me ... I know they're shocked. I'm not usually the rough type.

There's just something about her, though...

I press down even harder and then lean into him, reaching down and lifting his upper half up off the tiles with a fist clenched in his collar. "You're blacklisted," I grit out loud enough for the rest of the crowd to hear.

Javi stops struggling, sensing that my anger is reaching its peak. "W-what?" he stutters. "No. You can't do that to me. I'm on the football team. I'm one of your friends—"

"Not anymore," I growl, resisting the urge to lay into him again. Make no mistake, I want to. I want to make him bleed. Rip him limb from goddamn fucking limb. But if I start now, I doubt I'll stop until he's dead and though I don't doubt my ability to murder a man in public and get away with it, I know how it'll affect me later. Ruining his future is good enough. For now. I release him and step away, lifting my foot off his sorry excuse for a prick after a good grind down that makes him flinch and whimper.

"Everybody fucking hear that?" I yell. "Javier Wilson is out. No one talks to him. No one fucking helps him. Nothing." I turn and glance back over my shoulder as Javi struggles to get to his feet. He lets the blood on his face run freely as he cups himself over his crotch. "You're as good as fucking dead to me," I state, pointing his way. "And you're not on the team anymore. Show up to practice and you'll be more than 'as good as.'"

"I-I don't understand, Abel," he huffs, fighting back tears as he tries to take a step forward and stumbles. "W-what did I do?"

My head tips back and I glare at him through slitted eyes. "You propositioned what's mine," I sneer. "Anyone who goes after or even thinks to threaten Rylie Moore answers not just to the other Eastpoint heirs, but to me as well."

With that, I turn and start off towards the house, passing Kellen Crawford as I go. "And you," I growl as I pass. "Make sure to pay up what you owe." Knowing him and the fact that Rylie didn't even know he was back, Crawford hasn't paid her for that night two months ago.

All actions have consequences and no matter how high he is on the totem pole of Eastpoint, I'm fucking higher. Rylie doesn't know it yet, but she's been well and truly claimed.

9

RYLIE

I STOMP across the grass of the front lawn, bypassing the red Mustang that sticks out like a sore thumb amidst all of the other far more valuable vehicles with irritation. Fuck this place. Fuck Eastpoint. Fuck the parties. And fuck one Sick Boy in particular. Why did I ever agree to this?

I shake my head. The answer's already there. Because I didn't really have a choice. Avalon may not realize it, or maybe she does and just doesn't care, but I don't have the ability to turn them—and now her since she's one of them—down. I'm here for one reason: protection. Already my nerves are on the fritz, wondering what the payback for tonight's little explosion will do to me. Abel seems the petty type.

My feet carry me to the edge of the property before I realize I really don't have a way to get back. I stuff my hand into my pocket and withdraw my phone to flip through my contacts. Looking at them, though, makes me feel more than a little pathetic. A full year at Eastpoint and there's no one else aside from the Sick Boys and Avalon. I really am shit at making friends.

Blowing out a breath, I shove the phone back into my

pocket and take a step off the curb, turning towards the interstate. A car comes speeding down the Crawford's driveway, kicking up dust and small bits of rock and grass as it cuts around some of the other cars with their ass ends sticking out into the street. I ignore it—at least until it stops right in front of me and the window rolls down.

A vaguely familiar face appears on the other side. Dash Bennington. If Brax and Dean are Abel's right-hand men, then Dash is his left. "What do you want?" I spit, unable to stop the vitriol from entering my voice. Surely, just like Abel, he'll find some way to put me in my place. To remind me that I'm nothing but a program chick under their command.

Shockingly, however, he leans over and pops open the passenger door, flexing his arm and throwing it wide before sitting back into the driver's seat. "Get in," he orders.

I blanch. "I'm not going anywhere with you."

He cuts me a cold look. "Abel told me to take you back."

Shit. I should've known he wouldn't let me off so easily. And I suppose it makes sense that he'd send someone after me. It wouldn't be good for his reputation if Abel were to leave the party and go chasing after some program chick. I turn my gaze back to the street, wondering how good my chances are of getting away. If worse comes to worst, I can probably call an Uber to pick me up. It's money I don't want to spend, but it can't be that much to get back to the Carter estate.

As if he senses the directions of my thoughts, Dash sighs. "I wouldn't if I were you," he says. "Just get in the fucking car, Rylie."

I don't want to. I *really* don't want to. The childish part of me wants to turn away from him and his offer, stomp my foot, and cry, but crying has never gotten me anywhere before. Nor has pitching a fit. In fact, the little one I pitched at the party is probably going to haunt me for the next little while anyway. I should just accept Dash's offer and take the opportunity to set up my cameras.

I must stand there contemplating my options too long because the next thing I know, Dash is grumbling under his breath and the driver's side door flies open as if he means to come around and stuff me into the car himself.

"Oh my God!" I snap. "Fine! I'm getting in."

The car door is in my hand and I'm practically launching myself into the passenger seat of his vehicle within the next second. I've already got a few crazy psychos to worry about; I don't need another.

"Seatbelt," he grits, but I don't even get the chance to clip it into place before he's pressed his foot down on the gas and the car is fishtailing out of the driveway onto the main road. If I was the type to believe in God, I'd be praying right now.

Finally, I get myself situated and locked into the seat—though it takes a bit with how fast he takes the curves. I begin to wonder if Dash is even his real name or if it's a nickname based on his driving skills. A thought pops into my head. "I'm not in the dorms right now," I say quickly, as he turns onto the highway.

Dash glances my way once before he cuts off an oncoming Jeep and makes his way into the fast lane. "I know," he says.

"You know?"

"The Carter estate?" he inquires, though from his tone, it's clear he already knows.

I sink lower into the seat. "Yeah."

"Abel told me."

"Oh," I say. Guess there's nothing else to it then.

Minutes of silence go by, but I get the feeling that Dash is observing me more closely than he ever has before. I half wonder if perhaps the news of where I'm currently staying will spread over campus by the time school starts. Guys like to think they're above the gossip girls like to spread, but that's bullshit.

71

They're just as much into other people's lives and faults as girls are. Rich or poor, pretty or ugly, everyone is prey to the interests of other people's lives and misfortunes.

"It's temporary," I say after what feels like the longest time. "I'm only there for the weekend."

Dash grunts. "I didn't ask." No, he didn't, but from the hole he's boring into my face, he might as well have.

When the car pulls into the Carter estate, I reach for the door handle, fully intending to bounce and leave Dash to run back to his master as soon as fucking possible. The second my hand lands on the latch, however, the locks click into place. I freeze, an automatic fight or flight mode activated as the car's locking mechanism snicks, alerting me to potential danger.

Slowly, I turn back to face Dash, noting that his hands are firmly squeezed on the steering wheel, so hard that his knuckles are starting to turn white. "Hey, buddy," I say, "you gonna let a girl go free or am I under arrest?" No one ever said I was good at the whole fight or flight mode. Sarcasm it is.

Dash pulls his hands away and turns to face me. "You run shit for the boys," he says slowly.

My brows practically leap to the top of my forehead. "Yeah..." I hedge.

"Do you work for others?" he demands.

"Depends on what you mean by 'work,'" I reply, eyeing him speculatively.

Cool brown eyes stare back at me for what feels like the longest time. Then, finally, Dash turns back to the windshield and glares through it. "You can run background checks under the radar, right?" he asks, but before I can either confirm or deny, he's already talking again. "I need you to run one on my ... father." The last word is pulled through his teeth.

I think back to what I know about Dash Bennington, and honestly, it's not much. Dash is an old friend of the boys. Closer to Abel than the rest. The Sick Boys have them—secondary friends who ride the wave at the back, not as close as their inner circle, but close enough that they can be called upon. The question is, why is Dash coming to me and not to either Abel or one of the others.

"I don't do conflicts of interest," I warn him quietly.

"It's not," he says quickly, closing his eyes for a moment before reopening them and turning them my way. "It's not," he repeats. "I just need to know everything you can find out—past and present, lovers and mistresses, business associates, *everything*—about him."

I consider him for a long moment. "It's a four hundred dollar down payment," I state.

"Done," he says.

"And a promise that you won't refer me to anyone else," I say. "I don't take referrals anymore. I'm only doing this because you're Abel's friend." And after tonight, I'm going to need someone to owe me something because I have a feeling Abel is going to want his pound of flesh when he gets back. I did probably embarrass the shit out of him tonight. That is, if someone like Abel even bothers getting embarrassed. Honestly, I doubt it. But he'll likely love any excuse to torment me, and I just gave him one.

"Done," Dash repeats.

I glance at him, considering his face, wondering what about his father could be causing him such distress. No one ever comes to me for anything good. I've set it up that way, I know, but at the same time ... sometimes I wish ... I sigh. Sometimes I wish for things that I can never have.

"I'll contact you in a few days," I say as he hits the unlock button and I pop open the passenger side door and step out.

"Hey, Rylie." I stop and turn back, watching as Dash's eyes slide from my face to the windshield once more. "Thanks."

I shake my head. "Don't thank me," I warn him. "I'm not doing you a favor. You're paying for my services."

He nods once and I slam the door shut behind me.

I don't wait for him to drive off as I head inside and he doesn't wait around anyway. It's a silent understanding. He did his job and now it's over. He's nice enough to me, but in my world, everyone else is temporary. They're just people passing by through the road of life. They're good for a while, even useful at times. Everyone else is a tool to use. Even the Sick Boys. Even Avalon. And even, as much as the thought of admitting it makes my chest ache, Abel Frazier. I need to remember that. I'm not someone who sticks around, and to them, I'm the same. Just a tool to use and then throw away.

Those thoughts swirl around my head as I make my way towards the garage, pulling up the code Avalon texted to me and plugging it in before I step back to wait for the metal door to rise, letting me in. The Carter mansion is quiet without anyone in it. It's cold, too, I realize, shivering as a blast of air conditioning hits me right in the face. Even the dorms aren't this cold.

Goosebumps rise along my arms and the small tiny hairs there begin to rise. I blow out a breath and head for the stairs. There's really no telling when Abel will decide to come home, and I need to get those cameras up and running before he does. I make the trek up the stairs and find my bag where I left it, just inside Abel's bedroom.

I stare at it for a moment, knowing that if he finds my little cameras, he'll probably be pissed. Then again, I can always use the excuse that Avalon asked me to watch him. These—thanks to me—are practically unhackable. Not impossible, but incredibly hard, and who else would know about them but me anyway?

I pull out the first one, turn it on and then get to work. Abel may not like how closely his friends watch him, but at least they care enough to. My chest tightens the tiniest degree more. *It must be nice. To have people give a shit about you.*

10

By the time I make it home from the party, after having Dash drop me off and another one of my teammates ride back with him after delivering my Mustang, I'm drunk and hungry. Not just hungry—fucking ravenous. Unfortunately, the type of hunger I'm currently experiencing has nothing to do with food and everything to do with the hard cock in my pants.

After Rylie left and I'd made shit clear to the dick who thought he could fucking proposition her, things had quieted down, but unlike most guys—the more I drank, the hornier I became. There were a number of bitches willing to jump into my pants. Only problem is, *little Abel* only wants one pussy.

I stumble up the stairs and hang a right, working myself through the maze that is this fucking house before I come to my bedroom. Throwing the door wide and letting it bang against the wall, I step inside and flip on the light. I don't know why I expected her to be waiting for me, but I did. So, when I look to my bed and find it empty, I'm annoyed.

Annoyed enough to go hunting for her, and of course, I find her nowhere near my bedroom, but instead across the fucking house, in one of the smallest extra rooms this place has. This time, instead of throwing the door wide, I try the handle and find it locked. Locked? In my own fucking house? Is she serious?

I waste no time picking the lock. It doesn't take much—the small multitool I usually keep in my pockets for emergencies is enough. Never thought I'd be using it for something like this, but if she thinks she can keep me out, she's got another thing coming. I slowly crack the door and step into the dark interior, letting it shut silently behind me as I step up to the single window between the small double bed and the desk across from it.

Moonlight pours into the room, illuminating the lavender locks of Rylie's hair as it spans across the pillow beneath her. I lift a strand, rubbing it between my fingertips, and wonder ... *would she welcome me into her bed if I tried now?*

I consider that as I stare at the side of her face. Small brown dots line her cheeks. Some darker than others. Freckles. How have I never noticed that she had freckles? They're not prominent, but they're beautiful all the same.

My teeth grind down against my jaw. I want her like a fire in my blood. So, why am I standing here watching her sleep?

I blow out a slow breath and release her hair before turning and sinking to the floor with my back against the bed. "You don't know what you do to me, Riot Girl," I whisper into the shadows. She fucks with me deep inside. Whether she realizes it or not, there's something about her that has managed to crawl into the cavity of my chest and find a place there, and yet, we're still fighting it.

I am and so is she. Because we're both cowards in the end, and if I were to accept her, she could really hurt me. More than that, she could devastate me. My hands clench against the smooth softness of the white carpet. I should get up and leave her, I think. But that thought never turns into action and minutes later, I'm still sitting here, staring at the whitewash wood of the desk and the blinking light on her laptop that sits atop it.

A small whimper whispers into the room, making my back stiffen. I pull away from the bed to look at Rylie as her form shifts and turns over. That's when I notice the pinch of her brows and the sweat coating her forehead. Her hands clench and unclench against the sheets as her eyes move back and forth behind her eyelids.

It doesn't take a genius to figure out what's happening. Every single one of us that has ever stepped foot in this house has demons—and I'm no exception. I've had my fair share of nightmares to recognize one. Her pink lips part and another terrified noise erupts from her throat, the sound making its way into my chest, stabbing me with the urge to help her.

"Don't..." A single tear leaks out of the corner of her eye and runs down the side of her face. The sharp feeling in my chest digs deeper. "Please."

I don't know who she's begging, but if I could find my way into her mind and fight them off for her—in this moment, I would. During the day, this girl is fierce. She's dependable. Sharp witted. Dangerously smart. Her talent is top class; it's why she's at Eastpoint. I've never seen her like this. Lost in the throes of some dark dream. The two words she whispers into the room are filled with longing, with pain and despair. As if she's already given up on someone coming to her rescue, and yet she can't help but cry out anyway.

Her breathing grows choppy and her legs saw back and forth beneath the sheets. Almost as if she's running from something or, perhaps, someone. My gaze is drawn to her and I couldn't peel it away from her even if I wanted to.

It's just too fucking bad that I had to be the one to hear her cry for help. I take a step away from her, meaning to leave her to the fantasy of her own making—it'll be better if she fights those demons herself. Because the truth of the matter is that I'm no one's hero, least of all hers. Almost as if she senses my nearness, though, her hand reaches out, seeking, as a cry of shock and hurt breaks free from her lips.

Some demons wear pleasant faces, Abel. Those are the ones you have to be most careful around. My mom's old words come back to haunt me at the most inopportune time. At the time, I hadn't known what she meant, but as I got older, it made sense. She had been trying to warn me. Not all that glitters is gold—or some shit like that.

The world we live in is full of monsters, many of which are invisible. They stalk us, day and night, climb into our beds and lay with us. They crawl into our bodies and make their homes in our hearts, wedging themselves so deep that nothing short of clawing out your own organs will make them leave. But no matter what they do, or how they come to be, they always leave scars.

And right now, I think I'm watching Rylie battle with those scars.

I'm not good at comfort. I'm not good with tears. Yet, as more leak out from her eyes, sliding down her face—and knowing that if she were awake, she wouldn't have let a single one fall—I find myself unable to resist the urge to move closer to her. To reach out and take her hand.

As soon as my hand touches hers, the tears seem to slow and then after a moment, they stop altogether. That only leads to more emotions rising within my chest. I close my eyes for a moment, but when I reopen them I know there's no more fighting it—no more fighting *her*. I can't stop myself from gently nudging her back as carefully as possible so as not to wake her as I climb into the bed with her. It's a miracle she never wakes, or perhaps something is just finally going my way for a change. Because I know, beyond a shadow of a doubt, that if she were to open her eyes and realize who was with her, she'd curse me.

Right now, though, she slumbers, like a princess in a storybook, and I find myself curling up against her, inhaling the soft scent of ocean shampoo as I hold her hand and chase away those demons of hers. I count the breaths she takes, listening as they slow and grow more and more even. Warmth floods my system as her body moves towards mine. Her fingers weaving into the spaces between my own. Her body is slight, so very fragile and having it pressed against me is a lesson in patience and willpower.

My foggy mind can't seem to do anything but focus on her. My cock pounds against the zipper of my jeans and I ignore the bastard. I'm wicked, a heathen, but even I'm not disgusting enough to fuck a sleeping girl, especially not one who seems to be fighting some internal battle.

Rylie's a cuddler, I realize moments later as she curves into my chest, burrowing against me as if she wants to find a way inside.

You're already there, I want to tell her. *And been there for a while.* Like a parasite.

I don't know for how long I lay like that, letting her use me as a shield for the darkness in her mind, but when the sun starts to come up, throwing a cascade of varying colors shining through the thin curtains of the window, and birds start to chirp, I know it's time to go.

It hurts to remove her hand from mine—to pull my fingers from her grasp as I get off of the bed and move back. For a moment, I stop and watch to see what she'll do and I'm rewarded with the little pucker of her brows once more, accompanied by the shifting of her arms as she moves them up and down, seeking and searching for something, someone. More specifically, for me.

Before I do something I know I'll regret, I turn and leave her room. I'm no longer drunk, but I am exhausted. And as I head towards my own room, peel my clothes away, and fall into bed, the soft sound of Rylie's even breaths follow me into a world of my own making.

I dream of purple hair and green and gold eyes. Pale skin and freckles that disappear under the sunlight. And what a wonderful dream it is.

11

RYLIE

"Oh, my God. That's fucking hilarious." Avalon's laughter echoes in my eardrums as I set up my new, and *very* temporary workstation in the spare room I'm borrowing for the weekend.

"I take it, I've got permission then?" I prompt her when another snort of laughter hits my ears.

"Of course," she replies and I can just picture her waving her hand through the air to accompany her tone. "I told you to do whatever you needed to. Cameras are a smart way to go. He'll hate them."

"I'm the only one who has access," I remind her. "I'll take them down when I leave."

"No," Avalon says. "You can turn them off when you leave if you want, but if we have to leave again, you'll just have to do the whole thing over again. It's best to leave them where they are for now."

I blanch. "I might have to do this again?" I grumble.

"It's a possibility," she replies. A moment of silence follows and I set the phone down, hitting speaker so that I can free up my hands as I click across my keyboard. Something's bothering her and the fact that she hasn't yet hung up must mean she wants to talk about it. Getting her to admit anything is like pulling teeth so I just need to wait until she's ready. "The doctor isn't sure yet if Dean should play this year," she finally says. "I wouldn't give a shit and he says he doesn't, but..."

It's not hard to see the issue there. To Dean Carter, the football team is like a training ground. If he and the other guys are kings, the football players are their knights. Being suddenly unable to do something you've grown up doing your whole life is sure to rock anyone's composure. No matter how stoic Dean Carter may seem, he's still just a young, twenty-something year old guy at the end of the day. He's not impervious to disappointment and pain. And when one hurts, they all hurt—including Avalon.

"He cares," I finally say when she still hasn't picked the conversation back up.

Avalon sighs. "Yeah, he does." Which means she cares too. "Dean's wanting to get a second opinion while we're here, but I doubt they're gonna tell him anything we haven't already heard."

"The bullet almost killed him," I remind her. "Most people would just be happy to be alive."

"Yeah, well, we're not most people," she says. Understatement of the century.

"Are you still coming back on time?" I ask as my fingers fly across my keyboard.

"Yeah, no need to worry, you won't have to put up with fuckboy central all by your lonesome for much longer."

I wince at the comment. I don't know why, but it feels wrong to think of Abel as little more than a fuckboy and I know she doesn't mean it in any true derogatory way. What with Avalon firmly ensconced as Dean's Queen, Abel and Brax are her brothers as much as they are his. She loves them in her own fucked up way.

"Speaking of fuckboy central..." Avalon's tone changes,

becoming more amused and almost smug. "Want to tell me what happened at last night's party?"

I stiffen. "He told you?"

She chuckles. "Hell no, he didn't tell me shit. Dean got a call from one of the guys on the team. Apparently, Abel went all caveman after you left and scared the fuck outta them."

"He did?" I blink at my screen and then turn my full attention to my phone. "What do you mean? What did he do?"

"Oh no, I want your version first," she says, "Talk."

A groan rumbles up in my chest. I press my hands flat against the desk in front of me and lean back, tipping the chair I'm in up on its back two legs as I turn my gaze to the ceiling. "It ... complicated..." I start. It's not. It's really not. The fact is Abel Frazier makes me lose my fucking mind. I close my eyes, blow out a breath, and tell her exactly what happened. When I'm done, I wait with bated breath to hear her reaction.

She's quiet for several long moments and then hums. "Huh," she says. "That's interesting."

"It ... is?" I sit up and let the chair drop back down on all fours. "You don't think ... I overstepped?"

"No, not really. You were nicer than I would've been," she replies.

Right, I think. Because the first party she went to here ... she lobbed a freaking Molotov Cocktail at Dean's ex-girlfriend's car. Surprisingly, though, Avalon doesn't say anything more about me dumping a drink on one of Abel's girlfriends. Instead, she changes the subject.

"You've got the cameras up and running now, right?" she asks. "What's he doing right now?"

"Uh..." I refocus on my computer and click across the multiple apps I have set up until I come to the one that records and saves the cameras in his room and open it. "He's sleeping in," I say. It's not surprising considering he got in at the ass crack of dawn.

"Are you serious?" Ava grumbles. "It's like 3 p.m. there right now. Go wake his ass up."

"Absolutely fucking not." The words shoot out of my mouth before I can stop to think better of it. "If he's asleep, he's easier to keep an eye on. I am not going in there to wake the raging beast. Who knows what the hell he might do."

Ava snickers. "Any other girl, I'd worry about, Ry, but I have a feeling you'll be just fine. Go wake the asshole up. He's gotta get up anyway. School's starting next week, he can't keep fucking sleeping in."

"Do I really have to?"

"Yup. Go wake him up and tell him to check his phone."

"Ava..." I glance from the phone on the desk to the image on the screen with mounting trepidation.

"Is there a problem?" she prompts.

A problem? Yeah, you could say that, I think as my gaze travels over the black and white image Abel presents on my screen. It's not the best quality, but I can see him as clear as day, his white skin pale against the dark sheets of his king-sized bed. It only took three cameras to cover the entirety of his bedroom —which is as big as an actual apartment. From this one, I can plainly see that the top sheet he's sleeping with has slipped down. I feel heat in my cheeks.

"He's fucking naked, Ava." Again.

Another snort.

"It's not funny!" I snap.

"Oh, I beg to differ," she replies through snorts of renewed laughter. I've never heard her laugh so much. I guess good dick does that to a girl. Too bad I can't fucking relate.

"I'm hanging up on you."

"Wait!" she says quickly. "You really do need to wake him up! He—"

"I got it," I say, cutting her off, and before she can say anything more, I hit the 'end call' button.

There's really no use putting it off. If Abel's got shit to do, it's clear he was either too drunk to set an alarm for himself or he just plain didn't care enough. I stare at his image on my screen. Asleep, he looks like any other guy his age, albeit way more attractive. His face is the kind girls would moon over from the covers of international magazines. He may not like to hear it, but the fact is, he's pretty for a man. The sharp angles of his jawline, the high cheekbones, the deep-set eyes. He's fucking blessed, there's no denying that.

I close my laptop and get up, stretching my back out as I head for the hallway and peek my head out. I don't want to do this. Correction: I *really* don't want to fucking do this.

Despite the fact that the Carter estate is beautifully decorated, modern, and clean—I feel like I'm a sacrificial virgin walking to her own demise as I head back towards the direction of Abel's room. I'm far from a virgin, but the thought is still there.

Like a frightened rabbit, my heart jackhammers inside of my chest. Why? I don't fucking know. Abel Frazier does that to me. *Suck it the fuck up, Rylie,* I command myself. As I step in front of his bedroom door, I inhale sharply and straighten my shoulders, tossing them back along with my hair. I do the one thing I've always been halfway decent at—I fucking fake it.

I pound my fist against the wood of his door. "Abel!" I shout. "Get up! Ava said you've got shit to do." A low moan rumbles from beyond the door and my thighs tighten in response. I pound against the door again after a moment when I get no other response and again nothing.

Fuck this, I think, reaching for the doorknob. I turn the handle and shove it open letting the light from the hallway shine into the darkened interior. I stomp across the room, taking care to avoid looking directly at the bed as I stop in front of the windows, grip the blackout curtains, and throw them open.

"What the fuck!" Abel growls, and from the corner of my

eyes, I see him reach for the sheets, pulling them up and over his head as if to block out the sun using other means. *There, I think. Just what I was going for.* Now, he's covered.

I turn and prop my hands on my hips. "Avalon called," I state.

"Of course she did." His irritated grunt comes from beneath the sheets a second before his head pops back out and he lets the sheets drop to his lap. My eyes automatically fall to his chest and my heart picks up speed once more. Sweat collects at the back of my neck. My chest swells with each breath.

In and out, Rylie, I tell myself. *In and fucking out.*

Abel groans again, the sound far deeper and crisper now that there's no door separating us. It unexpectedly makes its way from my ears straight to my belly. I tighten all over. "What the fuck does she want now?" he demands.

Abel rakes a lazy hand through the unkempt yet somehow still fucking beautiful mop of white-blonde hair at the top of his head. It's really not fucking fair. I wake up looking like a half dead raccoon and he wakes up looking like a supermodel.

"I don't know," I snap a reply, turning my face away as I let my eyes trail around the rest of the room in favor of staring at his face or his chest again. "She said to check your phone."

"Dammit," he mutters before reaching for the nightstand, grabbing his phone from its charger, and unlocking it. I catch sight of his knuckles. Red lines mar the skin there. *Did he get into a fight after I left?* I shake my head. Even if he did, it's none of my business.

I wait a moment and then edge towards the exit. "Well, now that you're up," I say. "I'll just..."

"Hold it." I freeze, a slew of curses threatening to fall from my lips as Abel's eyes lift from his phone and glare my way. "You're going with me."

"I have plans," I lie. "I'm just here to make sure—"

"Did I fucking ask if you had plans, Rylie?" he cuts me off. "No, I didn't. I said you're going. End of discussion. Go get dressed."

I frown and look down at my clothes. "I am dressed," I point out. "You're the one who's not dressed."

Abel drops his phone on the bed and glares at me as his eyes track down my body to the black, ripped skinny jeans and white band tank top that clings to my form. He doesn't say anything, but in the next instant, I'm stifling a scream as I whirl away from him when he tosses the covers back, revealing that I'd been fucking right—Abel Frazier slept in the nude.

"Why do you keep doing this!" I snap. "Put on some clothes."

Abel makes his way across the room, the sound of his footfalls reaching my ears. The muscles of my body wind tighter and tighter as they grow closer and closer until I can feel the heat of him against my back and the humid warmth of his breath as he leans down next to my ear. "Why? Don't like it?" he challenges.

I clench my hands into fists at my sides. "You know I don't."

He hums in the back of his throat, the sound reverberating over my already stretched thin nerves. "You're a pretty liar, Riot Girl," he says. "I'll give you that much, but a liar is still a liar."

I don't respond. I have nothing to say to that. Instead, I step away from him and keep my eyes firmly fixed on the wall as I stride out of his room, slamming the door as I go.

12

"TAKE A PICTURE, IT'LL LAST LONGER." I snort at the sarcastic quip from the purple-haired demon in my passenger seat and return my attention to the road.

"You know, you've become a mouthy thing in the last few months."

"Whose fault is that?" she replies tartly, crossing her arms over her chest even as she folds one leg over the other.

My gaze goes immediately to the vast expanse of pale skin revealed from beneath the hem of her short black skirt as the fabric drifts slightly up. *God bless the modern world*, I think even as I clench my fingers against the steering wheel. "Are you suggesting that I'm the one to blame for your attitude?" It's curious. Just a few short months ago, she was a scared little mouse, but with Avalon's arrival, she's become far more disrespectful. Normally, I'd be set on correcting a little nobody like her, but ... I can't help but want to hear more from her. I like the way she fights against me, like a small creature struggling against a much bigger predator.

Since the first time I met her, Rylie's been the type to choose flight over fight, but now ... now I see how she's changed. So imperceptibly, I wonder if she even realizes it. She meets my eyes far more than she ever has before and it turns me on.

After several long moments and no response, I find myself glancing back in her direction once more. "What's wrong?" I taunt. "Cat got your tongue?"

She frowns and glares out of the side window. No answer.

"It's rude not to respond when someone's talking to you," I remind her.

"Yeah, well, it's also rude to force someone to go places she doesn't want to and not tell her where they're going," she mutters in response.

A laugh bubbles up out of my chest and I shake my head as I flick the Mustang's blinker and turn off the highway into a dinky parking lot. I slow my speed and cruise through the lot until I'm parked behind a rust brown pick-up truck with a dent in the side door.

Rylie frowns at our surroundings. "A body shop?" she says, scanning the sign above the open garage that reads "Carlton's Body & Design Shop".

"Yup." I pop off the last of the word as I toss the Mustang into park and turn off the ignition, removing the keys as I reach for the car door. "Come along, Riot Girl." I glance back as I get out, and smile at the cute curl of her lips as they turn down into a grumpy frown at that nickname. There are few things in life that make the world enjoyable, but irritating the fuck out of her is one of them.

I head off towards the glass double doors at the front of the building, the smell of oil and the sound of loud rock music drifting from the work area. "Hey, yo, Abe!" I turn at the sound of my name and lift a hand as a few of the guys pop their heads around their current jobs and wave my way. Normally, I'd stop in for a quick chat, but today isn't the day for that.

I sense Rylie's curiosity as she looks their way before

returning her laser focus attention to me. She's got questions in her eyes, but her lips remain shut like the good girl she is. She knows to keep them to herself, at least for the time being anyway. My hands hit the doors before my body and I shove it open, stepping to the side and holding it wide as I wait for her short legs to catch up.

"Yo, Tanner!" I call when I don't see a body at the front desk. There's a thump from the open doorway behind the desk and then the sound of a cheap metal folding chair scraping against the linoleum floor. A wide frame steps into view and a brilliant, albeit yellow smile. Carlton Tanner is a big man, built like he was made to work a railroad with his bear-like body and I cut a look out of the corner of my eye just to watch Rylie's reaction. Just as expected, her eyes widen slightly and her jaw drops. Yeah, he's got that initial effect on people.

"My boy's back," Old man Tanner says as he rounds the countertop. He pauses, his gaze swinging to the short shadow to my right as Rylie shrinks back. "And he brought a girlfriend."

I laugh. "You know I don't bring my girls around you, Tanner," I say as I reach out and take the older man's hand, shaking it roughly before I withdraw my keys and slap them on the desk. "I'm just here to drop off the Mustang for a checkup."

"Righto, my boy, righto." Tanner nods, but his whole focus is on Rylie. I get it—she's hard not to look at. My eyes trail down and get stuck on her ass. The back and forth sway of it makes me want to bury myself inside her and stay there. A grin comes to my face when she looks at me sideways. If she only knew what I was thinking, she'd probably slap the fuck out of me. That, too, I can't help but find attractive. "You need a rental?" Tanner's question pulls me back from my thoughts and I lift my gaze to his.

"Yeah, I can't stick around," I answer. "Got other shit to do today."

Tanner's attention returns to me and without hesitation,

he flips his hand up and smacks the backside of my head. "Oye!" he chastises. "There's a lady present, boy. You know better than to be cursing. Your momma taught you better than that."

I flinch and rub at the back of my head. "Yeah, yeah," I wave him off, dodging another smack with a grin when he goes to do it again.

A big, fat finger lifts and wags in front of my face. "Don't be disrespecting a lady in my house, ya hear me, boy?" he says.

I shake my head but acquiesce. "Yes, sir, I hear ya."

Tanner eyes me for a moment as if trying to gauge my sincerity and like the little devil I am, I shoot him a smug grin and shrug. "Aight then, lemme get the paperwork you gotta sign," he finally says. "Be right back."

Rylie waits until the old man disappears into the back office before speaking up. "You just let that man hit you," she says, her tone suggesting shock.

I shove my hands into the pockets of my jeans and rock back on my heels before cutting a look her way out of the corner of my eyes. "What'd you expect I'd do?" I ask. "Punch him?"

"Well," she begins, staring towards the back office entrance, "yeah. I did."

"Old man Tanner doesn't mean anything by it," I explain.

"Yeah, but you're—" I'm about to yank a hand out of my pocket and slap it over her mouth when Tanner walks back out and slaps down a small stack of papers, cutting her off.

"Alrighty, son," he says, reaching for a cheap metal pen holder next to the ancient computer system set up there and then hands me a dust covered blue pen. "Sign these and I'll go grab a set of keys from our borrows—any preference?"

"Truck or SUV," I reply as I start scanning the documents and scribble my initials at the appropriate sections.

"If we're doing a full workup," he says. "It'll probs take 'til the end of the day. Ya came in late again, boy." He frowns my way. "What I tell ya 'bout waiting 'til the last minute."

My lips twitch in amusement. What a fucking jackass, acting all tough and fatherly in front of Rylie. "You don't normally give me this much shit, old man," I say as I finish scribbling my signature on the last paper. "There a special reason today?"

He holds his fist up in my face. "What'd I say about that kinda language in front of a lady," he grumbles. "Yer asking for a knuckle sandwich, boy."

I laugh. "Of course, old man. Haven't had anything to eat today and yours are always the best."

Tanner shakes his head and pushes away from the desk as he ambles over to the wall of hooks to the side of the back door. "Yer getting worse every time I see ya," he mutters, snatching a key fob from one of the hooks. He comes back over and tosses it my way and I reach up, catching the thing midair. Rylie's attention is like a burn along the side of my face. If I were to look her way, I bet those massive hazel eyes of hers would be centered squarely on me. Her attention is not unwanted, but here, it's also not for the reason I'd like. Perhaps, it was a bad idea to bring her along.

"Thanks, old man," I say, pushing the papers towards him, "Just shoot me a text if it's gonna take longer. You don't need to put me at the top of your list. I can come back and pick it up tomorrow if need be."

"You been 'round this reprobate long, Miss?" I scowl when Tanner ignores me completely and turns to Rylie.

"I ... uh..." Her eyes widen a fraction and she takes a slight step back, so unconsciously I don't think she's realized it until she accidentally bumps into my side.

"Aw, there ain't no reason to be 'fraid of an old man, Missy," Tanner says, holding his hands up in a sign of innocence. He grins, showing off the pale yellowness of his teeth and the chip he's got in his upper right canine. "Old man Tanner ain't never hurt a lady."

I frown as Rylie blinks and then pink stains her cheeks. Never in my life did I think I might be jealous of an old man, but right now I can't help the thoughts that pour into my mind. *What the fuck is she blushing for?*

"Leave her be, Tanner," I say, forcing my words to come out light. "She's shy."

"Ah, so you like the shy type?" Tanner rocks back on his heels and then strokes one hand down the side of the beard that covers the lower half of his face from his jawline to just under his nose. "She's a pretty little thing, looks a bit too young for you though. How old are you, sweetheart?"

I feel Rylie stiffen at the question. "She goes to my school," I tell him quickly. "She's old enough."

"Did I ask you, boy?" Tanner replies, arching one furry brow. "I was talking to the lady."

"I'm nineteen." Rylie's response is quiet, barely a whisper but Tanner hears it.

"Nineteen? Aye, she's old enough then." He turns to me and winks. "Better treat her right or she'll be running off with someone much less reckless."

"Oh yeah?" My muscles relax as he moves back around the counter. Each step takes him further and further from Rylie and I don't want to delve into why that calms me. Nope. Not at fucking all. "Well, don't you worry, old man. I've got her on lockdown."

Tanner laughs, the sound loud and boisterous. It makes Rylie jump at my side. "Already thinking about putting a ring on it, huh?" he asks and before ... perhaps with anyone else, I would've cursed him out and told him 'fuck no,' but Rylie Moore ... I glance her way, noting how her attention has turned to the floor and she's got her tiny fists shoved into the light jacket she's got on over her Gothic Girls R Us outfit.

"There are other methods I might use to entice a woman, old man," I say slowly, watching her and waiting to see if she'll look at me over the comment. And just as expected, her head comes up and her cheek turns my way. A mixture of irritation and confusion fills the glare she sends my way.

"Well, whatever you do, little boy, you better protect what you claim," Tanner says with a wave of his hand. "Now, you two get on out of here. We gots work to do. Take your girl on a date or something. You know where the borrows are at—back of the lot. Yours's the Ford in lot seventeen."

"Thanks, man," I say absently as I reach down and grip Rylie by her elbow and steer her towards the exit.

"You—" She starts, but I can't let her say shit until we're in the clear.

"Wait," I mutter under my breath as I shove the door open and gesture for her to head out. She eyes me but doesn't push it.

Rylie steps outside and I follow, turning the corner and heading around the side of the open garage, waving as a few more of the guys spot me and call out their greetings. All the while I can feel Rylie's impervious gaze on my face. Definitely a bad fucking idea to bring her here, I decide. I don't know what the fuck I was thinking.

As soon as we're around the side of the main building and facing the back parking lot, I blow out a breath. "Alright," I say, "go ahead."

I half expect her to launch into immediate demands, but instead, she surprises me. "So ... you come to a pop shop for your car?"

"What?" I stop at the first row, clenching the borrowed key fob in my hand.

She looks from me to the garage at our backs. We're far enough away now that the guys can't hear us. "It's just..." she frowns as she starts speaking, "I expected that you probably went to one of the expensive dealerships to detail your car."

94

I stare at her for a moment before replying. "I work on my car myself a lot," I finally say. "But I always bring it here if it needs a full checkup ... you sure that's what you wanted to ask?"

"Well ... I mean I just..."

"Go on and say it." I sigh as I start walking again, passing the lot numbers and scanning the ground for the right one.

"I don't know what you want me to say," she admits. "Am I surprised? Yeah. I mean, I never expected you of all people to let some old guy smack you in the back of the head and treat you like his..." Her voice drifts off and I glance back to see her staring at the ground biting her lower lip in deep concentration.

"Grandson?" I offer.

Her head lifts and she nods. I close my eyes and suck in a calming breath. Of course, she would be surprised. It only makes sense. She's seen me as Abel Frazier, Eastpoint Heir, and wealthy trust fund millionaire since our first meeting. She doesn't realize it yet, but there are layers to people—yes, even me.

"My mom liked this shop," I tell her. "She always brought her Mustang here and when she died and I got it, I kept bringing it here."

"So, they know you through your mom?" she asks as I start walking again. Her little footsteps patter behind me as I stomp down the line, wishing that the old man had given me a fucking rental closer to the garage so we could be in the car for this type of talk. Maybe I should've waited. Oh well, no going back now. Rylie's curiosity is in full force.

"Yeah."

"Do they know about your ... um ... background?" There it is, the all-important question.

My feet drag to a stop at the back of lot seventeen. "You think they'd treat me like this if they knew who I was?" I ask turning to face her.

She blinks. "What?"

I debate on it for several moments before finally deciding on the truth. "No," I finally say. "They don't know who I am." Old man Tanner and his workers never even knew my mom was rich when she came to them. So, it only makes sense that they have no clue that I am, and I want to keep it that way. As much as I'd like to believe they wouldn't treat me any different, I know the truth from experience. The second money is involved, people change.

"These guys?" I gesture back to the shop. "They don't have a fucking clue who I am. As far as they're concerned, I'm just like them. Their world is small. They don't know who the fuck Abel Frazier is. All they know is that I'm a college student. I play football. And that car—means the fucking world to me."

Rylie looks up at me, her face impassive. I don't know what I expected from her, but it's not ... this. It's hard to get a read on what she's thinking. Several moments pass—a long enough time that I'm debating on just getting into the truck now that we're here, but then finally she speaks.

"Why?" One syllable. One question. A whole lot of meaning.

I drag a hand up through my hair. "I just never felt the need to tell them otherwise. Sometimes, it's better to have people like you without all that other shit in the way." And money was just shit—shit that piled up and blinded others to what really fucking mattered. Sure, the guys and I may have grown up with gilded walls, but even those were a cage when you couldn't step outside of the role you were born into.

Is it lying? Yeah, probably. But sometimes, little white lies are all we can rely on. They're like glue holding me together sometimes. Keeping me from spilling my guts all over the road. But she doesn't need to know about that. She doesn't need to know how dirty I actually am. How this body of mine has been used and degraded. I turn away from her.

She doesn't say anything, but I can sense her attention and, though I ask myself why the fuck I bothered telling her that little hidden truth about myself, I don't mind the newfound curiosity she has towards me. In fact, I want to exacerbate it. I want her to think about me and only me. All the time and in every way possible because that's how I think about her. Constantly. Invariably. She's becoming a habit, and it puts me on edge.

"Get in the car, Rylie," I command. "And just do what I say for now. Tomorrow your carriage will turn back into a pumpkin and you'll be back in your dorm room when the queen returns."

She's quiet for a moment, and then, just because I know she can't help it, she speaks. "I'm no Cinderella, Abel," she says. "But if this were a fairytale, you would be a beast ... not a prince."

I smile, but there's no amusement in the expression. She's right. All too fucking right.

13

RYLIE

THE WEEKEND ENDS AND AVALON, Dean, and even Brax—whose whereabouts no one knew about, not even Avalon—return. I'm relieved of duty and finally allowed to go back to my dorm room at the newly-built Havers. I hadn't been in the replacement dorm for long after the fire at the beginning of the summer, but I'm already back to feeling like I'm home, and staying away from it is not conducive to a good sleep schedule. My days as Abel Frazier's babysitter are over, and there's no way I'm actually sad about it. But ... I am curious.

The things he showed me, the sides of him I saw, linger in the back of my mind as I pack up my bag and head to my first class of the semester come Monday morning. Thankfully, the other side of my dorm room remained empty when the other students moved in. I have no doubt that's thanks to the Sick Boys. Can't have their one and only information broker staying with anyone else. They'd learned from that mistake from Avalon.

I'm alright with it, though. I don't mind the solitude. In fact, I relish in it. Unlike most people, I leave the extra bed and dresser empty. I don't claim places. I rarely spread out. I learned early on in life to take up as little room as possible. That way, when it's inevitably time for you to go, there's less attention on you and less to clean up.

The sweltering summer heat beats down on the back of my neck as I stride across campus, heading for one of the business buildings. This will be the last semester that I have to take classes outside of my major and I can't wait for the chore to be over.

I walk into the classroom, find a table in the farthest corner, and immediately make a beeline for it. Just as I'm getting ready to drop my bag on top of the desk, a shadow appears over me. I jerk and spin towards it, sighing in relief when I see it's just Dash.

"Hey." He lifts a hand in greeting. "So, I guess you're back on campus now?"

My muscles loosen, relaxing after the brief scare, and I nod. "Yeah." But he doesn't care about where I'm staying. No. There's a reason Dash Bennington has approached me. "I've got your information," I state. "Do you want it now or..."

"You can give it to me after class," he says. "We can grab lunch. I want to review everything you've found."

I blink. "You want to grab lunch with me?"

He nods. "Yeah, I might have some questions about what you found."

I stare at him for a long moment. Dash is a handsome guy. Kind. I've run into him a time or two before, and from what I know of him—though he's not as wealthy as the Sick Boys—he's got a background that's all green. Trust fund. Fancy cars. Girlfriends with connections. Most guys his age that had been given all that he had would be at least a little cocky, maybe arrogant, but he's never displayed those qualities. He's quiet, reserved. A watcher.

From what I now know about his father, I understand him a

bit more. He doesn't want to ask me any questions. He just wants to make sure I'll remain silent.

I blow out a breath and nod once more. "Okay, that's fine," I say. "We'll do lunch. I'll give you the info then."

"Great." He shoves his hands into his jeans pockets and ambles back a step or two. "I'll hit you up after class." Then he's turning and moving away, back towards a few of his teammates gathered in the third row across the room. I watch him go for a moment before slowly turning back to the desk and taking my seat.

The professor strides into class with less than three minutes to go and starts off by slapping down a mug of coffee, grabbing a dry erase marker, and writing out his name on the board. I reach for my bag and pull out my laptop. It might seem like I'm taking notes, but the reality is I'm checking up on the information I've got for Dash.

I'd really planned on printing all of this out before I presented it to him. For now, I condense it all into a file and send it directly to his phone. My fingers hover over the keyboard as the sound of the professor droning on about chapters and future homework assignments pervade the room.

There's an incessant itch at the back of my neck. It's a warning system. For as long as I can remember, it's always acted up when something went wrong. It happened when that email came through about Daniel getting out of jail, and now, it's telling me I need to check on him again. Even if all I really want to do is ignore it and pretend like Daniel Dickerson doesn't exist—like he has nothing to do with me and there's no possibility of him tracking me down and finding me. I know better, though, than to ignore the vague warning even if it's probably just my own anxiety.

Before I know it, my fingers are scanning through the various channels and I type in his name. Immediately, a cornucopia of information comes up. His mother no longer lives in the house he was raised in. After me, her ability to foster kids from the system was revoked and she had to move. Of course, I expect that he's probably staying with her. A man with his record now—even if it happened when he was a teenager—is going to have a difficult time finding a place to stay without registering. As it stands, he should be registered even if he's with her, but she'd never make him. She never believed me anyway.

My throat clogs as my entire world narrows down to the words and numbers on the screen. I memorize the address and then calculate the distance between it and Eastpoint. Nine hours and thirty-two minutes driving distance. It's not far enough, but truth be told, I don't think anywhere in the world would be far enough.

I double check my identity. Even though I kept my first name, my last name is different now. It should be enough to keep him from finding me. Somehow, though, all I can recall when I think of him is the fixation. Not the months of public judgment I faced after everything had come out. Not even the nights where he'd crawl beneath my covers and push himself against me. Those things were easy compared to the possessiveness he displayed.

"And that's time for us today." The professor's voice rings throughout the room, his words penetrating my skull along with the sounds of the other students in the classroom as they get out of their seats and begin collecting their stuff, shoving it into bags, and talking loudly as they head for the hallway. I glance to the side and note that papers have been dropped on the edge of my desk—the syllabus and a collection of other things I'm sure have to do with the future of this class. Another thing becomes increasingly clear. I just spent the entire class period doing the one thing I hated most about my past demons—obsessing.

I snap my laptop closed and grab the papers, stuffing them into my bag alongside my computer. Seconds later,

Dash steps up to the desk with his backpack hanging over his shoulder. "Ready to go?" he asks. Grabbing my bag, I gesture for him to lead the way and he does, catching the classroom door by the edge and holding it for me as we step out into the hall. "My car's parked in the lot behind the building," he says.

I nod and then trail behind him as he leads me through the building and out through one of the back doors that puts us close to the back parking lot reserved for upper class students. Dash reaches into his pocket and withdraws a key fob, hitting the unlock button that makes a small silver Porsche beep and its lights flash.

When we reach the vehicle, he steps in front of me, blocking me from the passenger side door so he can reach the handle and pull it open. I pause, frowning up at him. Dash arches a brow at my expression. "Don't question it, Rylie," he says. "Just get in."

A sigh works its way up my throat, but there's no use arguing. It's not a big deal that he feels the need to act the gentleman with me. It's just ... not something I'm used to. I settle into the lush leather interior as Dash snaps the door shut and strides around the front of the multi-hundred-thousand-dollar vehicle and gets into the driver's side.

"What are you hungry for?" he asks pleasantly as he starts up the engine.

Another frown takes over my face. "It doesn't matter," I tell him. "It's just food."

"Then you don't mind if I decide?"

I wave away the question. "As long as you don't take me to some country club, I don't give a shit."

The corner of his mouth curves up and he revs the engine, sliding out of the parking lot with ease. Minutes later, we're pulling into a familiar place. "Of course you'd bring me here," I grit out.

"You did say you didn't care if I decided," he points out. "And it's not a country club."

"It is a club, though," I mutter. "And an exclusive one at that."

"It's not that exclusive," Dash says.

"Do they even serve food here? Is it even open?" I demand as he shuts off the car and gets out.

I grab my bag and follow him. I suppose it doesn't matter if they do or not. My gaze trails halfway up the surface of the industrial-sized brick building to read the unlit sign.

Urban—a club owned and operated by none other than the Sick Boys' leader.

"They'll have something," Dash says. "And Dean asked me to stop by to make sure they got everything they needed for Friday anyway."

"What's Friday?" I ask before I can stop myself.

"Party," Dash says as he withdraws a completely different set of keys and unlocks the front door, holding it open for me to pass through. "School's back and so is everyone else. I suspect the guys want to make Avalon's status official."

Like it wasn't practically official before school ended, I think sardonically. "Do you know?" I ask, watching him curiously as he disappears into the dark building, leaving me beside the only light—the entrance. The sound of his footsteps echo into the massive interior I know is beyond the shadows.

"Know who she really is?" Dash replies, his own question an answer to my own.

"Yeah," I say, though I already know the truth.

A moment later, lights come on, making me flinch against the sudden illumination. He pops his head around the corner and waves me on. "I do," he says, proving just how much they trust him. "Now, come on. Sit at the bar and I'll grab something from the kitchen."

"If you wanted privacy for the conversation we're about to

have," I say as I move forward, following his command as I step into the main hub of the building's room, "we could've gone back to Havers." I shiver as the chill of the air conditioner kicks on and blows air down across my bare flesh. Unwrapping the jacket I've got tied around my waist, I head towards the bar Dash mentioned and set my bag on the floor before slipping into it.

Grabbing a stool, I start to pull it off the counter and set it on the edge—not stopping until the whole row is down. By the time I'm done, my arms beneath the jacket's sleeves are sore and there's sweat on the back of my neck. Maybe I should actually take up working out. I might be skinny, but I'm far from healthy if something like this tires me out.

Clambering onto a stool at the very end of the bar, I reach down and heft my bag up onto the surface, reaching inside and withdrawing my laptop. I click across the screen until I've deleted all evidence of my earlier searches and the only thing left is the reason I'm here. Dash moves about in the back, the sound of kitchen utensils clanging together followed by a low curse as he drops something.

Curiosity binds me. Dash Bennington is as close to the Sick Boys without actually being one of them as possible. What is the reason for his presence here? Minutes pass as I wait, scanning the giant open space for something to do and focus on until he comes back out, carrying two plates.

He sets down the first one next to my computer before the second goes to the surface in front of the seat to my right. "Eat first," he orders, gesturing to the sandwich on the plate. "Then we'll talk."

My stomach rumbles, announcing its vote on what we should do and with a sigh, I push my computer to the side, pick up the sandwich, and start eating. The two of us eat in virtual silence, the only sounds disturbing our quiet lunch are those of our movements. Plates scraping against the bar's countertop.

Then Dash hops up, eyes turning across our meal as if he's forgotten something, and he disappears back into the kitchen, returning with two dark bottles. He pops the first, hands it to me, and then the second before taking a long swallow.

"I don't drink much," I say, staring at the bottle.

"It's a beer, Rylie," he says. "You need something to wash down the PB and J."

Memories of years that aren't as far behind me as I'd like them to be rise to the surface of my mind, and as if it'll shut them up faster, I grab the bottle and press the mouth to my lips, tipping it back and draining half of it in one go.

"Whoa, I didn't think you'd go so hard so fast, girl," he says. "Slow down."

I lift away with a gasp and already, I feel my muscles relaxing even more. I set the bottle down without responding to his comment and reach for the rest of my sandwich. By the time I've polished it off, Dash is done with his own and sitting at my side, watching me curiously. I have the sudden urge to tell him what I told Abel the other day—to take a picture if he wants the image in front of him to last longer.

"Thanks for lunch," I say uncomfortably. He gives me a small smile and nods as he reaches for my plate to stack it onto his own. He grabs his empty beer and mine as well and disappears once more.

I haven't had a drop of alcohol in well over a year, my last experience pushing me to an edge I don't exactly care to repeat, but right now, I'm finding it hard to recall why I thought it was so dangerous. If anything, I feel more relaxed than I have in months.

Dash returns and retakes his seat. Time to get to work.

"Check your phone," I say, shoving away my thoughts and pulling my laptop back front and center. "I've sent the info to your email. The file's encrypted so no one can open it unless they have a password." I wait for him to pull up the email on his phone before telling him said password and making sure he can see my findings.

Ninety percent of what I found out about Dash Bennington's father are things that anyone with half a mind could find; it's the last ten percent that I suspect Dash was after. I wait for an undetermined amount of time, watching him curiously. I don't know what I'm looking for—a reaction maybe. But there's nothing. His face remains passive. His eyes lock on the screen as he reads the records and words written there.

It's not so much what I found as what it implies. Like a lot of the students at Eastpoint, Dash's family has connections to celebrities and other elites. Dash's father is the CEO of one of the premier talent agencies in the world and with a face that could rock the modeling world if he wanted, I've always wondered why Dash has remained as down to Earth as he is. Why he chose Eastpoint instead of fame.

I glance down to the phone in his hands as I carefully reach up, touching the top of my computer, debating on closing it. "Do you have any questions?" My voice is quiet in the great big open space that Club Urban is with just the two of us here.

He swallows and then puts his phone down, clicking the button on the side to make the screen go dark. The first movement he's made since he started reading. "No." It's one word. One syllable. Yet, there's a breadth of information held within it.

None of your business, Rylie, I warn myself. Dash slowly sucks in a breath and bows his head. His hands hang down between his legs and I can sense his true desire. I bet he's wishing right about now that he'd asked for this information in public. He can't know that I understand what he's feeling. To him, I'm sure, it must feel like he's all alone in the world.

A part of me wants to let him continue thinking that. It's not necessarily out of cruelty, the feeling. Sometimes feeling alone has a way of putting pressure on a person. Pressure to do something. To rise up. To fight back. Sometimes, when your back is against a wall and you're at the edge of your breaking point, you'll find you can do things you never thought possible.

Even bravery can be found in the darkness if you look hard enough.

I finally shut my computer, and Dash speaks. "I'll send the rest of the money I owe you by tomorrow," he says quietly. "I..." He reaches back and stuffs a hand into his back pocket.

I hate that I notice how shaky his hands are as he pulls it out and sets a fifty on the counter. "I'm sorry," he says. "But I don't think I can drive you back. Can you..." He doesn't look at me and just waves at the cash on the counter.

I could. I could just take the money, pack up my shit, call a ride, and leave. Leave him to his devices and his thoughts and his ... obvious torment. Maybe I should. After all, Dash is Sick Boy adjacent. A lackey. Outside, but close. Any involvement with him—no matter that this doesn't technically concern them —will only eventually lead back to the others and I've got enough on my plate as it is. I should leave it alone.

My breath sounds loud to my own ears as I tell myself all of that. But I'm stupid. A true dumb fuck sunk so low in shit creek that, paddle or no paddle, there's no getting out now because even though I know I probably should get up and walk away ... I can't. I just fucking can't.

My fingers lock onto the edge of the counter, biting into the hardwood as I stare at the shiny surface. "I know it's none of my business," I start.

"Thank you for finding this for me," he interrupts without looking my way, "but really, you should take the money and go now, Rylie."

I watch him out of the corner of my eye for a moment before releasing the counter and turning towards him. I don't get a single word out before he's already talking. "I don't think I have to tell you what will happen if you decide to sell this information elsewhere, but I'll say it nonetheless," he says, his tone growing cold as he looks at me. "It would be in your best interest to keep this to yourself."

I suck in a breath and then slowly release it. My motto has always been—ever since I can remember—don't get involved in other people's drama. Do not invite trouble, and whatever else you do, don't be a hero. Though I'm not necessarily planning to break that motto, I know I'm toeing the fucking line. Getting as close as fucking possible without stepping over it. One harsh wind will send me over the edge.

A part of me begs my rational mind not to say anything more. I shouldn't offer anything to him. No help. No guidance. No sympathy. That part of me is scared. Frightened that opening myself up to anyone—even someone who so obviously has suffered similar traumas—will only result in more pain.

"You should tell them," I say, ignoring the tone and glare he's giving me that both suggest I should stop.

The stool scrapes against the hard floor as he gets up from his seat. He tucks his phone away into his back pocket. Dash doesn't say anything, but he knows exactly who I was talking about.

"He's not going to stop," I tell him. "Men like him never do." If anyone knows what a monster is capable of, I do ... and I suspect ... so does he.

A cool gaze finds mine. "I know," he says, and I have a very distinct feeling that he really does. Dash Bennington knows all too well because, even though there was no actual evidence of him being a victim of his father's sick perversions, I know, deep down, he was.

Dash isn't an arrogant man. He holds no cruelty nor resentment. He's beyond that. Unlike me. All I have is resentment, buried so deep inside of me that it comes out in fast bursts of rage that I've tried to stifle as long as possible.

All this pain. All this misery. The agony that we've suffered in the darkest parts of the night.

For me, it left me hollow. Empty of anything except fear and anger.

For him, though ... darkness like that only made him kind. And that kind of response to a trauma like ours frightens me even more than my own.

"Then listen to me now," I order. "Tell. *Them.*"

He stares at me before narrowing his eyes. "Who is them?" he demands as if he wants me to say their names.

I look up pointedly and then gesture to the building we're in. *"Them,"* I repeat, meaningfully. "At the very least, you should tell Abel."

I half expect him to dismiss me, but instead, he merely stands there for a moment more, his eyes scanning my face. I don't know what he expects to find. Perhaps proof that I'm just like him. Finally, though, he nods. "I'll think about it," he says.

It's not a confirmation, but neither is it a rejection. I hope he does, I realize. As much as Abel Frazier disturbs me down to my core—I know he would never let a friend like Dash Bennington suffer an injustice like this.

14

RYLIE

I'm GOING TO DIE. *Those are always the first words that penetrate my brain.* I'm going to die and he's going to be the one that kills me.

I run down a long hallway, but with each step, my legs grow shorter and shorter until the walls and ceiling all start to feel as if they're out of reach. My breaths come in heavy pants and tears leak down my face, unrepressed. My lungs can't keep up. I'm exhausted—tired from running—but this hallway never fucking ends.

Laughter echoes up the walls behind me, but I dare not turn back to look. I know he's coming. He's following me, his slower steps almost mocking my own frantic hurried pace. I need to get out. I need to get away. Where is the fucking door?

"Rylie..." Oh God, no. I hear that voice. The same voice I heard every night for almost a year before I finally told someone. He's coming. "Sweetheart." Daniel's eerie voice has morphed into something straight out of a horror movie. He doesn't sound like the Daniel of my memories, but something far more sinister.

Some people believe that children have nightmares because of developing fears combined with a younger mind's overactive imagination. Overactive, *I think.* Ha. That's just another phrase for unrealistic.

Panting, straining, I push my legs to go harder, as hard as they can. Until I think they might fall off or break under the strain. I don't need to breathe, I decide, as long as I can get away. So, I hold my breath and I squeeze my eyes shut and I just focus on moving my legs. Feet slapping against the tiled hallway floor, vomit burns up my throat with each passing second.

Sometimes, in these dreams, he doesn't catch me. I just end up running forward forever with the cruel laughter following me. Those are the best ways for this dream to end. Tonight, however, I should've known that's not what it would be.

The daily stressors in my life—Daniel's release, Avalon's request, Abel ... they're all weights pulling me down, slowing my movements. So, when dream Daniel's rough hands wrap around my arm and pull me back into the darkness, I'm not even surprised. My feet pop off of the floor as I'm yanked backwards and the hallway disappears only to be overtaken by a multitude of shadows. My lips part and a fat finger slips inside, sliding against my tongue, choking me.

At least it's a finger, though, *I think.* And not something else.

More tears burn at the backs of my eyes and then slide down my cheeks. My chest tightens painfully and the second the finger is removed, I gasp for air. Danny's lips press against my cheek and move up to my ear.

"Oh little Rylie," he whispers, *"did you like our little game of tag that much?"*

I shake my head, unable to speak. My fingers curl into fists against my sides, my nails stabbing into my palms until I can feel the breakage of skin and the slick blood. Why? I can't help but wonder. Why was it me? Why did he return to my bed every night and not go to someone else? What is it about me that attracts bad people?

111

"Why aren't you answering me, Rylie?" Danny slides around in front of me, his dull brown eyes black in the darkness. There's no light anywhere, so it doesn't make much sense for me to be able to see him so well, but this is a dream after all, and there's no rule that says dreams have to adhere to the rules of reality. "You ran from me; that was because you wanted to play tag right? I caught you." His hands dig into my sides, pulling me against his chest. "What's my reward?"

Shivers of disgust chase down my spine as he reaches up and curls a lock of my hair around his finger. This Danny is different from the real one. He's just like the monsters in a child's nightmare. Where the real Danny is normal looking—neither fat nor skinny—this one is a bulbous lard with thick fingers and wrinkles and hairs sprouting from spots along his sagging neck and face.

Ugly. Disgusting. Repulsive.

Those are the thoughts that come to mind. That is what he is and it is also what I feel whenever he touches me. Dream Danny's hand grips the front of my shirt and rends it down the middle. I push back, fighting him as he groans and delves into my pants and grips the fabric, tearing it apart as well.

"Oh, Rylie," Danny groans, rubbing himself against me. "Rylie. Rylie. Rylie. I love you."

This is it. This is the issue. The reason why Daniel always came for me and never anyone else. Because for him, it's not about just getting something during his 'special time', it's about getting me. I'm not just an obsession for him. I'm a compulsion. He needs to hold me *down*, force me to choke back sobs as he shoves himself, unceremoniously, into the place between my legs. As he makes the world inside of me burn into a swirling inferno. Until I hate myself inside and out.

His groans are impossibly loud in my ears. I try to squeeze my eyes shut and drown them out, but it's impossible. Bile burns my esophagus. I turn my cheek as he thrusts hard against me and *something sharp stabs into my lower belly. It hurts. It hurts so fucking bad, but no matter how hard I fight, no matter how many times I punch at his chest or clench my teeth against the agony in my belly or scream or beg—it never ends. It never ends until he's ready to let me go.*

"And I'll never let you go, sweet little Rylie," he whispers against my ear. "You're mine."

I BOLT UP IN BED, WAKING FROM THE NIGHTMARE WITH A silent scream on my lips. It all happens so fast—one moment, I'm asleep, trapped in the dream that mixes the past with my own half-deluded fears, and the next I'm back in my dorm room at Havers. Gasping and hunched over, I squeeze my fingers into the fabric of the t-shirt I wore to bed, feeling like my chest is going to explode.

Try as hard as I might, the tightness doesn't ease. Instead, it travels from my chest to my throat and then drops down to my stomach. Before I even realize what I'm doing, I'm half stumbling out of the bed. My knees hit the floor hard and I snatch the trash can under my desk and start puking.

The vomit that comes up is green and red—the same bright cheery colors as the theme of Christmas. It's dirtied in my mind, though, with the knowledge that it's nothing more than the Twizzlers and Mountain Dew I had for dinner.

I don't know how long I stay there on the floor, but it's long past when I finish emptying the contents of my stomach. I'm too tired to get up, so I just lay there, with my arms draped around the trash can and sweat drying on my face. When I do finally decide to get up, the darkness outside of my window has started to lighten and I can hear others in the dorm already awake and moving about as they head to the shared bathrooms for their morning showers.

Exhaustion pulls at my limbs as I climb up and stand on

trembling legs only to collapse back onto my twin-sized mattress. For over a year now, Eastpoint has made me feel safe. Or as safe as one can be under the thumb of three insane, rich assholes. Now, everything is ruined.

I don't know if it started with the email or with this strange non-relationship I have with Abel Frazier. Perhaps it began way back when Avalon first arrived. All I know is that I'm at a breaking point. If I want to keep my sanity—if I want to stay here—I need to be sure.

After several minutes of letting my heart rate slow to a normal speed, I stand and move to my desk, gently toeing the puke-stained trash can out of my way as I take a seat and open my laptop. The more I know about Daniel Dickerson, the better I'll feel. If I could, I'd have a tracker put on him so that any time one of my old dreams comes back to haunt me, all I need to do to feel safe again is look up where he's at and make sure he's not coming back.

Something tells me that if I really want to feel safe again, if I want to make these nightmares stop once and for all, I'll have to do something else entirely. My eyes stray to where my phone sits, plugged into its charger on the corner of my desk closest to my bed.

I lean back against the low back of my desk chair and turn my gaze to the sky, but I'm met with only the white tiled ceiling. Monsters are funny creatures; the difference between fictional monsters and real ones is fictional monsters are easily detected and easily defeated.

Because if I truly sit long enough and think about it, Daniel wasn't the first person to treat me cruelly. He was just the one who took it a step too far as well as the only one who tried to make it seem like he was kind in the midst of his abuse. The mean foster parents before and after him had been uncaring, but they hadn't been quite so ... vicious.

A sudden and peculiar thought enters my mind. An insane

thought. An absurd question with no answer. What would have happened had I let Abel kiss me that night two months ago? Would I have been another notch on his belt? Or ... would I have been able to tell him the truth? Would I have been able to ask him for the impossible?

After all, the Sick Boys had made Corina disappear like she'd never existed. Sure, I knew it was likely Avalon that had been the one to kill her, but she was no cleaner. She didn't make people disappear. She made them pay. No, it was them who erased everything else.

So I have to wonder, could they—or rather, could *he*—do the same to my monsters? Would he if I asked?

15

ABEL

DESPITE THE FACT that I just had old man Tanner do a full body workup on my baby over the weekend, I find myself under the hood of the Mustang only a few days later just looking for something to distract me. I'll never be a professional mechanic or detailer, but there's something soothing about putting my hands on a big work of machinery, something about the simplicity of a collection of parts working in perfect synchrony.

There's nothing to fix. Hell, there's nothing to even take apart. He's got my beauty running as smooth as she would've been her first day off the lot. So, what the hell am I doing?

Cleaning. My. Fucking. Car. Making her spotless from the inside out because if I can't put my hands all over a chick that I actually want, then at the very least I can take care of the only girl I've given a shit about for a long time.

Aside from Avalon that is.

Unfortunately, thinking of the demon queen must actually summon her because that's where she finds me, hands covered in wax as I work the paint like a pro to make it shine, and she's trailed by none other than Braxton and Dean. The bastards. I have no doubt that they've probably expressed their *concerns* about me considering I've been in a foul mood ever since Rylie moved back to Havers.

It's not that I miss her. I don't. Three days with a chick isn't enough time to warrant missing her when she's gone. Nope. Don't miss that smart mouthed brat at all.

"Whatcha up to, Frontman?" Avalon asks as she follows me around the Mustang to take a seat on a loose stool resting against the wall at my back.

"What's it look like?" I reply. "I'm waxing my car."

She hums in the back of her throat, and out of the corner of my eye, I watch as Dean moves over to her, taking up position at her side with his back against the wall and his arms folded over his chest. As if he can't stand to be away from her. Must be fucking nice. I pour some more of the butter wet wax onto the rag in my hand and get back to work.

"Heard about that party you went to this weekend." Brax's low grumbling voice lifts over the top of the car, coming from the other side where I can't see him as clearly now.

"Yeah," I reply, sensing the pattern that these three are taking. "It was fun. I had a grand ol' time. I would've asked you to come along but you were ... oh, wait, you just took off and didn't tell anyone where you went, didn't you? Huh. Guess you actually have to be here to go places, don't you?"

I'm actually not bitter that he wasn't there, but I already know where this is going. They heard about my claiming of the little program girl. I put Rylie on lockdown and made sure the whole campus knew.

"I was running down a lead," Brax replies.

I grunt a non-response and slide the rag across the red paint in front of me even harder.

"A lead?" Avalon pipes up.

"On Ace," Brax says.

My hand slows against the paint and I stand up, finally

straightening from my crouch. I eye where Brax stands, hips against the side door of my black '67 chevy impala, mirroring what I know is Dean's exact stance behind me.

"And?" I prompt when he offers no more. "Did you find anything?"

Emotionless hazel-gray eyes meet mine and hold for several seconds before finally turning away. "We'll see soon." It's vague, but it's unsurprising. Brax doesn't like giving too much information until he's had time to gather it.

I sigh and toss the rag to the floor, next to the bottle of wax. "Alright, fine." I hold my hands up in surrender. "Say it."

"Say what?"

I turn at Avalon's pseudo-innocent tone and glare at her. She grins my way, unabashed. Cheeky little minx. "Don't act like you didn't come in here to read me the riot act." *More like the 'Riot Girl' act,* I think. "So say whatever it is you think you need to say—give me whatever fucking advice it is you think I need and be done with it. I'm over this subtle bullshit, it's not like any of you are any good at it."

Avalon snorts. "You're right," she says. "Subtlety is not our style."

I give her a bland glare. "Then just get it over with," I repeat.

"Do we need to read you the riot act?" Avalon asks, tilting her head to the side as she fights a devious little smile.

I narrow my eyes on her. "Dean should spank you more," I tell her.

She gives in to the urge and smirks at me. "Like that would really help you."

No, but at least she'd be busy getting pounded into the wall by the big man and not down here, getting mixed up in my shit. As if she knows what I'm thinking, too, Avalon cups her hands around the edge of the stool and rocks forward slowly, planting

118

both of her feet on the floor. "So, are you gonna tell us what your deal with her is?"

"There's no deal." It's a lie and I fucking know it, but I'm not quite sure I'm ready to go there yet. Soon, maybe when I've got her figured out a bit more. Perhaps when I've got Rylie well and truly under my thumb, and I feel like she won't disappear and run away—maybe that's when I'll be ready to admit my fucking deal with her.

Avalon arches a brow. "Bullshit."

"Baby..." Dean looks at me even as he issues the warning to her.

"No." Ava hops off the stool and moves towards me. "Something's been going on for a while now. Since the start of the summer, you two have been circling each other like a pair of rabid hyenas."

"More like a cat and a mouse, savage girl," Braxton comments.

Dick, I think. Even as the defensive thought arises, though, I know they're right. That night at the Crawfords made me realize a few things.

One, Rylie Moore is hiding a lot more secrets than we know of. Regardless of what her file says or doesn't say.

Two, she's a lot softer than she looks and she makes me think crazy ass things—like what it'd be like to have all that softness over me, under me, and on top of me.

And last, but certainly not least, something's got her scared. Oh, she hides it well. Real fucking well because I suspect Avalon has got no clue, despite the fact that she's her closest friend—hell, her only friend. I want to know what that fear is. I want to know *who* it is, and then I want to rip them limb from limb for reasons I'm ... not ready to delve into.

Avalon crosses her arms over her chest, and my eyes dip down to the curve of her breasts as they rise up against the low neckline of her t-shirt. A growl from Dean has me pulling my gaze back up lazily and grinning from her to him. "Sorry, man," I say with a shrug.

"Don't let him distract you, D-man," Ava says. "He's just trying to get out of admitting his feelings."

"Ew." I flinch away from her and back up, stopping just before my body hits my freshly waxed car. "Don't talk about girl shit with me, Ava," I say. "You know it grosses me out. I thought you were different. Yeah, I know you have tits and a va-jay-jay and all that shit, but I didn't think you were like *a girl* with *feelings*."

Avalon's fist shouldn't be such a shock—and to my mind, it's not. My body, however, is a different story. Breath rushes out of my chest as she sinks her knuckles right into my abdomen, just as hard as any man. "Fucker," she mutters with irritation. "Stop trying to distract us."

I cough out a laugh as she pulls back and I rub against the place she hit. "What the hell was that?" I tease. "A love tap or are you just expressing your *feelings* again?"

"You wanna get hit again, bitch?" Avalon asks, glaring at me. "'Cause I can make it happen."

Before she can follow through on that little threat of hers, however, Dean's arms come around her middle and he pulls her back against his chest. "Baby, he's trying to fuck with you." The irony of the fact that she basically just said the same thing to him not two minutes ago isn't lost on me.

"Yeah, well, it's fucking working." Avalon sends another glare my way but allows herself to sink into his embrace, and goddammit if my chest doesn't tighten up just seeing the two of them. I have to look away as I straighten and reach down to grab my wax and cloth. I'm not gonna get done here any time soon, it seems.

I take my shit and move over to the row of cabinets installed against the back wall, opening the one on the farthest left and sliding the closed bottle inside before shutting it. "I don't care if you're interested in her," Ava says as I move to wash my hands in the sink next to the cabinets. "But if you're just looking for another chick to fuck, choose someone else."

I come to a stop in front of the sink and without thinking, I turn back, half-shocked by her words. "The fuck?" I blurt. "You think I'm tryna fuck with her or something?"

Ava watches me, the glare gone from her eyes, now replaced with something akin to curiosity. "I don't know what you're thinking, Abel," she admits. "You've been weird since shit went down and Frazier Senior bit the dust."

"I'm just dealing with shit," I tell her, irritation swelling in my chest. "I'm not going to fucking hurt your friend." Unless that hurt is sexual in nature. I could just picture lavender-haired Rylie with bruises on her thighs from how hard I've fucked her. The image in my mind is enough to make my whole body tense. Yeah, there's no denying I want her physically. All that other shit, though, is a distraction.

"Maybe you won't mean to," Dean says quietly even as he holds onto Ava's hips where his hands have drifted to.

Anger swells within me and the image of Rylie disappears as if it never was. I point his way. "Go fuck yourself," I snap. "You don't know shit about what I'm feeling or what I'm dealing with."

"Then tell us." I jerk my head to Brax as he speaks for the first time in several minutes. Damn motherfucker always somehow manages to disappear in a room full of people. Despite his size, despite his demanding presence, it's like he's got a switch inside of him that he can switch on and off and become invisible even if it's with Dean or me.

"You want to know how I'm feeling?" I demand, shooting my hands out wide. "So the fuck would I? How the fuck do you feel, Brax? About Elric? How do you feel knowing your dad killed one of his brothers and then tried to kill Ava?" I gesture to her as I talk and somehow, the fucking pile of shit that's been sitting inside of me for the last few weeks comes up. I can't stop it. "For fucking *money!*" I yell. "They tried to take her from us like they've taken *everything.*"

My mom. My fucking innocence. My childhood. Every good thing I've ever had in my life has been tainted by the name of Eastpoint. My relationships. My friendships. My family. Shit—even whatever this shit I've got going on with Rylie is stained by who and what I am. None of it would even be mine if I were not the son of an Eastpoint Legend. *Well, some legend he turned into,* I think viciously.

I turn and slam a fist down against the side of the sink hard, and the skin over my knuckles splits. I bow my head. "Fuck them," I hiss through the pain. "I don't..." I can't get the words out. I want to say it, and my lips try, but no air is left. I want to say that I don't care that they're dead, but even that feels wrong somehow.

My chest hurts. A steady, dull repetitive thudding starts up in my temples. I don't want to be here anymore. My fingers clench against the sink.

"Abe—" Dean's voice is cut off, though I don't look up to see why. Then I hear it—the soft pad of footsteps on the concrete floor.

Slender, feminine hands come around my body and the press of a smaller and much more delicate body touches my spine. Avalon may act tough, and she may be a woman—shorter and less muscular by physiology, but she's not fragile. She's not weak. Not like I am right now.

My head bows down even more because as much as I don't want to admit it, as much as I want to shove her off and stalk away and not accept this ... act of love—or whatever the fuck it is—I can't do that either.

"It's okay," Ava says quietly. "You're okay, Abel."

A distant memory resurfaces. Those words, spoken by me, over and over again until my voice was raw. The recollection is hazy, barely there and then I feel a masculine hand on one shoulder and another on the other—two different hands, two different men, both brothers.

"It's guilt," Braxton says. "That's what you're feeling. Guilt."

"It's okay to be sad about their deaths," Avalon agrees. "Even if they were shitty fucking dads."

"I'm not sad," I say. And I'm not. I don't feel sorrow for my father or Brax's. What I feel is ... loss. Loss of what they could have fucking been. They could've been better and now they never will be and that leaves a hollow feeling inside of my chest that I didn't realize I've been trying to fill up in the only way I was ever taught.

Bodies. Female bodies crawling all over me. Plump cherry red lips on my dick. A pussy in my face. Tits against my chest. Drugs in my lungs. Alcohol in my veins. I've been clouding my eyes over with all of that shit for so long, I forgot that this is what it's like to deal with all these *emotions* without it.

I release a shuddering breath. "If I promise to make an appointment with Viks, will the three of you leave everything else alone?" I ask without lifting my head.

"Are you actually going to show up?" Ava mumbles against my back.

"Did you?" I shoot back.

Instead of answering, though, the little brat releases me, and soon enough, Brax and Dean retract their hands as well. I reach for the knobs on the sink and turn, quickly rinsing my hands clean of oil, wax, and blood before wiping them dry on my jeans and turning to face everyone once more.

Ava looks less than pleased, but she also doesn't look nearly as angry as she was earlier. Progress, I suppose. "Are you actually interested in Rylie?"

I should have known it was coming, this question. She's like a dog with a bone. Ava doesn't get attached to people, but to her, I guess Rylie's proven herself. And as for me...

"If you're asking if I want to fuck her, the answer is always yes," I say, cocking a smile her way. "Thick or skinny, you know I like 'em all. If you're asking if I want to date the program girl ... that's a different story. I don't do dating."

"You've never locked a girl down either," Braxton points out. "I mean other than Ava—but we all know how that turned out."

My eyes shoot to his face, but he merely grins my way. The fucker knows exactly what's going on. Ava looks to Dean for confirmation, and just as expected, he nods in agreement. I'd say they were traitors if it weren't for the fact that this is Avalon they're telling.

"I don't want to get into it right now," I finally say when the three of them turn their curious and insistent eyes back on me. "I don't know where things are. Do I want her? Yes. Am I interested in her beyond a one-night stand?" Also yes, but I don't know how to say that without Avalon getting her hopes up. So, all I do is sigh and turn away. "We'll see."

"Okay, fine," Ava says at my back. "I'll let it go for now, but Abel?" I reach the other side of the car and look back. Avalon stares at me, her cool blue-grey eyes serious. "If you change your mind about her, or if you decide you don't want her, then let her go. Don't fucking lead her on."

Something inside of me rebels at those words. *Let her go?* Rylie's face flashes before my eyes. Her frizzy purple hair. Big sunken eyes in a porcelain face. Dainty features. So very breakable, and so very desirable. *Never,* a voice inside screams. It's a child's voice, the one that latches onto anything and everything that shows it affection. *She's not mine to keep,* I remind him. *Not yet.*

"Fine." I force the word out—for Ava if not for anyone else.

"Then again, that's even if you can get in her pants." Ava's words are accompanied by a shit eating grin.

I turn and cup the front of my jeans. "Don't you know by now, Princess?" I say with a laugh. "I can get into any chick's pants. It's my superpower."

She arches one dark eyebrow. "Bet on it, then," she challenges.

I lower my arms and look at her. "Bet on if I can get into the goth girl's pants?" I ask. "Do you want to give me your new cash hoard that fast?"

Ava shrugs, unconcerned by my words. "Scared, Frontman?"

I scowl. "Not even a little, Princess. Fine, then. What's the deadline?"

She hums and reaches up, tapping one finger against her full, pink lips. "I'll be generous," she says. "How 'bout 'til the end of the semester?"

"Deal," I say. "I'll put a hundred—"

"Just a hundred?" she cuts me off with a laugh. "Man, you don't have much confidence in your skills, do you?"

I grind my molars. "A hundred fucking thousand," I snap. "That good enough for you?"

Her evil little eyes twinkle with glee. Fucked up bitch. She's so goddamn lucky she's boning my brother. "Done," Ava says with a grin. "I can't wait to watch you two burn."

Before I can make a comeback, Dean slings an arm over Ava's shoulders and pulls her into his body. "Screw the hacker if you want," he says. "No judgment man. Even if you two end up as nothing—or you fuck and fade—she's still contracted so we'll make do. Whatever you decide to do with the girl is up to you. We'll back you. It's what we do."

"Thanks." I push the word out, and I mean it. Despite the fact that my chest feels tight at the idea of fucking and fading from a chick like Rylie Moore, I appreciate the fact that they're willing to back me no matter what.

These three are family. They're all I've got and even if I completely burn myself reaching for more—letting my greed overtake me even as I try to steal something precious from the world to claim as my own—I know they'll help me regardless of my choices. That's just who we are.

Now, the decision of what to do with one purple-haired, gothic wannabe program girl is completely up to me. I can't stop the smile that comes to my face. Maybe they were right. I've realized that avoiding her is too hard. Playing a game of cat and mouse is far more fun. And I know just the next step to torment my favorite victim.

16

RYLIE

THE SECOND I step into my communications class on Thursday, I know I've made a terrible mistake. I don't really need the class, but I knew it would look good on my transcripts. After all, companies like to hire students who are well rounded in their university careers. I can't just rely on a recommendation from Eastpoint and the fact that I attended on a full scholarship. Unlike most of the student populace, I actually have to make an effort for my future.

Unfortunately, all of that effort has led to a massive error.

Overlooking who might actually be in the class with me.

"Well, look who it is."

Kill me, now, I beg the universe, but it must be deaf, blind, and stupid when it comes to these men—or specifically this one. At least, it feels that way when, after a moment of silence, there's no sudden lightning bolt to strike me down as per my request.

"What are you standing over there for, Riot Girl?" Abel continues from the back of the classroom where he sits, surrounded like a king by not one, not two, but three chicks.

And as if the three of them have one single brain between them, they sit up and turn their heads my way.

A scowl overtakes my face as Abel ignores the obvious glares they're sending my way and gestures to the chair to his right. "Come have a seat, Ry-Ry."

Without hesitation, I dump my bag on the front row table, glaring right at him as I do, and hope that he notices that it's as far from where he sits as physically possible in the room before turning and plopping down in the seat. But just because I'm not facing him doesn't mean I can't hear the laugh that echoes behind me.

Abel is an Eastpoint heir. He draws attention wherever he goes. Right now, I wish that attention would grow fangs and swallow him whole. At least then it might remain off of me. No such luck is to be had today, though. I can feel eyes on me like razor sharp points. Eyes that seem to dig past the surface of my skin and sink deep.

My throat closes as faded memories of past eyes come back to me. *Not here,* I tell myself. *Shit.* My fucking nightmares don't normally give me flashbacks mid-day, but for some reason, I can't seem to stop my muscles from bunching up under the loose black t-shirt I'm wearing. My breath saws in and out of my chest.

My gaze jerks up and moves to the clock above the board on the wall. This class is a short one. Only fifty minutes. I can hang on for fifty minutes. A moment later, I know I'm wrong because the telltale sound of heavy footsteps thump behind me and then warm breath assails my ear as Abel leans down against my back.

"If you think ignoring me is going to get me to go away, Riot Girl," he says, "Think again." My eyes cut to him as he turns his attention to the skinny guy wearing glasses sitting on my right. "You," he snaps.

Glasses guy jerks and I watch as his eyes widen behind his

lenses. "Wh-who me?" he stutters. I blow out a breath. I already know what's coming.

"Yeah, you," Abel says. "Get lost."

"I-I'm sorry?" Glasses guy looks confused and then glances between me and the massive hunk of annoyance standing against my back.

"That's my seat now, dude," Abel says. "Find a new one."

Glasses guy doesn't need to be asked again. He scrambles up and out of what was originally his seat, scoops up his notebooks and bag, and scrambles across the room to an entirely new row. I clench my teeth as my panic fades and Abel slides into the seat at my side.

"What are you doing?" I ask under my breath, hoping his groupies have stayed far enough back that they don't hear me. Considering that I'm not choking on expensive perfume right now, I expect that they have—probably at his request. Which boggles my fucking mind.

"Hanging out with my new friend," Abel replies with a smile, draping an arm around the back of my chair.

I gape at him. "You're not serious." He can't be fucking serious. It's just not possible. "Are you pranking me?"

Abel's cool blue eyes watch me from his periphery. "No pranks, Riot Girl. Now pay attention. Class is about to start." And he's right because, just then, the professor walks in, slams his bag on the front table, and turns to scribble on the board. He's talking, but despite how close I am, I can't hear a word he says. The entire breadth of my attention is on the man at my side.

He confuses me. Enrages me. Makes me feel things I thought were broken inside of me, and now he's what? Trying to be my friend? I can't be friends with a man like Abel Frazier. It's just not possible. Avalon is the closest thing I have to a friend and even her I keep at a distance. It has to be that way, especially now, especially on the off chance that I have to disappear again.

Time seems to crawl by during the class and I can't tell if it's because of who I'm sitting next to or because of my own scrambled thoughts. Abel moves and his arm slides against mine, making me jerk away.

Eyes up front, Rylie, I order myself. *Focus.* It's a fucking impossible feat, though.

As soon as the professor stops writing on the board and ends class, I'm shoving my shit back into my bag and hiking it up over my shoulder. "Whoa there, Speed Racer." I jerk to a halt, nearly slamming into Abel's chest as he stands up, blocking my avenue of escape.

Blowing out a breath, I tilt my head back and look up ... and up. God, he's the fucking short one, why is he still the size of a goddamn line-backer? Oh, right. Because he is one. He smirks, and I blink at the appearance of a small, barely-there dimple in his cheek. It's shallow, almost more of a shadow than an actual dimple, but my attention latches onto it anyway. It's cute.

"Where's the fire?" he asks, redirecting my focus back to him and off of his features.

"Right here," I state. "And I'm trying to get away."

His grin widens as he leans down, placing one hand—palm down—on the table next to us. "You should know better than to try and get away from me, Riot Girl," he warns me. "As punishment, I'm going to require something from you."

I grimace. There's no telling what he wants. "Information?" I guess, almost hopefully.

He laughs. It's a startling sound—loud and boisterous—echoing through the room as the other students grab their stuff and file out. "Hell no," he says. "Not unless you're willing to give me your real file."

My body goes on lockdown at those words. "Real file?" I

repeat, but the sound of my voice comes to my ears from far away—like I'm screaming down a long, dark tunnel.

Abel leans in closer until I smell cigarettes and whatever expensive ass perfume those chicks from earlier have left on him. "I may not be as smart as you, Riot Girl," he says, lowering his voice so that only I can hear him, "but I'm not stupid. Your file is far too clean for a girl like you."

He's right. The realization crashes down around me. I should've known better. I should've put something in there. A minor arrest record scrubbed clean because I was underage. Something. But I'd been too worried about how permanent it would become after college. I wanted to look poor, but not damaged. To people like the Eastpoint heirs—like Abel—poor people are easy to manipulate. As much as the social justice warriors don't want it to be true, money rules the world. Greed has become as natural to human existence as breathing.

I have nothing to say to Abel now, so all I do is tip my head back even further and stare back at him, waiting.

His smile widens. "So, what'll it be?" he asks, reaching up. His fingers brush over my chin and under, holding it so that I don't lower my gaze. I resist the tremble of visceral want that pulses through me. It's unnatural. I hate it, and since he's the one making it happen, that hate now extends to him. I narrow my eyes. "The file or something else?"

A scoff leaves my lips and rather than calling it back, I jerk my chin from his grasp. "Sex?" I snap. "You think I'll whore myself for you? How fucking original. I'm not—"

Abel growls and I realize my mistake a second too late as he turns and crowds me against the desk. I jerk my head up and look around, but find that while he was talking—everyone else has already hightailed it out of class. Fuck.

A firm hand locks onto my wrist and pulls it up and out. My eyes shoot to Abel's face as his other hand palms my hip. He rocks against me and my body lights up. Fire crawls up my spine and spreads into my head as I feel my skin begin to heat. "Didn't know you thought I was such a fucking piece of shit, Ry-Ry." The nickname is a taunt on his tongue as his anger comes through. His cool blue gaze flashes with electricity that threatens to burn me. I've offended him. My lips part in surprise. I didn't know he could *be* offended. He acts like nothing fucking touches him.

"I-I'm sorry," I stutter out, trying to shove down the strange emotions he's calling forth. Arousal. That's what this is. Real, actual lust. The feel of Abel's body against mine—big and foreign. The weight of him doesn't feel suffocating. Why is that?

"Look at me."

I don't want to. I really don't want to. I don't want him to see. I don't want him to know. I squeeze my eyes shut, and when I don't move to follow his command, his fingers find my chin again, tilting it up despite my resistance. I can feel his breath against my face. It's hot and smells faintly of menthol and...

"Did you drink whiskey before coming to class?" I ask, stunned.

His dark chuckle finally has me peeking my eyes open. Abel Frazier is a beautiful man—practically sculpted by the Gods themselves. It's truly not fair. His beauty. His intensity. All of it is focused on me. "I'm not blackmailing you for a quick fuck, Rylie." The way he says my name makes my heart pound faster. This is dangerous—so fucking dangerous. Is this what Avalon felt when she was faced with the Sick Boys all alone? No, probably not. That crazy bitch probably relished in the adrenaline that is now coursing through my veins. "If I wanted a quick fuck, I wouldn't come to you," Abel finishes.

Cold water washes over my system at those words, cooling the burning lust that had swelled within me. Right, I think.

Because I'm not the type of girl guys want unless they have no other options. Abel's got every option. Why would he—

My thoughts stutter to a stop a moment later as Abel presses his hips into mine and I feel the hard ridge of a distinct erection sliding over the front of my stomach. My mouth drops open. My eyes widen and my attention shoots up to his face as the grip he has on my chin goes from slight to hard. His fingers cup the lower part of my face as he moves closer, bending until his head is right next to mine, his lips scant centimeters from my ear.

"Because when I fuck you, Riot Girl," he says, sending chills skating down my spine, "there won't be anything quick about it. It's going to be long and hard and so fucking dirty, you'll be wondering why you thought resisting was ever an option."

My legs are practically gelatin they're so weak. Those filthy words whispered against my ear are the very reason resistance is the only option. I don't even have the opportunity, though, to come up with a response before he's talking again.

"And for your information, sweetheart..." I close my eyes as his voice vibrates in his chest and against mine. He's so close —*too* close. "I'm not the type to bargain for sex."

"Then, what—"

"The party," he says, cutting me off before I can ask what he wants. "If you don't want to hand over your real file then be at Urban tomorrow night."

I would rather pluck out my own eyeballs and feed them to the annoying squirrels that inhabit the small grassy area in front of my dorm than go to another party at Urban. A thought occurs to me. I can just doctor up another fake file. I don't really care if he knows about everything else, about my actions after Daniel. It's only the earliest parts of my life that need to stay buried. If I could scrub my memories of him as well as I'd scrubbed the proof of what he'd done on paper, I would.

Hacking can only do so much. It's only the paper trail I can burn away; reality is so much harder to erase.

"When do you want my file?" I say, forcing the words to come out slow. I don't want to seem too eager to give up my fake secrets.

Abel pauses and finally—thankfully—pulls away to glance down at me, one blond brow lifting. Heat steals across my face, but I hold firm. The darkness disperses from his expression, almost as quickly as it'd come. He laughs and then shakes his head, stepping back and taking all of the heat he provided with him until I'm left shivering against the cold air conditioning of the classroom. "On second thought," he says, "keep your secrets, Riot Girl. I'd rather have you at the party."

I cross my arms over my chest. "I'd really rather not."

"No?" That stupid smile on his face and that stupid barely-there dimple have my full attention as he talks. "You don't say? Are you trying to tell me you're not a partier, Riot Girl?"

Not anymore, my internal conscience supplies. Outwardly, however, I remain silent. Glaring at him. Daring him silently to force my hand. I should've known better. No one can play a player like Abel.

"Does it matter?" I shoot back.

He shrugs. "Guess not since you'll be coming anyway." His grin is boyish and that, too, is a lie. He's so fucking devious and we both know that this little game we're playing is going to leave either one or both of us hurt, or, more likely, just me—wrecked and ruined like always. "Cheer up," Abel says, backing away as he shoves his hands into his pockets, "you were fun at the last one. Maybe wear a swimsuit this time, though. I'll make sure to have the Jell-O pit put together in advance."

Irritation swells. "I'm not go—" I don't get to finish my sentence. Before I can manage it, he's already turning as he strides away, waving his hand behind him as he goes.

"See ya tomorrow night, Riot Girl," he calls over his

shoulder. "Wear something hot enough to make me want to take it off with my teeth later, yeah?" He pauses just outside the door and looks back. "And it was rum ... not whiskey."

I gape after him, left with little more than a command and the image of Abel Frazier flashing those perfectly straight white teeth of his as he rips my panties down my legs and buries his face between them. I sag against the desk, my chest pumping up and down. Some unknown emotion drags up my back and wraps around my throat, squeezing tight, as I shift my legs and realize something else as well. My panties are soaked.

17

ABEL

YOU THINK I'll whore myself for you? Rylie's words echo in my mind. My fists clench as I push out of the classroom building. No, she's not the type to whore herself out, but I am.

A disgusting emotion clogs my throat, bears its talons, and sinks into my muscles, diving deep until it hits the fucking bones beneath my flesh. Vile. Revolting. Worthless.

The onslaught of memories come to me hard and fast. I've got another class, but instead of heading towards it, I direct my steps towards the parking lot and I don't stop until I'm at my car. Gripping the handle of the driver's side door, I rip it open and slump inside. The coils inside of my chest wind impossibly tighter and my hands shake as I reach for the console and rip it open, delving into it until I've got a small blunt in my grasp. I put one end between my lips and light the other, inhaling as my head drifts back against the seat.

"Fuck." The word slips out—the only sound in the interior of the car. Normally, the Mustang gives me a sense of safety, but I didn't get here fast enough. I didn't light up fast enough. It's coming—old memories that have no business crawling out of their graves, but crawl out they do, and like zombies they consume me, dropping me right back into a nightmare painted in gold.

15 years old...

I DON'T WANT HER, BUT I DON'T HAVE A CHOICE. FOR MEN like me, freedom is nothing but an illusion. Amidst the sparkling glasses of champagne and diamond chandeliers that even the portrayals of the rich in movies and on television can't hope to match, there is one irrefutable fact: *Everything comes at a price.* Tonight's price is Ella Chaplin.

As I walk across the marble floors of one of the most exclusive hotels in Eastpoint, the strings of that price tighten around my throat. Every step makes me a little light-headed. I'm suffocating. It's not normally this bad, but Brax and Dean aren't here. They're somewhere else, and right now, I wish I was with them.

My father's hand lands on my shoulder, gripping tight as his fingers dig into my muscles until the pang of his irritation is a physical ache rather than a mental and emotional one. "We're here to do a job, Abel," he states. "Remember your responsibility and you'll see them again."

I close my eyes and inhale. There it is—the reason Brax and Dean weren't invited to this little get together. Or, if they were, this is the reason why they didn't come. Because this isn't something they can do. It's not something they were born for. This is my secret shame, my motherfucking duty.

"As long as you keep Ella Chaplin happy," my father continues. "Everything else will go according to plan. Find her, seduce her, and do what needs to be done. I'll have someone text you when I'm finished."

He'll have someone text me, I think. Because he can't bear to do it himself. Doing something like that—having a fucking conversation with his own son—is beneath him.

And whether he realizes it or not, I hear the truth between the lines: I'm beneath him.

I shift and move my shoulder out from under his grip. "Abel." Lionel Frazier doesn't yell, but he doesn't need to. Just my name in that silver-tongued mouth of his feels like a thousand knives hanging over my head. I freeze just before the entryway but don't look back. It's a little rebellion. As many as I can find, as many as I can get away with—I'll take them all. He may have me under his thumb now, but it won't be that way for long.

Unlike him, I have friends. Not just allies. Not just heirs thrown together and forced to work alongside one another because of some centuries-old tradition. Dean and Braxton are my brothers—not by blood, but by circumstance. I trust them with my life and doing so lets me know that I'm not alone, even when I really fucking feel like I am.

"Don't forget the goal," he says coldly.

My mouth twists into a scowl. "I know what I'm fucking doing," I snap, and with that I leave him, striding into the ballroom that's been rented for just this occasion and into my own personal version of hell.

Lights. Camera. Action. Every single person on this stage is an actor. We're all gliding around in our tuxes and designer accessories like we're having the time of our lives when, in fact, we're slowly leeching our own lives away. That responsibility my father is constantly preaching to me about is simple—everything I do must be for the good of Eastpoint.

No matter how offensive.

No matter how dirty it makes me feel.

No matter how grotesque my insides become.

It's all for the purity of the Eastpoint lineage.

And though it may not be me, I hope one day ... someone comes along to sully the Eastpoint name. Hell, the second I get the chance, I'll be happy to burn it all down myself. I'll take my father's veritable mountain of money and I'll watch him burn atop it. For now, though, I just need to turn my eyes forward and focus on what I have to do.

There's that funny saying chicks in upper class England used to say—close your eyes, spread your legs, and think of England. This is true for me, except instead of England, I have to think of Eastpoint. And I don't spread my legs, I go down on my knees for a pair of them. It's repulsive—the things I've done for the sake of tradition and honor. Nothing about it feels honorable, but I've learned one thing—I'm damn good at getting between a woman's legs and just as my father expected, Ella Chaplin, the daughter of Eastpoint's wealthiest rivals, will be no different.

As soon as I catch a glimpse of her, the game is on. She sees me and I turn around. I know this game well, so well, I could probably play it in my sleep. Catch and release.

It's all in the way you reel the fish in, Abel ... My mother's words slip into my mind at that precise moment. Almost as if she's watching from wherever she is now. She was never quite the socialite every other woman I've been surrounded by my whole life is. She was wild, untamable. She enjoyed hunting and fishing and working on cars and was far more beautiful when she was covered in engine grease and smelling like gas fumes than the number of vultures circling the ballroom I'm currently in.

I can sense their interest, the way they drift closer when they realize I'm alone. I'm not with Dean or Braxton or even my father. That's the point. I start moving, reaching up and snagging a champagne flute off of a wandering tray as a waiter passes by. I down it in one go and drop it off on a table as I keep walking. Another flute appears in my grasp and is gone just as quickly. I'm moving in a circular motion, greeting people I recognize as I pass, but making my isolation clear. There's no one on my arm and that means the spot is open and available.

The bodies and faces of those surrounding me disappear until the only thing left are shadows with big white eyes, scanning our every movement. I don't want to fucking be here. It's all a fucking act. Every single, expensive perfume smelling, money grubbing, cock fucking second of it. I feel dizzy. How many glasses of champagne have I had? Sickness curdles in my gut, threatening to spew out. Those faces, those eyes, they're all watching.

"Abel Frazier." I stiffen at the sound of my name, but I know that voice. I turn slowly towards it, lifting my glass as I finish it off, and then set it aside.

"Ella Chaplin." My tune mimics hers as she stands there, dressed to kill in a long black sheath dress.

Her bright red lips curl upward. "What are you doing here?" She saunters forward and perhaps, if it hadn't been made clear to me that this is expected, then I might've actually enjoyed what I'm about to do.

Cocking my head back, I look down at the girl that's a good two years older than myself. She's petite, her tight body dressed perfectly in a dress that likely costs more than most Americans make in a year. "Alleviating boredom," I say.

"Mind if I join you?" she inquires, moving closer until her perfectly manicured hand lands on my chest. Given the choice, I'd tell her no. I'd shove her away and leave this suffocating prison-like room and fuck whatever plans my father has for hers. But I don't have a choice. My freedom is not my own.

So, instead, I grin down at her and let one of my hands drift up to her side, gripping her hip and pulling her closer. "I never mind a beautiful woman on my arm, Ella." I arch a brow. "Do you promise to help me with my boredom problem?" I ask, lowering my voice and putting my lips right next to her ear. And just as expected, she shivers.

"What did you have in mind?" Her question is a bit breathless and also a bit ridiculous. She knows very well what I have in mind.

"It's a hotel," I say. "What do you think I have in mind?"

Ella Chaplin rolls her eyes and pushes back slightly so that I'm not quite so close. Still, I notice her hands never leave my body. She's just as easy as the rest. A little bit of reputation and flattery on my part and she's putty in my hands.

Carefully, with slow movements, her hand slips up into the side of her low-cut dress and she produces a keycard from her bra. Her tits push up against my body as she leans forward and slips it in front of my face. "I know just the place," she says with a grin.

"Great, then let's get out of here." I curve my arm around her waist and spin the two of us towards the door.

Halfway to the doors, I spot two men walking towards us. "Abel!" My father calls out and waves as he and George Chaplin step in front of us, cutting off our exit. "I didn't realize the two of you knew each other." My eyes narrow, but I plaster a smile on my face anyway.

"Of course, we go to the same school," I say, tightening my hold on Ella's waist. Her head tips back and she smiles up at me. What I don't say is that Ella is a fucking senior, and I'm a sophomore. We have no classes together and have hardly spoken before tonight.

George Chaplin grins at the two of us before shaking his head. "Of course the two of you are sneaking out, aren't you?" he guesses. "I suppose a big shindig like this one isn't what the kids are into these days." His attention goes back to my father. "If they were old enough to drink, perhaps..."

I barely resist the urge to roll my eyes. He should know well enough that age means utter shit at places like this. I've already had more than enough alcohol to palate what I need to accomplish tonight and no one stopped me. But instead of pointing that out, I just laugh and agree. "I hope you don't mind, Mr. Chaplin, but Ella and I were going to head out and maybe grab something to eat together."

Mr. Chaplin nods and then glances at his daughter. "Whatever makes my little girl happy makes me happy," he says.

Ella giggles and presses herself so close to me, she's half climbing my body. "We promise to be good, Daddy," she coos, making it quite obvious to me that she's planning to be the exact opposite of good.

Hold it in, Abel, I tell myself. *Hold it the fuck in.* I can feel my father watching me, his penetrating gaze assessing and evaluating. This is good for him, though. Everything is going according to his plan. If Chaplin thinks his daughter and I might become a couple then the merger my father is attempting to close tonight will go well. All I need to do now is get Ella Chaplin out from under the eye of her father and up to her hotel room, fuck her stupid, and wait to be released from my fucking duty.

"Well, we won't keep you kids any longer," my father says, patting Mr. Chaplin on the back. "Shall we move on and let them go have their fun?"

"Of course." Mr. Chaplin shoots me a sharp look. "You take care of my daughter, Frazier. You hear me?"

I nod politely. "Of course, sir."

Almost as soon as he's out of earshot, Ella Chaplin leans up against my side. "You can take care of me, Abel, can't you?" she breathes hotly. "I've heard you're very good at taking care of a woman's needs."

Irritation slides through me and the first thought I had when I stepped into this place comes to mind. I don't want her, but I don't have a choice. My fingers tighten on her side and my strides lengthen until I'm half carrying her towards the elevator. The second we're inside and the doors slide shut, I turn her and slam her back against the wall, my mouth coming down hard over hers. I push it all out—the anger, the disgust, the wreckage that's festering inside my soul—as I kiss her. Only when she's moaning and compliant in my arms, do I finally pull away.

When I speak my voice is gruff—just enough to disguise the violence I'm repressing. "You heard right, sweetheart," I say. "You heard very fucking right." And then I go to my knees in that elevator and I show her just how well I can take care of a woman's needs ... for the sake of fucking Eastpoint.

18

"JUST GIVE IN AND COME." Ava's words drift up from the speaker of my cell and fill my half empty dorm room.

I scoff. "Did you do that when Dean demanded you do the same?" I shoot back.

"Fuck no," she says with a laugh. "But Abel isn't Dean." *And I'm not her,* I want to say, but somehow, I manage to keep those words in. I don't hate Avalon. In fact, I respect the hell out of her—not that I'd tell her that. She's got a big enough ego as it stands. But I do envy her.

She came here just like me—with nothing—and now she's the one and only Eastpoint queen. Just because she didn't demand that title and earned it instead doesn't mean I don't see the miles of differences between us. She relishes confrontation. She takes the blows head on and keeps going, but not me. I can't. I'm a hider. A runner. I've been broken before and I will never go back to that cold, dark place. I'd rather light everything behind me on fire and keep going.

"If it makes you feel better, Dean's making me go too," she says.

I snort. "Like he could make you do anything," I mutter as I reach into my dresser and pull out a pair of cheap black tights—they're old, and unlike the girls who prefer to buy their clothes pre ripped, mine are ripped due to excessive use.

"True," Ava replies, "but he can be very convincing when he wants to be. I've never dated a guy with a tongue piercing, but it—"

"I don't want to know." I shut that shit down fast. Girl talk is one thing, but talking about her sex life with the King of Eastpoint is a completely different matter.

"Would you rather I talk about Abel?" she asks.

Yes. "No," I say aloud, almost shoving the word out before my real answer can escape.

She chuckles and then sighs. "Don't overthink the invite," she says. "They probably just want to keep an eye on you."

"An eye on me?" I narrow my gaze on where my phone sits across the room, face up on my desk, as I stand to finish pulling up my tights. "Why would they need to do that?" *Did Abel tell them that my file was fake?*

"Dunno," Ava says as I reach across the bed and snatch up the Falling in Reverse t-shirt I'd tossed there earlier and fit it over my head. "Are you hiding anything?"

I pause as my hem drifts down to my stomach to meet where my tights reach my waist. A moment of silence passes and then I speak. "Even if I was," I hedge, "it wouldn't be safe to tell you, not with you shoved up Dean's ass all the time."

If Ava's offended, she doesn't sound it when she barks out yet another laugh. I swear she's laughed more in the last couple of weeks than in the half a year I've known her. "Fair," she replies. "And for what it's worth, I get it. It's not easy letting someone in."

I plop back down on the edge of my twin sized mattress and grip handfuls of my hair, separating them out on either side of my head. "So, this whole party at Urban is to announce you as an Eastpoint heir?" I ask, redirecting the conversation back to the original topic at hand.

Over the line, I hear a puff of frustrated breath. "Yeah, I guess," Ava responds. "I don't really give a shit, but Dean says it's important. I mean it's not like he's gonna stand up and basically beat his chest and say 'this is my woman, hear me roar' or some bullshit, right?"

I bite my lower lip, unwilling to tell her that I absolutely think Dean Carter would do that. The man is head over heels, balls to the wall, dagger in the heart in love with this chick. One of my hands drifts up to my chest as my nails sink into the fabric, pulling it tight against my back and loose in my front. What they have is the kind of love that lives and dies with one other person. It's nothing I could ever understand.

"—Rylie? You gonna say something or—"

I blink and release my shirt, letting it bag against my frame as Ava's voice cuts through my thoughts. "Sorry, I got distracted," I half-lie. "What'd you say?"

"I asked if you wanted me to pick you up tonight or if you were gonna take the bus to Urban."

"I'll take the bus," I say immediately. "The last few times you gave me a ride, I had to anyway." Because she ditched me, not once—but multiple times.

"Oh, right, yeah," Ava's voice wavers. "Sorry about that."

I shrug before realizing she can't see me. "I get it," I reply aloud. "We weren't really friends then."

"But we are now," she says.

I press my lips together, but I don't deny the statement. If Ava wants to be friends with me, she'll do it on her own terms. I get up and move across the room, rifling through my dresser until I find what I'm looking for. Pulling up the mini white and purple plaid skirt, I zip the side and then turn and pick up the phone.

"I gotta finish getting ready," I say.

"That means you're definitely coming, right?" she asks.

As if I have a choice, I think. "Yeah, I'm coming," I say instead. "I'll see you when I get to Urban."

With that, I press 'end call' and set my cell down, leaning against my desk chair. The Sick Boys are keeping an eye on me? That almost seems more dangerous than it's worth to be here. Eastpoint doesn't feel safe for me anymore, but I can't tell if that's just my own internal fears or if it's facts.

My fingers drum a beat against the surface of my desk, and then I lift my phone once more, scrolling through until I reach my contacts. It's almost pathetic how few numbers I have in my phone, but for each one I've had, the same number has been transferred again and again, but never used. I want to use it now, I realize, and before I can think better of it, I run my finger over the name and hit call.

"Hey, this is Christine, I can't come to the phone right now, but if you leave your name and number I'll get back to you. Thanks!" Christine's voice is loud in my ear and it's changed since the last time I heard it. She sounds older but brighter than when she was a teenage foster kid in the same group home as me and that monster.

I bite down on my lip until I taste blood as the answering machine beeps over, letting me know that I can leave a message. "Hey, Christine, it's ... Rylie from ... well, I don't know if you'd remember me, it's been a while." Thirteen years, seven months, and three days to be precise. "I just ... wanted to ask you something, but I guess you're not around. Don't worry about it. I'll, uh, try to call back later."

Once again, I end the call and sag against the desk, only this time, I feel tears pop up into my eyes. I didn't realize how hard it would be to hear her voice again. Christine—though she'd only been a decade older—had felt more like a mother to me than any of the foster parents I'd had. I don't know if it was because she'd been in my situation for longer, another girl in

147

the system and could relate, but she'd been the only one who had seemed to care and believe me.

Wiping at my eyes, I force strength back into my legs and stand up before leaning across the desk and propping open my laptop. I double check the tabs I'd put on Daniel, and stare at the numbers and location names on the screen as if to reassure myself that no matter where I go, I'm safe here in Eastpoint. I may be chained to the Sick Boys, but at least I've traded up for monsters who won't hurt me. It's better to be used than hurt.

19

RYLIE

IT'S LOUD. The music. The people. The light rays that span down from the ceiling, rotating in a timely fashion—left, right, left, right, circle around. It's like overstimulation for the brain. My stomach growls as I make my way from the front door, after waiting only God knows how fucking long to get in, reminding me that I forgot to eat dinner. Again.

I need a drink, I think, but before I can head towards the bar, I spot a familiar head of white blond hair. My gaze tilts up and his eyes meet mine. He tilts his head one way and then smiles before pointing to the stairs.

I blow out a breath. I've been summoned.

As I head through the crowd, working my way from the very front of the club towards where I see two of Eastpoint's football players manning the entrance to the Eastpoint Heir's private balcony that overlooks the dance floor and bar, I scan the area. More than a few heads turn my way, but their eyes are filled with nothing but contempt.

Most of the student body is here, and almost all of them are dripping with money. Couture dresses that would rock the bodies of models in New York City clubs. Diamond tennis bracelets. Real Rolex watches and shirts and jeans that cost more than a down payment on an apartment.

Sometimes, when I think I've gotten used to the way the rich and powerful live, it's shoved right under my nose, reminding me I'm never good enough. Not in my second-hand store combat boots, ripped tights, and the thin white band t-shirt that I'm currently wearing. I gave it a shot tonight—white instead of black with even a pop of color with the band's old bright pink lip and green tongue logo. And still, I'm the odd man out.

Halfway through, bypassing the bar, some chick pops up out of nowhere and slams her shoulder against mine. I stumble and nearly fall on my ass—would have if not for the fact that there are so many people in the crush around that I'd actually just slammed into the guy behind me.

"Hey, fucking watch it!" the guy snaps, but my entire focus is on the girl in front of me, the one who purposefully ran into me.

I glare at her but she merely smirks. "Oops. Sorry, didn't see you there." Yeah fucking right. I'm practically the only one here whose entire shirt is like a neon fucking sign under the black lights. Before I can lash back or say anything, however, she scoots by, leaning down to press her lips close to my ear as she hooks one claw like manicured hand around my shoulder. "But maybe if you were back in your hole and not here, it wouldn't have happened. Know your place, program girl."

The two girls with her overhear her words and twitter like they're some sort of flock of birds and then, together, they stride off—back into the crowd, disappearing as if their only purpose was to give me that warning. Perhaps I would've been intimidated if I actually gave a shit, but all their antics seem to do is sour my mood even more.

I practically stomp the rest of the way to the entrance of the back staircase and glare up at the football players who stand on either side like bouncers with their arms crossed. They take a look at me and then glance at each other before pointing towards the stairs.

"They're waiting on you," the one on the left says.

Great, I think. That can only mean one thing—and it explains why that chick went out of her way to give me that less than intimidating warning. Abel's up to something.

I mount the stairs in what feels like utter darkness; the only light I can see comes from both behind me and above me at the mouth of the narrow staircase where it opens to a vast space filled with luxurious lounges and dark rustic tables that match the industrial setting of the club. To the right are long bars jutting out from the wall and lining the edge of the balcony where a few girls in skimpy dresses are talking and drinking next to a familiar face.

Braxton glances away from the girls, meeting my gaze and giving me a nod of acknowledgment before he returns his attention to them. Odd. He's not usually the playboy type. Maybe they're workers; they don't look young enough to be students at Eastpoint. Not that it's any of my business, I remind myself a moment later as I turn and scan the rest of the space.

While I've been to Urban a couple of times over the last year, I've never been allowed up here. This is the Sick Boys' sanctuary. Where they can sit up high, watching their kingdom without allowing their subjects to touch them. And as far as I know, the only other program girl to be allowed up here is Avalon, who isn't a program girl at all.

Almost as if she senses my thoughts, Ava lifts her arm from where she sits on a suede black couch pushed as far from the balcony part as possible with a massive, tattooed man at her side. Dean Carter looks far more relaxed than I've ever seen him. Never thought I'd be one to admit it, but he looks like a normal college boy—albeit a little rougher around the edges—when his gaze is on Avalon.

"Hey, come sit over here," Ava calls, and because I don't see a reason to deny her, I do.

I stride over, avoiding the one man who makes unwanted emotions rise up within me as he stands against the private bar chatting with the pretty blonde bartender who looks ten seconds away from laying herself out for him to take his shots from. She completely ignores the guys milling about and waiting on the other side of the bar. My hands curl into fists at my sides and I sit down on the couch harder than necessary, nearly bouncing off the edge as I try to focus on something else, anything other than how aware I am of Abel Frazier.

Avalon grins my way. "What do you think?" she asks, gesturing around. "Isn't it ridiculous?"

I arch one brow. "It's elaborate," I agree.

She snorts. "Right? I mean, who the fuck has a private bar?"

Guys who are richer than gods, that's who, but I don't say that. Instead, I lean forward, crossing my legs as I focus on her. "Are you the one who told the guys downstairs you were waiting on me?" I ask, wincing at the almost hopeful note in my voice.

Ava takes one look at me and gives me a smirk. "No*pe*," she pops the end of that word and it tells me all I need to know.

I feel eyes on the side of my face, but I refuse to turn and meet the cool, ocean gaze I know is waiting for me. He's practically burning a hole into my skin with his focus, but I'm not going to give him the satisfaction of knowing I'm just as aware of him as he is of me. At least, I hope he's aware of me that way. It wouldn't be fair if it was all in my head. Maybe I need to go back to therapy, or a real doctor—find out if there's something wrong with my head.

"So, what am I doing up here?" I press, leaning to the side as if I'm adjusting my position when really, I'm just seeing if the heat from Abel's stare follows. It does.

"You were invited, Moore," Dean says. "That's what you're doing up here."

Ava smacks his stomach with the back of a hand before leaning away from him, the couch creasing as she moves from his side towards me. "If I have to stay up here with their rich friends by my fucking self, I'm gonna shoot someone in the head," she groans. "I needed at least one person up here that annoys me less than everyone else."

"Just one person?" I repeat. "I thought you had three."

Dean chuckles darkly. "If you think she doesn't threaten to shoot us on a daily basis, then you need to spend more time around her," he says with a shake of his head.

I open my mouth to respond but am quickly interrupted by the shrill sound of a call coming through. "Hold on, baby," Dean says, leaning down to kiss Avalon's cheek as he pulls out his cell. "I'll be right back."

She sits up and turns towards him immediately. "Is it the doctor?"

He palms the back of her head and instead of answering, takes her mouth in a heated kiss. My eyes widen at the sight and I can't help but turn away as a flood of heat steals over my face. Once again, though, I end up staring at a man I know I shouldn't. Abel's body is facing the bartender, but his eyes are fully on me. As soon as my eyes meet his, he lowers his head and tilts it to the side as if he's assessing me.

He has a way of seeing deeper than the surface, down into my bones and soul. With no words, no actions, no anything—I feel like he's peeling my skin back and diving into the parts that hurt, the pieces of me that make me scream out for someone to help me, save me. I once thought I could be the only thing I'd ever need. I once thought that affection was a luxury I couldn't afford, and one that wasn't necessary to live a full life. All I needed was money and protection, but lately, he's making me question that.

Abel has all the money and protection in the world. He has friends that would kill and die for him and he would do the same for them. Yet, when I look into his eyes, I see nothing but a vast cavern of loneliness that matches my own. It's disconcerting.

"Asshole." Avalon's mutter, filled with both a longing and irritation, brings me back to the present.

I return my attention to her to find that Dean is already off the couch and across the room, striding towards the exit with his phone pressed to his ear. "Why's he an asshole?" I ask, curious.

She lifts a hand to touch her lips before leaning back into the couch. "Because he didn't fucking answer me and he knows I hate it when he uses his body to distract me."

I can't help it. I burst out laughing. Of all the things I expected her to say, that was not it. Avalon cuts a look towards me and raises one sharply defined eyebrow. I know her well enough to know that she doesn't fuck with much make-up and defining her features like every other girl our age. She's just naturally fucking beautiful. It's not fair. But it's the look of amusement that crosses her eyes as she watches me laugh over her ridiculousness that gets me in the end. As my laughter tapers off, I reach up and wipe beneath my eyes. My fingers come away with black smudges.

"Glad I could amuse you," she mutters.

I shake my head. "All you do is amuse me sometimes," I reply. "And others, you terrify me."

She considers my last statement for a moment before shrugging. "Good."

"I'm sure if it's really important, he'd tell you." I nod to the way Dean went.

Her eyes trail across the big open space and her lips purse together. "Yeah, I know he would," she agrees. "I just want to know everything sooner rather than later. I don't like this waiting game we're playing with the doctors."

"I thought he was cleared to go back to football?" It's not a question, but it comes out like one.

Avalon lifts one shoulder and lets it fall. "Different doctors say different things. He wasn't cleared here, but when we were in California, we saw a specialist and they think he might be able to play. His primary thinks he needs a few more months, but..." She doesn't need to say it. I don't know Dean well—only in the way an employee knows her boss—but I do know his type. He doesn't like being out of control. He's used to being able to move his body and bend it to his own will. He's fit, an athlete—much like Braxton and Abel. It must be difficult for him to have to give up a part of him because of what they've all been through.

Yet, if I do know anything, I know he wouldn't trade it. I'm one of the few people who knows the reasoning behind why he'll most likely be sitting out this next year on the field, and I know why Avalon's face pinches down at the reminder.

"It's not your fault," I tell her quietly. It's almost too quiet in the noise of the club, with the music and talking, but she hears it because she responds almost immediately.

"It fucking feels like it is," she hisses through her teeth, crossing her arms over her chest. "If it wasn't for me, then he wouldn't be in this shape."

I shrug. "People will risk their lives for what's important to them. I bet if you asked him if he thought it was worth it, he'd say it was." Without a doubt.

Ava shoots me a look. "Stop being such a smartass," she snaps.

It's on the tip of my tongue for me to tell her to 'make me.' Only, depending on the mood she's really in, she actually could. Instead, I just shake my head and smile. The smile doesn't last, though, because the longer we sit there, shooting the shit as we wait for Dean to come back, the more an itchy feeling on the back of my neck makes its presence known.

Every few seconds, I glance over to Abel. Sometimes, he's watching me. Sometimes, he's not. The feeling doesn't go away though. It feels like a million eyes are centered on me and the club is dark enough with enough people that I can't tell what direction it's coming from.

As soon as Dean makes a reappearance and Avalon's attention is back on him, I move to stand. "I think I'm gonna head down and grab a drink," I say quickly.

Avalon blinks up at me in surprise. "You can just grab one up—"

"I'll be right back," I cut her off without letting her finish. I need to move. I need to just … figure out if what I'm feeling is just ancient anxiety or something more and I can't do that if I don't put some space between me and my distraction.

Before Avalon can call me, I'm at the top of the stairs and descending back to the first floor without another word. In the time I've been upstairs, more people have entered the club and the heat and noise from before is nothing compared to what it is now.

Bodies crush against my sides as I walk across the floor, moving between groups to reach the bar furthest from the balcony. Twenty feet past the dance floor, someone slams into my side and I nearly go down in a heap.

Thankfully, a pair of strong hands grab my upper arms and lift me back up and a chest turns, blocking the drunken dancers from doing much more harm. "Are you okay?"

I glance up and meet a familiar face. "Dash?" He grimaces as someone bumps into his back and locks his hand tighter on my upper arm, steering me towards the bar.

"I notice you've been spending more time with Avalon lately," he comments lightly when we finally reach the counter and find an open space.

"Is that a problem?" I shoot back, turning my gaze up at him.

He doesn't look down. "No, never said it was," he replies. "Just an observation."

I bite my lip and lift a palm, calling one of the bartenders flitting back and forth down the counter. Dash remains next to me, and I wait for him to tell me why. When several seconds pass, and he still hasn't uttered another word, I blow out a breath.

"If you're worried about me telling them your secret, I won't," I say.

Finally, his head tilts down and his gaze finds mine. He doesn't need to say anything for me to know that's exactly why he approached me, and why he helped me. He's just making sure that I won't blab about his father and the gruesome truth of his home life.

"If I went around telling all of my clients' secrets, then I wouldn't make any money," I assure him. "I advised you to tell them, but if you don't want to, that's your choice. I'm not going to force the issue."

Dash's gaze remains on my face for what feels like a long time. He doesn't say anything until the bartender finally comes to take my order. Then, instead of talking to me, he simply turns to the girl and goes, "Whatever she wants, put it on my tab."

I blink. "Dash, you don't—"

"Have a good night, Rylie," he says, cutting me off as he takes a step back from the bar. "I'll see you around." And then he disappears back into the crowd.

"So, what do you want then?" the bartender asks, arching a brow expectantly.

I sigh. "Vodka tonic," I say. She nods and heads off without asking for my ID or glancing down at the black X across my hand. Anywhere else, I'd be carded, but this is an Eastpoint club. No one cares and no one will get in trouble since Eastpoint owns the town and the police here.

The bartender comes back a minute later, sets a glass full of clear liquid down before me, and then flits off. Still, the eyes are burning into my back so without a second thought, I lift it and take a sip as I turn back towards the crowd.

No sooner is my back to the bar, than a guy comes out of nowhere, shoving himself up against my front. I gasp as the glass in my hand fumbles and then tilts and the cold wash of vodka and tonic water drenches my chest.

"Fuck!" I snap slamming the glass back down as I snatch my shirt and try to keep it from plastering to my front, but it's too late. Of all the nights to wear white, I cross my arms over my chest as the fabric quickly turns see through and glare up at the offensive party. "What is *wrong* with you?" I growl.

A cap of curly brown hair dips down and eyes clouded over with intoxication rove from my boots up my calves and thighs to my chest and then to my face. "My bad, baby," he slurs. "Maybe I can buy you something else."

"Yeah, a new fucking shirt, asshole." Despite my words, my fingers clamp down harder on my arms as I keep them crossed over my chest. Already I can feel the weight of stares being directed my way. "Just fucking forget it." I turn to go when a hand clamps on my shoulder and pushes me back against the bar counter.

"Now, wait a second. I'm tryin' to be nice here."

"Get the fuck off of me," I snap, but dumbass obviously doesn't speak the language of the sane because he ignores my demand and pushes himself harder against me. Rage wells up from within as well as the consistent buzzing of attention I feel from others.

"Come on, I said I was sorry," he says with a grin. I squirm against him, my gaze jerking left and right as I try to find an opening. "Are you really gonna go and leave me here, looking like an asshole?"

"You *are* an asshole," I inform him, seething as I shove him back again. Before he can summon a reply, a dark voice speaks over my head.

"Take your fucking hands off of her before I fucking remove them."

Oh, fuck. This night just became ten times worse.

20

ABEL

She's running like a scared cat and I would say it's not like her, but that would be a lie. It is like her. Rylie's a runner. She's easily frightened and easily overstimulated. I'm shocked she even heeded my order to come here, but when she spends the first half of the night with Avalon, I figure out why. Avalon convinced her.

All I can do is stand over by the bar watching her, staring at her like exactly what I am—a predator. I want to eat her up, consume her, and inhale her into my soul until there's no part of her I don't possess. I always thought Braxton and Dean were the crazy ones, but I guess I've got the gene too. All it takes is the right woman and my vision hazes over with desire and insanity.

She senses my attention. I can tell by the way she keeps flicking a glance my way as if to make sure I'm still here.

I'm still here, Riot Girl.

I'm just waiting on her. Whether that's her approach or her final decision, I'm stuck in this limbo, trying to predict what she'll do next.

It doesn't take long for her to get uncomfortable under my

gaze. She stands, says something to Avalon the second Dean returns from whatever phone call he took, and then disappears back down the stairs. I don't like not having her in my sights, especially not in this kind of place, so I find myself ambling over to the overlook of the balcony.

Braxton breaks away from the girls he hired for the evening —a heartbreak for them, but probably good. I hate it when he brings his prostitutes in. He won't fuck the girls from school though because then everyone would know about his *issues*.

"You're getting to be as bad as Dean," he comments.

"Fuck off."

He chuckles and does no such thing as he reaches into his pocket and pulls out a slightly crumpled cigarette pack. Instead of cigs, though, when he opens it and pulls out a slender white roll up, I realize it's weed. "Want one?" he asks, offering me a second one. I take it without thinking and put one end between my lips as I reach into my pocket for a lighter.

Coming up empty, I lean over to him after he lights his and press the end of mine to the cherry red end of his. I inhale, rocking back on my heels. Loud bass music thrums through the club. The hard beat rocking the walls as the bodies down below grind together. Rylie's easy to pick out in the crowd. Where all the other chicks are wearing dark dresses meant to slim their figure, her t-shirt stands out like a sore thumb, bright under the black lights as she squirms through the crowd heading towards the bar.

The fuck did she need to go to the bar down there for? There's one right up here.

I don't realize I've asked that question aloud until Braxton answers.

"Easy," he says. "Because you were standing at the bar the whole time and that girl is so fucking aware of you that even standing twenty feet from you doesn't make her forget the fact that you're watching her like a hawk."

161

Yeah, I realize. I am. Especially now that she's down there and I'm up here. Staring at the back of her head like an aerial predator ready to swoop down and carry her away. I put the joint back to my lips and inhale again. Smoke fills my lungs, the effect relaxing my muscles as I turn my attention to the man at my side.

"I'm becoming obsessed," I admit aloud. I think it's the first time the words have left my lips and that makes them potent.

Brax snorts like that much has been obvious from the start and I shoot him an irritated look. "Considering you've got people watching her at practically all hours of the day and night, yeah, I'll say you're fucking obsessed, man."

"How do you know that?" I demand, feeling my back stiffen. He's been mostly absent lately, but that doesn't mean shit. If Braxton wants to know something, he'll find out at all costs.

He turns and blows a cloud of smoke directly in my face. "How the fuck do you think?" he asks. "They don't just work for you, my man." He turns back, hooking his arms over the balcony railing. "But don't worry, I don't think Dean knows. He's a bit wrapped up at the moment."

Almost as if to punctuate his comment, the soft sound of a feminine moan filters over my ears. I glance back to see that Dean's got Ava on his lap and his tongue down her throat—no doubt trying to distract her from whatever bad news that phone call must have been. The two of them have been duking it out over his recent injuries for the last two months.

I return my gaze to Braxton. "You don't seem all that concerned with my newfound obsession," I point out.

His shoulders lift and fall. "Should I be?" he asks. "Of the three of us, I honestly thought you'd be the first one to find someone and settle down."

I blow out a long breath, letting the stream of smoke exhale from my lungs into the air above the dance floor. "What do you mean by that?"

Brax's gaze is cool, his brows drawn down low. His lips curve into a half smile. "Nothing bad," he says. "Just that you were the type that always wanted a family. Kids. That kinda shit."

I blanch. "I don't think any of us are going to go that far," I tell him.

Kids need parents that are whole, parents that aren't fucked beyond all recognition. Parents with souls and kindness. That's not us and it never will be.

Silence drifts between Brax and me for several long minutes as we finish off the joints and then put them out in a shot glass as a chick dressed in a low-cut club dress walks by, holding up a tray. "You think about talking to your girl?" Brax finally asks.

I cut a look towards him out of the corner of my eyes. "'Bout what?"

"'Bout that secret she's keeping," he says.

I grit my teeth. As if it'd be that easy. I could ask Rylie to tell me the truth all day long, but as she proved earlier this week —agreeing so readily to give me her real file as if I didn't know what she was thinking—she's incapable of giving it to me.

Braxton whistles, making me turn my attention to whatever he's locked on down below. As soon as I do, I feel my muscles tense all over again—the relaxing effects of the weed disappearing in a split second. Dash is talking to Rylie, keeping his back to the crowd and to me as he stands over her at the bar.

"Relax, dude." Brax laughs. "If Dash was there for your little claiming ceremony the other weekend, then he knows she's yours. He's as loyal as they come." Yeah, that may be true, but I certainly don't like the way she doesn't appear to be all that concerned with him being so close to her. Him *touching* her with his hand on her arm. In fact, I find myself imagining ripping that arm of his clean off and then beating him to death with it.

Braxton shakes his head. "Yup," he says lightly. "Obsessed as a motherfucker."

And this close to going down there and beating the absolute fuck out of a man I've known since elementary school. All over my obsession. Thankfully, though, Dash turns and says something to the bartender and then heads off, leaving Rylie alone. My muscles barely have a minute to relax once more when, just as she gets her drink, another fucker comes out of nowhere.

It isn't until her drink goes down her shirt, turning the white fabric see through, and the guy pins her against the bar that I lose my shit. Braxton doesn't even try to stop me. The second the fucker's hands are on her, all bets are off.

I head for the stairs, feeling violence sing in my veins. *It's on, motherfucker.*

21

"TAKE your fucking hands off of her before I fucking remove them." His voice is deep, far different than his usual, easy-going tone. It's threatening. The guy in front of me jerks his head up and his eyes widen when he realizes who's there.

Abel doesn't waste any time as he grips the guy's arm and half pulls, half shoves him back away from me before he steps in front of me.

"Whoa." The asshole who'd been hitting on me and made me spill my drink is suddenly very alert. His hands are up as he backs away. "Sorry, man, I didn't know she was your bitch."

I almost feel sorry for him. *Almost.* Until that last comment, anyway. "What the fuck did you call her?" Abel demands.

"I-I'm sorry, I-I—"

"I'm not the one you need to apologize to, you fucking prick," Abel snaps, gesturing to me.

The guy's eyes turn to me and he grimaces but nods. "Yeah, sorry," he says, "I didn't mean to ... uh ... make you spill your drink."

"And let me guess," Abel says. "You didn't mean to call her a bitch either?"

The guy is obviously unsure of how to respond. He wavers on his feet, glancing back and forth between me and Abel. I bite my lip, debating on what to do. Before I can decide, however, Abel scoffs and jerks his head towards the club's exit. "That's it, get the fuck out."

The club music continues, and it takes me a second to realize why the fuck it seems so loud. It's because no one in our vicinity is talking. They're all focused on the scene before them. That itchy anxiety is back full force. I half shrink down behind Abel, darting my gaze from side to side, but sure enough, all eyes are on us. Fuck me; I wish the floor would open up and swallow me whole.

"Come on man," the guy in front of Abel wheedles. "It was an accident. I already apologized."

"Are you stupid or deaf?" Abel replies. "I don't give a fuck. Get the fuck out or I'll throw you out myself."

By now, Abel's practically vibrating with rage. It's a different side of him I've never really seen before. I place a hand against the small of his back and without hesitation, he reaches behind him and grips it. His palm is hot against my knuckles, and he doesn't let go.

"Get the fuck out," he repeats for the third time, his voice deepening. "Or I'll break your legs and make you crawl out."

"I'd do what he says, Duncan." My body freezes at the sound of a new, but familiar voice.

Oh no, I think. No. No. No. *Fuck* No.

Now, there's not a single person in the vicinity not aware of what's happening. So many eyes are on us, staring—both in surprise and in a sick sense of curiosity to see what will happen next. And unfortunately, I'm smack dab in the middle of it all. The feeling of wanting to sink as deep into the shadows as possible practically overwhelms my senses.

I try to tug my hand free of Abel's grasp as none other than Luc Kincaid steps out of the crowd—people parting to let him through as they do for no one but the elite. Abel's hand merely tightens against mine and when he glances over his shoulder, it's with a warning in his icy eyes. I know what he wants me to do—sit still and be a good girl while he handles this fucking mess. Honestly, I don't mind him handling it. In fact, he's more than welcome to, but I don't want to be here for it. I want to run. To get away.

"I didn't even do anything," The guy who'd been hitting on me—Duncan—says.

Luc doesn't bat an eyelash. "Doesn't matter. You're done here. Do yourself a favor and get out while you can."

"You're not gonna actually let one of the Eastpoint's tell you what to do, Luc, are you?" Duncan stares at Luc in shock. Guess he never got the memo. My eyes trail up to the balcony to see Avalon, Dean, and Braxton all looking over the edge. Dean lifts what looks like a beer bottle, tips it back, and takes a long swig. No one even cares that Kincaid's here because ever since the beginning of last summer, things have changed.

The power dynamic has shifted. The Eastpoint Heirs and the Kincaids are no longer rivals. Maybe they're not exactly friends, but they're certainly not enemies anymore. Too bad no one prepared this guy. I almost feel sorry for him. That is, I might if I weren't more concerned about myself—or how much attention this little pow-wow is drawing.

"What do you mean by that?" Luc Kincaid turns fully to face the guy who started this whole mess. He tilts his head and a cruel smile twists his lips. "Do you think I should do something about an Eastpoint heir telling me what to do?"

I swallow reflexively, beads of sweat popping up along my spine. My heart hammers in my chest. Closing my eyes won't help. I know if I close them, all I'll be able to do is picture thousands of stares all directed towards me. Vomit curdles in my gut, threatening to come up. I stop trying to let go of Abel's hand and latch onto it instead.

His back straightens as soon as I do and I know he feels it. I press against him as close as possible until my breasts and forehead are against the soft fabric of his t-shirt. I keep my eyes open, but my gaze is on the floor. There's really no use in hiding, but I can't help it.

I feel like I'm surrounded by a pack of hungry, wild animals and even if their attention is no longer solely centered on me, as soon as they finish their current prey off, I know I'm next.

"W-what? Dude, of course!" I hear Duncan say. "They're shit compared to you and Augustine!"

"Is that right?" Luc's deep baritone grows deeper. Darker. The fingers of my free hand find one of the belt loops to Abel's pants and hook on. He's not doing anything. He's not saying anything.

Why? I think absently, trying to distract myself. The answer hits me a moment later. What had he said that night in front of the Crawford house? People don't learn to fear him until it's too late. Some might think it's weak of him to stand back and let someone else handle his problems, but in reality, it's smart. It conserves energy. It doesn't mean he can't handle it. He will when the time is right, but for now, it's fine to let Luc Kincaid take over.

It probably serves more than one purpose as well, knowing Abel. How sneaky he can be. I rub my forehead back and forth across the middle of his back. He's tall enough that the top of my head doesn't even reach his shoulders and he acts as a semi-wall between me and the rest of the crowd gathering.

Luc says something to Duncan, but I don't hear it. Suddenly, though, Abel turns and slams me against the counter, bracing himself on either side of me as Duncan careens past us—two larger, broad-shouldered guys that are wearing St. Augustine's colors lift him up and cart him out. He's throwing punches and cursing up a storm.

Luc glances over to Abel and me as Abel straightens and

faces him. A moment of silence passes. Anyone else might thank Luc for stepping in, but Abel won't. He's not the grateful type and it's not like Luc didn't choose to step in all on his own. The two of them lock eyes for several long moments, tension arcing through the air until finally, Luc smirks and lowers his head.

"See you 'round, Frazier," he says, clapping Abel on the shoulder before he follows behind the others.

Abel stares after him for a split second before his gaze finds mine. The heat of his eyes travels downward and I realize I'm still soaked in the front. I cross my arms over my chest just as he reaches down and grips the hem of his black shirt and rips it up and off.

The dark fabric descends over my head, blocking my view momentarily. "Put your arms through," he orders. "Then go wait for me by the front door. I'll drive you back to the dorms. I gotta talk to Dean and Brax real quick."

I want to deny him, but before I get the chance, he's already walking away. It's only then that I realize he's wearing a wife-beater under his shirt, and somehow, someway, he still maintains his air of regality as he strides through the club.

Now that Duncan and Luc Kincaid are gone, I've become the center of people's attention. So, instead of chasing after him and telling him where he can stuff his orders, I quickly yank the newly given shirt down, covering my front, turn, and flee towards the front of the club.

No one stops me now. No questions are asked—just their eyes following me as I practically run from the bar towards the doors. I don't stop until the nighttime air is in my lungs and the solid dark pavement is under my booted feet. Only then can I feel the first breath of actual fresh air enter my lungs, and even that relief is momentary.

"Hey, Rylie." I stiffen at my name being called and slowly, as if my head is stuck on an axis, turn and face the man standing not ten feet away, with a cigarette between the fingers of one hand and a lighter in the other.

I thought I was keeping things relatively quiet, but apparently not if Luc Kincaid knows my name. It would be one thing if Abel or someone had said it inside, but that hadn't happened while he'd been there which can only mean that he knew it before now.

"What do you want?" I bark, wrapping my arms around my middle as I turn to face him.

His lighter flares to life and I glance around, noting that the two guys that were working for him are gone along with the asshole from inside. I don't know where he had them take him, and I don't care, but I certainly don't like being alone with him —which I am since there's no longer any line or bouncer waiting outside. I passed them all in the hall of the club on my way out.

"I just wanted to ask you something," he says after a moment.

I watch as he puts his cigarette to his mouth and inhales, the end of it flaring bright red before dimming as he takes it away and releases a cloud of smoke. The muscles in my leg jump as I tap my foot, waiting for whatever it is he's gonna ask.

When seconds slip by and the only sound is that of passing cars, the dull music thrumming inside beyond the door, and my own breathing, I can't stand it anymore. "That shit is gonna kill you," I snap. "So if you could tell me what you wanted to ask before you drop that'd be great. Any time now would be even better."

Luc chuckles and looks down at the cigarette in his hand as he blows out another round of smoke. "Yeah, it probably will," he agrees. "But maybe guys like me deserve an early death."

No, I doubt it, I think. There are people much worse than Luc Kincaid—hell, people much worse than the Sick Boys and far more deserving of death. And I know they're not all the shining stars of the upper echelon that others seem to think. Their hands are dirty, stained with blood, and their minds blacker than anyone can imagine. Still, there are monsters far worse out there. Monsters hiding behind masks of civility and kindness, and they prey on the weak.

Despite the warmth in the air, I shiver and turn fully with my back to the parking lot as I face him. My eyes skate towards the door, but Abel's not here yet, so I'm stuck. "I'm not going to make you feel better if that's what you believe," I say. "I just want to go home without bloodshed. It's not a difficult request and you're the one who said you had something to ask me. I suggest you do so before my..." What do I call Abel? My boyfriend? No, he's not that. My master? Definitely not. With my luck, he'll fucking walk out just as I say it and then that'll open a whole new can of worms. "Just say what you're gonna say before my friend comes to get me," I finish lamely.

Luc's lips twitch. He breaks away from the wall and walks into the lamplight surrounding me, stepping out of the shadow of the building. Gold blond hair several shades darker than Abel's is pushed away from his face. I tip my head up as he approaches.

"I heard you can find people," he says quietly.

"Oh yeah?" I tighten my grip around myself. "Where'd you hear that?"

"Ava."

I blink and my shoulders drop. I blow out a breath. "I'm usually relatively good at finding people," I admit begrudgingly. Usually, though, is the keyword in that sentence. Whatever Luc's about to ask me for now, I already expect I'm going to agree, but that doesn't make my failure to find Avalon's friend any less harsh in my mind.

I know I'm good as a hacker. Fuck, it's the one thing I'm confident about. My skills with a computer. Diving into the deep web. Tracking people. Trailing their cyber breadcrumbs or even the ones others leave behind on their behalf, but even I'm not able to work miracles and bring ghosts back to life, and this Micki girl ... at some point, I'm going to have to tell Avalon that it's impossible to find someone who just doesn't exist.

"I don't care what it costs," Luc says, distracting me and pulling me back from my internal thoughts. "But I need you to find someone."

"Who?" I ask, refocusing on his face. My eyes widen when I see the expression there.

Anguish. Pain. Torment.

It's visceral, the agony on his face. Something I never expected him to show someone like me. As much as I believe neither Luc nor Dean would admit it, they're similar. It's in the way they walk and hold themselves. The height of their arrogance. The tone in their voices. The expectation of being followed and respected.

But I'm a nobody. Invisible, or if not that, then nothing more than a passing fancy or threat, depending on the perspective. Whoever this person is obviously means a lot to him, and if I can tell by the way he's standing before me, ash dropping from the forgotten cigarette in his fist as he clenches it between his fingers, he already suspects something.

"Give me your phone," I say, startling him.

He blinks, and the expression disappears. Luc looks down at his cigarette and sighs as he drops it and then steps over it, crunching it under his shoe as he reaches into his pocket and withdraws his cell, handing it over. I take it and swipe through his contacts quickly, typing in my number.

"Send me all the information," I say before I can talk myself out of it.

I'm just trying to make a connection, I tell myself. *It'll be good to have a favor from Luc Kincaid.* And maybe that's really part of it, but I know better. Deep down, I know I can't stop

172

from helping someone in that much pain. It reminds me too much of one I know all too well.

Luc takes his cell phone back and slips it into his pocket once more and I turn away, taking several steps until I reach the sidewalk and stare across the street. I want to go home now. More than anything. I want to fall asleep and just ... stay there, in a dream that's nice and warm and safe, for a long while.

I'm tired. Not the kind of tired that one gets from staying up all night, but the bone-deep kind. The kind of tired that never really goes away but stays like a cloud in my mind, fogging over every waking moment. Making me forget good things and only remember the bad.

I hate this kind of tired. When I look back, Luc is gone. I release a breath I didn't know I'd been holding. My chest eases and my heartbeat has finally slowed down. More than anything, I wish someone would pull me out of this fog. Lift me from the brink of unhappiness and show me the light. Show me what it's like to actually be loved. Loved like whoever Luc lost obviously was. At least, by him, they were.

Urban's door opens and closes behind me, slamming and clanking—metal against metal and then a familiar scent invades my nose. "Ready to go?" Abel asks as he reaches my side.

I turn to him as he holds up a set of keys and jingles them in my face. I slap his hands away and roll my eyes. It takes a split second for me to realize what I've done but all Abel does is smirk and then start off down the row of cars, hitting a button on the key fob that lights up a pair of headlights on a dark SUV.

I've gotten comfortable with him, I realize. Enough so that I don't even think about slapping him or insulting him or pushing back against the constant pressure he has me under. And he doesn't even seem to care. *Why?* I wonder. *Why doesn't he care that I don't bow to him anymore?*

Abel stops at the front of the SUV and turns back. "Let's

go, Riot Girl," he orders, calling across the space between us. "Get your ass in the car."

Riot Girl. That nickname. His presence. His protection. It can't be ... but maybe it is...

"Abel."

He arches a brow and turns to face me. "What's up?" he asks.

I stare back at him, my feet stuck on the ground. It's like that light I was craving. I hope ... a part of me wants to be wrong, but there's another part that really hopes I'm not. Because I'm so tired of being alone. Afraid. Forgotten. And I ask the one question rolling through my mind beyond the fog and the confusion and old scars.

"Do you ... like me?"

22

RYLIE

ABEL DOESN'T ANSWER ME. Or maybe he's just putting it off. I'm not sure. The silence in the interior of the SUV is so loud it screams through my ears. When I asked the question, he'd just stood there and stared at me for the longest time. Then, he got into the car and that had been his non-answer.

It isn't a yes, but it also isn't a no. Is he waiting for me to give him a signal, to tell him what *I* want? I cast a look at him from the corner of my eye as he drives with one hand clenched on the steering wheel and the other propped up on the driver's side door with his knuckles under his chin.

I can't get a read on him. What he's thinking, what he wants; I don't know any of it and that bothers the fuck out of me.

"Wasn't it you who said 'take a picture, it'll last longer?'" Abel murmurs, startling me.

My face heats and I turn away, staring at the passing scenery—the trees and buildings and the sign of Eastpoint University as we pass through the columns to make it onto the campus. "You didn't answer me," I point out, ignoring his comment.

"I'm thinking," he replies.

About your answer? I want to ask, but I'm not sure if I'll get one to either question. Maybe it was wrong of me to ask now. I mean even if he does say yes, what happens then? It's not like I can just date him. Abel Frazier doesn't date. But if he did, would he try to date me? Can I even be in a relationship with someone with all of my own baggage?

Questions shoot through my mind one after the other, leaving no time to answer them so all I'm left with are what ifs and confusing emotions.

The SUV turns into the parking lot of the new structure of Havers and I look up at the massive columns and fresh white siding. On the inside, it's almost an exact replica, but the outside has definitely been updated to match the rest of the campus. Perfect. Pristine. Untarnished. Everything I'm most certainly not.

As soon as the vehicle comes to a stop in one of the new reserved parking spaces, I grab at the handle and snap my seatbelt off. "Thanks for the ride," I throw over my shoulder as I hop out.

I snap the door shut and stride off towards the front, fumbling around in my pocket for my phone and wallet where my student ID is. My feet hit the sidewalk and I pause as the distinct sound of a car door shutting reaches my ears. I look back to find Abel, hands in his pockets and an amused smirk on his face, following after me.

"W-what are you doing?" I ask.

"I'm answering your question," he says.

I blink. "But you—" I shake my head. "You're not coming in with me," I state instead.

"You sure 'bout that?" Abel doesn't even stop when he reaches the sidewalk as well. He strides right past me up the walkway and towards the double front doors. When he reaches the front he swipes his own ID, which is like the black credit card of student IDs because, for someone like him, it's an all-access pass. He turns, holding the door open for me, and nudges his head towards the interior.

I know there's no getting away from this. Maybe if I'd never asked that stupid question, I wouldn't be dealing with him now, but the fact is—I did. Something possessed me to want to know if this Sick Boy had an even sicker interest in no one else but me, and now I'm regretting it.

I trudge up the path and slip past him into the building, ignoring the girl at the front desk who lifts her eyes from whatever show she's watching on her computer to see who it is. She gasps when Abel marches through and nearly fumbles as she slaps her laptop shut and stares openly when he follows behind me through the second set of doors that lead to the rest of the dorm.

Abel's stare on the back of my neck makes me feel flushed as I hurry up to the second floor and down the hall. Thankfully, no one seems to be around. It's a Friday night, though, and even the program students have a life, so I shouldn't be surprised.

My hand lands on the door to my dorm room, but I don't unlock it or turn the knob. Instead, I stand there, contemplating where this is going. If I open this door then Abel and I are going to be in a room alone together. This room is my personal space. Practically the only sanctuary I have. Letting him in here, right now, after that dumb question, and after how he protected me at Urban feels like I'm acquiescing to something else. Something I'm not sure I'm ready for.

"You gonna stare at that door all day or let me in, Riot Girl?" I jump when a firm, masculine hand lands on my neck and pulls back my hair, brushing it away from my skin so that he can lean down and let the warmth of his breath descend on the side of my throat.

I close my eyes as his chest presses against my spine and his shadow encases mine against this door. Something electric buzzes under my skin, little waves of sparks that rotate and move through me. He's so fucking close I can practically feel his flesh on mine and what's worse is ... I *want* to feel it.

I want to go back into that dark place with him, and I want to find out if he's just another punishment or a reward—if I'll finally get something that doesn't make me feel worthless.

"Rylie?" Abel's curiosity is there in his tone, lifting his voice to a new pitch as he gently folds his fingers over mine and turns the key and the knob at the same time, letting the door swing inward.

"What are you doing, Abel?" I ask, my voice rough with meaning. "What are *we* doing?"

Once again, as gently as possible, Abel urges me into the room, steps inside along with me, and then lets it close and lock behind him until it's just the two of us in this space, *my* space.

"I think we're finding out if I actually like you, Rylie, or if you're just a challenge."

I pause at that, not liking the latter part of his answer. "I don't think ... we should." I can't help the way my words tremble on my lips. I don't want to find out that all I am is just a challenge to him. I don't think I could bear it if that's all this feeling is.

"Rylie." I don't look up when he says my name, nor do I when he turns us both and pushes me back against the door or when he arches his arms up over my head. "Rylie, look at me."

I shake my head, resisting the pull of his command.

"You don't want to?" he asks. "Or are you scared?"

I bite down on my lower lip so hard, blood floods my mouth, coating my tongue. The answer is right there. I *am* scared. Fucking terrified of him and the fact that my first reaction when he puts his hands on me isn't disgust, it's ... a heady mixture of lust and longing for more.

His thumb reaches down and touches my lip where my teeth scrape against the raw, split flesh. He swipes across the open wound, pulling his hand away, and only when I see that his skin is covered in the red of my blood, and he's drawing it up and towards his mouth, do I find myself gazing up at him as his tongue flicks out and licks it from his fingertip.

"There you are, Riot Girl." There's no light, save for the small sliver of illumination coming in from my window, and he blocks that. Yet, I can still tell that his entire focus is on me. He bends down, his hot breath rushing over my face as he speaks. "You want to know if I like you?" he asks.

I swallow roughly, unable to answer verbally so I nod.

"Yeah, Rylie, I think I like you."

"Because I'm a challenge?" I question.

"Would that upset you if you were a challenge?" he asks instead of answering. I stiffen. *Yeah, it would.* But I'm not sure if I'm ready to admit it out loud. My teeth sink into my already sore lower lip and he grasps my chin. "Stop doing that."

Startled, I release my lip. "What?"

"Biting your lip—stop doing it," he orders on a growl.

"Why?"

He leans ever closer. "Because every time you bite your lip it makes me want to overrule your mark with my own."

Warning bells are going off in my head. Big, flashing neon signs that are screaming at me to turn back now. I ignore them all as my breath catches and I tip my face back even more so that it's easier for him to see. "Then why don't you?" The taunt is out before I can stop it. It's idiotic. Dangerous. Yet, I can't help the thrum of the heartbeat in my chest beating faster as Abel's big body freezes over me.

Slowly, his head turns to the side and the light illuminates part of his face, enough that I can see the smile there. "You're always full of surprises," he says quietly, almost a whisper that I'm not supposed to hear. Then his mouth is on mine and I can't think anymore.

The kiss is wet. Wetter than I thought it'd be. In all of my nineteen years, I've never actually kissed someone. I've had sex —loads of it. So much that I often feel like the only thing my body was created for was to be a doll-like tool for others to use and get off inside of.

My therapist back in high school said that sexual promiscuity after abuse as a child is a sign of the victim trying to gain mastery over what they couldn't control when they were younger. I don't know if she was right, but it did feel better to have the choice for myself when I let other people fuck me— even if I never physically enjoyed it.

This, however, is completely different. A kiss isn't sex. It's somehow even more intimate because there's no turning away from it and pretending like it isn't happening. There's no way to not feel the emotions coursing through me because he's right here in front of me. Abel pulls back and I stare up at him, shaking and trembling with confusion and need.

"Rylie." The way he says my name makes me want to sink into him and let him take all of my past fears away.

"What?" My response is a hoarse whisper.

"Are you a virgin?"

I shake my head. "No."

Abel tilts his head slightly as he stares down at me. "Then let me ask something else," he says. "Have you ever kissed someone?"

My eyes fall to the floor. "W-why?" *Was it bad?* I wonder. *Can he tell?*

"'Cause I want to know," he replies. "It's a simple answer— yes or no."

It's not simple. In fact, it's far from it. It's embarrassing. I haven't been a virgin for most of my life. I knew what sex was before I even knew what anything else was. It's not right, but it's true. This, though, feels even more depressing. I can't kiss. I shouldn't have even tried.

"If you're done here," I say, turning away. "Maybe it's time for you to go back to your party. You guys held it for a reason. I'm sure the others aren't too happy with you taking off like that."

Firm fingers wrap around my wrist and pull me back. Abel settles more firmly against me, pressing me into the wall as he reaches down and lifts my face to meet his once more. "Fuck what the others want," he says. "Look at me and answer my question."

I swallow roughly. "No, okay," I snap. "No, I've never kissed anyone. Fucking happy now? Are you happy to know that I'm so messed up that I'll have sex with any guy that asks but not kiss them?"

Silence. My short outburst hangs inside of it, swelling and making everything feel heavier. Then, finally, Abel drops my wrist and blows out a breath. "Yes," he says.

"W-what?" I gape at him.

"I said yes," he repeats. Then he grimaces. "Well, yes, I'm happy that you've never kissed anyone before, but not that other shit. I don't care about who's come before me, Rylie. But kissing—I can't wait to teach you how to kiss."

"Teach me?" I ask. Excitement rolls through me. He's not backing away. Despite the fact that I pushed him, he's still here.

Abel's hand touches my cheek, fingers brushing down my jawline. "Yeah," he says, his lips twitching. "Now open those pretty lips of yours, and I'll show you how you kiss a man, Riot Girl. I'll show you how to kiss *me*."

The next thing I know, my lips are parted and Abel's tongue moves into my mouth, invading and taking over all of my rationality. His breath is hot and his skin against mine is even more so. The feeling of his hand on my face, of his lips on mine, and of our bodies brushing against one another takes me to a new realm. It's a beautiful place where nothing hurts and no one wants to use me. He just wants to make me feel good.

And I do, I realize a moment later. I feel amazing.

Kissing Abel Frazier is powerful.

My hands come up, clutching at the long strands of his hair and I sink even deeper into his kiss. He tastes like alcohol and mint and I want more. I crave more. A low, rumbling groan vibrates in his chest and his hands leave my face as they fall to my hips, grasping me, and lifting until my legs are encircling him.

I'm latched onto the front of his body like a fucking monkey and I'm not letting go any time soon. He turns us both, taking his steps one at a time as he feels his way through the dark until he hits my bed, and then my back is on the mattress and he's coming down on top of me.

For a brief moment, when my eyes open and his head lifts, it's not him I see, but someone else. A scream chokes in my throat and my hands slap at his shoulders, shoving him back before my current reality catches up with the old one.

"Rylie?" Abel has gone still above me, his body frozen in position, neither moving to push me further nor pulling away.

"I'm ... okay," I say, breathing through my mouth as I slump into my pillows and unlock my legs from his waist. "Sorry." That's it. Just 'sorry.' Because there's no way in hell I can explain my old demons to him.

Finally, after what feels like forever, Abel moves back and the moment is broken. Tears of embarrassment and frustration burn in the backs of my eyelids. The one guy I actually want to even kind of sleep with, and I fucked it up. Rage pours through me, causing my hands to tremble as Abel gets off the bed.

I expect him to make some sort of excuse and then take off. Hell, I'm ready for it. I've prepared myself for the disappointment. So, it comes as a complete shock when Abel reaches down to the hem of his wife-beater and yanks it up and over his head, letting the fabric drop to the floor of my dorm room.

With no words, he drops back down on top of me, his bigger body curling around mine. "Turn over," he urges.

Confused, I do. I flip my body until his front is pressed to my back once more and we're spooning on the narrow twin sized mattress.

"You want to tell me what that was about?" he asks casually as he reaches down to the hem of the shirt he put over mine earlier.

"N-no," I stutter as I let him lift it away from my stomach and gently tug it upward until he's got it off of me and thrown over the side of the bed.

He hums in the back of his throat and I shudder from the noise as he grabs at my original shirt, still slightly damp and smelling of vodka tonic, and lifts it just enough to worm his hand underneath. I suck in a breath as his fingers brush my belly. Everything in me tightens, even my core. I can practically feel him inside of me and we're not even that far yet.

He's a fucking temptation and I'm losing the will to resist him.

"Breathe, Riot Girl. I've got you."

23

ABEL

She's soft to the touch, and she makes something inside of me —something I didn't even know I had—come out. The desire to protect. To claim. To make her my own. It's different than just pretending she's mine so others will back off. I actually want it to be true. I want *everything* she has to give—even if that includes pain and despair.

For tonight, I'll settle for driving them away—her regrets and her darkness. I'll know her secrets soon enough, but for right now, she can just be. And all I need is to see her face when she comes apart. When she realizes that I'm the only fucking one who can make her feel like this.

My hands dip into the waistband of her skirt and tights, moving until I slip past her panties and touch the core of her. I grit my teeth as my fingers reach heaven. She's not just wet; she's fucking soaked. All this cream slipping out from between her legs and I know it's for me. What a good girl she can be when she has the right motivation.

Slowly, so as not to startle her, I press my thumb against her little clit and start to rub it in circles. Rylie's back arches against me and her ass presses into my crotch. I'm hard as a rock. I want nothing more than to rip her clothes away, unzip my goddamn jeans, and shove myself so far into her, she won't know where she ends and I begin.

Over her shoulder, I watch as her eyelids slip down, hiding her gaze, but she can't hide her expression. Pretty pink lips part, pale cheeks flush, and she clamps down on my digits. Her pussy tightens and releases in a repetitive, fast movement. As if she can't tell if she wants to keep me inside or push me out. I wait a moment more and then I start to move.

As soon as I do, her eyelids fly back open, but her gaze is far away. She gasps as I shove my fingers inside, rubbing against her clit, and then withdraw them again. After a while, her hips start to undulate, mimicking the movement of sex as she rides my hand.

"That's it, Riot Girl," I whisper, pressing my lips down against the skin behind her ear. "Fuck my fingers. Take your orgasm."

She shudders at my words and I can feel where her muscles down below squeeze at the sound of my voice. A small smile spreads across my lips. "Do you like that?" I ask. "You like listening to me while I tease your pussy?" Another squeeze. More gasps. She more than likes it. She fucking loves it. A new rush of wetness coats my hand. I hiss through my teeth at the feel. I want it on me. All over me. I can't fucking take this anymore.

I yank my hand out of her underwear so fast, it leaves her shaking. "What are you doing?" she half whines and then stiffens at the sound of her own voice—as if she's not used to hearing herself like that.

Before she can fully grasp onto her usual tightly held control, I push her onto her back and slip down the bed, grabbing her thighs and lifting them up over my shoulders. "Abel!" She stares down at me in complete shock, but I don't care. She may not be a virgin, but it's obvious no guy she's ever been with has taken the time to really take care of her, not like I will.

I pinch the thin fabric of her tights—it's already worn through into holes in several places. It's not hard at all to rip a new one right where I need it. She gasps again and arches up on the bed. My hand spans down over her stomach and I shove her back down.

Glaring up at her through her own thighs, I growl. "Don't fucking move."

Hazel eyes widen and then roll back as I hook two fingers into the crotch of her underwear and yank them to the side before burying my face between her thighs. Did I say this was heaven? God, I was so wrong. It's so much more than heaven. It's fucking nirvana on my tongue. Just having all of her cream on my hand was far from enough, it's so much better in my mouth, down my throat.

I'm so hungry for her. Starving. A raving beast.

I lick up the center of her until I find the little hidden pearl of her clit. As soon as I do, I give it some special attention, laving it before sucking it into my mouth and humming as I reach up with my free hand and sink two fingers knuckles deep into her tight little pussy.

Her trembles grow worse and I can't help but smile against the gushing wetness that soaks my lower face. I want more. I thrust my fingers into her channel, back and forth as I try to lick up the cream that leaks around them. Her pussy is clamped down impossibly tight and her thighs are a shaking mess around my ears.

Slender fingers sink into my hair, nails scrape against the back of my skull, and I pause as a shiver chases down my own fucking spine. Shit. I'm half ready to come in my own pants and I haven't even done anything else yet. Normally, I don't get off by going down on a chick, but it's not hard to realize that Rylie isn't just an average chick. She's not just another warm body in bed, not a notch on the belt my father made me start. She's just Rylie and when I pull back, sinking my fingers back into her wet flesh as I rise up over her, I see her eyes are open and unguarded.

It's so different from her usual expression that I feel a responding throb in my dick. I can't take it anymore. I keep pistoning my fingers in and out of her, hard and fast. I want to make her come. I want her to cry out with release under me, and I want her to taste her own pleasure, too.

With one hand between her legs, I grab onto her chin with the other and tilt her face up, shoving my mouth down over hers. She shudders under my ministrations, making me feel like the most powerful man in the world. And just like the good student she is, she responds to my kiss by mimicking my earlier movements. Her tongue seeks out mine and I let her have it. She draws it back, welcoming it into her mouth as she sucks the remains of her juice off of it. A moan bubbles up in the back of her throat and on the next thrust of my fingers, I pass my thumb over her clit pressing down hard, and feel the rewarding rush of liquid as she tightens all over.

Rylie rips her lips from mine and cries out as she comes all over my hand. Only when she's done and sated and panting in a mess on the bed do I lift my hand from between her thighs. I slip the two fingers that had been inside of her into my mouth and savor the last of her release. She watches me with wide-eyed wonder and curiosity. It's that curiosity that kills me because it makes me wonder if she doesn't want to taste herself again. Filthy little things like that make everything inside of me tighten.

But that's enough for now. This is enough. For a girl like Rylie, taking the slow route is better. It's something I've never done before, but for her, I'll try.

I withdraw my fingers from my lips and wipe them against my jeans before rolling her towards the wall and sinking back into the mattress. Closing my eyes, I breathe through my nose as I will my cock to stop throbbing, but even after several minutes of nothing more than just lying there with her in my arms, the little fucker doesn't soften.

"Um ... Abel?"

"Hmmm?" I hum against her back as I tighten my hold, pulling her more firmly against my chest as I relish in the feel of her body against mine.

"What are you doing?"

I bite down on my lower lip to keep myself quiet, but it doesn't do shit because, in the next moment, a snort escapes. She peeks back and gapes at me. "Are you *laughing?*" The way she says the word, I might as well be jacking off against her sleeping ass or something. Then again, that's not a bad idea.

The image comes to mind and it's a hot one—Rylie face down and ass up on this tiny fucking bed, naked and open to me as I stroke my cock, rubbing it between her asscheeks until I come down the small of her back.

"Abel!" Rylie's fist arches back and punches me in the shoulder so abruptly—and me, being the dumbass that I am, caught up in my own little fantasy world where she lets me do dirty, filthy things to her, doesn't even see it coming.

"Fuck!" I curse as her movement forces me back an inch or so—an inch that I fucking needed on this damn prison sized mattress because it sends me falling over the edge. And to keep her safe and not drag her with me, I release her as I go, slamming into the hard floor with my spine. A groan lifts up my throat and I turn over, stretching my shoulders as I grab onto her desk chair and slowly get back up. "Most chicks aren't usually so violent after they've had an orgasm, you know?" I say as I shake my head.

Rylie's head pops up on the bed. "I—what? No. You were—

"

"I think the term you're looking for is cuddling," I answer

her earlier question as she fumbles through an awkward response.

She stares up at me in the dim lighting, and I can practically see the cogs circling in her brain. "What..." she begins, but the question drifts off. Rylie sits up and turns until her legs are over the side of the bed. Her fingers grip the hem of her skirt and pulls it down and I know it's because she's aware of how wet she still is and the fact that there's now a newly made hole in her tights. Bet she won't be wearing those anymore. And if she does, then I'll know exactly what she's asking for—my mouth back on that beautiful little pussy.

I step forward until my shadow overpowers her and her head tilts back, wary eyes meeting mine. Leaning down, I press my hands into the mattress on either side of her thighs. "I can't explain it," I admit, "the things you do to me." I close my eyes and sigh before reopening them. "You confuse the hell out of me, Riot Girl."

She blinks. "I don't mean to," she confesses.

The corner of my lips twitch in amusement. "I know," I tell her. "Which just makes my emotions all that much more concerning. All I know, Rylie..." My right hand leaves the bed and arches up, cupping around her throat as I keep her gaze directed upward, at me. Always at me. "Is that I want you."

Her eyes widen. How she can be shocked by this revelation after I just made her come all over my mouth and hands is a mystery to me, but I still kind of like that about her. I like the mystery she presents, the confounding paradox of this seemingly fragile girl, and the small snippets of power that lurk beyond her facade.

She's a hider—a careful planner. She doesn't get too close and she doesn't open up often. But for me, she will. I'll make sure of it.

"Open your mouth, Rylie." The command is easy on my tongue, but for her, it's not as simple as following. I watch the debate that goes on in her expression. It only lasts for a brief moment, but when she decides to do what I say, I feel like a fucking king. Her pretty pink lips part for me and she tilts her head back even more.

That is an offering I can't resist. My head descends and my mouth hovers over hers for a split second before I dive forth and devour her. She gasps when I kiss her—almost like each one is a shock to her system. Like she can't quite believe it. To be honest, neither can I.

She hates me. Hates what I represent—power, money, and control—but here she is for me now. Opening her mouth. Parting her lips and letting me consume her soul. I kiss her with reverence, so as not to scare her away. She's been such a good girl for me tonight. Letting me eat her pussy. Letting me suck her cum from the fucking source. This is a reward.

I run my tongue down the length of her lower lip before delving back inside and when she responds by nipping at me, I jerk and almost shoot off in my fucking pants right then and there. The hand I've got clamped against the back of her neck tightens and I pull away with a chuckle.

"I want you to realize something, Riot Girl," I say even as I try to catch my breath. Kissing Rylie is like running a marathon with no water. "After tonight, everything changes for you."

Her chest pumps up and down as she, too, sucks in breath after breath. It's good to know I'm not the only one affected by this chemistry between us. "W-what does that mean exactly?" she asks. My eyes latch onto her tongue as it comes out to run the same path across her lower lip that I had just traced. I clench my jaw against the urge to do it again. When the desire still doesn't disappear, I close my eyes and draw in a breath.

I suck it in and hold it for three seconds. One. Two. Three. Repeat.

"Abel?" Rylie's voice penetrates my mind. I reopen my

eyes. "What did you mean by that?" she repeats again. "I mean ... you don't date, so what are you—"

"You're right," I interrupt her. "I *don't* date." Never have, and honestly, for a long time, thought I never would. I'm not sure if telling her that we're dating would make her run or not, so I hold off on that thought. We don't need the label, not right now. All I need to know is that she's mine and no one else's.

It's possessive, the need to own her—body and soul—but I'm not demanding and giving nothing in return. No. I'm benevolent, or at least, I will be to her. I'll own her, but in return ... she can have me. What's left of my wicked, dark heathen soul is hers and all she has to do is be mine.

24

RYLIE

"You can't stay the night," I repeat my decision for what feels like the hundredth time.

"Why not?" Abel responds. We've moved from where we were, the tension of earlier abated. I'm at my desk and he's ... lounging back against my bed. Almost like he fucking knows what seeing him in this casual setting is doing to me.

"Because we're just..." I don't know how to explain it. No, that's not quite it. I don't want to explain it—my nightmares. "Because I said so," I finally settle on.

"Psh." He snorts and lifts one leg over the other, crossing them at the ankles. I frown, turning and heading towards my dresser. I reach inside, grabbing a few things, and head for the door. "Where are you going?" I turn back in time to see him sit up with a scowl.

I arch a brow. "Since you won't leave, I'm going to go get changed in the bathroom. Hopefully, you'll be gone by the time I get back."

He groans and slumps down once more. "You're being a buzzkill, Riot Girl," he whines.

"Then nothing's changed," I snap back, turning the

doorknob and yanking the door open before he can say anything else.

Once I'm out in the hall and the door is shut behind me, it all comes rushing to my head in an instant. Abel Frazier is in my dorm room. More than that, Abel fucking Frazier put his mouth on my pussy and made me come like I've never come before. I don't ... exactly know *what* we are. Not dating, but not casual either. Or are we?

My mind turns over and over as I head down the corridor to the shared bathroom. I step inside, shivering at the chill despite the fact that it looks like someone left the window cracked to let some of the outside heat seep in. Shaking my head, I slip into one of the stalls and change into a pair of low riding sleep shorts and a ratty, old t-shirt. Afterwards, I step outside and wash my face in the sink, doing my nightly routine. It feels odd acting normal when there's someone waiting for me just a few doors down. At least ... a part of me hopes he didn't listen and that he's still there. I'm torn. I want him and yet, at the same time, he frightens me. Still, I can't help but move faster than usual, eager to get back just to see, even though I know I'm not going to change my mind about him staying the night.

When I get back to the room, I see that Abel is, in fact, still there, thumbing through his cell as he helps himself to my shit. "Are those my M&Ms?" I ask dourly as I stuff my clothes into the laundry hamper—sans tights, of course, because those are now forever ruined.

"Yup," Abel says with a grin right before he pops another handful into his mouth. Jackass.

"Abel." I stride up to the side of the bed and stand over him with my hands on my hips.

He grins up at me and swallows the candy in his mouth. "Rylie," he deadpans back.

I suck in a breath and go for the easiest solution. "*Please* go home. I'm tired and I want to go to bed."

His response is to scoot over and pat the sliver of mattress space left. "Then come to bed."

A groan leaves my lips and I push my hands up my face, pressing my palms into the sockets of my eyes. "I won't be able to sleep with you here," I confess.

The sound of fabric shifting has my fingers spreading as I take a peek to see what he's doing. Abel sits up and moves towards me, swinging his long legs over the side of the bed as he reaches up and grasps my wrists, pulling my hands away from my face.

"If I leave you alone tonight, will you come over to my place tomorrow?" he asks.

"The Frazier estate or the Carter estate?" Neither are preferred options, but if it gets him out of my room... "For how long?" I hedge.

"A couple of hours at least," he replies. "And my actual home—Dean's place. Not that shitstain my dad left."

Only he would call a million dollar home a shitstain. "Do I have to talk to anyone? You're not having a party there, right?"

"We don't have parties at Dean's," Abel says. "So, are you coming over or am I staying the night?"

My head rolls back on my shoulders. "Fine, I'm coming over. Can you *go* now?"

His chuckle ripples over my eardrums, and I have to repress a shiver as it threatens to overwhelm me. Why is it that now, every time his voice dips, all I can think about is that humming thing he did between my legs?

Abel catches my hands and uses me to drag himself up from my bed. He stands over me for a moment, cupping my face in his palm as he leans down. My eyes drift closed all on their own as his lips take mine. It's a light kiss and I can feel the smile on his mouth as he does it.

"See you tomorrow, Riot Girl," he whispers against my lips. "Pick up when I call."

With that, he releases me and steps around my body, snapping up the rest of the bag of M&Ms I had sitting on my desk as he walks out, leaving me alone. I wait until the door clicks shut behind him and the sound of his footsteps outside fades before I slump onto my bed, grab my pillow, and start screaming.

What. The. Actual. Fuck.

My heart is beating a million miles a minute. My palms are sweaty, and I am ... abso-fucking-lutely losing it. This is so beyond what I ever expected.

I didn't just kiss Abel Frazier. Hell, I didn't even just let him come into my room and slip into my bed. No. When I go big, I go fucking stupid big. I let him into my bed, between my legs, and I loved every second of it. And yes, if I'm being honest with myself, I'm almost ... excited about tomorrow.

Maybe it's a date.

Is it weird to be excited about something like that?

Lifting my pillow away from my face, I roll onto my back and stare at the ceiling. I'm nineteen years old and I've never been on a date. That's kind of pathetic.

I don't know how long I lay there, staring at the ceiling, but as my eyes slowly begin to drift closed—exhaustion weighing me down, a buzzing jerks me back awake. With a groan, I sit up and rub my eyes with the back of my hands. This night feels like it'll never end.

I reach across the bed to where my phone sits, propped on the edge of my desk. My eyes go immediately to the time—1:05 a.m.—before they check the caller ID. As soon as I see who it is, my body stiffens all over. It's Christine. I never actually expected her to call me back, but now here I am, staring at her name after so long. I was the one who called her first, yet my finger hovers over the answer button. I'm unsure. Reopening old wounds is never a good thing, but Christine was one of the few good memories I have of that time.

The email telling me that Daniel is out still sits on my laptop, a constant reminder of what I went through, but maybe he doesn't even think of me anymore. Maybe he's different. I'll never forgive him, but I just want to move on. Yet, if that's true, then why did I call Christine? Because I want to make sure. I have to make sure.

My thumb hits the green button and I put the cellphone to my ear. "Hey, Christine, thanks for calling me back," I start. "I didn't think you'd call me back this late, but I appreciate it. I just called to—"

"Hello, little Rylie." The rough, deep masculine voice is not Christine's. It's so much worse.

Ice cold air washes down my spine, freezing my world. It covers my words, silencing them. It slips between the crevices of my bones, tightening everything all over until I'm trapped in a little bubble of frost. Chained and caged without a single metal link to keep me in place. No, this kind of capture is one that's inescapable because it's all in my mind. Until it isn't.

"What? You're not going to say hello back? That's so mean of you. It's been over ten years."

My lips part but even air can't escape. I'm choking on nothing. Suffocating as the world around me turns black, the darkness creeping ever closer.

Come on, Rylie, I hear an inner voice snap. *Do something! You can't just sit there. Say something.*

It's too late to act like I don't know who he is. Even if I tried, he'd see right through me. Daniel always saw through all of the lies I tried to come up with to explain why he couldn't come into my room. Sometimes, he'd merely play with me. When I said I was sick, he'd tell me he'd be my doctor—but apparently doctors like to shove things up little girl's pussies so that never worked.

"What are you doing with Christine's phone?" The words finally manage to scrape out of my throat. I can feel my eyes burning with unshed tears. The room around me grows fuzzy. I inhale, but the oxygen feels like fire in my lungs.

"I like to keep an eye on old friends," Daniel replies. "Christine never did move far away. Guess she never expected to pay for her part in your betrayal."

My teeth sink into my lower lip as my chest squeezes impossibly tight. "Christine didn't do anything to you," I say. "And I didn't betray you. You were sick and you should've never touched me to begin with."

"We were in love, Little Rylie—"

"*No!*" The scream comes shooting up my throat. "You were obsessed with a child, you sick pervert!"

Silence on the other end. I fucked up. It's been too long. I knew I shouldn't have let my emotions get the better of me, but it's too late now. Oh fuck, what have I done?

"Is Christine alive?" I demand.

"Not for much longer, Rylie." Daniel's voice is cold, angry. He thinks nothing of telling me what waits in store for the girl who helped me escape him. "In fact, I think it would teach you a lesson to hear this."

There's no time to ask what he means because in the next moment, there is a sharp noise—the sound of a ... is that a nail gun? Sharp air pressured noises echo into the receiver and I hear it when he pulls the trigger. *Snap. Snap. Snap.* Sounds of high pitched, yet slightly muffled feminine screams come over the line. Vomit crawls up my esophagus. I slap a hand over my mouth as I slip off the bed and fall to my knees. The rough cold floor bites into my skin.

"Fucking. Goddamn. Bitch." With each word that Daniel curses, he pulls the trigger.

"Stop," I rasp out, but he doesn't hear.

"Stupid. Fucking. Cunt." More nails. More screaming. Then Daniel's back on the line and Christine's distant sobbing echoes dimly in the background. "Do you hear that, Rylie? Do you hear your friend? You were such a fucking bad girl and this is what your punishment is. You think you can get away from me? No."

"Please stop hurting her," I beg, hating the way my voice trembles. I can't help it. I'm catapulted back to the little girl I was thirteen years ago. Scared and at the mercy of a psychopath.

"Are you going to come back to me?"

I don't answer. He'll know I'm lying if I agree right away, even if it's just to get him to stop. But obviously, I take too long answering because he blows out a frustrated breath. "I knew you wouldn't see the light yet," he says. "But don't worry, sweetheart. As soon as I'm done with Christine, I'm coming for you next. You won't be without me for long, Rylie. We're meant to be together."

The line goes dead, and I can't hold back the vomit any longer. I drop the phone and upchuck everything I have in my stomach, which, as usual, isn't much. Tears track down my cheeks, falling into the puddle of yellow bile and puke on the floor beneath me.

For a long time, I just sit there, crying as I dry heave even long after the contents of my stomach have been emptied. There was a reason I was so afraid to hope that things had changed, that he had changed. Because, deep down, I knew the truth.

Daniel will never forget me, and worse, he'll never forgive me.

Through my tears and through the agony in my chest and the fear in my brain, I sense myself moving. My hands find the corner of the bed and I pull myself to shaking, trembling legs. I can't stay here anymore. I have to go. My sanctuary here has been compromised. It was the second I thought it'd be a good idea to contact Christine.

This is my own fault. It always is.

25

ABEL

I put the cigarette to my lips and inhale the smoke, letting it fill my lungs. The darkness of night washes over the backroads of Eastpoint as I fly through on my way home. With the window rolled down, and the wind slipping inside, I feel freer than I have in a long damn time. The only thing that could make this night better is if Rylie had let me stay. Falling asleep with her in my arms, even if it was on that cramped, lame excuse for a bed, would've been the perfect ending to a night that started as utter shit.

When I pull into the Carter Estate, I note that the lights are on. Everyone's home. I don't bother to pull the car into the garage. Instead, I park it right out front and drop what remains of the cigarette in my hand to the gravel beneath my feet as I step out, and crush the burning end under my shoe.

I hear laughter when I enter the house—drunken laughter. I close my eyes for a moment and just relish in that sound. It's been too fucking long since we've had anything as real as the sound of Avalon's giggling. Whatever devious thing she's doing, I know we'll all put up with it if it keeps her laughing like that. Rounding the corner into the living room, I spot her on the floor with a drink by her side as she holds Braxton's hand captive. He watches her with obvious amusement—his hookers nowhere to be found—as she carefully paints his nails black.

"Having fun?" I quip as I drop onto the sofa.

Her head pops up and she smiles my way. "Where've you been, Frontman?" she asks. "Is Rylie not coming?"

I scrub a hand down my face. "Not tonight, Ava," I tell her. "She's tired."

She gives me a look before she returns to painting Brax's nails. "Wonder who made her that way," she replies.

I grin. Maybe it makes me a dick to be proud of the fact that I know I'm the reason for Rylie's exhaustion, but I don't care. All this, and I haven't even had a real taste of her yet. Not the way I want to.

"Baby." Dean's voice echoes through the room before he appears, carrying a giant blanket. "Ready?"

She puts the finishing touches on Braxton's nails and hops up. "Yup." She pops the last of the word as she strides towards him. When she stops at his front, she leans up on both of her feet, rising to her toes, offering her lips to him, which he, of course, takes as an open invitation. There is still a heavy pang of envy in my chest when I see them like that. I'd never want to take away his happiness, or hers, but at the same time ... what they have is what I want.

A true partner. Someone to call mine.

The couch dips down next to me, redirecting my attention to Braxton as he blows out a breath and moves the forgotten glass that Avalon left behind on the floor to the coffee table in front of us. "Nail painting?" I taunt with a raised brow. "I mean I know you like our resident crazy princess, but dude, seriously?"

Braxton snorts. "If it keeps her occupied long enough, I'll let her paint my nails. Besides, I hear the chicks are digging it these days. Bet your girl would be all over me if she saw me like this." He takes one hand and wiggles his fingers right in front of my eyes.

With a laugh, I shove his hand away and shake my head. The way he said it, though, settles something inside my chest. Yes. I like that. Rylie as 'my girl.' Brax's accepted it. Hell, I know Dean expects it, and Ava—I glance her way to see that Dean has dropped all pretenses and the blanket he'd obviously brought for her is laying forgotten at their feet as Avalon tries to climb his front and wrap her legs around his waist. Her tongue in his mouth and his hands palming her ass.

My gaze pans away and back to Brax. "What'd she have after I left?" I ask. "She's far drunker."

Braxton fights back a smile as he relaxes back into the cushions on the couch and lifts the drink to his lips, downing half of it in one go. "Dean wanted to distract her so I thought I'd challenge her to a shot duel."

"And he allowed that?" I ask, shocked.

Brax shrugs, looking far too smug. "He was pissed at first, but she must've said something to cool his anger because he's ... well ... there they go." And just like that Dean is striding past the two of us with Avalon latched onto him like a spider monkey, all limbs and hands and lips as they practically devour each other. I shake my head.

"If I didn't know better, I'd say they were well on their way to having a bus load of kids," I say.

That does earn a snort of laughter from Brax. "Avalon as a mom?" he waves a hand in front of his face as he doubles over. "Hell fucking no. I'd be scared of any crotch goblin that spawns from that woman's womb." I can't help but laugh along with him. For sure, if Avalon ever decides to have kids, they'll probably come out knives drawn and all.

"Come on," I say after the two of us have calmed down. "Let's grab another drink and sit outside. I'm feeling another cig."

Braxton doesn't resist the offer, and soon enough the two of us have new beers in hand as we step out onto the back porch overlooking the several acres of woods that are behind the property. I tip my head back and suck down a mouthful of bitter liquid, letting it slip down my throat, reminding me of an earlier time in the night when something much smoother had slipped over my tongue. Shit, it's like I can still taste her.

"So," Braxton begins, slipping out a new pack of cigs and slapping it against his palm, "you two figure out what you are yet?" he asks.

I tip my head to the side, cracking my neck as I set my beer down and reach for a cigarette and lighter off the patio table before us. "Not exactly," I hedge, flicking the lighter and watching the flame flare to life.

"You look like a man ready to stake his claim," he comments. I can feel the heat of his gaze, his assessment. He's not wrong.

Rylie Moore. Program girl. Hacker. Secret employee. Whatever she is to us doesn't matter anymore. Because she's a hell of a lot more now. My fingers and tongue have been inside of her. That's not just for fun. It's pure ownership.

"She's mine," I agree easily.

"You going to tell her or just let her figure that out on her own?" he asks.

I lift my shoulders and let them drop as I put the cigarette to my lips and inhale. Relaxation rolls through me. I open my lips to respond, but before I get the chance my cell phone buzzes in my pocket. With a frown, I fish it out. At this time of night, only emergency contacts ever call. When I see the name on the caller ID, however, I know something's wrong.

I hit the answer call button and put the phone to my ear. "Troy?"

"Your girl's on the move," are the first words out of his mouth.

"What's going on?" I demand, snuffing out my barely started cigarette into the ashtray Brax shoves towards me.

"Not quite sure yet, but she just left her dorm about twenty minutes ago. I figured it wasn't anything to worry about, but I don't have a good feeling about this. She's at the bus station."

"The bus station?" What the fuck could Rylie be doing at the bus station? I pull my phone away and check the time. It hasn't been that long since I left. "What is she doing there?"

"Buying a ticket—a couple of them actually. I followed her to the ticket booth," he replies before hesitating for a moment.

"Troy? What do you know?"

He breathes out a sigh. "I'm not sure exactly," he answers. "But the girl seems spooked. I watched you bring her home and she seemed fine then, but something must have happened. Oh, she's trying to hide it, for sure, but the girl is scared out of her mind. She keeps checking her surroundings. I know this kind of look. She's running from something."

From me? I wonder silently. No, that doesn't make any sense. When I left her, she'd agreed to see me tomorrow. Something must've happened between then and now. Something else. Maybe whatever secret she's kept hidden from us has finally come back to bite her in the ass.

A cold anger descends over me. Even if that is the case, she shouldn't be running off on her own. No. She should be coming to me. "Watch her," I command. "Do not let her out of your sight. Call me if she gets on a bus and make sure you know where she's going."

"You don't want me to stop her?" Troy asks.

No, she's running for a reason. Whatever that reason is, she thinks she needs to be away from here, away from Eastpoint, and away from me. I'll let her run for now, but there's no way I won't be following. Besides, Rylie's a smart girl. Troy's got orders not to hurt her and if she's that scared, there's nothing he can do to keep her that she won't find a way out of.

I know her well enough to know that when Rylie is determined, there will be nothing capable of standing in her way. Nothing except me.

"No," I answer him. "Just keep watch and call me as soon as anything changes." I hang up and stand from the table, the chair scraping back as I move towards the back door.

"What's going on?" Braxton's question reminds me of his presence.

I turn with my handle on the doorknob. "Rylie's on the run," I tell him. "I'm going after her."

He stares at me for a brief moment. I don't know what he's thinking, but in the next instant, he sighs and shakes his head before following behind. "Whose car are we taking?" he asks. "Yours or mine?"

I already know the answer to that. "Mine." My car. My girl. My fucking fight to win. And I will win it. Rylie doesn't realize this yet, but the second she let me into her room tonight, into her bed, and between those pretty little thighs of hers, she became mine. And I don't let what I consider mine run away. Even if it means I have to tie her to me in the most permanent way possible. Rylie Moore is no longer her own woman. She's Sick Boy property. She's Abel Frazier Property.

26

SWEAT COATS the back of my neck. Anxiety cramps my stomach. The bag at my side is far too light as I board the next bus. I packed in a rush. Only the necessities. Money, a few changes of clothes, but most importantly—false identities. My best bet is to get across the border and from there, maybe find a place with a low cost of living. With all of the money I've saved up for the last couple of years—especially the bonuses I'd received from the Eastpoint heirs—I'll be able to lie low for a while in a place like that. The issue is gaining access to those funds and making them untraceable.

A couple thousand in cash sounds like a lot, but it'll go fast if I'm not careful. Hell, even if I am, it'll go fast anyway. There's no telling how long Daniel plans to keep this up. If he's waited thirteen years to come after me, then he's not likely to stop any time soon. It's not like he'll just show up at my empty dorm room, snap his fingers, say 'oh, darn,' and head back without another thought. No.

He's obsessed, and as the object of his obsession, I know I can't take chances.

The burner phone in my bag remains silent, and for the

first time in my life, I don't have anyone trying to get in contact with me for something or another. I feel guilty for leaving certain people behind. Ava, for one. I haven't had a friend in a long time, but I'm sure the guys will manage to find all the information I managed to scrape together on that girl she had me looking for on the laptop I had to leave behind. The extra I'd purchased a while back sits in the bottom of my bag, unopened and unused.

Technology is my friend, but it can be a double-edged sword. Any connection to my past will be traced back quickly. I need to be careful with my movements and how I use this ability of mine. I close my eyes and rest my head against the cool window of the charter bus. Across the aisle, an older man in a dark jersey has a baseball cap pulled down over his eyes. He's facing away, but I keep my eye on him regardless. I don't recall seeing him get on, but I know he's been changing each station with me for some time.

Did Abel sic someone on my trail? Could he already know I'm gone?

I've been traveling for a while now. Did he get on the same bus as me back in Eastpoint? Or did he join later? I can't remember if I saw him immediately. I eye the man again, but he doesn't look like anyone Abel would have any contacts with. He's older, gruffer, and practically snoring as he rests in much the same position as me. Maybe I'm just being paranoid, but thinking of Abel brings a fresh pang to my chest. Dawn is approaching. I've been on the road for what feels like forever and my muscles ache with stiffness. I can see the sky lightening on the horizon. If he doesn't already know of my disappearance, the morning will bring it and Abel will know I ran.

Almost, I think. *I almost fucking had something there.* Eastpoint was the longest I'd stayed in a place in several years. I'd grown comfortable. And when Abel had shown his interest ... everything that happened a few nights ago ... it almost seems like a cruel joke that the universe is playing on me. Give me something just for the night only to turn around and take it back the next day.

Nothing good is ever for keeps—not for me. My lips twist in a facsimile of a smile in my reflection in the window. There's no point in mourning the loss of what never was anyway, yet I can't help but be angry. Furious. I wanted it. So fucking bad. And it's not fair.

You could've stayed and told Abel the truth, my inner voice reminds me. And then what? I think back tartly. Explain my past to him. Watch him shrink from me in disgust? Even if he didn't. Even if he understood and accepted all of the gruesome scars that sit in me, spoiling and growing rotten from lack of care, what then? Would I have been able to accept myself? No.

Daniel would've still shown up. He would've found a way. Money and power has nothing against crazy. In fact, staying would've put Abel in danger. And even if he was moderately interested in me for a short time, I know whatever curiosity I presented to him would have been nothing more than temporary. Like he said, he doesn't date. Why the hell would I be the exception?

Answer: I wouldn't be.

I made the right choice. Running is the best course of action. For me and for Abel. Now, he won't have another burden. Now, I can go back to life on my own. Like how it should've been.

My eyelids slide shut. I didn't realize how fucking tired I am until now. The rhythmic sound of the tires turning on the pavement and the air conditioning of the bus lulls me into a half-asleep state. Just a few more hours and I'll be somewhere completely new. Somewhere I can disappear.

I don't realize I've fallen asleep until the sound of voices talking reaches my ears. I jolt up in my seat, my hands clamping down on my bag to make sure it's still there. A nightmare hovers on the fringes of my mind even as I try to adjust to the waking world. The man across the aisle from me is gone. Obviously, my earlier thoughts were unfounded.

I rub the remaining sleep from my eyes as people come up from the back of the bus moving for the exit, and glance at the sign flashing above the driver's seat. Detroit. I'm so fucking close, I can practically taste it. Exhaustion pulls at my limbs though. How much longer will I be able to keep going and stay safe? I shouldn't have fallen asleep. Someone could have snuck off with my belongings and right now, I'm in no position to handle any more problems. It would probably be good to stop here for a few short hours, find a place and crash long enough to get my energy back up.

At least for now, I know Daniel won't know where I am. I'm ahead of him, even if it's only temporarily.

Getting up from my seat, I move my bag from my lap to my back and stretch as I trail the other passengers onto the platform. It's loud and bustling even this early in the morning. People hurrying back and forth between buses, small children crying, frazzled parents trying to rush. The stale smell of gasoline and body odor permeates the air, and underlying all of it is the coolness of northern air.

I'm out of my little Eastpoint bubble, and instead of feeling relief, I feel almost ... homesick.

Shaking my head and throwing off those wayward, unwanted thoughts, I move away from the platform and head for the exit. There has to be a motel somewhere nearby or, better yet, a hostel. Though less private, a hostel will be far cheaper than a motel. And honestly, being around others might offer another measure of safety. Losing myself in crowds is just another method of survival at this point.

I bypass a wall of payphones as I make my way out of the station and onto the street. Morning sunlight hits the back window of a parked car not far from me, throwing the reflection into my eyes and I wince as it burns my corneas, turning away and heading down the street. The smell of coffee enters my nostrils and calls to me, but I can't stop for any luxuries right now.

Though I've never been to Detroit, and at first the busy streets and fast paced movement of people confuse and throw me off, it's relatively easy to decipher how it works. Keep your head forward and down, don't pay attention to strangers, and don't offer a smile.

Despite my desire to avoid the smell of coffee, I know I've got to find a place sooner rather than later so I can get back on the road. I hang a right into a small coffee shop and set up at a back table, pulling out my unused laptop and logging into the business's customer Wi-Fi. I search for nearby hostels and click through several photos before finding one within walking distance. As soon as I have the address, I close my laptop and squeeze out of the shop and back onto the street, hurrying. The sooner I get there, the sooner I can sleep, and without any of its regular caffeine and sugar, my body is already crashing.

Hammock Hotel & Hostel is off the beaten track, down a back alley and out onto a side road that's obviously just as rundown as the building itself. White brick with a flat red roof and one single faded green door that has obviously been painted one too many times greet me as I march up the solid steps and turn the knob.

The sounds of laughter and the smell of weed and cooking eggs slap me smack dab in the face the second I'm inside, but I don't care. It feels ten times better just being off the street. I check in at the front desk with a dude far more obsessed with the ancient Gameboy in his hand than with the actual process. He gestures towards the stairs.

"Beds are up there. No extra guests. Rooms three and four are occupied so leave those alone. Bathroom has towels and toiletries and shit," he says absently, jamming the keys and buttons with his fingers in fast motions.

"Thanks," I mutter as I ascend the narrow stairwell and head past the occupied rooms. I peek into a few and note other people's belongings scattered about. Some doors are locked and some rooms smell like someone smoked an entire bush of weed. I pinch my nose and back out, not stopping until I find one of the smallest rooms at the end of the hall with two bunk beds across from each other. Thankfully, each bunk comes with a dark navy blue curtain to draw up and hide the user from people coming in and out.

I clamber up to the top bunk on the right, as far from the door as possible, shove my bag to the end of the mattress that sinks in the middle and rip the curtain down until nothing more than a sliver of sunlight shines through.

Curling in on myself, I finally give in to the urge to mourn the loss of what I had. Eastpoint. Avalon. Abel. The dorm room. A home I thought I would have for a few more years at least is now behind me. I know I shouldn't have gotten so attached, but I did. There's no denying that fact now.

A single tear leaks out of the corner of my eye and slides down my cheek, but anger has me wiping it away roughly with the pad of my thumb.

It's not fucking fair, I think, wrapping my arms around my knees as I draw them up to my chest. And just as I close my eyes, I swear the universe whispers back, *nothing ever is for the broken ones...*

27

ABEL

IT's dark by the time Braxton and I make it into the city. We've been just a step behind Rylie for the last several hours, having to reach each station and then wait until Troy called to inform us of her direction. One bus after another, I'm starting to wonder if she'll ever stop when Brax finally gets that final text saying she's taken a breather, settling into a shitty Detroit hostel of all fucking places. It would've been much easier if we'd known where she was going, but as far as any of us can tell, she's fucking winging it. She has no plan.

That—the knowledge that she never had the intention to leave me—is almost enough to calm me. *Almost.* I'm still furious —more so than I've been in years.

I'm not usually the angry one. That title belongs to Dean. Right now, though, I feel as though I could take him out and anyone else who thinks it's a good time to test me. And whether she realizes it or not, Rylie has been testing me. Every second. Every minute. Every hour she's been on the run and without so much as a text, phone call, or anything to me ratchet up my fury at her.

I was under the impression that we had made certain things fairly clear that night in her dorm room. Obviously, I was mistaken. Something I will not be again when it comes to her.

"Pull in here," Brax directs as he gestures to a lone figure on the side of the street with a dark hood flipped up to cover most of his face. I direct the Mustang into a gravel parking lot between what looks to be a pawn shop and an abandoned warehouse. Warehouse district Detroit is not the place to be after dark. Rylie's lucky Troy said she didn't stop here until the light of day. Her ass is already gonna be red enough after this little fucking trip.

I park the car and withdraw my keys, popping my door and stepping out as Braxton does the same. Together, we head to the figure. Troy waits until our approach to turn and meet us. He drops his hood back with a frown and digs into his pocket for a moment, retrieving his cell.

"She entered about half past eight a.m.," he reports. "Hasn't been seen since. She stopped at a coffee shop up the street before she came here."

Probably to search for a place to stay, I surmise as I turn towards the building in question. I gesture for Braxton to take Troy's phone. "Download the pictures he's got," I state. "Send them to someone else—Rylie's back up. I want to see if anyone else was following her."

"She's definitely running from something," Troy agrees.

I know she is. The only question is, *what is she running from? Or is it who?*

My eyes scan the front of the plain, drab building, noting the electric sign in the front bottom left window advertising open rooms. "Did you go inside?" I ask.

"No," Troy replies. "Didn't want to spook her if she saw me. I think she was catching on. I tried to change clothes at one of the stations a few hours back, but I almost missed her and didn't want to take the chance again."

I nod but don't respond. The front door to the house opens and a greasy looking man in overalls and a gray beanie strides down the front steps, hanging a right and ambling off down the street. My teeth clench. This is where she'd rather be than to just tell me the fucking truth and rely on me. My hands clench into fists at my sides.

"What's the plan, Abel?" Brax moves up to my side as he speaks.

"Did you send the images already?" I ask without turning towards him.

He waves the phone in front of my face, breaking my concentration and earning a hard glare. With a smirk, he tosses the cell back to Troy. "I downloaded them to my phone and sent them to our backup," he answers. "Now, are we going in there to get her or what?"

I consider the answer. We've got three options. Option one, we wait until she comes out on her own. Option two, we go in there, balls to the wall, and drag her ass out kicking and screaming. Or Option three, I take care of this myself.

Since option three is my own personal favorite, I think I'm going to go with that. Regardless of whatever we do, though, we need more information. I'm going to get it from her, one way or another.

"You want us to wait out here?" Brax asks. I debate on that. It would be good to have a pair of hands on deck just in case she gives me the slip.

"Yeah," I say. "Watch the front and back. If she comes out without me, tackle her ass. Meet back at the Mustang in thirty."

"You think that's all it'll take to convince her to come out with you?" Troy asks, earning a snort from Braxton.

"He's not exactly thinking legal, my man," Braxton says, clapping Troy on the shoulder.

Dawning realization enters Troy's eyes and he straightens. "Understood."

"I think you're wrong on the timing though," Brax states, turning to me once more.

I arch a brow. "Oh?"

He grins before making a show about checking the time. "It's a little after noon. You can at least take an hour, can't you?"

My insides tighten at his meaning. We haven't gone that far yet, but ... my attention returns to the front of the house. Maybe it's time to show her who she belongs to. Maybe this will show her that leaving without a fucking word is more than unacceptable; it's a betrayal. When I don't respond verbally to Braxton's amused taunt, he speaks again.

"Are you staking a claim?" he asks. "A real one?"

That's an easy answer. I swallow back my anger and stretch the muscles in my neck as I lean against my heels. "Yeah," I say, tossing Brax the keys to the Mustang. "I am."

If Rylie wants to run, that's fine, but there's no way in hell she's going anywhere without me.

I start off across the road, dead set on the building currently housing the little pain in the ass I've been annoyingly obsessed with for weeks. I take the stairs two at a time until my hand is on the doorknob. It opens into a dreary, and slightly musty smelling interior front room where a dude is focused on a game in front of him.

Inhaling through my nose, I stomp towards the front counter and stop in front of him with a scowl. The dude catches sight of me out of his peripheral vision and jumps, slamming his game down before putting a hand to his chest.

"Jesus fuck, man!" he snaps. "You scared the shit out of me."

I don't respond. Instead, I reach into my wallet and pull out five hundred-dollar bills and drop them on the surface between us. The man's eyes widen when he takes in the money. "Uh ... we're not a—" he starts.

"My girlfriend is upstairs," I explain slowly before slipping into my lie. "We had a fight and she ran out. I'm here to take her home. Take this and get the fuck out. We'll be gone within the hour."

The man continues to stare at the money, and I can sense the fight within him. He's not sure whether or not to believe me. The ancient dial clock on the wall behind him clicks with each second that passes, but finally, he reaches for the money and quietly folds it up, and puts it into his pocket.

"If I hear screaming," he says. "I'm calling the cops." It's a bold statement, but the fact that he doesn't meet my eyes tells me it's all talk. Enough to make him not feel like a piece of shit for selling some chick he doesn't know out.

"I recommend you take a lunch break," I say, reaching up to clap him on the shoulder. I tighten my grip, waiting until he winces and then lifts his head to meet my eyes. "I insist."

He gulps before jerking his chin down in a nod. I release him and ignore his breath of relief as I head for the stairs. As I stop at the bottom two guys and a chick appear at the top. I step to the side and wait for them to descend, watching as they wave to the desk guy on their way out the door.

"They were the only other ones here," desk guy says quietly, and before I can say anything, he turns tail and heads out the front door along with them.

Dangerous, I think. *So fucking dangerous of Rylie to put her trust in nobodies like them.*

I ascend the stairs and start my search. I'm quiet. Meticulous. Opening doors, picking the locks if I need to, double checking each and every room—regardless of whether or not it's a bedroom. Bathrooms. Laundry rooms. Open spaces. There's no telling what my little runaway is thinking. I certainly don't know anymore. Finally, I come to a door at the end of the hallway.

Before I even open it, I can hear soft noises. Whimpers. Tears. Soft, ragged breaths.

The door creaks open and I spot the single bunk with its curtain drawn. The whimpers cut off and I know she senses my presence. She's awake. And the time has come for my little Riot Girl to recognize her mistakes.

28

RYLIE

MY EYES POP OPEN. My instincts are like an old friend coming to me in a split second. I go from exhausted, nightmare-filled sleep, to awake in a matter of seconds. It's quiet. Too fucking quiet.

The sounds of other people in the house are gone. There's no laughter. No games being played. Nothing but breathing and the low churn of the ancient air conditioner working itself to decay. My heart hammers inside of my chest. A cold sweat breaks out over the back of my neck.

As slowly—and more importantly, as quietly—as possible I reach down and latch onto my bag, thread my arms through the bag straps, and tighten them. I should've chosen a bottom bunk, I think. It would've been a better advantage.

I'm debating on my next actions when the curtain to my bunk is yanked back and sharp sunlight pours into my little cubby hole of darkness, temporarily blinding me. But that isn't a good enough excuse for me. I don't think. I just react. I see the lingering figure of a man outside of the bunk and I rear back and let my fist sail.

My knuckles connect with a hard jaw. I don't even think

about the fact that this man is taller than I remember Daniel being, but then again—maybe Daniel's grown in the past thirteen years. He was still just a teenager when I last saw him.

I punch so hard that I fall out of the bunk, tumbling to the floor with a loud thud. The second my legs hit the hardwood floor, I reach up, latching onto the ladder I used to crawl up into the bunk to pull myself up from the floor, and despite my aching back and probably already forming bruises, I launch myself towards the door.

"No you don't," a familiar, and completely shocking voice, snaps as two arms band around my middle, yanking me back against an equally familiar hard chest.

I blink, blowing hair out of my face as I look back, trying to determine that my ears are, in fact, not deceiving me. Angry blue eyes glare down at me and my whole body sags. "Abel?" I breathe in surprise. "What *the hell* are you doing here?"

Sensing my lack of fight, he loosens his hold, but doesn't take it away completely as he sets me back on my feet and turns me to face him. Then, without any fanfare, he shoves my back against the bedroom's closet doors and snarls down at me.

"That should be my fucking line, Rylie," he growls. His shadow blocks out almost everything, dimming the sunlight pouring in through the windows, giving my eyes enough time to adjust to the fact that he's really here.

Now, my heart starts pounding for a whole different reason. "Y-you can't be here," I stutter out, the realization finally hitting me. *I was fucking right! He had sent someone after me. Or maybe he has a tracking device on me somewhere. Not my bag. That's new and he's never touched it. My clothes?* "How did you know where to find me?" I demand.

A hard hand slaps the door above my head as he leans down. "I'm not going to answer a goddamn question out of your mouth until you start providing a few answers of your own," he informs me. "I suggest you start talking."

My shoulders lift and fall with my harsh breaths. I can't keep looking at his face. I turn away, but as soon as I do, the fingers of his other hand are on my chin, directing my attention right back on him. The fucking egotistical jackass—as if he can't stand for my eyes to be anywhere else.

"Why did you run?" he demands.

"That's none of your business," I say before I realize that saying as much pretty much solidifies the fact that I *did* run. "Not that I was running," I say quickly, trying to cover my mistake. "Maybe I just needed a break."

"In the middle of our first semester back?" he asks. "Right after I ask you on a date?"

My throat closes. I don't know how to answer that other than to lie, but this lie is going to hurt him. I don't want to hurt him. I bite down on my lip, worrying it back and forth as I try to figure out how to get around it.

I don't realize what I've done until a low vibrating growl sounds from his chest. "What did I tell you about biting that lip?" The snarl that rips from him is purely predatory. It's startling. Almost ... frightening. Especially when he leans down and uses his own teeth on my sensitive flesh. I gasp, releasing my lower lip enough that it gives him room to sink his own pearly whites down into the soft, pink skin.

Heat rises up within me. A completely inappropriate reaction, especially right now. Despite knowing that, however, my body doesn't seem to get the memo. My thighs tighten and a gush of wetness slips down into the crotch of my panties. I close my eyes and sigh as he bites down hard enough to split the flesh and then soothes the broken skin with his tongue, licking away my blood before he shoves that tongue into my mouth.

All thoughts of getting away flee in an instant. He sends them running and screaming from the room and devours my thoughts with his lips and tongue until I'm a wet, trembling mess. Somehow my hands have crept up his back and my nails have sunk themselves into the fabric of his shirt.

He's so rough that even as he deepens the kiss, our teeth clash together. It's almost like he's trying to crawl inside of me, like he's trying to invade my body with his own and take it over. A shiver crashes down my spine. I don't have time for this. If I'm awake, I need to be on the move and if Abel has found me then that can only mean that Daniel can as well.

Using the last of my mental and physical strength, I release him from my clutches and, instead, shove the flats of my palms against his chest, pushing him back as I gasp for oxygen. "I need to go," I manage to croak out. "A-and you need to leave as well."

"Oh, we're not going anywhere, Riot Girl," Abel informs me coldly as he reaches up and wipes a bit of my blood from his lower lip. "Not until you start answering my questions. Starting with, who the fuck you're running from?"

My back goes ramrod straight and I withdraw from him—crushing my spine against the closet door despite the pang it sends through me. There are sore spots along my back and side from where I fell from the top bunk. Abel's eyes peer into me like he's trying to see through my flesh and bone and penetrate the core that lies within. Like he can see through to my tarnished, broken soul.

"I..." *Do I tell him or do I not?* The question weighs heavily in my mind. A part of me wants to, but another part of me is too ashamed. *What will he do if he knows just how damaged I actually am? Will he still want me? Will it even matter?*

My heart gallops inside of my chest, trying to get out, but it's captured in the prison of my ribcage. I can't think. My head clouds and fogs over with emotion. Panic seizes me. Grips me by the throat and steals the very breath from my lungs. No. I don't want him to know. I don't ... I can't. There's no way I could possibly shame Dash for hiding his own deep, dark, dirty secrets because even I can't seem to voice it to someone who tracked me down for this very reason.

I clamp my lips shut and shake my head wildly, shoving against him even harder. "No!" I scream. "Let go!"

"I'm not letting go!" he yells back, pulling back and punching the closet door. I jerk when the sound of breaking wood splinters through my mind. "Not until you tell me the fucking truth, Rylie!"

"No!" I shove him away from me, watching as he stumbles under the surprising force of my push.

Panting, I back up towards the door, but he stops me with a pointed look and a finger. "Don't you dare walk out of that fucking door, Rylie," he growls. "If you walk out of that door right now, I won't hesitate to trap your fucking ass, hogtie you, and drag you back to Eastpoint and keep you locked up until you talk."

"You wouldn't..." I start, only to stop when he drops his hand and takes a single step towards me, arching his brow.

"Try me," he says coldly.

I can feel the burn of tears in the backs of my eyes. Fuck him. It's not like I wanted any of this to happen. But there is he —*here* he is—like ... like what? A knight in shining armor? No. Abel is no knight. He's a fucking wicked prince and he doesn't know how to take no for an answer.

Well, I'm tired of being his pawn. I'm not some fucking toy to be shoved around a board and commanded to do whatever it is he wants me to. "I'm not at Eastpoint," I hear myself say—as if the words are coming from someone else. I recognize my voice, but I don't recall giving myself permission to say the words that are coming out of my mouth. "You can't tell me what to do."

"God fucking dammit, Rylie, just tell me!" he demands. "Is it that fucking hard?"

"I'm not your fucking toy!" I scream, clutching at my chest as I bend over from the force of my words.

Abel stands up straighter and stares back at me. "I wouldn't come all the way here for a fucking toy," he states.

Oh no, I think. *No no no no.* He can't be looking at me like how I think he is. His eyes are assessing, dropping from my face down to the rest of me and back. He takes a step towards me and I take a step back, growing ever closer to the door. He stops.

"Rylie." My name is like a prayer on his lips and it makes the tears in my eyes burn even hotter until it takes all of my practically nonexistent strength to shove them back. "Rylie, I just want you—"

"I'm not like Avalon, Abel!" The words burst out of me with vicious intensity, cutting him off. I don't know why he keeps looking at me like that. Almost like he's expecting another girl, but there's no one else here. There's just me.

Abel's brows lower over his eyes, scrunching together. I wish I could punch that stupid look of confusion off his face. "I didn't say you were."

"You fucking act like it," I say. I turn away and shove the palm of my hand against one eye socket. I'm sure I'm probably smearing my makeup even more than it already is from the number of hours I was on those fucking buses and even sleeping. I probably look like a half dead raccoon, but at this moment, I don't care.

"What the hell are you talking about?" he demands.

My chest pumps up and down. My hand drops away from my face. "People fear Avalon," I say. "They feared her before anyone even knew she was an Eastpoint heir. They feared her before Dean and the rest of you accepted her. Because she's strong. I'm not strong, Abel. I'm not her, and I can't be. Not even for you. I can only be what I am." Weak and pathetic. A coward who always runs from her problems.

Silence descends and it's so loud in my ears that I swear it's going to make me combust. I hate it—the quiet—because it's only ever when there's no noise, no distractions, that I realize that I'm alone ... and I probably always will be.

"You don't need to be like Avalon to be strong," Abel says, his voice quiet, but growing nearer.

I snort. "I don't need you patronizing me either." I turn and look up at him.

"I'm not patronizing you." His face is serious, his expression emotionless but at the same time, there's a hardness to his features as if he's daring me to deny him. To refute his statement. I don't need to. No matter what he claims, I know the truth.

Abel moves towards me and out of instinct, I take yet another step back. He freezes and then with a frown he continues forward, and this time ... this time I let him. I resist the urge to turn and run because I'm curious. Yeah, maybe curiosity killed the cat and maybe it'll kill me too, but honestly ... I'm so fucking tired, I just might let it.

He doesn't stop until he's standing over me, hovering like some giant statue. He's not as tall as Dean Carter and certainly not as tall as Braxton Smalls. Maybe to anyone else, Abel Frazier is the Sick Boy who disappears into the background. But not to me.

He's not the playboy or the good time guy. He's not what everyone else thinks.

I know who he really is. I've seen the broken pieces of this man, and as much as I want to deny my own feelings, I find them beautiful. That doesn't mean I deserve what Avalon has, though. The loyalty she forces from other people without even trying—me, Abel, Dean, Braxton ... she's so much better and stronger than me in every way. She's not afraid of the monsters that linger in the dark. She faces them with a cruel smile on her lips.

"Avalon is dangerous like a spiked club," Abel says, making

223

me look up into his cool crystal blue eyes. "You're dangerous like a fucking poison, Riot Girl." I blink. "You slip into my veins and you drive me crazy from the inside out. I can't get you out of my head. You're in my fucking dreams and I want more."

My lips part in shock and when he leans down, I stumble backward, tripping over my own feet and falling sideways into the wall. Abel shoves his forearms down against it, trapping me once again. "M-more?" I stutter. He can't mean what I think he means, but I'd be stupid not to believe it. I mean ... there's no other explanation for why he's here—why he followed me, tracked me down, and found me.

I'm just ... scared to believe in him.

His head lowers until his face is right in front of mine and when he glances up, it's through light blond lashes that are longer than any man should have. "I want you in my bed, Riot Girl. Every fucking day. I want to wake up to you and touch you and I want to carve my fucking name into your soul. I want to be the man you turn to for help." My breath escapes me in a rush at that proclamation. "Now, please ... tell me who I have to kill to get you to come back to me."

I shake my head, but all that earns is a harsh curse from him that echoes throughout the room—throughout the fucking house.

"God, why won't you just fucking use me, Rylie!" he screams. My eyes widen in shock as he clenches his jaw until I swear his teeth crack. "Use me," he continues. "I don't give a fuck. That's what I'm here for. I want you. You fucking want me." He glares at me when I open my mouth to deny that claim. "And don't even fucking think about lying to me," he says.

I don't think I've ever actually seen him this angry. With his face flushed and his eyes like rock hard diamonds, glittering with intensity and animosity—all of it directed at me. "Decide," he growls. "Right. Now." I swallow roughly. "Are you with me or are you not?"

I feel a clock start to tick. There's an invisible countdown clicking through both of our minds. I don't know how I know, but I do. Each second brings the two of us closer. His chest to mine. His face in front of me, blocking out all else.

"I can't..." I whisper as if that'll stop the clock, but it doesn't.

Five.

He bends his head forward. "Give me an answer, Riot Girl," he demands.

Four.

I shake my head, gasping for breath. "It's not that I don't ... you're just ... you could get hurt."

"That's not a yes or no," he states. "And fuck hurt—I'm already hurt. You fucking hurt me the second you left without talking to me."

Three.

My chest aches. "I didn't mean to hurt you." It's the truth. I knew he'd be angry, but I didn't think he'd come here. I didn't think I meant that much—not just to him, but to anybody.

He's right here, though. His lips scant centimeters from mine. I can sense his desire to take; it's a violence in the air.

Two.

"Yes. Or. No." His eyes are on mine. Demanding. Seeking. Searching. Wanting.

My mouth opens, and I form the word. I have to say it. I have to tell him no, but I can't ... the word never makes it past my lips.

One.

He slams his head down and lets his mouth overtake mine, silencing any more chance I have of backing out. There is none of that anymore. I didn't answer in time. Now ... now I'm his. And if I'm honest with myself, it's because I wanted it that way.

29

RYLIE

"Not here," I say, pulling back from his kiss, feeling dizzy and senseless.

Not ever, I mentally force myself to correct, but it's a flimsy thought at best. Abel has me trapped. The walls are closing in, but they're so warm and inviting—practically promising me sanctuary if only I'll open up my ribcage and expose each one of my deepest, darkest shames. What is nothing to him is the entire world to me.

Abel stares back at me, analyzing my face as if he's trying to determine my innermost thoughts. People say that the eyes are the windows to the soul. Right now, I hope all he's seeing in them is pure exhaustion and not the discomfort and fear. Dipping his head down, a rush of his breath slaps me in the face as he presses his forehead to mine.

"If you run again..." His words trail off, but the threat is clear.

I nod. "I'll stay with you," I say quietly, but in the back of my mind, a little voice creeping with uncertainty has to add, *for now...*

"Fine." He pulls away from me and a wash of cold air slaps

me in the face. He gestures to the floor, where my bag lays and I scramble to grab it, shoving everything that spilled out back in and hefting it back up over my shoulder. Abel's hand reaches for mine, gripping it tightly as he pulls me along behind him. "Let's go."

I don't say a word as Abel leads me out of the hostel, but I do notice the reason why no one intruded on Abel and me during our fight. There's no one here. Even the check in guy is gone. I eye the empty counter as I'm dragged past it and out the front door.

It's only when I turn my head away from the building towards the street that I spot another familiar face. Braxton Smalls leans against the side of Abel's red Mustang with his arms crossed and one corner of his mouth pulled upward into a smirk. When he spots us, he lifts a hand.

"Yo," he calls. I blink and in the next instant, he pulls out his phone and dials up a number. "Got her," he tells whoever it is on the other line. "You can come back to the car now."

Dean? I wonder. Avalon? I peek at Abel. He wouldn't have brought them here, would he?

When another man walks around the side of the hostel and jogs across the street, I realize the truth. I scowl at the familiar man from the bus as he dips his head and nods my way.

"Miss Moore," he says cordially.

I clench my teeth and shoot Abel a furious glare. "Don't look at me like that," Abel says. "If he hadn't been on your tail, I wouldn't have known where to find you."

"That was the point," I tell him.

He shrugs, unabashed, and then motions towards the Mustang. I grimace. Of course, we'll all fit, but it'll be tight. As if he's reading my mind, Abel gestures to Braxton. "We'll sit in the back," he says. "But when we get to the hotel, I think you and Troy should see about getting a second car to head back in. It'll be a long ass drive back."

That's when I put on the brakes. I stop and rip my arm from Abel's, taking two steps back as I clutch at my bag's straps. "I'm not going back to Eastpoint," I state. The very idea makes panic crawl back up from my stomach and into my throat. Eastpoint is no longer the safe place it used to be for me. After that phone call from Daniel, I have no doubt that he's smart enough to track me there. Christine wasn't hiding, but it doesn't take a genius hacker to track a cell phone call.

"Calm down," Abel says. "We're not going back. At least, not right away."

He reaches for me and I take another step back, nearly stumbling over the gravel parking lot, but I catch myself before he can touch me. "Not ever!" I snap.

Abel levels me with a look. "We're not going back right now," he repeats. "Only Troy and Braxton are heading home—Brax has classes, after all, and he has to cover for the both of us. We'll talk about the rest of the plan when we get a place to stay for tonight."

I eye him uncertainly. I know Abel and he's not usually one to compromise. He's used to getting what he wants, and I have no doubt that I need to be careful around him. Because if things don't go his way, he'll probably follow through on his promises of hogtying me and dragging me back to Eastpoint and the very center of danger.

"Rylie." I lift my gaze and meet Abel's as he holds out his hand, not moving towards me, not pushing me, but waiting for me to come to him. "You're tired," he says. "Please let me take you to a place that, at the very least, doesn't have bed bugs or easily bribable douchebags."

That last comment has me inhaling sharply and I grit my teeth as I send him yet another seething glare. I can't seem to stop them when it comes to him. How is it that months ago, I was too scared to lift my head and even look him in the eye, but now I feel no hesitation in telling him just how much I fucking hate him with nothing more than a look? Of course, I should've expected that he had something to do with the fact that the hostel was empty. I thought people meant safety, but he's just proven yet again that no one can be trusted.

I avoid his hand as I move forward, circling his body as I head for the car. Thankfully, I find it unlocked when I reach for the passenger side handle and pop open the door. I grip the head of the front seat, yank it forward and clamber into the back, shifting until I'm as far into the corner as possible, clutching my bag in front of me as I try to figure out where we go from here and what kind of truth he's expecting when we get to wherever we're going. At the very least, it should be fine if it's his name on the room. It's not like Daniel will expect me to be with anyone. He delighted in the fact that I didn't like playing with others even when I was a little girl. It meant that he could have me all to himself. I close my eyes and grind my teeth at the reminder.

Outside of the car, Abel and Braxton talk quietly. The man with them—Troy—is silent, but I can feel his curious gaze on me the entire time. Finally, when they're done with whatever decision they were making, the door opens once more and Abel's white blond head appears as he crouches down and climbs into the back with me. Braxton and Troy follow with Brax in the driver's seat.

With three massive men inside the Mustang's small interior, I feel their heat like a wave crashing over my skin. The warmth is soothing and I find my eyelids sliding shut as Braxton turns on the car. I blink and jerk when firm hands are on me a second later, but it's just Abel as he reaches across me, gripping the seatbelt and pulling it down to clip it into place.

His eyes meet mine, and when I try to look away—out of the small triangular window—he reaches up and clasps my chin, bringing my face back around until there's nowhere else for me to go. Then he leans down and nips my injured lower lip, dragging a gasp of surprise from my lungs. A mistake on my part, I realize a moment later as it gives him just enough room to invade.

Abel's tongue sinks into my mouth and twines with my own as his uncompromising fingers hold me tight, forcing me to take everything he has to give me. When he's done, my chest is rising and falling in rapid movements and I can't seem to catch my breath.

"When we get to the hotel," he whispers, "You should know we're finishing this. You and I."

I don't have to ask to know what he means. A little tingling thrill of excitement bolts through me. Despite it, however, my lips part to refute his claim. His thumb moves up and touches my lips, holding them shut as he stares down at me, eyes hard and unreadable.

"And if you try to deny me," he says, his voice dropping lower as the Mustang begins to back up, the car's movements drawing him closer to my chest. "I'll have to punish you. So, think about that before you open this pretty mouth of yours, Riot Girl. I'd think about that very hard if I were you."

Abel releases me and though I can feel his body moving back into his own seat and hear the sound of his seatbelt being clipped, I feel as though he's still there. As if his hands are on me and holding me hostage. Except ... unlike everyone else in this world, I don't dislike being his captive. In fact, if things were different, if *I* were different, I think I might love to remain in the place he so obviously wants me—in his arms.

If I thought I might get a reprieve from Abel when we got to the hotel, I was wrong. The second we're parked and out of the car, I start walking double time towards the sliding glass front doors to stay as far ahead of him as possible. It takes him no time at all to catch up, though. And as soon as he does, he casually tosses an arm around my shoulders and drags me back to his side, slowing us down so that the others can walk ahead.

"Already running?" Abel comments lightly. "Remember what I said about that. You seem to forget about my threats. It's almost like you don't take them seriously." As if to prove his point, he looks down at me, causing me to tilt my head back, and then reaches up, swiping a finger across my bottom lip. The same lip he'd bitten earlier.

Everything inside of me clamps down, tightening until my muscles ache from the automatic contractions. I turn away, ripping my mouth from his fingers as we enter the building. I keep my face straight forward and my feet marching towards the front desk. I just need to get through this, convince him to let me go, and then I'll be on my way.

I don't like the thought of wasting time here, but it's better to spend what little time I'll need to convince him, and take advantage of the free hotel room for the night. Hell, I can't remember the last time I had an actual meal. I don't think I even stopped once to grab a bite to eat the entire way here. Maybe I'll order up some expensive room service. It's not like he can't afford it. My stomach rumbles, appreciating that idea very much.

"Don't worry," Abel says. "We'll get you some food." Heat creeps up my face. I hadn't realized it'd been that loud. I don't say anything as he directs me to the elevators and waits. Minutes later, Braxton and Troy approach. Brax tosses Abel a keycard that he catches midair.

"Seventh floor," he states. "End of the hall." He looks down at me and grins. "I'm right next door." I frown, not sure what to do with that information or why it's important. Frankly, right now, I just don't care so I don't even bother to ask.

Someone slaps the button for the elevator and when it arrives, the four of us pile inside and head up. The entire time to the room, Abel makes sure to keep his arm around me, keeping me pressed tight to his side. Almost as if he's afraid the second his skin isn't on mine, I'll run. Granted, though, he's got a reason to believe that. I may not like it, but it's a smart move on his part.

The elevator dings, signaling that we've arrived on our floor. Before I can pull away or move into the hall, Brax jumps ahead and Troy follows with a yawn. It makes sense that their lackey would be tired; after all, he was following me through every stop for the last twenty-four hours. He's probably had just about as much sleep as I have which is to say very fucking little.

"Have fun, kiddies," Brax calls as he waves over his shoulder. "Remember to pay the fee if you break shit."

My jaw drops. "We're not going to break anything!" The words fall from my mouth before I seem to remember who I'm talking to, but Braxton doesn't seem at all upset by the outburst. In fact, at my statement, he throws his head back and laughs.

"That's what they always say," he says a moment later, stopping in front of the door that must be the entrance to his room. "Just try to keep it down if you can, I can usually sleep through anything, but I'm pretty fucking tired and I doubt..." He lifts his head and flicks a look to the man at my side. I look up, but Abel's expression is closed off as he gently nudges me past Brax to our door. "I doubt he'll be letting you go any time soon, Rylie," Brax finishes, causing a new wave of heat to rise across my face and then spread down my neck.

"Mind your business, Brax," Abel says through clenched teeth as he shoves the keycard into the door alongside him. Braxton pops open his door and leans inside, flicking the light on. I glance beyond him, noticing that Troy isn't saying a word. In fact, just as the door in front of Abel and me opens, Troy disappears into his own room, shutting the door without another word. God, how I wish I could disappear like that, but if I tried it, Abel would just come after me. I release a tired sigh.

"Night!" Brax calls back as Abel takes my shoulders in his hands and mechanically moves me forward into a large end suite. The door shuts firmly behind us, and the locking mechanism beeps into place.

My eyes adjust to the light in the room, and I turn my head, taking it all in. One large king-sized bed takes up the main part of the room, but considering that this is a hotel worthy of Abel Frazier, the room isn't necessarily dominated by it. In fact, the room is more than twice the size of my dorm room. A giant flat screen television is anchored to the wall across from the bed, and floor to ceiling windows span the back wall, along with a sliding glass door that leads out onto a balcony.

"The curtains are blackout," Abel answers an unspoken question of mine—whether or not I'll be able to sleep with that much sunlight streaming in. I nod back without responding and loosen my death grip on my bag, letting the straps fall down my arms. I swing it to the side and drop it into a chair just inside the door.

"Do you want to take a shower?" Abel asks.

I scan the room, spotting the open double-frosted glass doors that lead to a massive interior bathroom. What I want most is to crawl onto that king-sized bed and crash. Hard. I doubt, though, that Abel will let it be if I fall asleep. Maybe a shower will wake me up enough to deal with the conversation we're about to have.

"Yeah," I say on another sigh as I move towards it.

"I'll call for food," Abel says as I step into the bathroom and turn to shut the doors behind me. His hand snakes out and catches the edge, and I pause. "Anything you want in particular?" he asks, leaning forward, staring down at me.

A shiver threatens to overwhelm me at the heated look in his eyes. "Anything's fine," I say.

He eyes me for a moment before nodding, and finally, he releases the edge of the door, allowing me to step back and pull them both closed. Cold air washes over my skin and I turn to the bathroom that looks almost half of the size of the room. A large tub lined with jets sits next to the toilet and takes up most of the right side, and across from it is a double sink with black marble counters. The second my gaze hits the wall at the far back, however, I'm heading forward, my entire focus on the glass enclosed shower that runs from one side to the other.

Shedding my clothes, and leaving them in a dirty heap on the tiled floor, I step into the shower and reach for the knobs. Adjusting the water pressure and warmth is fast and easier than I expected. Within a minute, the water is descending over my head at the perfect temperature, soaking into my hair and running down my back. I wince and sigh as the heat moves past my skin and into my muscles.

Turning and peeking over my shoulder, I notice an already dark bruise forming just above my ass, on the side I landed on when I fell out of the bunk back at the hostel. Swiping water out of my face, I shove my hair back and reach for the small bar of soap sitting on the ledge to my left. Focusing on lathering up my hands, I wash my body and rinse before realizing I'm no longer alone.

A dark shadow appears on the other side of the frosted glass of the shower and my breath catches as Abel pops open the doors and steps in *completely fucking naked.*

"What are you doing?" I snap, slapping a hand across my chest and another down below.

Abel doesn't seem that concerned with my actions because he just steps further into the shower and shuts the door behind him before nudging me back and taking over the fall of the shower. He snatches the shampoo bottle and turns to me.

"Turn around," he orders.

I eye him warily, then slowly, I face away. The wheezing

234

squirt of shampoo being removed from the bottle reaches my ears a moment before his fingers touch the top of my head, smoothing down my hair and spreading the semi opaque liquid through the strands.

My hands remain firmly in place, but there's no denying the pleasure of feeling him so close. His fingers work over my scalp, massaging until I have to repress a moan every few minutes. When his hands drop to my hips, my body stiffens all over again. His thumb brushes against my bruise as his lips land on the top of my shoulder.

"I'm sorry," he whispers.

I close my eyes, wishing he would just be the guy I thought he was months ago. A cocky asshole with no care for anyone around him and no damaged past to make him relatable. One dimensional. If he were that it would be so much easier to hate him, to avoid him, to resist him.

"It's not your fault," I reply.

His mouth opens against my skin and instead of denying my words or agreeing to them, he drags me under the spray and, removing the hosed shower head from the wall, he uses it to rinse the suds from my hair and the rest of my body. His movements are gentle, almost reverent as he takes care of me. A hand grips my shoulder and turns me to face him.

"Drop your arms, Rylie," Abel orders.

"No."

His lips twitch, but I'm not sure if it's in real amusement. I seem to suck all of that out of him lately. He reaches up and touches my wrist, wrapping his fingers around the first one covering my breasts, and pulls it away. There's no resisting, either, he's far stronger than me. So, I just sigh and let it go as he does the same to my other one.

My eyes widen, however, when he doesn't drop my wrists and instead, pulls them both up and twists them until he can capture both with one of his hands as he backs me against the tiled shower wall. "A-Abel?" Electricity races through me. Awareness. Desire. Heated intuition. It's happening. Now. I knew he said it would, but it almost feels too fast. I'm not sure yet.

I've let so many men inside of my body, but Abel isn't just any man. He's ... him, and if I let him inside, I have a feeling there won't be a way to get him out. He won't leave on his own. I'll have to pry him out using any dirty means necessary. A part of me, though, wants that. I want someone to fucking fight for me. To want me the way he seems to.

"Open your mouth, Rylie," Abel commands, his voice hoarse as he runs his free hand down my chest. I'm viscerally aware that I'm not as full chested as the girls he's been with. My tits aren't flat, but they're barely enough for him to cup in his hands. He doesn't seem to care, though, as he grazes them, gripping a nipple and twisting until my mouth opens on a cry.

That's all the invitation he needs to dive down and take over. His tongue drags across my lower lip, tracing the wound he made earlier and then slipping inside like he had in the back of the Mustang. Water slaps our sides, slipping down my hip and leg.

"You've gotten better at kissing," he says as he pulls back. "Maybe it's all this practice."

I blink and stare up at him. He's going to kill me. His fingers leave my nipple and trail to the other one, pinching and twisting it until my back arches and my feet creep up until I'm on my toes, following the strange mixture of pleasure and pain that come from him.

"The food will be here in an hour," he informs me quietly, as if he's not sexually torturing me but just relaying the weather or some other menial topic.

My mind is fogged over with desire and confusion and heat and want, and he's ... talking about food. I can't think straight. "Before it gets here, you and I are going to have a long talk," he

236

informs me. "Where you're going to tell me everything I want to know, and if you're a good girl..." He releases my nipple and grabs my face, fingers sinking into my cheeks as he directs my gaze up at him. "I'll let you come a few times before I take your pretty little pussy."

Fuck. Me. Sideways.

30

ABEL

I've never claimed to be a good man. I know, in the grand scheme of things, I'm not. I've never been and I don't want to be. A good man would quietly let Rylie finish her shower alone. He would feed her and tuck her in and not demand the things that I'm about to. He would feel guilt for the things I'm planning to do to her.

I feel no such guilt.

The only things that resides within me right now ... are lust and anticipation.

Big hazel eyes stare up at me. Full and round and wary. That's good. She should be. I'm angry and horny. Two emotions that each on their own are dangerous. Together? Together, they can only spell trouble. The thing with me, though, is that I like trouble. I like it a fuck of a lot.

I release her arms and reach down, gripping her under her thighs, and lift her against the wall, pushing her back as I lock those legs of hers around my waist. Her hands drift down to my neck and she clings as I spin us. I smack my hand against the knobs as we go, shutting off the water, before striding out into the main interior of the bathroom.

Her naked flesh slips against mine, wet and cold as she shivers in my arms. That's alright, though, she'll be feeling too hot in a few minutes. In fact, I plan to make her feel like she's bursting into flames before this is over. Whatever I have to do to lock her to me. By the time the sun sets and rises once more, she'll know who she belongs to.

I walk to the sink and set her ass on the ledge, reaching down and gripping her thighs, pushing them wide. She gasps as I hook my hands beneath them and pull them up, setting first one foot on the edge of the counter and then the other.

"What are you doing!" she practically screams as she tries to put them back down.

I slap one thigh, earning a surprised gasp, and glare at her. "Don't fucking move," I grit out. "In fact, put your hands under your knees," I order. "Hold yourself open for me."

"W-why?" she stutters, eyes wide even as her hands move to do as I told her to. "What are you going to do?"

She should know better by now. "You're not stupid, Rylie," I say as I lower myself to my knees. Braxton knew what he was doing choosing this place. The sinks are the perfect height for what I have in mind. "You know exactly what I'm going to do."

The second my mouth lands on her pussy, the sharp inhale of her breath fills the room, but I don't let it slow me down. I know what I'm doing down here on my knees. It's what earned me my reputation after all. I spear her deep with my tongue, rolling into the sweetest tasting pussy I've ever had in my life. I eat her, devouring everything in my path, until those thighs of hers are trembling and I can feel the effort it takes her to keep her hands under her knees.

She's shaking. Trembling under my mouth as I suck her clit between my lips and scrape my teeth down the center before diving back into her entrance. She's open for me. Maybe not mentally or emotionally. Not yet. This is the bridge, though.

This is all the connection I need to get her to admit that she's mine and this is only the beginning.

"Abel!" Her scream is only the first of many and it comes just as a fresh gush of juice flows out over my tongue and drips down my chin. I attack her even harder, pushing her into the next one. When you've got a woman on the edge of the precipice like I do Rylie, it only takes the start to push her down as many times as you want and I do. I push her again and again. Until she's a sweating, shivering mess. Until she can't hold her legs up anymore and instead, reaches down, shoving the palm of one hand against my forehead, pushing me away.

"Please, God, I can't..." I capture her wrist, pulling her hand away from my face as I lean up and kiss the pulse point there.

"You can, Riot Girl," I tell her quietly. I know she can. Maybe she thinks she's got the whole world fooled. Maybe she thinks she's got me fooled, but I see her. I see past the facade she's got up. She's far stronger than she portrays. There are demons in her eyes. Maybe not the same ones as my own, but mine react to hers.

They're beautiful, those demons of hers, and I don't want to save her from them. I want to show her how to harness them. To use them. To relish in their darkness because it's only in the dark that we truly understand ourselves.

I rise to my feet, shoving myself forward, and stepping between her thighs. My gaze settles on beautiful tight little rose pink nipples against white skin, and before I do anything else, I find myself leaning down and circling one with my tongue. I tug it into my mouth and feast on her flesh. My tongue still tastes of her pussy juice. I drag it from one nipple to the next and can't stop the grin that comes to my face when her hand creeps up and sinks through my hair.

She locks on, tightening her grip until she tugs me away from her breasts and up to meet her gaze. "If you're going to fuck me, Abel," she states, eyes glazed over with lust as well as something else. *Is that determination in my little mouse's gaze?* I wonder. "Then do it. Don't tease me."

My grin turns into a full-on smile as I circle my hips, pushing my cock against her wet entrance. She's practically dripping onto the floor beneath us. She's just how I want her most—soaked to her core and needy.

"But I like teasing you, Riot Girl," I snicker, reaching down and lifting my cock. I let it slap wetly on top of her pussy, watching the way the feel and sound of it makes her catch her breath. Her eyes dart down to it, and it does something to me to watch her swallow roughly. "Don't worry," I whisper, leaning down until my lips are touching the tip of her ear. "You'll be able to take me."

And before she can deny it or start to shake her head, sending a cascade of her half dry lavender hair flying across her face, I pull back, set the head of my cock to her core and push forward. She gasps, nails sinking into my shoulders as she arches her spine.

"There we go, Riot Girl," I say through a solid breath. God, she squeezes my dick so fucking tight. It's like slicing my way through heavy waters. She's so fucking vise-like she just might break me. But what a way to fucking go, right?

I can't stop what we've already started. It's far too late for that. "It's okay, baby," I whisper. "It's okay."

She whimpers and leans up and away from the counter and mirror, plastering her body against my chest until her hardened nipples scrape against my skin. "It's too much," she pants. "Please, Abel. I can't. It's too deep."

No, it's not. It's not deep enough. I look down and grimace. "I'm only halfway in," I inform her.

"What?" She jumps and yanks back, jerking her gaze down to see that what I'm saying is, in fact, the truth. Her hands turn into fists and come down hard on my shoulders. "Pull out," she demands. "That thing is a fucking monster. I can't do anymore."

"Yes, you can," I tell her. She doesn't have a choice anymore because there's no fucking way I'll cave to that little demand of hers. I'm not pulling out.

"Wait!" She stares down hard at my dick for the longest time. If I wasn't such a confident bastard with far more experience than she's probably comfortable with, I'd think there was something wrong with me. I know there's not though.

"It's not as big as you're thinking," I lie, as I resist the urge to chuckle. Only I would have to try and convince a woman to fuck me by telling her my dick is small. It's fucking hilarious and someday, we'll look back on this and laugh. Right now, though, I'll say whatever I must to ensure that we continue. "You're just small, Rylie." So fucking tiny. Like glass in my hands as I skim my fingers up her sides, over her ribs, and back down again to her hips.

"Condom," she says suddenly, yanking her face up so quickly that she almost headbutts me in the jaw. Only by the grace of my natural instincts do I manage to dodge that one.

"What about condoms?" I muse, adjusting my hips and sinking in another few inches. Her inner muscles squeeze tight. A whimper escapes her lips and her fists turn back into nails. I'm gonna be wearing her marks before this is all over.

"You're not wearing one," she tells me. "You need ... you need ... *fuck* ... stop moving!"

And I'm not going to, I say silently as I finally drive my cock home. I don't want a single thing to come between us. If she's gonna do this with me, she's going all the way. Like I said, I'm a bad man, but for her, I'm so much worse. I'm possessive. Something I've never been for anyone else in my fucking life. She drives it out of me. Looks up at me with those stunning, captivating eyes of hers that practically beg me to make her mine.

It's the way she talks. The way she walks. Hell, the way she simply exists and breathes in this world is practically demanding that I shove myself so far deep inside of her that we become one person. I'm just doing what she's silently begging me to do. I'm claiming her in every way necessary.

"Look at that," I say as she arches against me, gasping for breath and hissing through her teeth as I circle my hips. She took me. All the way to the fucking hilt. "I knew you could do it, Riot Girl."

"Oh ... fuck." Her head drops down against my chest and I can hear the exhaustion in her tone. We're not even close to being done.

I fuck back and forth, shoving my cock into her perfect pussy only to withdraw and repeat the process until she's clinging to me, whimpers and moans falling from those precious lips of hers. I feel the tingle of release slap me at the base of my spine. It arches up, taking over even as I try to hold back, to make this first time with her last. It's hard. Impossible. Like a man dying of thirst standing before an oasis of the purest waters. Irresistible.

My hand snakes down between us and my fingers lock on her clit. "No, don't!" she screams. "I'm gonna..." She does. A split second after I pinch that little bundle of nerves between my thumb and forefinger and tweak it, she comes all over my cock, shaking as her eyes roll back into her head. "Abel ... Abel ... Abel."

I drive into her hard, releasing her clit and returning my palms to her hips as I lift her in time with my movements. I pull her into me, shoving inside as deep as I can go and grinding until my release finally comes in a heated wave. My grip on her skin becomes bruising and my teeth begin to tingle. The desire is there. I want ... I need ... I open my mouth and set my teeth down on the curve of her throat, biting down until I feel the responding squeeze of her pussy muscles sucking on my cock, emptying me of the last of my load.

Only then do I finally sag into her arms. Panting and sweaty, she reaches up, combing her fingers through my semi wet hair. I look at her through my lashes and lowered eyelids. Despite the gentleness of her hands, there's an irritated look on her face when I meet her eyes. A dark chuckle escapes me at that.

She just blew my fucking mind, and of course, she's pissed at me.

"What is it now?" I ask lightly as I continue to stand there, leaning against her and the sink for balance because right now it feels like my legs are going to collapse at any second. That's how far she's driven me to insanity. I've fucked countless other women, but only Rylie has ever truly made me feel like this.

"You didn't use a fucking condom," she snaps.

I sigh. "You're right. I didn't."

"What if I get pregnant?" she demands.

"Would you want a boy or a girl?" The question comes out sarcastic, a way to drive the direction of the conversation I was hoping we could wait a while for, but I mean it. I'm curious to know if we had kids, what would she want?

"What?" Rylie pushes me back slightly, and I go willingly, sure that if I keep trying to stand, I'm gonna fall. So instead, I reach forward, lifting her back against me and turn, striding towards the toilet, and sit on the closed lid as I keep her on my lap, taking a breather.

"Do you want a boy or a girl?" I repeat the question, grinning up at her as her position on my thighs makes her slightly higher than my own.

A little V forms between her brows and she stares at me as if she's looking at a code she can't quite figure out. I kind of hope that's true too. It only seems fair, after all. If she pushes me into a new fog of confusion, I hope I'm just as hard to decipher as she is to me.

"Are you saying you want kids?" she asks. "Now?"

With her? I'll take whatever I can get. I sigh and lean forward, letting my forehead rest on the place between her slight breasts. And again, my lips twitch as her hands automatically rise up. She seems to have a fascination with my hair. Maybe I should grow it out.

Despite the fact that I drove the conversation this way for a reason, I know it's probably not a good idea to tell her the truth. To tell her the thought of my seed taking root in her small stomach and watching it grow and shape into the life that we made together turns me on. It'll send her running and I don't want to start out that way again.

So instead of answering her, I reach around her body, palm her ass and lift her against my chest. I can tell the moment she feels my re-hardened cock as it rubs against the small flat of her tummy. It doesn't stay there for long. With her so close, it's impossible to resist the temptation she presents. I'm tired of trying to resist. I'm tired of her pushing me away. We've made it this far and there's no fucking way in hell I'm letting her go back.

"Open for me, Riot Girl," I demand, lifting her further. "Take my cock and put it inside of you."

Her lips part and a haze descends over her expression. There's an inner war going on inside of my girl. I rub my mouth against hers, letting her taste the evidence of her arousal on my lips. "You know you want to," I tempt her. "Talk is overrated. Let's do something that'll make the both of us feel even better."

Stop fighting it, I silently plead. I'm dying here and she's my only cure.

That moment she finally makes her decision will go down in history as the moment she hooked my heart and attached it to her own. She stares back at me as her tiny hand reaches between us, slipping over the ridges of my abs until she palms my cock, straightens and guides the head to her pussy and once it's there, I slowly release her ass and she sinks back to the hilt, taking me deeper than I've ever been.

"That's it, Riot Girl," I praise her, loving the way her head goes back and how the strands of her hair brush against my thighs as I fuck up into her. I want more. I want to turn her around and fuck her from behind. I want to dive down and kiss that juicy ass of hers and worship the very ground she walks on. "Taking me so ... fucking good." I grit out the words and with every groan she releases I know I'm doing it right. I'm going to take this girl so far into heaven that she'll never realize that I'm the devil she should be running from.

"Abel..." The way she says my name makes me tighten all over. My muscles are jumping and spasming as she squeezes tight around me.

More. I want fucking more. I want it all. I want her everything.

With gritted teeth, I stop her on the next descent and lift one leg. Her head pops back up. "What are you—" I don't give her the opportunity to finish her question. I'm already spinning her, turning her to face forward with my cock still in her pussy and now her ass pressed right against my abs.

One hand slaps my knee and the other hits the little half wall between us and the tub. Fucking in the bathroom of a hotel wasn't how I predicted we'd start this relationship of ours, but again ... anything it takes. I want to claim her everywhere. In this bathroom. On the bed. In the hallway. Fuck, I'll take her across every surface in this world.

Unlike Dean, I don't shy away from prying eyes. I want to claim her publicly. Take her so violently and completely that no one can hide from the fact that this woman is mine. They can look. They can see. But if they fucking touch what belongs to me, I'll chop off their limbs and shove them up their asses.

The only thing keeping me from acting on those darker desires of mine is her. Rylie probably wouldn't care for a show of exhibitionism. At those thoughts, an amused smile spreads my lips wide, but the sound of her cry as I fuck up into her pussy, arching my hips so that she's bouncing against my lap, taking my dick inside her very core, draws me back to the present.

"I'm gonna fall!" she cries. Her nails scrape my skin, sinking in. Her spine trembles with fear as she tries to adjust, but I don't let her. I keep her feet off the floor and keep her completely dependent on me for balance. I like the way it makes her inner muscles clamp down, holding onto me.

I lean forward, pressing against her back as I draw her hair to the side and kiss her neck. "You're not gonna fall, Riot Girl," I promise her in a whisper. "You're gonna fly."

31

RYLIE

ABEL's talented fingers enter my pussy for what feels like the hundredth time in the last several hours. We'd long since moved from the bathroom and into the bedroom. Room service had come and gone, but the food sits across the room, growing cold as, instead, he makes a meal out of me. Again.

He's going to kill me. He's going to fuck me to death and oh, what a way to go. If Abel Frazier decides that killing me with sex is the way I need to go, then who am I to tell him otherwise? Who am I to tell this monstrous sex god not to take my life and send me straight to heaven?

I groan, spearing my fingers back into his white blond hair as he dives deep, licking up a path between my thighs. Everywhere is sore. My muscles are practically screaming at me for relief, but he doesn't seem to be in any mood to stop. I'm exhausted. Practically falling asleep as he eats me out. No man has ever done this for me, and now I think I'm ruined for any other man that might want to.

This is Abel's true power. The ability to rob me of breath, of words, of sanity. Another moan bubbles up out of my throat as another orgasm overtakes my body. It rises up from my belly, heated warmth that floods the rest of me as my limbs lock up and my thighs tremble. He steals everything from me.

Once it's over, I sag into the mattress, soaked in my own sweat and wetness as he crawls up my chest. He kisses one nipple and then the other and I flinch at the overstimulation, but he doesn't comment. No. Not Abel. He's only got one thing on his mind, and that's to take as much as he can.

"Come on, Riot Girl," he whispers gently, almost reverently as he urges me over onto my front.

I groan, this time in agony as he adjusts me to his desires, sliding a soft down pillow beneath my tummy to tilt my hips up so that my ass is pointed towards his lap as he drags rough fingers down my sticky spine and over the curve of my asscheeks.

"Are you tired?" he asks as he slides right back into me.

I whimper as his cock hits a place deep inside of me. Fuck him. It's too fucking big, but he doesn't listen. He hasn't used a condom. Not fucking once. If I were any other girl, maybe I'd be panicked, but I'm not. I wonder if he knows. It's the only excuse for his dangerous actions tonight. He's come inside of me so many times, if I were normal the two of us would have every right to worry, but not Abel. Every time he fucks his release into my pussy, he just groans with ecstasy.

Yeah, I think. *He has to know.* Unlike most girls, my period has never been regular. I go several months without one. No birth control has ever been able to regulate me. I'm just ... not normal. There's practically no possibility of me getting pregnant, but I had asked because shouldn't *he* be worried? With his money and family name, I have no doubt that many girls have tried to trap him before ... why would he be so lenient with me?

My nails sink into the sheets as Abel saws in and out of me and little pops of pleasure creep up along my spine. He drags my thoughts back to the present. I gasp for breath, unable to keep it in my lungs for long.

"Of course I'm fucking tired," I groan through a wave of pleasure as it crashes over my system. "We've been going at this for hours." I've lost all sense of real time. I don't know if it's still day or if night has fallen. There's no clock on the bedside either to give me an idea of the time and the blackout curtains have long since been drawn shut.

Abel's chest vibrates against my back as he chuckles, coming down hard over me until he's all the way inside. I arch up, pushing back against the bottom of the mattress with my toes as I feel him enter me the deepest anyone has ever gone. It's so deep it hurts, but only for a moment. Then even that pain turns to pleasure as he reaches around beneath me and tweaks my clit, sliding his thumbs through my wetness to the bundle between his fingers, and plays with it.

It's like he's the master musician and I'm his instrument. He knows how to play my body perfectly. There's no questioning. No hesitation. It's enough to drive me to the brink. Tears leak out of my eyes as I bury my face into the pillow in front of me and scream out my frustration.

"We have a long way yet to go, Rylie," Abel informs me, breathing against the back of my neck as he sets his teeth to my flesh and bites down.

My pussy clamps down on him as he leaves yet another mark. There's no telling how many bruises and bites I have all across my body. Before he dragged me from the bathroom into the bedroom, I'd spotted the front of my body. I'm covered in the marks of his making.

Abel's hand releases my clit and moves back around to my ass. He's got some strange obsession with it. He can't seem to stop touching it. Massaging it. Just as he's doing now. Fingers grip my cheeks and I stiffen as he spreads them.

Glancing back over my shoulder, I stare back at his face. "What are you doing?" I demand.

He lifts his head and cool blue eyes glimmer with desire as he thrusts his hips against my backside and slides his cock back and forth into my innermost depths. I clench my teeth, trying to keep my mind on the present and not lose myself once again to the sexual haze that has seemed to descend over the both of us.

"Fuck!" I slap the bed. I can't. I can't do it again. I've come so many fucking times since we started this, I regret ever agreeing to it. "Please ... Abel..."

He moans. "I love it when you say my name, Riot Girl," he tells me. "Say it again."

I shake my head, hanging it over my bent arms. "I can't..." I practically sob. "I can't do it again. I can't come anymore."

"Yes, you can, sweetheart," Abel promises confidently. "You're so strong, baby. You can do anything. You can come again and again. I'll make sure of it. Don't you worry. I'll take care of you."

I'm not worried about his ability to take care of me. I'm worried about my ability to actually walk after this. I cry out as he sinks inside me and lifts me up. One of his hands touches mine, our fingers intertwining as he pulls me onto my knees and off my hands.

Abel guides my hand to my usually flat stomach and presses my palm down. "Do you feel me, Rylie?" he asks. "You feel my cock so deep inside of you?"

With shock, I realize that my stomach does feel slightly distended. I look down and it's not noticeable, but when he pulls back and thrusts inside, I feel like he's hitting my cervix. There's immense pressure. It's too much. I throw my head back against his chest and huff out a breath.

"It's too much," I say. He releases my hand and re-grips my hips, slamming inside of me. That pressure is still there and it's not too painful, but I've never felt anything like it before. Soft hands touch my neck, my cheek, fingers grip my chin turning me to face him as he stares down at me with brows drawn low.

"Is it really too much?" he asks. "Or are you just afraid of what you're feeling?"

That is a loaded fucking question. "Why are you even doing this?" I ask instead of answering. "Haven't you had enough?"

His eyes sharpen. "No." Abel's jaw clenches tight as he squeezes the word out through gritted teeth and almost as if to punish me for the question, he pulls out and slams home, fucking into me in one long stroke that has me falling over.

My palms slap the mattress as he releases my face and grabs ahold of my hips. "I'll never have enough of you, Riot Girl," he growls. "You should accept that now. You want to know why I'm doing this?"

Heat swarms me, melting away my thoughts and I gasp, panting for oxygen. There doesn't seem to be any.

"Because *you. Fucking. Ran. From. Me.*" Each word of that last statement is punctuated by another hard thrust. His hands move back down to my ass again and my head pops up as he takes ahold of my cheeks and spreads them.

His thumb moves inward, grazing over my asshole. My breathing speeds up. "What the fuck do you think you're doing?"

A dark chuckle escapes him, lingering in the air. The sound sends a vibration of something wicked through me. He's no fucking hero. He's a villain and his evil laughter echoes in my head. "I'm just wondering how hard I can fuck you here and how much noise you'll make for me," he replies.

"Who says I'll let you fuck me there?" I counter even as the feeling of his cock sliding through my pussy once more determines that I've already fallen so far for this man. How he's managed to fuck me so many times back-to-back-to-back is a fucking miracle. And if he needs time to let his dick recuperate, he always dives down with his hands and tongue. *Is it his goal to make me go crazy?*

Fingers dig into the cheeks of my ass, spreading them further apart as he drags his cock from my entrance completely and for the first time in what feels like forever, I feel empty. I didn't realize how accustomed I'd grown to the physical sensation of being penetrated and filled up by his cock. Now that it's gone, it feels ... wrong.

"Oh you'll let me before too long," he says, all confidence. Nonetheless, he draws his thumb away. I feel him behind me, his knuckles bumping against the inner skin of my thighs as he lines up the head of his cock with my dripping pussy. I groan, long and low, as he sinks into me.

It's been too long and not long enough at the same time. I shiver as I feel every bump and ridge of his cock as it penetrates me, moving deep within me, conquering my pussy like it's his territory for the taking.

"So noisy," he says with a quiet laugh. "You don't want to wake Braxton up do you?"

Heat spreads over my face at the reminder. That's right. Braxton is sleeping in the room next to ours, and we haven't exactly been quiet.

Abel leans over me, smashing his dick deeper into the tightness of my cunt. I gasp at the movement, feeling his cock hit something inside of me that sends fireworks dancing along my skin. "How about we make a bet, you and I?" he whispers, and I have to fight through the pleasure-pain clouding through my brain just to hear him. "If you can keep from waking Braxton up—ergo, you let me have my playtime uninterrupted —I'll let you drive the Mustang for one hour."

Those words pique my interest. He loves that fucking Mustang. It's his pride and joy. I look back over my shoulder and assess his expression. Is he serious? I'm not particular about the actual vehicle itself, but I know something that most don't. That car was gifted to him after his mom's death, and from what I know—Josephine Frazier was the only woman before Avalon that the Sick Boys respected and loved.

Even if I don't care about driving that car, it means something to him. "Why?" I ask.

He pulls out and slams back into me, causing me to cry out, my hands slapping against the headboard as we finally reach the top of the bed. All that thrusting and movement has led here.

"Why?" he repeats on a chuckle. "Because you want me vulnerable, don't you?"

I stiffen, his question hitting me in a raw sort of way. *Do I?* I ask myself. *Do I want Abel Frazier vulnerable?*

Silence descends between us as Abel presses down against my back. His hands are still on my ass. He's waiting. Waiting for my response, for my answer, but I don't know what I want. *What do I want from him?*

The answer comes to me a moment later. I want to do to him what he's doing to me. He deserves to feel like he's losing his mind. Abel Frazier may not realize it yet, but he's met his match in me. I'm over feeling like a doormat. Being his bitch or his employee.

"What do you say, Riot Girl?" he taunts once more. "Are you game?"

I'm more than game. I want something even better than driving his car. I want to extract a promise from him. Pushing my hands against the mattress, I leverage up on my knees and thrust back against him until the backs of my thighs meet the fronts of his.

"I want something else," I wager.

Hard hands slap my ass. "Fuck," he curses under his breath. "What do you want?"

A small grin flits across my face. What do you know ...

having this kind of power is a little heady. Addictive, just like the man handing it over to me on a silver platter.

"You want to know what I'm running from?" I challenge. "I'll tell you, but only you. When we leave here. We're not going back to Eastpoint until I decide." No matter how much I want to return to the place I now think of as my home, I can't, not until it's safe.

A growl lifts up from the man behind me. "You're not leaving me again," he snaps.

I roll my eyes. "I know that, asshole," I reply. "You can come with me, but no one else. It'll be too noticeable if all of us are missing."

"You're telling me to send Troy and Brax back on their own?" he clarifies.

I nod. "Yes." Him, I can handle. Him ... I might be able to tell the truth.

"Hmmmm." The hum in his chest filters through my ears as his hands move over my sore flesh and up my back until he locks onto my shoulders and uses his hold to pull me back on his dick, thrusting and rotating his hips as he grinds himself into the deepest parts of my pussy, driving out all logical thought.

"Fine," I finally hear him say. "Deal."

I gasp, sucking in breath. No more waiting. I don't know when I started liking this, when I forgot to fear him and began enjoying watching him get riled, but I suddenly do and there's no backing down from this bet. "*Game. On*," I huff out.

"That's what I like to hear," he says just before he anchors his hands on my hips and withdraws from my pussy until only the head of his cock nudges against my folds.

Abel slams into me and repeats the motion almost immediately. Fast. Too fast. He pounds me against the headboard—hitting that spot inside that only he seems to know about, the place that makes me melt. I bite down on my lip until I taste blood. If I'm going to win this little bet, I can't stop.

255

The second I open my mouth, it'll be over. And I have a feeling that Abel knows just how close he's driven me to the edge.

So, I clench my hands on the solid wood headboard of the hotel bed, and I let him rail me. My hips are jerked back and forth so roughly with his movements that I'm surprised I haven't gone straight through the wall and into Braxton's hotel room yet. I know it's part of his strategy to get me as close to the wall separating the rooms as possible. His fingers dig into my skin. Fresh bruises and promises of more to come linger between us.

It feels so fucking good though ... and so fucking hard to keep my mouth shut. He hits that place again inside and my lips pop open, a small sound emerging. I release the headboard with one hand and cup it over my mouth.

Abel laughs. "What a dirty little girl," he taunts. "Loves getting her pussy creamed, doesn't she?" He fucks me hard, and one hand isn't enough to keep him from slamming my head into the wall. I move forward, his dick following as I press my entire front to the headboard, my ass canted outwards so he can continue. I'm so close to orgasmic bliss it isn't even funny. This one threatens to be the biggest one yet.

"You like it like this, don't you?" he continues, panting with the effort he's expending. "Hard and fast. A pretty little brat with cream dripping down your thighs. I think you want him to hear you." His breath is hot against the side of my face as he leans forward. "I think you might even like others listening to the dirty sounds you're making. I bet you want people to watch what a dirty girl you can be for me. But it's only for me, isn't it? This pussy is mine."

I part my lips, but thankfully no noise escapes. Unfortunately, neither does any air. I'm choking. Choking on nothing but the filthy words spilling from his beautiful lips.

"Say it," he growls.

I shake my head. *Fuck no,* I think. If I say anything right now. If I even let one single sound through, I'm going to lose. I need to think of something

"*Fucking. Say. It.*" He pounds into me. "Tell me whose pussy this is!"

He's almost got me. I'm on the edge. His hips stutter and my eyes roll back into my head. I'm grasping at strings of control, barely holding on. His words only seem to drive me closer and closer.

His chest shakes against my back, sweat slicking down over our skin. Abel clamps down on my sides and this time, he uses his hold to lift me as he pulls me away from the headboard and wall and falls onto his ass, keeping me locked onto his lap. As soon as he sits, his dick shoots up into my pussy harder than ever.

Fuck. I slap a hand against the bed, gritting my teeth to resist the urge to scream. "Careful," he says, sounding just as close to the edge as I am. "You're gonna lose if you make too much noise. Braxton's a light sleeper."

A moment later, it's too late anyway. He hits that place inside of me, grinding against it at the same time that his hands come around and his fingers latch onto my nipples. My lips part and I scream. I scream as I come apart under his touch and the demands of his body.

With my head thrown back and his cock so far into me I can't tell where I end and he begins, it takes me some time before I calm down. When I do drift back to reality, it's to the sounds of Abel groaning out his own release against my body. His hands have returned to my hips and he keeps me anchored to his thighs as he unloads inside me, the hot gush of his cum rushing through me and mixing with my own release.

I don't even have the energy anymore to fight him. I sag into his arms, my head lolling back against his chest as my eyes slide shut. Exhaustion overwhelms me. Just as I'm slipping into the darkness of unconsciousness, the light brush of fingers touch my brow, gently pushing back my hair as firm, masculine lips touch my temple.

"Sleep, Riot Girl," I hear Abel say. "I'll wake you when it's time to go."

Asshole, I think just before that sinking oblivion finally takes over and I realize ... he really did fuck me until I passed out.

32

RYLIE

DESPITE ABEL's promise to wake me, I'm the first of us to wake up. My limbs slide against silky cool sheets and my back presses against what feels like a space heater before the memories of the day before come flooding back to me. My eyes open and I peek back at the man lying against my back, spooning my ass with his arms around my waist.

A quick check under the sheets confirms my assumption. We're both naked. Strangely though, I don't feel dirty. My legs and thighs are sore as fuck. In fact, just laying here with them rubbing together makes me wince at the chaffing. There's no clock on the bedside table, but I spot both of our cell phones there, each plugged into their respective chargers attached to the wall.

Is this what it'd be like to be Abel's girlfriend? I wonder absently. The normalcy and the calm I feel in his arms upon waking and seeing our phones there, lying side by side as if it's the most natural thing in the world makes a pang enter my heart. This is what I could've had, I realize, had Daniel not returned.

I squeeze my eyes shut and shove back the force of my own

panic, fear, and frustration before slowly—as gingerly as possible so as not to wake the sleeping monster at my back—reaching for my cell. Pressing the power button, I check the time and my eyes widen when I realize it's already eight o'clock and the date tells me it's the next day.

Almost as if to remind me that instead of eating, I fucked for a good several hours and then slept even longer, my stomach growls. Loudly.

Abel groans and shifts against my backside, his hands contracting on my stomach as he tightens his hold and pulls me back against him. "Five more minutes," he mutters, burrowing his face into my hair.

A shiver skates down my spine as his lips brush the base of my skull. *How the fuck can I be turned on by that? How the fuck can I be turned on by anything after that marathon yesterday?*

Shoving my internal desires down, I reach back and smack his arm. "I'm hungry," I say before lifting my head and glancing around the room. The tray from the room service we never ate yesterday is gone too. Makes sense, though. No doubt it'd have been a gooey, congealed mess by now depending on what he'd ordered. My stomach, however, isn't nearly as understanding as it rumbles again in protest. "Abel."

He sighs. "Fine," he huffs before retracting his arms and sitting up.

I watch as if in a trance as he lifts them up, stretching. My eyes fall to the lines of his abs as they contract and soften with the movements. Fingers nudge my chin until I'm staring at an amused Abel. "Eyes up here, Riot Girl, or you may never get food."

Oh ... dear fucking Jesus babies. He's dangerous in more ways than I originally contemplated. Is this what he's like when he's truly happy? I wonder. Because it's a startling contrast. He seems almost boyish as he tosses back the covers and crawls out

260

of the massive king-sized bed. He has no shame as he strides across the room to a shopping bag I hadn't noticed before. Maybe it was delivered after I'd fallen asleep. He riffles through it and pulls out a new, fresh pair of jeans. After ripping the tags off, he tugs them on—sans underwear—and then goes back for a simple black t-shirt.

The clothes themselves don't look expensive, but when he wears them ... he looks like he should be walking the runway of a Paris fashion show. How is that fair?

"Enjoying the show?" Abel asks, drawing me out of my thoughts as he turns around and finishes doing up the front of his jeans.

I swallow roughly, reaching down to gather a handful of the sheets, and drawing them up to cover me, aware of just how naked I am and how very *not* he now is. I half expect him to launch across the room and rip the sheets from my grasp and tell me that I shouldn't be so shy in front of him, not after everything I let him do to me last night—not after everything I *enjoyed* letting him do to me. Surprisingly, though, he doesn't.

Abel smirks and then circles the bed until he reaches the bedside table. He bypasses his cell sitting there and picks up the landline, punching in a few numbers before putting it to his ear. I listen to him order breakfast, absently turning away to observe the room we're in.

I caught glimpses of it the day before, but the majority of what I'd actually paid attention to had been before we started the hour upon hour sex-a-thon. Leaning to one side, I put a hand to my neck and crack it before sliding my legs to the side of the mattress, dragging the sheets with me.

While he's still on the phone, I take the opportunity to head to the bathroom to clean up a bit, sheets and all. I wince as my thighs tremble when I go to sit down on the toilet. There's so much wetness between my legs and I know that it's not all from me. Whatever people say, the rumors about Abel Frazier are fucking accurate. He's a fucking monster in bed. Once I'm done, I wash my hands, wrap the sheets around my front and head back out into the room.

Just as the bathroom door creaks open, Abel says something to the person on the other end and hangs up the call. "You've got new clothes in that bag as well," he informs me.

"I have stuff in the bag I brought," I tell him, but curiosity has me getting up and making my way across the room anyway. I reach for the bag and pull it open. I don't recognize the name on the front, but considering the bag looks more like a purse than the plastic grocery type bags I'm used to getting my clothes in when I go shopping, I'm going to take a wild guess and say that these aren't from Walmart.

I pull out a pair of leggings that are softer than any I've owned before. Biting my lip, I hold them out, taking in the little white skulls that litter the fabric in an inconsistent pattern. I love them ... and I fucking hate Abel Frazier, because this almost makes me love him too. It's the considerate behavior that gets me. I'm not used to it and I don't know how to react to it. So, I do what I do best. I don't react. At all.

I simply pull out the rest of the clothes—a black sleeveless dress that laces up the sides, a bra, and a matching thong. Taking in the lacy underwear, I shoot a dark glare over my shoulder before flinging them on the bed. Abel leans back against the opposite wall, watching me. There's an expectation in his gaze, a gleam. I'm not sure what it is he thinks I'll do, but I hope I disappoint.

Turning, I let the sheet fall, enjoying the gleam in his eyes turning heated as he licks his lips. I don't stay naked for long. I snatch up the obviously preemptive underwear, pull them on quickly, and then yank up the leggings before donning the bra and dress.

"There are shoes in there as well." Abel gestures to the bag and I frown before grabbing the edge of the bag and dragging it towards me as I peek back inside. Sure enough, there's a small box at the bottom I'd missed under copious amounts of flimsy packaging paper. I lift the lid and scowl before slamming it back down.

"I'm not wearing those," I grit out as I turn and storm towards the bathroom. I find my forgotten boots sitting against the tub, and I grab them quickly and head back into the bedroom to sit on the bed and pull them on.

Abel watches me the entire time, smiling even despite my irritation. Maybe it's because of my irritation. He does seem to love pissing me off.

"You'd look good in heels," he comments with a shrug in response to my angry glares.

"I'm not a doll for you to dress up," I snap back, but the truth is ... it's not about the heels. The heels were ... they were fucking beautiful. A deep dark purple with the backs ridged to look like a spine. It almost hurt to look at them. That was why I'd shut the lid as fast as possible.

I can't get greedy here, I remind myself. I've already taken it too far. I stayed too long and I put myself in danger. Heels are a no. I need to be prepared to run at a moment's notice. There's no telling where Daniel is. He found and probably killed Christine easily enough because it doesn't make sense for him to torture her like that just for me to hear only to leave her alive, and he wasn't even obsessed with her like he is me.

A cold dread slips down my spine as I finish putting on and lacing up my shoes. Abel moves in front of me and his mouth opens when he sees my face, but before he can say anything there's a knock on the door. My head pops up and my heartbeat speeds up, not stopping until the person on the other side of the door speaks.

"Room service, Mr. Frazier."

My panic edges back, but only marginally.

Staying back and around the corner, I listen as Abel opens

the door and takes whatever the man on the other side has. I hear him decline the trolley and then another familiar voice intrude.

"Oh, are those eggs?" The door opens wider and Abel steps back to allow Braxton into the room. My face heats at the reminder of the night before and ... my bet with Abel. He takes the tray from Abel's hands as Abel says something to the hotel employee before heading into the bathroom and coming out with his wallet.

At least I don't need to worry about dipping into my own funds for this little off-schedule foray, I think, as Braxton walks past me and sets the tray on the lone table with four chairs surrounding it. This hotel room is like its own mini apartment.

I follow behind him, tilting my nose up to the smells emanating from the tray as he lifts it, revealing two full breakfasts with bacon, eggs, pancakes, toast, and orange juice. I don't even wait for Abel. I sit my happy ass down and reach for the first plate. By the time Abel has finished tipping the hotel employee and shuts the door behind him, I've devoured one of the plates of bacon and have moved onto the toast.

"I don't think I've ever seen you eat this much," Abel chuckles as he approaches.

I lift my head, a mouthful of toast in one cheek and a fork in hand as I start in on the eggs. Across from me, Braxton has taken his own seat and is devouring the second breakfast that I assume had originally been intended for the man standing over the both of us, watching with clear amusement.

I don't say anything and continue eating. All the while, I'm eyeing both Abel and Braxton out of the corners of my eyes. Once I've stuffed myself past what is my normal capacity and I feel almost sickly full, I push away the last plate and wash it all down with a glass of orange juice.

Abel is the first to speak. "So, Brax..." he hedges. My back stiffens as I start to pile the empty plates back onto the tray. "Did you hear anything interesting last night?"

Braxton chuckles. "I heard a little mouse scream," he replies, "but other than that it was a quiet evening."

Heat steals across my face. Me. He heard me scream. Which means I lost that damn bet. I finish piling the plates and replace the tray cover over everything before standing. I turn to Abel and inhale, but almost as if he senses my words, he stops me with a raised hand.

"Don't worry, Riot Girl," he says. "I'm willing to compromise even though you lost."

My hands turn to fists at my sides. "I wouldn't have lost if you weren't such a crazy psychopath," I snap.

There's a complete and utter lack of remorse on his face as he leans back and crosses his arms over his chest. "Regardless, you did lose," he reminds me. "But I'll be kind."

"What does that mean?" I demand. Does that mean he's willing to let me leave? Or will I have to slip away again somehow? This whole situation has brought it home just how out of practice I am. Or maybe it's just him. Abel is like a dog with a bone; once he latches onto something or someone—that someone being me at the moment—he doesn't let go.

"It means you and I will be leaving this hotel and traveling north," he replies. "While Braxton and Troy head back to Eastpoint."

I blink, surprised by how easy that was. It's not exactly the ideal situation, but getting as far as possible from Eastpoint is the point. Maybe it'll actually be easier with Abel by my side. I could cross the border into Canada, and with my skills, have a new name and identity in a matter of hours. I just haven't had the time. I eye Abel with wariness. He can give that to me. The only question is—will he let me go once it's all said and done?

Braxton nods, drawing our attention as he lifts his hand. "I figured you'd decide something along those lines," he comments as he lowers his arm once more. "So, I took the liberty of having Troy go out this morning and rent an SUV for us to drive back."

"Then that settles it," Abel agrees. "When he gets back, we'll check out. You guys head home—cover for Rylie and me with classes—and we'll head north."

My gaze bounces back and forth between the two of them. "You don't even know where I'm going," I point out.

Abel turns to me and arches a brow. "Were you not heading north?" he asks.

I was, but he doesn't know yet just how far up I was planning to go. I shake my head. "No, you're right, I am," I say. "But—"

"Don't worry," Abel cuts me off. "I'll get the rest of the story when we get on the road."

"You taking the Mustang?" Brax asks as he digs into his pockets

Abel nods as he catches the keys Braxton tosses him out of the air. "Of course. I doubt whatever Rylie here is running from is really looking for me. As long as we stay low, I'm sure we'll be good. She's got a laptop with her and I have my cell, we'll be in contact."

My mind is a whirl of emotions and confusion. All of the fear and panic I've felt for the past few days have collided and I find myself drifting over to the bed and sinking onto the corner of it, watching as Abel and Braxton talk. They make plans, discuss times to check in, and for the first time, someone else has taken over for me.

I've been in charge of myself for as long as I can remember. Eating. Sleeping. Dressing. Everything that parents did for their children, I did for myself. I've never had someone just waltz into my life and start making decisions for me. A part of me is irritated by it—angry that he has the fucking audacity. But I'm also not surprised. Abel has proven that he knows how to take charge and as he stands there in front of Braxton, hands gesturing as they talk, I'm starting to see the real difference between his persona at school and the real man.

Here, he proves himself to be the son of a multi-billionaire. I'd always thought trust fund kids were spoiled assholes who had more money than any child should ever have, but the fact is … he was raised on how to lead. He knows what to do in a crisis. He has the power and money I've never even thought of touching. And unlike me, he knows what to do with it.

Braxton stands suddenly, bringing me out of my internal thoughts. He passes the bed, pausing as he looks down at me and laying a giant hand on the top of my head. The damn thing is so massive it cups the entire back of my skull. He gives me a small smile and then rubs against my hair before he turns and leaves the room.

"Start packing your stuff, Rylie," Abel says as he pulls out his cell phone and strides towards the wall where our chargers are plugged in. "We're leaving within the hour."

I have no words for that. No reason to refuse and every reason to accept, but I still can't help but ask, "why?"

Abel pauses and looks back at me as he stops moving across the room. He slowly lowers his arm, cell phone still in hand, and then he takes a step towards me, stopping when he reaches my knees. His cell falls from his palm and lands on the bed next to me as he bends over and grips the edge of the mattress on either side of my legs.

"Why?" he asks.

I nod. "Why are you doing this?" I ask again. "Why me?"

He tilts his head at me, cool gaze assessing. As if he's trying to figure out if I'm being serious, but this is as serious as it gets. He doesn't yet even understand the dangers that lie in wait. I've put off telling him for so long, now I feel almost stupid for doing so. But last night changed things. It made no sense to tell a man I wasn't even sure was interested in me about my past. I thought I had more time as well, and now that has all blown up in my face.

My past has been a ticking time bomb and we're down to the wire. The path I walk is treacherous. Each step unstable. Each move unknown.

Yet, he walks in like it's easy. Like it means nothing for him to take over my life and run the show. And I'm so tired that I'm just ready to let him. I want someone else to take control for a while because I'm tired of doing it all myself and failing anyway.

Abel lifts a palm and cups my cheek. "You really have no idea, do you?" From the tone of his voice, it's clear he doesn't expect an answer and even if he did, I have no idea how to respond. "Rylie..." He moves closer until his face blocks out everything in the room. Until he's all I can see.

Truth be told, he's all I *want* to see. He's so heartbreakingly beautiful that sometimes I just want to shut out the world and stare at him with wonder. How could this world be so ugly and create such a perfect specimen. Wild features. Thick brows. The dark hair at the root of his white blond locks. The chisel of his jawline. Everything about him is meant to entice. I wonder if he hates that. I can't imagine so because he uses his looks like a weapon. Eyes like daggers. Lips like poison. Abel Frazier is meant to seduce and destroy.

"I'll tell you why," he says, voice dipping low, "when you tell me why you ran."

Silence descends between us and for several long minutes, Abel stands there like that, holding my face like I'm something precious. When I don't say anything, he pulls back, turns, and continues what he was doing.

The moment now has passed, but it'll come again. I know, the time of my confession is on the horizon, and I can't run from it forever. For now, though, I want to at least make sure I can run from Daniel.

33

ABEL

I WATCH in the rearview as Troy and Braxton drive the opposite way before Rylie and I pull out of the hotel parking lot in my Mustang. Rylie offers no direction, so I take the first exit on the interstate heading further up. We're butting up against the border to Canada anyway, but regardless of what she seems to think, it's not easy for anyone to just pop over to another country.

At least, not if you don't have the background and funds like I do.

The fact is ... I lied to her. She has no idea, but we're only postponing our return to Eastpoint and I have no intention of taking her any further north. She has no idea what she's doing. She's just running blindly. Well, I'll let her do that for now, but it won't last. Just like those tightly sealed lips of hers, I'll eat up this space between us.

It seems I've gone and done it. Fallen. Hard and deep. Fast. I'm drowning in her ocean and there she sits, barely two feet away, with her forehead pressed into the glass of the passenger side window as she watches the cars speed around us and the pavement disappear under the wheels of my car.

I close my eyes for a brief moment, drawing in a breath, and steer the front of the Mustang away from the border. We're not going to Toronto. We're going somewhere else. Somewhere far more important. Four days. That's all I'll give her. If I can't convince her to return on her own with me in that amount of time then I'll have to tie her ass up and drag her back because there's no point in running when she should know I won't let her.

She belongs in Eastpoint. We both do.

The hours pass in a mixture of silence and light music played on the radio. Every city or so, she reaches forward to fumble with the channels as the radio signals change and go out. I watch with a small smile. She doesn't seem to notice it, but I don't let just anyone mess with the controls of my Mustang. Dean and Braxton are the only other people outside of my mechanics allowed to touch my baby. Anyone else would have their fingers broken. Not her, though. She's special.

I don't pull over for anything other than fast food and gas fill ups and she doesn't say a damn word. There's no commentary on where we're going. I can't tell if she just doesn't give a fuck or if she trusts me so much that she's not paying attention. If that's true, then it's almost enough to make me feel guilty for deceiving her. Almost.

It isn't until the last cup of coffee I grabbed at a drive through is dry and night has long since fallen that I decide to call it a night. Rylie doesn't complain or say a word as I direct the Mustang off of the interstate and to the first place I see.

We're in the middle of nowhere, so a fancy hotel like the one Brax booked for us in Detroit is out of the question. The headlights of the car wash over a one-story motel facing the road. Peeling semi-orange paint and bars over the glass doors of the lobby greet us. I peek at the girl in the passenger seat, but all Rylie does is begin to gather her bag and slip on the shoes she'd long since taken off as she preps to follow me inside. My own bag—a parting gift from Brax—sits against my back as I walk, and I know due to the heaviness that he put my gun in there as well. Looking around at this place, I might need it.

We check in, and instead of a card, I hand over a wad of cash—ignoring the leering look of the balding, greasy looking redneck at the front desk as he peeks at Rylie. My hand clenches into a fist, but she's tired and getting into a fight will only make her have to wait longer. At least this place will be far enough off the grid to make her feel as safe as she can from whatever it is that she's running from.

I snatch the key with a tab labeled with the room number from the desk clerk and turn, nudging Rylie back outside and down the line of doors until we come to ours. I almost go back and buy out several other rooms when I see the lights on in the room next door and hear the loud fake orgasmic cries of a woman. No doubt some prostitute is earning her rent in there. Rylie gestures for me to hurry up and I release a breath, shoving the key into the door. Unlocking the door and pushing it inward reveals ancient green carpet, wallpaper from the seventies, and cracked molding.

I groan. "Shithole," I mutter as I step inside, considering our options. We're nowhere near an actual city and I doubt there will be a much better place on the highway for at least another hour's drive. "Maybe we should sleep in the fucking car," I say.

"It's fine," Rylie says, dropping her bag into the lone chair shoved up underneath the room's air conditioning unit that sticks out of the window. It rattles and coughs out semi-cool air into the otherwise stifling room. "I've stayed in worse places."

That last comment has me pausing as I turn back to lock the door behind us. I hear her moving about the room, getting ready for bed as if what she said holds no meaning at all, but it does. It does to me. Quickly locking the door, making sure that the chain at the top is securely in place, I pivot back to the rest of the room just in time to see Rylie take off her dress.

My heart fucking stops in my chest. She's facing away from me and though she's still fairly covered, her hair falling over her upper back and her leggings pulled up enough to cover her from the waist down, I see it—the massive black and purple bruise just above the cleft of her ass.

I'm across the room in a heartbeat and I must have moved too fast for her to notice because when she turns to toss the dress onto the bed, she jumps. "Abel!" she gasps. "What—"

"Turn around," I order, cutting her off. She starts as my hands land on her hips and I force her to face away. My fingertips feather across her skin, so gentle ... so fucking light she might not even be able to feel my touch. I don't want to hurt her. Not anymore than she already has been. My thumb brushes against the edge of the bruise; seeing it again like this just hits home how stupid I was. I'd been a bit too preoccupied in the shower—it was hard not to be with all of her naked flesh before my eyes just waiting to be soothed and taken.

She looks back over her shoulder, big hazel eyes wide and round. Despite the dark circles under her eyes, she's stunning. Fucking beautiful. I've had any number of women on my arm. I've fucked rich older women who'd been supermodels in their youth. I've fucked their daughters. But Rylie Moore is the most beautiful thing I've ever laid my eyes on.

This dark mark on her skin, however, pisses me off. I don't like seeing it on her. I don't like seeing her hurt, but more than that, I don't like knowing that I did this. That this bruise is my fault.

I wrap my arms around her middle and draw her back against my chest as I bury my face in the curve of her throat. It takes a long time for the words to creep up, but when they do, I mean them. "I'm sorry."

She's quiet, and then, "It's okay," she says. "It's not your fault. I've had worse."

My arms tighten around her. That doesn't make me feel the least bit better. In fact, it makes the angry demon inside of me rage ever hotter. She's stayed in worse places than this dump of a motel. She's had worse than a bruise the size of a man's fist on her back. She's had what? Worse. Always worse.

I don't want her to have worse. I want her to have better. I want to *be* her better.

This girl and what she does to me ... she has no clue. She's so fucking oblivious. That night I had with her, it wasn't enough. I'm starting to suspect it won't ever be enough. I haven't fucking slept that goddamn well in so long as I did with her curled up in my arms, snoozing away. And as I had watched her sleep, played with her hair—with her and her vicious little attitude none the wiser—I had seen a future. A future where the two of us would wake up next to each other. One where she'd talk shit and I'd kiss the fuck out of her. And if I was being truthful, there was a reason why I was taking such chances with her.

I'm fucked up beyond belief. I want to lock her to me in any way I can. I want my cum in her pussy. Sloshing around her small belly. I want it to take root. I want to watch her get big. I want to tie her down and keep her with me forever. I want to see her smile and I want, more than anything in the world, to have her direct that smile at me.

I can't stand this anymore. I can't take it. "Tell me." The words are pulled from my throat, hoarse and so fucking hard.

Rylie stiffens against my chest and tries to pull away as soon as they're out, but I tighten my hold, not letting her. "Abel, I'm tired," she says, but the lack of anger in her tone tells me she's just trying to avoid the truth, and I can't do it anymore. I wanted to give her time to come to me herself, but I'm not about that life. The life where she avoids the truth and only takes what she can get.

"I'll do whatever you want me to do," I promise. "But please just ... tell me the truth. Why did you run, Rylie? What are you running from?" I lift my head away from her throat and firmly turn her to face me. She ducks her chin and I have to force it back up with a solid hand. Fingers on her throat, thumb at her jaw, she's given no more choices. "Riot Girl..." I press my forehead to hers.

The moment's ruined by a loud thump against the wall that jars the decades old box television anchored to the wall in the corner. A curse slips out of my lips as I raise my head and offer a glare at the wall. A mistake on my part because it gives her the room she needs to push away from me.

Rylie turns and grabs her bag, yanking it open and delving inside, pulling out a long black t-shirt a moment later that she slips into—covering her nakedness.

The moment, I fear, is over. She's dragged that damned protective layer of silence back around her. She doesn't look at me as she takes off her shoes and crawls onto the mattress. It creaks under her slight weight and I wince. Whoever is next door bangs against the wall once more, making the shitty paintings of woods and deer shake as well.

I pinch the bridge of my nose. I'm so fucking exhausted, but I want her to open up to me.

Four days, I remind myself. We've still got time before we get to where we're going. With gritted teeth, I stride to the wall, shut off the lights and then force myself to go to the bed and not dive on top of her. Instead, I take off my own shoes and crawl under the starchy sheets and curl an arm around her middle, dragging her across the bed until her ass is nestled against my dick. When it starts to lengthen and harden, she squirms.

"Unless you want me to do something about my predicament," I say into the darkness of the motel room, "I

274

recommend you stay still." That has her settling down rather quickly and she stops moving, the sound of her quiet breath moving in and out as she slips into sleep.

I lay there for the longest time, my tired eyes growing more and more exhausted. Sleep, however, seems eons away. I feel like I can hear every single thing in this motel. The two next door having sex that would put any other fucker to shame if I weren't me. I swear I can even hear the sound of bugs skittering in the walls and across the floors.

This place is a dump and for the first time in my life, I'm ashamed. I'm ashamed that I wasn't more aware of our surroundings, that I didn't plan in advance, but most of all that Rylie isn't even bothered by it. In fact, she seems almost accustomed to places like this and that has me wanting to know just what kind of life she lived before she came to Eastpoint.

I glance down at her, my fingers moving to her temple as I push her hair back and stare down at her sleeping face. She's pale with dark lashes that throw shadows down her cheeks. Such a slight frame. She looks and feels like glass—breakable and fragile. I sink deeper into the mattress and pillows, stuffing my face into that mass of lavender hair of hers and inhaling a scent that is uniquely hers as the exhaustion finally claims me and sleep takes over.

I'm drifting, aware and not for the longest time. I forget where I am. All I know is that I have the sweetest smelling woman in my arms. Her warmth against my chest, sinking deep beneath my skin. I'm so comforted by having another person in my bed, against my body, that I almost don't hear it at first. The sound of a lock clicking. But I do, and the second my brain registers what it is, I'm up and out of the bed.

I shoot across the room, snatching the handle of the motel room door as it turns and creeps open. The chain is in place so whoever is trying to break in doesn't get very far, but I'm in a foul mood. And as I hear the sheets of the bed shift and Rylie's sleep slurred, "What's going on?" my anger only intensifies.

Without a second thought, I unlatch the chain with one hand and reach for my bag next to Rylie's, withdrawing the gun I usually keep in my glove compartment, and flick the safety off. The chain is off and the door is yanked open in the next instant.

I grab the shadowy figure just outside and turn, slamming him against the wall next to the door as I shove the barrel of my gun against the base of his skull. "Move a single muscle," I say through gritted teeth. "And I'll blow your fucking brains out."

"Shit!" the man's voice is gruff, "I-I'm sorry, I got the wrong room."

"No, you didn't." I'm not fucking stupid. There was no way another key would have opened this door. I step back and recognize the haggard and bearded face similar to that of the desk clerk—a relative apparently. I have no doubt that his plan was to rob us blind while we slept. Perhaps they'd forgotten about the chain or maybe people didn't use it enough. When something slips from his hand and lands on the floor, I look down and realize that's not the case at all. The fucker had planned on cutting the chain.

"Abel?" Rylie's voice from the bed is confused.

"Get up," I tell her. "Get your shit and get to the car. We're leaving."

I don't hear a response and when I glance back to ensure she's doing as I've ordered, her eyes are on the man I've got against the wall. When she catches my gaze, she arches a brow. "Are you going to kill him?" she asks.

"I'm considering it," I say honestly. I'm not as kill-happy as Brax or Dean, but right now, I'm too fucking irritated to think rationally. It wouldn't have mattered if it was just me this man was trying to rob. I'd probably have beat him senseless and left, but it's not just me I have to consider now.

It's her. He put my girl in danger and for that, death is the only recourse.

At my words, the man I've got pressed to the wall whimpers. He begins to tremble, shaking so hard it's difficult to keep my gun steady against his head. "P-please I d-didn't mean noffin' by it. It's noffin' personal. I-I wasn't gon' hurt ya."

I whip my head to him and growl, pressing my gun even harder into the place between his skull and neck.

"Abel," Rylie calls again.

"What?" I snarl without looking back.

"If you kill him then that will only take up more time we don't have to waste," she says.

And fuck if she isn't right. But that doesn't mean I can just let him go. With an irritated huff, I pull away, waiting until the man sighs in relief and tries to turn back around. The second he's facing me, I punch him in the nose, relishing in the cartilage breaking under my knuckles. Blood pours down his face, but I'm not done. I grip him by the disgusting shirt he's wearing, heaving him up as I flick the safety back on my gun only to use the thing to pistol whip him until he's unconscious.

I drop his unconscious body to the floor and turn back to my girl as she slips out of bed, reaching for her shoes and slipping them on. Tucking my gun into the waistband of my pants, I help her gather her things, taking both bags and sliding them up my shoulder as I leave the key on the dresser, shove my feet back into my shoes, and urge her out of the room and into the parking lot.

"I'm sorry," I mutter as I hit the key fob for the Mustang.

Rylie glances up at me and offers me a small smile. I must be fucking hallucinating or something because she reaches over and touches my arm once, almost comfortingly. "It's alright," she says. "You woke up before he did anything, and even if you didn't kill him..." She drifts off, looking back at the open doorway to the motel room. "I doubt he'll be doing this again, and if he does, he'll probably think twice about who he's robbing."

God, have I mentioned how fucking hot smart girls are? Any other chick I know would've been a crying mess, but not Rylie. No. She assesses the situation and picks up on the clues to tell her exactly what's going down and then she manages to keep a level head. How? I don't know. Years of practice, maybe. What I do know is that I want more of it. More of her.

She heads around to the passenger side of the Mustang and climbs in. I grab the driver's side door and do the same, slinging both of our bags to the bottom of the backseat. "What now?" she asks.

Fuck, I don't know. I groan and scrub a hand down my face. "We still need to get some more sleep," I inform her as I put the key in the ignition and turn the car on. The radio clock reads back just past 2 a.m. We can't keep surviving on a few hours of sleep at a time.

"We could sleep in the car," she suggests, reminding me of my earlier proposal. I hadn't actually been serious, but when I think about it ... it might be our only option for now.

The thought has me hanging my head against the steering wheel with a dark laugh.

"What?" Rylie's voice is concerned. Her gaze burns into the side of my face, but I don't look her way.

I shake my head. "It's just fucking funny," I say.

"What is?" she asks.

"This." I gesture around us—to the dark parking lot with no safety light and the grotesque motel across from us with nothing but older model trucks and what looks like a retired undercover cop car with a smashed out back window in the corner of the lot. "I'm one of the wealthiest guys at Eastpoint. Richer than half of America, if not most of it. And here I am ... and all I offered you is a fucking night at a roach motel." It's so pathetic that I can't help but laugh.

"I don't care about that," Rylie says quietly.

That stops my self-loathing fueled laughter. "You should." I look at her. "You should give a fuck about where you are."

She frowns. "I already told you that I—"

"Don't you fucking say that you've been in worse places," I warn her.

She blinks at me, shock drawing her brows down and popping her pretty pink lips open as she stares back at me. I turn back to the steering wheel. "Put your fucking seatbelt on," I order as I do the same. I shift the car into drive and peel out of the parking lot.

I recall seeing a sign a few miles before we'd pulled off the interstate about a trucker's lot somewhere up the road. Not halfway there, it starts to rain. Big fat droplets slapping the windshield. I'm almost grateful when the sign for the trucker's station comes into view with lots of lighting and a gas pump.

I steer the Mustang around the back and park along the side of a row of eighteen wheelers. I shut off the car and get out, ignoring Rylie calling after me as I head towards the trunk. I pop it open, lifting it, and reach inside until I snag the kit I keep there for emergencies. Whether my mom knew it or not, she always warned me to keep bottles of water, blankets, and other necessities in the back of my cars. I don't do it for any other one, but the Mustang is different. The Mustang was hers, so I've always felt like I have to follow her rules about cars when it comes to this thing. Now, I'm grateful for her advice. Even if I can't find a nice comfortable and safe hotel for Rylie, she at least won't freeze to death.

Rain starts to fall harder on the back of my head and I hurry back towards the driver's side door after shutting and locking the trunk once more. I climb into the driver's seat and shut the door behind me, shoving the pack into Rylie's lap. Leaning forward, I remove the gun from my waistband and then arch over to her side, popping open the glove compartment and placing it where it belongs before closing it up.

"Take that," I snap. "And sleep in the back with it."

"What is it?" Even as she asks the question, though, she opens the waterproof satchel and peeks inside. She withdraws a blanket and a small airplane pillow before looking at me. "You keep stuff like this in your trunk?"

I arch a brow. "Why so shocked?"

She shrugs, unfolding the blanket over her lap as she starts to shiver. "I don't know, I just expected something a little more ... badass?"

I snort. "Badass? Like what?"

"Guns and ammo," she replies easily. "Maybe a machete or two."

I bite my lip. What a little fucking smart ass. "Get in the backseat," I tell her again.

Instead of doing as I say, however, she side eyes me. "Where are you going to sleep?"

"Where do you think?" I gesture to where I'm currently sitting. "You're looking at my bed."

"Abel, you can't sleep in the front seat. Why don't you lay in the back?"

"I'm fine," I say, already reaching for the steering wheel adjustments as I pop it up so that it's not sitting right on my dick. "We're probably only going to get a couple more hours. Just enough to last until we get back on the road."

"And what about this?" Rylie rips the blanket off her lap and shoves it in my face. "There's only one. Take it."

Before I can shove it back at her, my face is filled with ass and my brain short circuits. Lush, beautiful, curvaceous ass. Fuck. Me. My hand twitches, the desire to grip it, touch it, squeeze it riding me hard as she turns and drops the bag I handed her onto the floor in the back. At first, I think she's finally doing what I told her to and heading into the back so she can lay down and get some shut eye, but that turns out not to be the case when she plops back into the passenger seat a second later with something new in her hand.

"What the fuck did I—"

"Here." She cuts me off as she breaks off a piece of what turns out to be a granola bar and shoves it into my hand.

With an irritated growl, I hand it back to her. "Eat it," I tell her. "I'm not hungry. When you're done, get in the back"—I toss the blanket behind my head for good measure—"and go to sleep."

Rylie takes my half of the granola bar and shovels it into her mouth. I watch her chew and swallow before frowning my way. "You're not going to get any sleep like that," she says as if I don't already know that. As much as I love my Mustang, it is not a travel car and definitely not a luxury bedroom on wheels.

I sigh, reaching up to squeeze the bridge of my nose between my thumb and forefinger. "Can't you just listen to me?" I ask. "Just once."

"Not when it doesn't make sense," she replies easily. "I'll be fine up here. I'm smaller."

"You are not sleeping—fuck it." I cut myself off and make a split second decision. Without sitting around to contemplate what this will probably do to me, I turn and slip into the backseat, falling sideways across the fabric covering until I'm far enough in that I can get my legs down.

I pop those fuckers down and then lean forward, reaching for the side of the driver's side chair. I lift the lever on the side and slide it all the way up. Then I raise my head and glare at the woman staring back at me before carefully taking her arm and dragging her into the back along with me.

"Wait! What are you doing!" I lay down horizontally, head towards one window and feet towards the other. It's impossible to actually get too comfortable. One foot ends up planted firmly on the seat with my knee up towards the soft roof of the car while my other leg hangs over the other side and my foot touches the floorboards. I lift and arrange Rylie until she's laid out across my chest. As she sputters and tries to shove herself off me—to no avail since I've got one arm firmly locked around her waist, keeping her there—I dig around until I find the fallen pillow and stuff it behind my neck.

"Grab the blanket, will you?" I ask politely.

"No!" Rylie slaps my chest and squirms against me. "Let me up, you stupid, pig-headed—"

"You say the sweetest things, Riot Girl," I muse, knowing it'll piss her off. "But I'm tired and the sooner you grab the blanket and cover us, the sooner we can get some shut eye."

"I hate you," she growls.

That might actually hurt, if it was true, but I know better. "No, you don't," I say, scooting down to get as comfortable as physically possible in this cramped space. "If you hated me, you wouldn't feel so safe with me."

She freezes and I close my eyes, not wanting to see the look on her face that I suspect will be more than just surprise. After a moment of silence, she starts moving, but this time it's not with the intention of fighting her way off of my chest. The feel of the blanket slides over my legs and the cool air of the interior of the car is muffled.

Silence stretches between us as I keep my eyes shut, just listening to the sounds of her breath and the rain slapping the soft roof of the Mustang. Her heart pounds against my chest as she finally seems to give in and lower herself against me.

Her hair tickles the underside of my jaw and I want nothing more than to open my eyes and look down and watch her, but I know she's not asleep yet and if she catches me looking at her now, I have no doubt that I'll do something that will cause neither of us to get any sleep for the next several hours. I can already feel my cock shifting in my jeans, very aware of the soft woman in my arms and the scent of her in my lungs.

I am so far gone for this girl, I think. Any other chick, I'd kick to the side of the road, but her ... her I give in for. The man who's given in for no one else but my brothers ... and she's the one who breaks me.

34

RYLIE

"How do you know that?" Abel's quiet in the face of my question for several long, agonizing seconds. I refuse to take it back. I need to know. How could he possibly know what I'm feeling or how I'm different with him than I am with other guys? He doesn't know shit about me. I haven't let him find out. Unless ... I pull back and glare down at his closed eyes.

"Whatever you're thinking, Riot Girl," he says with a sigh as his eyelids lift and those cool toned irises of his fixate on me, "it's wrong."

"How do you know?" I demand again. "Answer me."

He stares back at me and we're locked in this strange, almost Twilight Zone-esque moment where there is nothing in the world but the two of us. Hell, this whole place—where we are, what we're doing—feels like a bad episode of that old show. I mean really? He was right to laugh about it earlier. If I give it more than a passing thought, it's really funny. Not so much in a haha kind of way, but in the ridiculousness of it all kind of way. A multimillionaire and a hacker girl on the run together, taking refuge in the backseat of a decades old Mustang behind a truck stop in the middle of bum fuck nowhere.

Finally, Abel lifts a hand and I jump when his fingertips brush down the side of my face. "I just know, Rylie." His answer is a whisper and the little girl in me shrinks away from the gentleness of his touch, not trusting it ... or him. But I'm tired of not trusting. Of not letting anyone else in. It's so cold here by myself.

My head dips down until my hair falls around my face, shielding it from his view. "Rylie?"

Just say it, I order myself. *Say the fucking words.* But they don't come. No matter how hard I try. No matter how much I wish to force the truth from my chest, to open up the cage I've kept myself in for so long. Even if I don't step outside, I can at least sit here with the door open, and maybe ... just maybe, he'll come inside with me and I won't be so goddamn lonely anymore.

I lift my head once more. My eyes settle on him in the darkness. The way his silver-blond hair shifts across his forehead and his crystal blue eyes level me with a look so intense they steal the very breath from my lungs.

"Rylie." My name is a curse on his lips, a whisper under the dim moonlight filtering in through the clear plastic back window of the mustang as the rain falls. We're alone—no ... not alone. We're together. "I wish..."

I wait, curious and wondering. What does he wish for? The man who can and does have everything in the world. What could he possibly want? His upper lip curls back and his teeth flash in the moonlight. The rain falls harder on the plastic and glass windows.

"Fuck it," he hisses through clenched teeth. "God ... fucking dammit. Just..." He leans up and forward, his hand moves from my cheek to the back of my neck as he holds me stationary so that he can brush his lips against mine. Once ... fuck they taste so good ... twice ... I'm losing all of my strength ... three times and that's it. I'm his. Only his.

Our mouths collide and it's pure passion. Like nothing I've ever felt before. His tongue invades and brushes against mine and hesitantly, I return the favor. I lower myself against him, my fingers scraping against the fabric of his shirt as I hold on for dear life. He kisses like he wants to consume me and I feel like too many of these drugging treasures and I just might let him. He's a fucking addiction, this man. Utterly impossible to resist.

A whimper escapes my mouth when he suddenly rips his lips from mine and forces both of us up until he's sitting and I'm straddling his lap. He grips the sleep shirt I went to bed in back at the motel and lifts the bottom part upward. I regret leaving my bra on, considering where I am now, but at the time, I'd just been thinking that the momentary discomfort would save time later.

"Shit." Abel glares at the front of my covered chest with irritation.

"I'm sorr—" I don't even get to finish my apology before he's already leaning forward and reaching behind me for something. I turn in time to see the console flick up. My lower back presses into it as he stretches his hand over the top and riffles through the contents and when he sits back, smacking it down on his way, he's holding a small pocket knife.

"I'll buy you another," he promises as he opens the blade and slides it against my skin. The cold metal makes me freeze, but then the fabric loosens and both sides of my bra fall away as he reaches up and then cuts the pieces holding the straps over my arms. Abel then rips the thing away, tosses it somewhere on the floorboards, and sits back.

Embarrassment shoots through me as he holds up my shirt and stares. I should tell him not to bother buying another one. It's not like it'll hurt me to go a couple of days without one. My tits aren't anything to write home about. They're barely enough to fill even half of his hand. With the way he's looking at me, though, it's almost like he's staring at a beautifully carved work of art.

He licks his lips and lifts my shirt even more until he presses the hem to my lips. "Bite down, sweetheart," he orders.

My mouth opens and I take the fabric between my teeth, doing as he says, out of both curiosity and an Abel Frazier infused haze of desire. Right now, I feel like I'm willing to do anything if it only means he'll bring me pleasure. And that, he does.

Abel closes the pocket knife and sets it on the seat next to us as he leans down and circles one nipple with his tongue. My back arches as his hands palm my hips, keeping me steady. The throb of his cock between my legs has me seeing stars as he works my nipples over with that perverted and talented mouth of his. Lips. Tongue. Teeth. He uses it all. He goes from one to the other and back again. I didn't even know they could feel this good.

"Do you even know what you look like right now, Riot Girl?" he asks, sitting back to admire his handiwork. I'm panting, sweating, and so wet between my thighs right now, I swear I'll cry if he doesn't fuck me soon. Abel, however, doesn't seem to be in any rush as he lifts a hand and brushes a thumb over one pink tipped breast. "So erotic. Like you were made for my pleasure. This shirt..." He touches the sides, lightly brushing the skin along my ribcage that's bared to him. "It frames your lovely tits so perfectly. When you hold it up for me like that, I know you want this. The black fabric against your pale skin. I get it now, why guys buy their chicks lingerie so much. I never really gave a shit about that before. Didn't make sense." He shakes his head as a corner of his mouth curls upward in a sardonic tilt. "But then again, I've never given a shit about the chicks I've fucked. Not until you."

I drop the shirt from my mouth, licking my lips from the

dryness the fabric caused. He frowns. "What do you mean?" I ask.

Abel stares at me for a moment and then slides his hands under my shirt, against my waist. I can see what he wants in his eyes and he's waiting for me to give it to him. I sigh and reach down, lifting the shirt up and peeling it over my head, dropping it out of sight as well. Then my hands are on him, against his neck and sinking into the soft locks of his hair.

"You should take off yours too," I say.

He grins and reaches down, acceding to my request. His bare chest is a gift from God. Chiseled, yet still human. I find my gaze drifting over the planes of his body. He may have looked at me like I was a work of art, but the truth is ... he's a fucking statue forged by ancient sculptors. Every hollow. Every ridge. Every dip and curve and hard, yet soft bit of flesh ... it makes my mouth water.

Shaking my head, I refocus on what I was asking earlier as I lean forward, bringing my still hard nipples—wet from his mouth—against his pecs. "Now, what did you mean?" I repeat.

He inhales and I jump when I feel his hands enter my leggings at the back, moving down to cup my ass. "Take these off and I'll think about telling you," he offers with an arched brow.

"What about when I run out of clothes?" I ask.

He shrugs. "Then I suppose it'll be tit for tat, Riot Girl. But if you want an answer right now, take off these fucking pants before I cut them off with that knife."

My eyes widen at the gruffness in his tone and the glimmer in his eye that tells me he's dead serious. In a frantic movement, I slide off his lap sideways, gripping the waistband and stripping them down before shoving them into one of the bags at our feet.

"There we go," he says as he re-settles his hands on my hips and drags me back onto his lap where now the only thing separating us are my flimsy underwear and his jeans. His cock presses up, rubbing against my clit through the fabric.

"Now will you answer me?" I practically pant as I grip his shoulders and refocus on the man in front of me.

How funny is it that not ten minutes ago I was tired enough to be ready to fall asleep in the front seat of his Mustang and now I feel energized, ready for whatever he's willing to give me? Not funny at all, in my mind. But another ridiculousness in this otherworldly place we seem to have found ourselves.

"Sure," Abel says as he palms the back of my head and drags me forward.

"What are you—" A gasp slips from my lips as his hands move back to my ass and he cups my cheeks, spreading them as his fingers dip down between my thighs, rubbing the soft fabric of my underwear against my pussy. My nails scrape his chest.

"My father was a businessman," Abel begins, but it's hard to pay attention when his fingers are making me wetter and wetter. The fucker. He knows exactly what he's doing. He doesn't want to tell me, but he's already made a promise so now he's doing everything he possibly can to get me to lose my focus. And it might have worked, too, if I wasn't so viscerally aware of this man and the small conniving ways he seems to mind fuck the people around him without even trying.

Dean and Braxton are the in your face guys, but Abel is sneaky. He'll have you admitting all your secrets without giving away any of his and I won't stand for that. Not now.

"Everything was in his arsenal. People. Places. Things." Abel works one finger beneath the crotch of my underwear, touching one side of my labia before he spears into my wetness and rubs the pad against my clit. I bite down on his shoulder, willing him to continue—both with his hands and his words. "I was no different," he admits. "My mom was in charge of me for the most part, but after she died, he let me know that I was to pull my own weight as an Eastpoint heir. All of us were." I don't have to ask who 'all of us' are. I already know. "Dean had his own cross to bear and so did Braxton."

Sweat slicks down my spine as another finger joins the one against my clit and together they rub along either side, pinching the precious bundle of nerves and making sparks of pleasure and pain shoot through me. I shudder in his embrace.

"God, you're so wet for me, aren't you, Riot Girl?" he asks as his fingers leave my poor, abused clit and move down to my entrance where he does, in fact, find me incredibly wet. Leaking like a goddamn faucet—something I've never done for any other man. Hell, even the times I did want it, I found it hard to get wet enough for it not to hurt—unless the guy had no girth or length to him. But Abel seems to have some sort of magic spell woven over me. Maybe it's hormones or pheromones or something because it's not natural, whatever it is.

"Keep talking," I say, breathless, as he rubs my entrance and then slowly inserts his fingers, sinking them deep until he's all the way to the last knuckle.

"Are you sure?" he asks.

"Yessss," I hiss as he withdraws and thrusts them back in. I lift my head and glare at him. "Continue."

He smirks, but despite what he's doing down below, it doesn't reach his eyes. Whatever it is he's talking about, it's clear that it bothers him. *All the more reason for me to know,* I think.

"I've fucked women older than my mom after she died," he says quietly, the admittance loud in the quiet interior of the car. "I've fucked women who have kids older than me. I've fucked women who were married and widowed. I've fucked their daughters and their nieces. Hell, I've even fucked an employee or two. Whoever my father demanded I seduce, I did."

I freeze, a coldness washing over me. Abel withdraws his fingers and then holds my hips in his hand with his head bowed. "How does that make you feel?" he asks. "Knowing that I was a whore for my old man?"

Angry, I think silently. So fucking angry. Angrier than I've ever felt against anyone—my foster parents, my teachers who ignored the abuse, even Daniel. None of them can hold a candle to the fury burning inside of my chest.

Abel doesn't look at me, and for a long time, he keeps his head lowered and his grip light as if he isn't sure if I want him to touch me anymore. With shaking hands, I settle my arms on his biceps and the touch seems to jerk him out of whatever internal turmoil he's in. His head pops up and he tips his jaw until I'm looking down at him, face full of anguish and pain and fear.

"I don't feel any differently," I tell him. I finger a white blond lock of hair, brushing it back behind his ear and watch as a sheen overwhelms his eyes until he closes them, refusing to let the tears fall.

Quietly, I press a soft kiss to his jaw, running my tongue up until I find his earlobe where I latch on and bite down until he inhales sharply and his cock—despite the direction this conversation has taken—jerks against me.

"My mom would've killed herself if she knew the things I've done," he whispers. I bite down harder until his hands tighten on my sides enough to bruise. "Fuck, Riot Girl."

Only when he says that do I release him and lick away the drop of blood I caused. "Your mother wouldn't have ever wanted you to suffer like that," I tell him. "She wouldn't have killed herself."

"She would've been ashamed of me."

Pure rage formulates in my gut and I shove a hand underneath his head where it rests against the back of the seat and grip his hair tight. Abel's eyes pop open in surprise and I shove my nose right against his. "No," I say through clenched teeth, "she wouldn't have been. She would've been ashamed of your father."

He looks me over carefully, eyes wandering and curious. "I didn't exactly resist," he says. "It was just sex. Meaningless sex. There are worse things a parent can force on their child."

I almost want to cry as those words slip out of his mouth. That's just it, isn't it? I ask myself. There's always someone who has it worse. If you're beaten and bruised, someone has a broken arm. If you've got a broken arm, there's another person who can't walk anymore. If you're at the lowest of the low, hey at least you're still alive right?

I've heard it all. Time and again. It makes a sickness take root inside my gut. The unfairness of life is so cruel. I thought it just shit on people like me—people with no past and no home and no one to give a fuck about them. Yet, here he sits ... and though he doesn't say it, I can see the dark shadows lurking in his eyes when he looks at me. The unanswered questions that still remain. Will I turn away from him? Will I see him as damaged or tainted?

After all, no matter how much money he has, a whore is still a whore.

"How old were you?" I ask. "The first time."

It takes a while for him to answer and when it comes, it rips another hole in my already damaged beyond repair heart. "Fifteen." That's it. No excuses for his father or his age. No other details. Just ... fifteen. As if that number means nothing when it really means the world.

At fifteen, you're still just understanding the world. At fifteen, you don't know who you are yet. Hell, I'm nineteen and I still don't really know who the fuck I am. Fifteen ... and so fucking vulnerable. No mom. Just a father who used him like a commodity, like an object.

My hands clench into fists automatically, to which he raises his brow and I release them. I'm glad, I think. So fucking glad

Lionel Frazier is dead because if he were alive now, I would take great pleasure in making him miserable. The things I would do to him. I'd wreck the very business he prized so fucking much over his own son. I'd violate everything. Sell his information on the dark web for fucking free. I'd do whatever it took for this man, for Abel, to get the justice he so rightfully deserves. The justice he'll now never have on the man who hurt him when he should've loved him.

"Did you ever..." It's hard to talk through the emotion that has crawled up my throat. If anyone can understand him, it's me. And fuck, but this means I can't keep the truth from him any longer. I was already on the brink of telling him about Daniel and about my own deepest, darkest shame. This will push me over the edge, I just know it. I close my eyes and inhale, forcing back my own tears before reopening them. "Did you ever talk to anyone?"

Abel's quiet for what feels like an eternity and then he shakes his head. "Dean and Brax knew, but we didn't really talk about it."

"Will you?" I ask. "After..." I let my words drift off, hoping he gets my meaning.

His fingers pinch against my sides. "That depends," he says.

"On what?"

"Are you going to give me a reason to go to therapy, Riot Girl?" He smirks in my face. "Are you gonna try and fix me?"

I cup his face and stare down at him. "No," I finally say. "I'm not trying to fix you because you're not broken, Abel."

His lips part and his brows rise up slightly as he leans away from me. His jaw goes slack and he just ... stares. For the longest time, he stares at me. What started out as a semi-erotic fast paced ready to get laid moment has turned into this. A staring contest, but I don't necessarily mind. I stare right back at him, letting him see the truth in my eyes.

I don't look at him and know his past and think he's broken because of it. It would be hypocritical of me to call him a whore. To tell him that he's damaged because of what he's done.

"Riot Girl..." That stupid nickname has found its way into my heart, and when he says it on a raspy breath, it delves even deeper, burrowing inside of my bones and forcing a path that's made just for him. "You..." He blinks and shakes his head. "You fucking amaze me sometimes."

I don't know how, I think. Or why he thinks that. But I'm glad. For the first time in my life, I'm glad that someone is looking at me the way Abel is. I relish it. I cherish it. And I want more. I want those eyes on me always.

Electricity races through the charged air and the roar of thunder overhead sounds so fucking far away as I drift forward, my lips parting as my hands move to his chest. I close my eyes, meeting him halfway as our mouths collide and that's it for me, I realize.

I've fallen and there's no coming back.

35

ABEL

MOONLIGHT FILTERS in through the windows, but it's still so dark here in the backseat of my Mustang. All I can see is her. All I can hear is the sound of her breathing, her soft whimpers and moans as she moves against me in the darkness. That and the rain. The soft pattering against the roof and the glass and plastic of the car seem to ramp up my ardor.

It's like the whole world has vanished and the only two people left on Earth are her and me. I like that. I like thinking that no one else will ever be able to lay their eyes on such a beautiful creature. It's possessive of me, but I don't regret it. Sure, I'd miss my brothers. I love Braxton and Dean. I love Avalon like a sister, but even the three of them can't compare to the woman in my lap.

Naked and shivering in my arms, Rylie gasps as I touch her again, sliding my fingers into her pussy and curling them upward. She jerks against me, her small, pert little breasts scraping against the skin of my chest. I like that, too, I realize. How surprised she seems at the tiny slivers of pleasure I give her. And that, without a shadow of a doubt, is pure selfishness. I should be angry. Furious that she is so lacking in love from elsewhere that she has to find it in me, but at the same time, I can't help but be joyful of my own luck.

"Are you going to come for me, Rylie?" I ask as I rub my thumb over her clit. With her underwear shoved to the side and my hand down between her legs, she rides my fingers like a prize-winning equestrian. Up and down. Backwards and forwards. Her hips move and she grinds against my fingers, chasing her release.

Curls of soft purple hair flutter before my eyes. The fall of light and shadow over her skin makes her seem almost transparent. Like she might disappear at any moment. Panic grabs my chest and squeezes up my throat.

No! Old memories resurface. No doubt caused by the recent conversation, they plague me—running through my mind in horrible flashes. All of them ... everyone that's ever been vulnerable in my life has either tried to use me or they've disappeared. I can't bear it if she goes away too.

I band my arm around her and shut my eyes, willing back the angry, painful thoughts as I fuck her with my fingers. She cries out and clamps down on me, her body going tense and tight as she latches onto my arms and strains against me as her release takes over.

I'm tired of losing people. So fucking tired of starting over again and again. Of losing trust and sinking into the man my father created. Fucking just to fuck, or worse, fucking for information and seduction. Fucking to have control. I don't want that between her and me. I want more.

"Take my cock out." My voice is hoarse. Demanding. Dark.

Rylie comes down from the high of her orgasm, watching me as I withdraw from her pussy. I stare back at her as I slip the fingers that are covered in her cream between my lips. Without hesitation, I lick her orgasm from my digits. Sliding my tongue between my fingers and making sure I get every single inch of it into my mouth and down my throat. A flush covers her cheeks as her chest rises and falls in rapid succession.

"Did you hear me?" I arch a brow as I slip my fingers out of my mouth and lower them to grasp her hips. "Take my cock out, Rylie, or do you want to stop?"

Despite my words, I know there's no fucking possible way we can stop this now. She wants me just as much as I want her. And thank fuck for that.

Her hands move to my jeans and her fingers quickly unbutton and unzip me. She frees me, reaching inside to grasp at my cock. Her small palm slides against my hardness and I grunt in arousal as she grasps it firmly, no more hesitation or fear from her. She slides her hand against me, pumping once, twice, almost three times, but I can't. I have to stop her there.

I reach across the seat and snatch the forgotten pocket knife. Flicking it open, I watch her face carefully, seeking out any sense of second guessing on her part. But there is none. She notices the blade; her eyes flick to it once, but just as quickly her gaze returns to mine and levels there as I use it to cut away the sides of her panties and peel them from between her legs.

"You're hell on a girl's underwear, you know," she says quietly, a hint of amusement in her tone.

I can't help but smile back. "Then maybe you should stop wearing any." I snap the blade closed and toss it back down. I don't know if it hits the seat or if it falls to the floor and I don't check. I don't care about anything but this woman and now that I have her—at my mercy and fully naked in my lap—I'm not going to let anything else distract me.

"Put my cock in your pretty pussy, Rylie," I command. "Ride me."

She hums in the back of her throat. "Hmmm. Are you sure that's what you want?"

I lift a brow. "I'm sure it's what you want," I tell her. "Unless you want me to turn you over my lap, slap your ass and then fuck you with your face pressed to one of the windows, I suggest you do it. We're in a car, sweetheart. There are only so many positions that will be comfortable for you, but if it's discomfort you want..." I drift off, watching her to make sure she understands my meaning.

She sucks in a breath and I groan as her pink tongue makes an appearance, sweeping across her full bottom lip. Rylie arches up and positions my cock at her entrance. Slowly, ever so fucking slowly, she sinks down. I look to where we're connected. It's a sight to see—those thighs of hers parted to accept me. Pale in the dark interior of the vehicle, and even more so against the tan of my hands as I grip her knees and spread her wider.

"Look at you," I order. "What a good girl you are, taking my cock so deep. Does it hurt, Riot Girl? Or do you like this kind of pain?"

When I glance back up at her face, it's to find that her expression is one of deep concentration as she moves her hips, sinking ever deeper. She's so fucking tiny, she squeezes around my shaft like a goddamn vise.

"That's it," I praise her. "All the way. You can take it, can't you? You can take everything I have to give you."

Her lips part on a half-pained gasp when she finally makes it down to the base of my cock. The inner ripple of her muscles squeeze and release me. Just like that first night, she whimpers and squirms as if it's too much for her to take, but I know better.

"You haven't looked yet," I remind her of my earlier order. "Look where my cock is entering you, sweetheart. Look at the beautiful sight."

Hair falls over her face, but I reach up, brushing it back as her eyes find mine and then gradually lower, until she's staring straight at the thatch of hair above the base of my cock and where her pussy meets my skin.

I lean forward, grabbing a fistful of her hair, and drag it

away from her throat until my lips are planted firmly on her skin. I kiss her there, gentle at first and then I open my mouth wider and sink my teeth into her luscious flesh. I bite down hard, the desire to mark her insatiable. I'm like a wild animal. I want to fuck her until she's so full of me she doesn't know what it's like to not feel me inside of her.

"Abel..." My name slips from between her lips, pained and agonized. "It hurts."

"Good," I whisper, releasing her flesh from between my teeth. "I want it to hurt, Riot Girl," I tell her as I wrap my arms around her waist and pull her harder against me, rocking my hips so I start to slide in and out of her ever so slightly. She moans, but I'm not done. "I want you to be sore and think of that soreness ... that pain as a gift."

"A-a gift?" She sounds out of it and when I pull away, cupping her cheek and tipping her head back so I can look her in the eyes, realizing that they're dilated and unfocused. Almost like she's in the midst of a drug-induced high. Except there's nothing here for her to get addicted to but me.

"Yes," I tell her, gentling my tone as I kiss her lips lightly. She leans into my kiss, making me smirk even as I pull away. "Everything I give you is a gift, even the painful parts."

With that, I grasp her waist and lift her from my lap until only the head of my cock remains and then slam her back down until she screams. Nails draw blood into my flesh as I fuck into her tight cunt.

With my feet planted on the floorboards of the backseat and Rylie straddling my lap, I fuck her like I did back at the hotel in Detroit—hard and without mercy. After that initial scream, she starts to whimper and moan. Bending until her hair falls over half of her face and mine, blocking out the moonlight as well as the truck station light, she slams her mouth against me.

Fuck. Her kiss is fast and unexpected. As my hips thrust

and I fuck up into her tight, wet, pussy, she spears into my mouth with her tongue. Grabbing ahold of my head—one hand on my jaw and the other in my hair, gripping the strands as if they're the only thing keeping her grounded—she fucks my mouth with her tongue the same way I'm fucking her pussy with my cock.

In and out. We both lose time. We lose our breath. We lose all sense of self as the only thing we can seem to focus on is each other. "Rylie..." I can feel the pleasurable tingles of my own release coming up on me, but I'm not done. I don't want to end this now.

With a roar of frustration, I rip my lips from hers and lift both of her legs, turning and depositing her against the seat. She gasps as I pull halfway out and slam home. The top of her head smacks the window and she reaches back, pressing one hand to the triangle glass frame as I don't stop.

I grab her legs and position them against her—knees to her chest—as I fuck into her, not stopping until I feel the flutterings of her orgasm as well around my cock. I look down as I withdraw and slide inside what can only be described as heaven on Earth.

"You're so fucking wet, Riot Girl," I tell her, loving the way she arches up at my words, her cunt practically strangling my dick as she tightens all over. She loves it when I talk to her like this. She may not admit it verbally, but there's no denying the reactions of her body. "You're soaking my lap, you know?" I tell her. "I bet the next time I take my car in to get detailed, they'll be able to smell you." I lean down as she gasps for breath. "All those guys at Carlton's Garage have seen you now. They'll know exactly who I fucked back here." And it's not a lie. She's dripping down my cock and the crack of her ass, so wet that I bet I could flip her over and use her own juices to fuck her ass.

Maybe I will ... next time, I decide, as I grit my teeth against a white-hot shot of immeasurable pleasure.

"Abel ... Abel ... Abel..." She says my name like a prayer. Like it's the only word she can remember. Like I'm her god. It's such a fucking turn on.

"That's right, Riot Girl," I continue, holding her knees down as I saw in and out of her pussy. I want to go over the edge with her, dive deep into this heady, dangerous feeling, and know that I'm not alone. That neither one of us is.

She said she doesn't want to fix me because I'm not broken. A sweet sentiment, but wrong. I'm so far beyond broken; I'm ruined. Soiled. Tainted. But that doesn't mean I'm not selfish enough to want to keep her anyway.

I direct her legs until her ankles are over my shoulders, and with one hand on her hip and the other snaking beneath until I can pinch her clit, I groan as my release finally finds me. It shoots down through my spine and I come. I come hard, thrusting into her core and feeling my own jizz fill her up. A hole soaked in my own release is warm. It's an entirely filthy thought, but I saw back and forth again, relishing in it as she throws her head back and screams again as she comes just as hard all over my lap.

When it's over and she sags back into the seat, her hand falls away from the window as I pant and drip sweat onto her chest, and I'm finally able to catch my breath. Her lashes flutter as her eyes close, but I hate that. I reach down, cupping her face.

"Look at me, Rylie." This time my words aren't an order but a request. For a moment, I think she'll refuse it, but after what feels like an eternity, she finally opens her eyes and looks up at me. I lower her legs until they're back around my waist and despite her unwillingness to move, I drag her up and reposition us into our original states. With my back against the seat and her on my lap, chest to chest. Wet, oozing cum slips between us and I know we're going to have to find out if this truck stop has a shower. I hate that. I'm not sorry for coming inside of her. It satisfies a sick sense of marking my territory. But I am sorry that she'll have to clean up in a place that doesn't match my specifications of perfect.

Still, there's one thing I can't deny. One thing I need to tell her. I close my eyes and drag her against me, hugging her to my chest even as she stiffens. "I love you."

Three simple words, yet they mean the world. I've never said them in this capacity. I've loved my mother. I've loved my brothers, and yes, I love Avalon. But I love no one the way I love Rylie. It's new. It's different. It's ... terrifying.

Her breath catches, but before she can say anything, I know I need to clarify the meaning of these words. "You don't have to say it back," I say quickly. "But I thought you should know ... whatever you're running from, I'll protect you from it. Wherever you want to go, I'll follow. You're it for me, Rylie, and even if you only want to use me, I'll allow it." The way I've never allowed anyone to before. All because she's burrowed her little damaged self deep into my heart and found a small hidden place for herself there—whether she meant to or not.

Several moments of silence pass and it takes forever for her muscles to unknot and relax. She slowly goes lax in my arms, so much so that I think she's fallen asleep. But then she speaks, and when her words come, they stab me right through the chest.

"I was six years old when I lost my virginity."

Shock snakes up my throat and wraps around my neck, squeezing until not a single whisper of a reply can be heard. Every single one of my muscles locks tight. I can't ... I can't even...

"I was in the home for a short time—only about three months before it happened," she continues. Her voice is level. There's no emotion, no shakiness. As if she's recounting grades on a report card or the expected weather of the day. They're just facts to her ... not life altering events that I'd never predicted.

I sit there quietly, stunned into silence as she does what I've been wanting her to do since I realized my interest in her went beyond the norm. She rips open the doors of her insides and spills all. She tells me about the teenage boy in the foster home she'd lived in growing up. She tells me about his strange obsession. She tells me about the abuse and the deviant things he'd forced upon her.

It takes every ounce of my willpower not to shatter the windows of the vehicle with a roar of outrage, but it takes far greater strength for her, I realize, to sit back and meet my eyes when she tells me the truth.

"I didn't run from you, Abel," she whispers. "I ran from *him*. Daniel is out now ... and he's coming for me."

There is no composure inside of me. No tranquility. Only rage, fury, and the insistent demand for vengeance. I lift a palm to her face and find that it's trembling. I stop, clenching it into a fist, and close my eyes, afraid to look at the clear hazel irises staring back at me.

When I reopen them, they haven't disappeared. She's still right here, looking at me with ... I'm not sure what. It's not expectation. It's an unreadable expression.

"Thank you," I whisper. "For telling me."

She nods but doesn't reply. As if she's waiting for something. For me, I realize. She's waiting for me. For my decision. She may not have said the words, but Rylie telling me this—telling me the truth—I hope I can take it to mean that she feels the same.

I touch her cheek, drift my fingers down to her neck, and hold her gently as I lean forward. I don't stop until our foreheads are touching and we're close enough for our noses to brush and her lashes to flicker against the skin of my cheeks.

"Let's go back to Eastpoint," I say, but before I'm even finished speaking, she's shaking her head.

"I don't think—"

"Trust me," I say, interrupting her. "Rylie. You can't run forever. Certainly not from a monster like that. I can..." Rip him to shreds. Erase his very fucking existence. "I can take care of him for you." What better way to destroy a monster than by relying on a bigger and meaner one?

"I'm not sure..." Despite her words, I can tell that she's not disinterested in my proposal.

"You want to go back," I press forward. "You don't want to be on the run like this." Even if it means I'll have to put it on the back burner—my original intention and the true prize of our bet—it's worth it. "You've trusted me this far," I say. "Trust in me again."

She bites her lip and I duck down, licking my way into her mouth as I stop her from bruising that pretty mouth of hers. When I pull back, her hands are back in my hair and her eyes are unfocused once more. "Say yes..." I practically beg her. "Say yes, Rylie ... let me be your savior."

Her lips part and she finally ... blessedly agrees. "Yes," she says and I can't help but hold her tighter and kiss her as the rain above our heads falls harder against the Mustang's roof.

In the back of my mind, though, I'm already planning. I don't necessarily like killing, but I also don't mind it. All in all, murder and the taking of life is something I'm ambivalent towards. This man—this disgusting excuse of human waste—however ... I have a feeling I'm going to enjoy ripping him limb from limb and pissing on his corpse.

36

RYLIE

A WEEK. That's how long I've been gone from Eastpoint, and when Abel drives through the town I've lived in for the last year and a half, I almost burst into tears. I don't know how he's managed it, but somehow, over the past several hours—I've lost all reason. Telling him about Daniel had been ... well, I want to call it a momentary lapse in sanity, but the reality is, it'll hopefully be the best decision I've ever made.

I glance down to where my hand is clasped inside his as he holds the steering wheel of the Mustang in his other. Despite what happened between us almost a full twenty-four hours ago, he looks fucking peachy. I'd half expected the trip back to Eastpoint to take longer, but I guess without all of the station hopping that the buses required, it's really more of a straight shot. We'd only stopped for momentary naps—where he'd demand I crawl into the backseat and cuddle him as he got some shut eye—food, and gas.

Now ... we're home, and ... we're driving right past the university.

I blink and crane my neck around as the gated entrance comes and goes and Abel doesn't even put on his blinker, swear, or swerve. "Hey!" I pull my hand from his grasp. "Where are we going? The university's back there!"

He frowns down at his empty hand before looking at me and then back to the road. His lower lip pokes out as he settles both hands on the steering wheel. "I told you, we're going home," he states.

"Yeah, my home is back there!" I say, exasperated.

"We're not going to your dorm room," he says with an eye roll. "That's not a home."

"The fuck it's not," I snap. "All my shit is there. I need to change clothes and—"

"Your stuff's at the house," he interrupts as he steers the front of the vehicle onto a new road.

I gape at him. "What?"

He glances my way and then looks back to the road. "I called the guys and Ava while we stopped for gas a while back," he admits. "I told them to move your shit into the estate. It's safer there, anyway."

I slump into my seat. I should've known he seemed too fucking happy. "You..." I shake my head in disbelief, but really, I'm shocked I didn't consider he would do this. I mean, it was almost exactly what they'd done to Avalon when she and Dean had hooked up. I shoot him a dark glare out of the corner of my eyes. The majority of my anger stems from the fact that he did it without telling me, and I know why—he did it like this because he didn't want to give me the chance to back out. I don't know what I thought. Perhaps after the situation was resolved, I'd quietly go back to my life and we could reverse time to when we were just contemplating the idea of seeing each other. But this is a step further. With the Sick Boys, once you're in—you're in for life. And once you're out—you're dead.

Is this how Avalon felt when they pulled this shit on her? I wonder absently. I'm even more surprised Dean is still walking around like he has a dick. I would've assumed she'd chopped that fucker off by now. The only reason I'm not considering it is … well, Abel isn't Abel without his dick.

I turn towards the window and press my lips together. Stupid asshole. Maybe if I hadn't gotten that dick, I'd feel differently. But it hasn't been that long since he'd last rocked my shit and my body can't seem to give up the memory of shuddering as I came under him or over him or next to him. He really knows what he's fucking doing with that thing.

Maybe I should make a website for it. It's massive enough. I'll call it "danger to women everywhere." Warn them all away. I doubt it'd be that easy.

"Are you pouting?" he asks a moment later.

"No," I lie.

He snickers and I whirl my head around and narrow my gaze.

"Just give it up, Rylie," he says. "You're in now, girl." He reaches for my hand and when I try to wrestle it away, my irritation resisting his touch no matter how good it feels, he only tightens his grip and sends me a warning look. "Don't act like you didn't see this coming," he warns. I watch as he lifts my hand and presses his lips to the backs of my knuckles.

Heat. White hot, fiery fucking heat licks up my spine. I jerk my hand away, almost accidentally smacking him in the process as I whip back towards the window and focus hard on the passing scenery. For a moment, I think he's going to let it go and not say anything.

Then he chuckles, and all he says is, "Your ears are red, Riot Girl."

Fuck me dead. Fuck me all the way fucking dead.

I remain silent for the rest of the drive and the second he turns into the driveway that leads to the Carter estate and I spot the front of the mansion, I start plotting my escape. It's not because this isn't for the best. I admit it makes the most sense. But there are so many emotions swirling throughout my head;

the reality of what I've agreed to is crashing down over me and I need a breather. The runaway in me has always been there, sequestered and always ready to take off at a moment's notice. At the merest hint of danger. I can't run away now, but I can take a step back. Just one and just for a short time.

Abel meanders up the driveway, slowing down as if he senses my impending exit. He pulls the Mustang around to the garage and it feels like I'm dying a slow death full of pain and agony.

Finally, once we're inside, and the car is officially parked, I unsnap my seatbelt and bolt. I move so fast, I nearly fall face down on the concrete garage floor from my stumbling, half numb legs. The door across the garage flies open and Avalon stands there, arms braced.

"Where the hell—"

"Bathroom!" I practically shriek as I dive past her, shoving her out of the way before I can think better of it.

It's a lame excuse, I'll admit, but I find the nearest bathroom, and the second I'm inside, with the door closed and locked behind me, I turn on the faucet and stick my still steaming face underneath ice cold water. I don't know how long it takes for the heat of my face to die down, but when I lift back up, I'm soaked from forehead to chin and dripping all over the marble countertops.

Snatching a towel from one of the holders to the side, I scrub my face clean and stare back at my reflection in the mirror.

A week ... that reminder still sits in the back of my mind. How could so much have changed in just a few short days? When I left Eastpoint, I was alone, scared, and convinced there would be no coming back.

Now, here I am, right back where I started, but when I look at my eyes in the mirror in front of me, I don't see the same fear reflected back. I see ... almost joy. *Hope.* It's not over. Not by a long shot. Daniel will come for me. I know his obsession well, but this time ... this time I'm not alone.

I hear the footsteps in the hallway a split second before a banging sounds on the door. "Don't even think of hiding from me, Rylie!" Avalon snaps on the other side. "You and that fucker, Abel, have got some explaining to do. If you're not out here in five seconds, I'm gonna bust down this door and beat your fucking ass and then I'll make you tell me what the fuck has been going on!"

I roll my eyes. I never knew Avalon could be so dramatic. Crazy, yes. Theatrical? No.

"One." She starts counting, but I don't let her hit two. I quickly unlock the bathroom door and yank it open. "Tw—why are you wet?"

I open my mouth to answer her, but a familiar voice shoots back his own interpretation before I can. "I make all the ladies wet, Princess," Abel calls down the hallway. "But most especially my girlfriend."

Motherfucker. Fresh heat eats up the sides of my neck as Avalon's eyes widen and then she smirks at me. "So you finally did the dirty?" she comments. "I mean, Braxton said as much but I wasn't sure if he was just fucking with me."

I cover my face with one hand and hold up the one with the towel still clutched between my fingers. "Please ... don't."

She laughs. "Alright," she agrees readily. When I part the fingers over my eyes to peek at her, she smirks. "But don't think that's the last of it. I'm just letting it go for now. Abel says he has something important to say. I suppose it's about you?"

I don't respond, but then again, I don't need to. She already knows the answer.

"Move your ass, Riot Girl, we're burning daylight," Abel yells.

I groan as Avalon reaches into the bathroom and snags the towel out of my grip. Without a second thought, she tosses it to the bathroom floor and latches onto my wrist, tugging me out into the hallway. "Listen to the boy toy, Rylie," Avalon says. "They get pissy when they don't think they're in charge."

I stare at the back of her head as she drags me up the hallway towards where I can hear glasses clinking and people moving about. "I thought no one was in charge of you," I comment back.

She snorts and pivots her head until I can see the side profile of her face. "No one is," she agrees. "I didn't say that I didn't let some of them *think* they were in charge. It's all mind games, Rylie. Mind games galore in the house of sickness."

Avalon turns back to face forward once more as we step into the main hub of the Carter estate. Only when we're in full view of the others and there's no more escape for me does she release me and move over to Dean's side where he stands at the counter, cutting up fruit. She grabs a piece off the counter and pops it into her mouth before leaning into his side. I watch as she tips her chin up expectantly and Dean chuckles, leaning down to accommodate her need as he presses his mouth to hers.

I find my eyes automatically trailing from them to Abel as he finishes unloading what looks like his bag and mine onto the living room floor. "Family meeting," he calls, looking up and towards me. "Let's get started."

If I thought sitting there and listening to Abel recount everything I told him would be awkward, I was right. It took several long hours in the car of him insisting that the others needed to know the extent of the danger I am—or rather we, since Abel insists that he's a part of my problems—now facing. I keep my eyes on him the entire time, too scared to look away as we sit on the couch and he explains what he plans to do about the man who was just a sick, twisted teenager when he tried to warp a child's mind and body to his perfect ideals. When he tried to warp *me*.

"So, what do you want to do?" Dean asks. "Officially, I mean."

"Officially?" Abel shakes his head. "We don't know shit about shit. The second this fucker steps foot in Eastpoint, he's dead. I want no connection to him other than that. If he doesn't come, then we just find him and bury him."

"He'll come," I say quietly, and suddenly all eyes are on me. I sink deeper into the couch.

"You sound sure," Avalon says.

"I am," I say. Daniel will come for me. He's coming to Eastpoint. "He called me and told me as much."

"Ahhhhh," Braxton sighs. "So that's why you ran."

I nod. "There was a girl from my old foster home that helped me and he called me using her number." I swallow roughly. "I don't think she's still alive."

"Man, that's some deep-rooted obsession," Avalon says, whistling. I raise my brows at her nonchalant tone. "What?" she asks, blinking. "You don't think so? I mean he's been waiting for how long to get back at you? Over ten years? Maybe he's mad at you because you sent him to jail."

"He was a teenager," I remind her. "He didn't go to jail officially until he turned eighteen. He was set for—"

"Yeah, yeah," she cuts me off. "The point I'm making is— Abel"—she points to him—"wants the fucker dead, yeah?" Everyone either nods or grunts in agreement. "You"—she points to me—"want him to go away, but you can't just pleasantly ask him to leave you alone, plus, he's gotta pay for that fucked up shit he did to you as a kid."

"Are you going somewhere with this?" I deadpan.

"You're the key," Avalon says. "We just lure him here with you and once he's here, we kill him." She pops another piece of fruit in her mouth from the plate on the coffee table. "Simple and easy."

It would be for her, but I've never killed anyone before. I

stare down at my hands clasped in my lap. I don't know if I could—despite what he did to me. I want to. There's no denying my desire to see the life of Daniel Dickerson snuffed out from this world, but could I do it if given the chance? Could I pull the trigger and know that I was the cause of someone's death?

I don't know how long I sit there like that in silence when Abel's hand comes down over both of mine. Jerking, I look up and meet his eyes. "You don't have to be the one to do it," he says quietly, as if he can read into the deepest darkest parts of my mind. "But one way or the other, he's going to die." Abel's cool blue eyes harden until it's nothing but a wall of ice. "I'll make sure of it."

And just like that, I know he will. Whatever we decide, Abel will figure out a path and all I have to do is help him forge it. I unlatch both of my hands and turn one over, weaving my fingers with his. "Okay," I say, turning back to the group. "Then what's the plan?"

ABEL DECIDES THAT I NEED TO BE WITH EITHER HIM OR one of the others at all times. Apparently, the house I'll be living in from now on with the four of them includes lockdown capabilities and a panic room if needed. After we devise a plan to sit and wait for Daniel's arrival—not my favorite part of the conversation—Avalon steals me away and takes me on a full, actual tour. The one I hadn't gotten when I'd stayed the weekend to look after Abel.

"Are you serious about the panic room?" I ask as Avalon leads me back into the kitchen several hours later.

She snorts. "As a heart attack," she says with a shrug. "I

know, they're fucking crazy. I guess rich people have a lot of enemies."

I give her a bland stare. "You know you're one of those rich people now too," I point out.

She smacks her lips at me as she pops open the fridge and rifles through until she finds a few limes and starts chopping them up onto a plate. I don't say how weird it is that she's cutting them on a glass plate. What she does with her shit is her own business, but when she starts to add salt to one side of the plate I start to question her.

"What exactly are you doing?" I inquire.

Avalon grins at me and then leans under the counter, coming back up to produce a full bottle of high class tequila. "Is that ... a worm?" I ask.

She laughs. "Yeah, I know. Weird as fuck right?" She shakes the bottle and the little squiggly thing at the bottom sloshes back and forth.

I grimace and then step around the counter to pull the fridge door open. I pop inside, spot a ginger ale and snatch it. "I think I'll stick with this," I say.

Avalon frowns. "Tequilas are for girl talk and shit, though," she says.

I shake my head. "You drink that gut rot shit," I tell her. "I'll drink this."

She blows out a breath. "Pussy."

"Bitch," I reply automatically.

She grins. "Cunt."

"Takes one to know one."

She laughs. "Damn, I knew it."

Tilting my head to the side, I pop the tab on my ginger ale. "Knew what?"

"That he'd take the bait," she says, going back to cutting up the rest of her lime.

"Bait?" I inquire, curious.

313

"He didn't tell you?" She looks back over her shoulder before tsking. "Damn, he's got some groveling to do in his future."

"What are you talking about?" I demand.

"Abel," Avalon says.

Frustration eats at me. I know she knows what she's doing—dragging me along like she always does. That's what Avalon's good at, getting beneath people's skin and seeing through their intentions and weaknesses. It makes sense. With the kind of upbringing she had—the kind we both sort of had—girls like us don't survive by being shy and docile. I got smart, she got hard. That's just the way of our world. You get hurt and you find a way to survive.

"Come on," Avalon says a moment later once she's got everything she needs. Lifting the plate in one hand and snagging the bottle of tequila in the other—sans any sort of shot glass or chaser—she gestures me towards the french glass doors.

I open it and let her take the lead, following her out onto a covered patio. There's a beautiful eight-seater table on one side and a giant lounge area on the other. Bypassing the table, she heads for the lounge couches and takes up residence in one corner—setting her plate on one side as she opens the bottle of tequila.

Lime. Salt. Drink. I watch her slug back a few shots and then take a seat at her side, remembering when that was me a few years ago. "What's with the drinking?" I ask, curious.

She bites back a frown as she takes another shot. "Honestly?" She lowers the bottle and sets it to the side, relaxing back into the cushions as if those few gulps of alcohol have finally chilled her out. She does seem to be a bit more high strung than usual today. "Dean."

I arch my brow. "He's already driving you to drink?" I tease.

"Yeah," she mutters. "He's been shitting mad about the whole football thing, not sure if he can play or not yet, and because of that…" She blows out an angry breath, "he's taken to focusing on other extracurricular activities."

"Didn't know the sex was so bad."

She shoots me a dirty look and I muffle my laughter by pressing the edge of the can to my lips. Damn, it's good to be home. Really fucking good. A pang tightens my chest. I thought I could leave this? Really? Was I stupid? Yeah. Yeah, I was.

"If it was just sex, I'd be fine," she mutters a moment later, pulling me back from my thoughts. "No. He's back on his wedding bullshit. I begged him for a Vegas wedding. I don't give a shit about all that other stuff. The invitations. The party. The ceremony. I don't even really want to get married, but I can't help but like the idea of claiming that fucker all for myself."

"Plus you promised him when you thought he was dying," I remind her.

She groans. "Never again," she says. "He's never allowed to almost die just to get me to do something ever again."

I laugh and so does she, but I know the truth. Despite her words, I know that whatever happened that night after the original Havers' dorm burned down and she was taken by that strange blond man with the gun scared the fuck out of her.

I remember seeing her at the hospital after it all—having to get myself checked out when I had nearly gotten shot. She'd been all over Dean, more so than I'd ever seen her. Avalon is a woman who doesn't need—not people, not things, not money, not anything. For her to cling to another human being like she would die without him was startling.

"Anyway," she huffs out as she comes back down from her laughter. "Back to you. I've got a confession to make."

"Is this about Abel needing to grovel?"

"Yup." She pops that last part of the word and then chuckles slightly. "But honestly, you might thank me."

I roll my eyes. If Avalon got involved, that's not likely. "Just spit it out," I say, taking another sip. My stomach tightens and my mouth floods with saliva and I quickly set it down as I curl inward until the nausea lessens. *Damn, when was the last time I ate?*

"So, I kinda sorta forced him to take a bet to get in your pants," Avalon says.

I pause. "I'm sorry, you fucking what?"

She grins. "Well, I knew he wanted into your pants and I knew you wanted into his. I thought I'd just ... pressure him a little is all."

"And he took the fucking bet?"

She flutters her eyelashes at me. "Like a duck to water," she states. "With a hundred grand on the line too. Though, in hindsight..." She taps her bottom lip with one finger. "I don't know who won because I totally bet that he would fuck you and I think he kinda bet the same thing."

I'm still confused. "Why?"

Ava drops her hand and sits up. My back stiffens when she leans over the couch and gets closer to me. "Because he was getting in his own way, Rylie, and so were you."

I arch a brow. "You're no cupid, Avalon."

She snorts. "Yeah, no I'm not, but I'm good at anything I put my mind to. You guys needed the boost or at the very least to fuck and get it out of your system and I needed to know."

I wait for it, but nothing comes as Avalon reaches for a lime and snags her bottle of tequila. Lime. Salt. Drink. And repeat. Then she reclines back against the patio couch cushions like a queen on her throne.

"Fine," I snap. "I'll ask—what did you need to know?" The curiosity is killing me.

She grins. "I needed to know if he was any good in bed."

"Are you fucking serious?" I stare at her. "That's why you made that stupid bet?"

Avalon throws her dark hair back and laughs so hard it

shakes her entire frame. When she glances back over to my face, all she does is laugh harder, until tears are rolling down her cheeks. "Dean's possessive," she wheezes out. "But I was always curious—I mean I'm pretty sure he and Brax have shared a girl or two—oh my God, did you fuck Brax too?"

"No!" I scream. I hear the french doors open, but the next words are already in my throat and on their way out the door before I can stop it. "I didn't fuck Brax!"

Abel, Dean, and Braxton step out onto the patio and freeze —and Avalon dies. Not literally—although I'm starting to wonder if, now that I'm living here, it would be easier to sneak into her bedroom and smother her to death because that damn heat I arrived with is back on my face and staining all across my skin.

All three of the guys' eyes move from me to Avalon and back again as Avalon roars with hilarity. "She—I—fuck." I grab the bottle of tequila and take a long fucking drink.

37

RYLIE

WHAT THE HELL IS NORMAL? I don't know if I even have a normal anymore. Two weeks ago, I was the chick that sat at the back of the class and avoided all conversation with my peers. Today—the Monday after our return—I'm Abel's girlfriend. It's surreal. It's confusing. It's ... uncomfortable.

Not being near him, exactly. We haven't really seen much of each other since we got back. These last two days have been filled with everyone else. Avalon and I have been hanging out and he's been off doing whatever it is that he's doing with Braxton and Dean. I barely see him for a few hours each night and morning before we're off our separate ways again.

This is different though. This is Eastpoint University.

Abel pulls into a student parking lot and slides the Mustang into a spot towards the front of the building. There's no sign or anything, but considering that the rest of the lot is filled to the brim, I wouldn't be surprised if it was officially his. My suspicion solidifies when I spot the black SUV the others had left in earlier in the morning in the spot next to his.

As soon as we get out, the two of us meeting at the front of his vehicle where he slings an arm over my shoulder and we head off to class, I can feel eyes peering at us. There's really no specific location—it's all over—but even that puts me on edge.

Abel leans down until his lips are against my ear. "Chill, Rylie," he says. "We've got everything covered. Dean and I worked all weekend with campus maintenance and security. New cameras are everywhere. Look—" He stops to point out several new cameras anchored into the corners of buildings and lamp poles. "Trust me." His hand squeezes my opposite shoulder.

"It's not that I don't trust you," I say, shrugging away from his hold as I pick up the pace and march a few steps in front of him. "It's just that I can't help the anxiety. I don't like knowing that he could pop up at any moment."

Instead of racing after me as I half expect him to do, Abel grins and pushes his hands into the front pockets of his jeans. If anything, he slows his gait, and in turn, I slow mine. It's not intentional, but more of an automatic instinct. I wouldn't have even noticed it if he didn't grin at me knowingly.

"You running from me or something, Riot Girl?" he asks.

I shoot him a look over my shoulder and then proceed to roll my eyes. "I should be asking you that," I say snidely.

He laughs. "I'm sorry I haven't given you any attention this weekend," he says. "I was working."

I turn back around and keep marching on. I don't care that he hasn't paid me attention. Who the hell does he think I am? One of his clingy exes? I'm not a girl that needs attention. My hands tighten against the strap of my messenger bag. I catch sight of our classroom building ahead of me and hurry towards it. Just as I reach for the door, a fast as lightning palm comes out, smacking the door into place as a second grips the door's handle.

My whole body tightens all over. "Let me get that for you," Abel breathes against the back of my neck, the warm rush of air making me tingle. He nudges me to the side and pulls open the door with a flourish. "After you."

I glare at him. "Stop it."

He blinks. "Stop what?"

"This." I gesture to the door. "You've never treated me like this before. I don't like it. It makes me uncomfortable."

"Rylie ... as proud as I am that you're finally telling me what you want," he says with a shake of his head, "this is nothing. I'm just holding open your door for you." He smiles. "Like any gentleman would."

If it's even possible, my glare hardens. "You're not a fucking gentleman."

"I—"

"Excuse me..." A small, short girl slips between us and into the open door Abel's still holding.

"Oh my God," I snap. I stride forward, wrapping my fingers around his wrist as I pull him away, forcing him to release the door handle as I urge him a few feet away from the building's entrance. "You don't have to act differently, Abel. I'm already freaked out enough over what people are going to be saying, you don't have to—"

Abel moves fast. The second I release his wrist, he's got me turned and pinned to the side of the building, cutting me off. "Why would you be freaked out?" he asks, sliding one arm up and over my head as he leans down all up in my space.

My brain short circuits. Wires cross. The words that I had been about to say dry up in my throat and I forget about everything but the way he smells when he bends and brushes his lips along the line of my jaw. PDA is seriously not my thing. In fact, I'd actively avoided it with every guy I'd ever dated or fucked in high school. This, though ... this is Abel and as he's proven before, he's not exactly one to stick to my rules. He's the exception in everything it seems.

"B-because," I sputter out. "I'm not exactly—" I gasp as his free hand grips my hip and he moves closer until his hips are pressed against my stomach and I feel something long and hard against my belly. "Are you fucking serious right now?"

The grin that he gives me is so fucking boyish, I hate that it dampens my irritation. It's not just a simple curve on the side of his lips, it's also the way he tilts his head and a lock of his white blond hair falls over one side of his face. "I can't help it," he says. "Little Abel likes you."

"Well, he needs to learn some manners," I snap.

Abel chuckles and the sound reverberates through his chest and into mine. "I tried to give you manners, Riot Girl," he reminds me. "You didn't like that either."

"I—you—fuck." He's not wrong, but at the same time, I know he's intentionally twisting my words. The question is, why? I groan and let my head thump forward. I don't even care when it accidentally bangs against his chin. At least, it has him backing up ever so slightly. I can feel his gaze on the top of my head and his hand releases my waist to move up and cup my skull, his fingers rubbing through my hair as they touch and massage my scalp.

This is the real Abel, I think. He's not thinking about others looking on or opening my doors or acting like a gentleman, he's just being him.

"You never opened my door for me before," I say quietly to his chest. "It feels like an act and I don't like it."

Abel's hand in my hair pauses at those words and after a brief moment resumes its ministrations. "You know," he begins, "I don't think I've ever really had a real girlfriend." I snort. "No, seriously," he insists. I lean back and look up at him, but his head is facing the wall at my back, his eyes focused intently as if he's reading something, or trying to remember something from a long time ago. "There were girls my dad wanted me to be with—a controlling mechanism for their parents or even just to get information—and some I really liked and some I hated, but I never got to choose them. I haven't been with a single girl that I think I actually gave a shit about," he says, finally turning his gaze down so that it meets mine. "Until you."

My lips part, but no words come. He leans down and presses a kiss to them, stealing the very breath from my lungs. My hands shoot forward, tangling in his hair as I rise up on my tiptoes to keep our mouths glued to one another for as long as possible. After a moment, he chuckles and breaks the kiss.

"Don't think I'm being weird," he tells me. "I acted like a gentleman for the chicks I was using, yeah. I did it to get into their pants and get what I needed from them, but Rylie, it'll take me a lifetime to get what I need from you. For you, I'm just doing it because I want to. Can you accept that?"

I breathe through my nose as I close my eyes and try to rearrange my chaotic thoughts. I lick my lips and reopen my eyes. "Yeah, fine," I mutter as I pull my hands back from his hair and slowly lower back to my own two feet. "For now."

Abel releases me and turns me back towards the door, pushing me slightly forward. "Then get a move on. We're late." I take a single step towards the door and stiffen as a hard hand comes down on my ass, smacking it as he sprints past me.

"Abel!" I yell, but there's no heat in it. This time, when he reaches for the door and holds it out for me, I don't say anything. I hurry inside and head towards our classroom. When we enter, the professor takes one look at who's with me and returns to his lecture as if nothing is amiss. Guess there's one good thing about dating Abel Frazier. As far as anyone at Eastpoint is concerned, he's one of the few students that could —and has—gotten away with murder.

We take our seats and I spot Dash several seats over. He glances my way and tilts his head before giving me a quiet nod and returning his attention to the front. Abel sits to my right and as I open my laptop, he reaches across the keyboard and squeezes my hand. He doesn't look at me, but I can feel the warmth in his palm and it's only then that I belatedly realize I've forgotten all about the eyes on us.

The worries haven't disappeared, but when he's by my side, they're not as heavy.

Before, I would've been a wreck. Not just because of the attention we're drawing, but because we're in the midst of a calm before a giant storm. There's still the danger of Daniel lurking somewhere behind us, speeding towards us in the dark with no lights and no brakes. There's no telling when it'll arrive. No telling the havoc that will ensue. And that's when I realize that this isn't my new normal yet. This is just the waiting period. That's the real reason for my nerves. I've never given much of a fuck what anyone thought about me before, anyway. Why would I start now?

The answer: I wouldn't.

It's just a defense mechanism. An excuse to explain why I feel the anxiety of this drifting limbo we're in. Until Daniel is taken care of, I'll always be looking over my shoulder.

Against my laptop's keyboard, I flip my hand over and weave my fingers between Abel's. Neither of us says a word. We don't take notes. We just sit there for the rest of the class—with the eyes of the students on both of us like they've been on him for his entire life. Only this time, he's not alone. And neither am I.

38

RYLIE

STENCH. *It was everywhere. In my hair. In my nostrils. I could feel it embedded even in my skin. No matter what I did, it seeped down deep into my pores. It was his smell, a sick marking he left on me every time. The combination of teenage body odor and something else. Something entirely rotten.*

With tears running down my cheeks, I stand in the small cubby of a bathroom at the Dickerson house and stare up at my reflection. My six-year-old face stares back at me. Hands raw from scrubbing at my skin, trying to erase Daniel's smell. I don't ... remember this.

Did I do this?

The face in the mirror shifts and changes. Muddy brown hair grows longer, lighter, taking on the iridescent color of a faded purple. My face gets leaner. My eyes bigger. I grow taller until I realize ... that's who I am now and this place is a dream.

Which can only mean one thing.

Panic chokes my throat as I turn to the door. I don't think before my hands are already pressing into the wood. There's no signal that he's there, waiting, just on the other side. It's just a sense. A knowing that I have.

No. I thought I was free. I thought I'd overcome this. Apparently not.

I shove my hands against the bathroom door, turning my back as I hold it closed. There's no lock. There never was at the Dickerson house. Oh, how I hated that. It was in here that Daniel touched me for the first time, coming in during bath time. He'd taken Marie out and told her to go get dressed and he'd help me. I hadn't felt comfortable, but I hadn't yet known what kind of monster he was.

Then as he'd dipped his fat fingers beneath the surface of the bath water, he'd rubbed my skin under the guise of helping me wash. He'd stared at me with cold, gleaming eyes—beady eyes; the same exact feeling I'd gotten from watching those animals in Africa on the TV as they'd hunted their prey overwhelmed me.

I'd frozen in fear. Shocked and confused when he'd slipped a finger down my tummy and touched the special place that no boy was supposed to touch. Now, I'm trapped back here. In this hellish nightmare.

"Rylie." I hear him just outside the door. The handle jiggles and I squeeze my eyes shut. Where is Abel? Everything would be alright if Abel were here. But he's not. This isn't a dream that I can control, it's a memory mixed with reality. Vomit threatens to shoot up my throat.

No, I think. Be calm. Think this through. It's not real.

"Rylie, come out!" A hard fist punches the door at my back. It may not be real, but the force behind me sure fucking feels like it. Fear squeezes my throat like a vise.

I'm not his prey anymore, I tell myself. I haven't been for a very long time.

A hand snakes over my shoulder, and I scream as I realize the door has disappeared. A nightmare wouldn't be a nightmare if it was as easy as hiding from my worst fears. A taller Daniel than I remember—the Daniel I'd seen in the report or as he'd been in that bright orange prison jumpsuit of his with broad shoulders, new tattoos that he hadn't had before, and longer hair straggling down over his eyes—appears before me. His arm bands around my throat and drags me against a wide, stone-cold body. Cold like a corpse. Yet hard.

Horror shoots through me at the feeling of his cock pressing against my lower back. "Did you miss me, Rylie girl?" Daniel nuzzles into my throat as his hand clamps down on my windpipe, strangling the air from my lungs until I can't breathe.

That horrible, vile stench of his—the very one I could never scrub clean from my body—overwhelms my senses. I thrash against him even as he chuckles. There's no air. No escape. No nothing. It's just him and me. Trapped. Alone.

"I missed you..." His free hand squirms down my body until he dives into the waistband of the pants I'm wearing and he hooks two fingers into the front of my pussy and holds me there as he inhales at the place where my neck and shoulder meet. The room in front of me spins.

Can you lose consciousness in a dream? I wonder absently. I feel like I might. I don't need to breathe, yet I'm reacting exactly as I would if he were really choking me.

My dream body slowly stops fighting him. My limbs go numb. And soon, all I can feel is Daniel against me—his ice-cold fingers fucking my cunt. And worst of all, when he drags them out and holds them in front of my face ... they're wet.

His fingers are soaked, but not with desire ... with blood. As if his fingers are weapons that he dug deep inside me. More wetness seeps down the insides of my thighs. I don't have to look to know it's more blood. I'm dying ... because he's poison. Daniel is poison who destroys everything good in this world. I was stupid to think that finding Eastpoint, that trusting Abel would save me when there's nothing that I can do. Nowhere I can run to get away from the truth buried deep inside my core.

I'm tainted by the worst of the worst. I was broken long ago *and remolded into the doll of his obsession. No one—man or friend—can save me now.*

"I knew you missed me," Daniel says in my ear. "Now you're all mine."

My lips part and this time, I manage to croak out a sound and it's piercing. Ricocheting through my mind, it's the loudest scream I've ever released. I scream until I don't hear anything but the sounds of my own agony.

THE ROOM WARPS. THIS TIME, INSTEAD OF MY BODY changing, the walls and floors and ceilings around me do. They fall away, revealing Abel's bedroom and the looming figure of him perched over me on all fours.

Only then do I feel his hands on my shoulders and the rocking of the bed as he shakes me. "Rylie! Rylie, wake up! Wake the fuck up!"

I gasp and the ringing in my ears cuts off. No, not ringing. Screaming. It was me. I was the one screaming. Distantly, I hear a loud banging, and then the door to Abel's bedroom slams open and I hear the double cocking of two guns.

"It's fine!" Abel barks.

On shaking arms, I lean up and glance over his shoulder to see Braxton and Dean standing there, both shirtless and both holding up handguns as they look around the room. Heat arches up my throat and I lay back down, my fingers gripping the sheets as both a way to stabilize my surroundings and to keep myself from launching off the bed and running somewhere where I can close and lock a door and die in a pit of embarrassment.

"What's going on?" A yawning and obviously freshly woken up Avalon ambles into the room.

"Rylie had a nightmare." It takes no time at all for Abel to understand what happened, and despite the fact that he's still sitting over me—and unlike Dean and Brax, he's completely naked—he doesn't move from his spot. "I'll take care of her. You guys go back to sleep."

I hear sighs and then footsteps, but instead of checking to make sure they're leaving I hesitantly look up to the man hovering over my body. He waits until the door shuts and clicks behind him before moving. With a groan, Abel slumps down against my body, face on my chest, turned to the side as the lower half of him nestles between my thighs. It's so fucking easy to curl my hands through his hair—I like it. Just feeling the strands between my fingers has a calming effect on me.

He doesn't say anything immediately. Instead, he just lets me lay there and catch my breath, but I know it's not over yet. Not by a long shot. Thankfully, he gives me several moments to collect my thoughts before he asks.

"What happened?"

I swallow around a dry throat. "You know what happened," I tell him.

He sighs, blowing out a breath against the skin of my collarbone as he arches up and grips my hip. I don't resist as he positions himself behind me and moves until we're both on our sides with my ass in his lap and his fingers flat against my stomach beneath the tank top I wore to bed.

"You're not going to tell me what it was about?"

"You're not stupid," I say. "You know what it was about."

"Do you want me to distract you?" he offers.

Do I? A part of me says yes, but really ... is it healthy to run away from my own mind? I want to, but what is it trying to tell me? *Should I be more concerned than I am about Daniel? Is there something I'm missing?* How the hell can he just accept this and deal with the damage I'm causing as if he's no big deal?

"You're not answering me." Abel's voice dips low and the sound shivers along my spine as he presses an open mouth kiss to the back of my neck.

"I don't think it's a good idea." How I formulate those words, much less push them out between my lips, I'll never know. Whenever I'm around him, I lose sense. Some people think that falling in love brightens the world. Makes everything new. It makes you see clearly for the first time.

That's a bold-faced fucking lie.

Falling in love is like falling beneath the ice of a frost covered lake. Your limbs go numb. You can't breathe. And slowly, you start to lose consciousness. It fogs over your mind, creating confusion. You can't really connect what's happening to your body to real life and suddenly, you're far away. In a new place and you're looking down on yourself wondering ... *where the hell did I go wrong?*

"Give in," he whispers.

"Said the spider to the fly," I reply.

The deep, reverberating chuckle that leaves him rumbles against my back and I have to hold my breath to resist the urge to flip over and face him. Why does he affect me this way? Why does he drive me to absolute insanity with just the sound of his voice? "Oh, Riot Girl, you're not a fly. You're so much more than that."

"If I'm so much more, then why am I here?" I ask seriously. "Tangled up in your web like any other girl."

"Because you're smart," he says. "You know a predator when you see one, and you know when that predator wants to eat you in the most delicious way."

My eyes slide shut as his hand delves down and tugs my shirt up. Warm, rough, masculine fingers slip into my panties and spear through my wetness. He groans against my ear. "Maybe you know far more than you'd like me to think," he says. "Definitely more than you're willing to admit. What I wouldn't give to hear you say it..."

Is that what he wants? For me to say it. I never have. Not once. I don't know if I can.

My lips part and I arch as he flicks my clit, and then rubs that little bundle of nerves in a circle—slow and then fast. My hips lift to meet his movements and I follow him, chasing the feelings he elicits in me. I can't stop. He's like a fucking addiction I can't stop myself from wanting. Sparks flicker to life behind my closed eyelids. Warm breaths escape my mouth in soft pants. It's never felt like this before. Like I'm poised on the edge of a cliff about to dive into an abyss. I've certainly never wanted it the way I want him.

"That's it, Riot Girl," he says, his mouth trailing alongside my jaw as he brushes my hair back with his free hand. "Ride my hand. Get my fingers soaking wet. Give me a taste of this sweet pussy."

My head thrashes against his shoulder and the bed. "I can't," I say, panting. "I can't." This is wrong. *He's* wrong—so fucking wrong for me. I shouldn't want this. No, I think. That's just my fear talking. Abel isn't wrong. He's ... everything that's right. The only right thing that I've ever let myself have.

"You can," he urges me, and suddenly, his fingers aren't just on my clit, they're pushing even further down—dipping inside as his thumb takes over the task of driving me insane. His thick fingers push into my core, spearing me, and the rumble of a groan in his chest vibrates through me as he finds out just how wet I really am. I was never like this before, but with him, with Abel, I'm starting to realize that it doesn't matter what I've done before. He's wrecked everything in his path to get to me, completely destroyed my barriers and rebuilt them, sealing himself inside along with me.

Even if this doesn't last, for as long as I live, there will be a piece of Abel Frazier buried deep within my soul.

Abel removes his hand from my pants and underwear and moves down my body. I shiver as he strips me naked. Peeling back the layers of my pajamas like he's removing my very skin and looking into the core of me.

"Look at me," he says and I do. I look and I see. I see his everything. The sinewy muscles and the dark gleam in his eyes as he lifts me onto his strong thighs into a sitting position until my ass is pressed down into his lap. I don't fight it when he adjusts me and his cock presses into my entrance.

Abel feeds me his cock, slicing through my pussy until he feels like he's reaching the deepest parts of me. Parts I didn't even know someone could touch, much less touch with their cock. Then he turns me, his arms under my thighs holding me in place until we're facing the large mirror across the room. I forgot about that damn thing.

My face turns away, but he nudges me forward again, moving until we're on the edge of the mattress and he's holding my legs up on either side of his thighs. "Look," he commands again.

I shake my head. I don't want to. The last time I looked in a mirror was in my nightmare and what I'd seen looking back at me was the real truth. I'm nothing more than a little girl frightened of the monster that crept into my bed at night, and I always will be.

"Rylie." Abel's voice is dark, deep, entrancing. "Either you look at your reflection in that mirror now or I'll make you. And while you might enjoy coming a few dozen times, I can assure you that after a certain point, it'll get painful."

As if I'm not already well fucking aware of that. Maybe he fucked his mind stupid that first night at the hotel, but I remember very well how much it had hurt—the pleasure and pain mixing and converging and making me lose my fucking mind.

Red-faced, and jaw clenched, I consider my options. I know he'll do it. What's worse is that I know he *can* do it. Where other guys struggle to make a girl come, Abel has a magic touch.

In slow, incremental movements, I twist my head back to face the mirror.

There's a small smile on his face, but instead of its usual cockiness, there's an excitement instead. A happiness I didn't realize was missing before. He lets my legs drop on either side of his and then wraps his arms around my middle as he holds my back to his front and begins to shift his hips. I gasp as he starts to move inside of me and automatically, my gaze shoots down to the place between our legs where we're connected. It's entirely perverted, watching this. Like we're starring in our own porno. Then again, I have a feeling Abel would've been a magnificent porn star. Unfortunately for him, if he were to try now, I'd wreck any chance of anyone buying his films. The porn industry is mostly online now. I'd bury those videos of his and like a backroom creep/fangirl, I'd hoard them all for myself.

I don't like it. The idea that someone else would watch him like this, that they would experience what I am with him. I grow still. *Am I ... jealous?* Holy fuck, I think I am. Shockingly, I've never actually felt this before. This intense possessiveness. But before I can really dig any deeper into the emotion, Abel fucks up into my pussy and reaches down, smacking my inner thigh hard enough that the pain has me arching up.

"You're not paying attention, Riot Girl," he chastises. "Am I doing a bad job?" I gasp for relief as his hand moves over my pussy. "Should I spank something else?" I tighten all over, unintentionally clamping down my inner muscles as well until his hand shoots to my waist and he groans. "Fuuuuuuuuuck." He hisses out the word like it's more of a prayer than a curse. "You like that idea." It's not a question, but a knowing. "Duly noted," he says, breathing through clenched teeth. "I'll keep it in mind for another night. For now..."

His cock slides in and out of the entrance between my thighs, moving faster and faster, and I reach back, needing something to hold onto. Abel lifts his hands and feathers his fingers over the tips of my breasts, pinching and rolling my nipples between his thumbs and forefingers.

"Look," he urges again until I'm forced, with a despairing groan of desperation—why the hell can't he just fuck me and let that be the end of it?—to turn back to the mirror. In the next moment, I know why. "I'm not a ghost from your past, Riot Girl," he whispers as his eyes lock onto mine in our reflection. "I'm your present *and* your goddamn future."

My chest clenches. Oh, how I wish that was true. Pleasure arches up through me, starting from the place he thrusts into and swelling up in my stomach before spreading outward. I want it to be true, I realize. I want it all. All of his promises and hopes and dreams. A single tear leaks out of the corner of my eye and I squeeze them shut—hiding from the image that he's shoving in my face and from myself.

But it's not that easy. It never is with a man like Abel Frazier.

"Riot Girl." I shake my head at Abel's call and keep my eyes closed until I feel one of his hands leave my chest, and his fingers touch my chin, turning me to face him. Only then do my eyelids crack open and I'm faced with the most beautiful person I've ever met in my life.

I'm well aware that Abel is not perfect. Not in looks and certainly not in personality, but there has never been a man so fucking stunning in my eyes than him. He's all of the good and all of the bad I never knew I needed. It's so overwhelming, it hurts to see him, but once my eyes are on him, I can't seem to drag them away again.

He smiles, his lips spreading and his teeth glinting in the dim light right before he leans closer and presses his mouth to mine. I'm lost. Completely and utterly lost to him. And I don't think I ever want to be found. "You don't have to tell me you love me," he says, panting as he, too, gets closer to the peak.

"But you do have to tell me that you're mine. So, say it, Rylie. Tell me right now—who owns you?"

That ... I don't have any problem admitting. "You do," I whisper back. Beyond a shadow of a doubt, this man owns me—body and soul.

39

RYLIE

PURGATORY IS SO MUCH WORSE than Hell. No one will admit it, but it's true. Purgatory is a waiting ground. Where you're neither dead nor alive. Neither safe nor anything else in between. And that is exactly what the next week is like for me.

And unfortunately, because things haven't yet come to a head, I'm under house arrest—rather, since I can technically leave the house whenever I want to so long as I have someone with me, friendship arrest. If that's even a thing. If it's not, Abel has made it his mission in life to make it a thing. If he's not glued to my ass, he's got one of the others on my case.

This is how I find myself on a Friday afternoon metaphorically chained to the desk in Avalon's spare room at the Carter estate clicking away on my keyboard as I finish catching up on all of the coursework I missed. I have no doubt that had it only been me, the professors wouldn't have been nearly as forgiving, but because Braxton had been the one to gather it all up for me and contact my professors for me, they hadn't said a damn word.

Across the room, Avalon lounges on the sofa pushed into the corner against the wall, playing some sort of game on her phone. I glance back, watching her as I debate whether or not I should bring up what I'm thinking. Before I can decide, however, she speaks without looking in my direction.

"You're gonna burn a hole in the side of my face." Her tone is amused.

I breathe in and release. "I'm trying to figure out how to tell you that I can't help you with that favor you asked me for a few months ago," I admit.

It's a blow to my ego, but it's the truth. In an effort to not think about the danger I'm in or the regular nightmares that have been coming back to me all week, I've thrown myself into anything and everything that'll distract me. And one of those things was re-diving into the mysterious missing case of Avalon's only friend from high school. I don't know if it's because there's so little to go on or if the girl really is a ghost, but she's nowhere to be found.

Avalon lowers her phone to her stomach and turns her head in my direction. "You couldn't find her?"

At first, I don't say it. It's hard. I keep thinking 'maybe, if I keep trying...' but no matter how many searches I've done, my information doesn't change. I've tracked down multiple women, but each of them have something that excludes them from the list of possibilities. Age. Race. There's always something missing or wrong. It's never taken me over two months to find someone. I'm starting to wonder if Avalon didn't dream this girl up. After all, it wouldn't surprise me to find out we were her first real friends.

"Why do I get the feeling that you're thinking something insulting?" Avalon inquires with a raised brow when I don't answer her question.

Because you're a strangely observant freak of nature, I supply the answer internally. Externally, however, I shake my head and distract her with a question of my own. "Do you have any more to go on?"

Avalon sighs. "I just know her name and the house she lived in."

"Wait." Excitement courses through me. "You just told me the area. You knew the exact location she lived?"

Avalon nods. "Yeah, if you pull up a map and we go by street view, I can probably point out which one it was."

I whirl back around in my seat and do that exact thing. As soon as I have the maps and street view up for Avalon's hometown, I wave her over. "Okay," I say. "I'm gonna go street by street—you direct me."

Avalon drops her phone onto the couch and moves up behind me, settling a hand on the back of the desk chair as she leans down and watches my computer screen. I follow her directions, moving the navigation arrow across the screen as we traverse the backroads of a shitty Georgia town until we're on a stretch of abandoned highway. It's an old highway, not used commercially anymore, and obviously run down if the potholes and overgrown weeds along either side of it are any indication. Considering images on the internet maps are almost always a few years old, I doubt it's been taken care of since.

"There it is!" Avalon's finger jabs at my laptop screen and I stop moving the arrow along. Quickly I snap a picture of the front of a run-down yellow ranch house. Actually, surprisingly —considering the other images of the highway and the trailer parks that litter the back roads in the area—the house isn't uncared for. It's clean and the lawn is mowed. There aren't any tractors or cars sitting outside in disrepair in the image, but something feels off to it. I don't put my finger on it until I notice the lack of ... anything it has.

Nothing on the giant wrap around porch. No bird feeders. No wind chimes. There aren't even curtains in the window. It looks cared for, but empty...

I shake my head and dig into the location, pulling up the

coordinates, and then find the address. "Will you be able to find her with the address?" Avalon asks.

"I'm not sure," I admit. "But it'll help. I have to find out who owns the house first. Maybe she rented and if there's a contract or agreement or something, I can find her full name and from there I can track her down."

"Just..." Avalon's grip tightens against the top of the chair and I can feel her knuckles dig into my back. "Do what you can?"

I glance up and see the play of emotions over her face. She's not usually one to give into them. Whoever this girl is, she must be pretty important. I decide right then and there, that no matter what happens—I'll find her. I'll find out everything about her and I won't even think of giving in again. Even if I have to spend the rest of my life looking.

"You know," I say as I save the information and sit back, stretching my muscles as Avalon returns to the couch and snatches up her phone, "it's kinda funny."

"What is?" Avalon asks absently.

"You and Luc both wanted to find someone," I inform her. "I didn't start until I got back, but he had even less information than you did. Just a nickname."

"Hmmm." Avalon looks completely focused on whatever her phone is telling her, then I watch with dawning horror as a wicked grin crosses her features. I drop my arms down at my sides and turn my chair to face her, gripping the sides of the armrests as if I'm preparing to start running.

"Why do you have that look on your face?" I demand as she slowly lowers her phone to her side and glances over my way.

She smirks at my half-activated flight mode. "Oh, no reason," she says casually.

What a fucking liar. My eyes dart to the door.

"Oh my God, Rylie," she huffs out. "It's not that bad."

"I don't believe you," I say. "And I don't know what it is yet, so I'll be the judge of that."

"It's nothing really, we're just going to a little party tonight."

I stiffen in my seat and my head pivots back around to face her. "No."

She smiles. "Yes."

"Absolutely the fuck not."

"Awww, it's so cute when you think you have a choice, Ry-Ry."

"Can I hit you?" I'm honestly considering it. Wondering if it would be worth the inevitable beat down just to feel the glory of punching her in her amused face.

Avalon's eyebrow lifts once more. "Sure," she agrees readily, "as long as you're aware that I hit back."

My mind screams *danger* at that. No. Not worth it. I groan and cover my face with my hands. "Please not another stupid party," I grumble.

"Don't worry," she says. "You're one of us now—you won't get left behind."

With a startling realization, I realize that she's right. That, however, only makes it so much worse. This will be the first party where I'm going as Abel Frazier's official girlfriend. There's bound to be some sort of trouble.

Avalon laughs at the expression on my face and marches over to slip a hand over my shoulder. I release my face and look up at her. "You need to lighten up," she tells me. "When shit hits the fan, you can stress out. For tonight, just ... drink and dance and get dicked."

There it is. Avalon Manning's wise words of wisdom. *Get Dicked.*

Hours later and a few pounds of makeup heavier—courtesy of a determined Avalon with time to kill—hard rock filters out from the front of club Urban. Avalon parks and we head up to the front. I duck as we bypass the girls in sky high heels and short skirts waiting in line as they glare our way. Or rather, my way. No one in their right mind would turn their glare on Avalon.

She flips her dark hair over her shoulder without a care and squeezes into the club ahead of me. With a sigh I follow, only to stop as a muscled arm comes down in front of me. "Back of the line," the bouncer snarls.

"I—"

"No." Avalon's voice rings above the music thrumming from inside the club and the people chatting outside.

The bouncer turns his head. "Sorry, Miss Manning," he says, pulling his arm back. "I didn't realize she was with you."

I shoot him a look. Doubtful, I think. I'd been right on her ass. He just wanted to exert his dominance over someone he saw as lesser than. Why? I eye him knowingly. Because he's seen me before. He's another program student on scholarship at Eastpoint. At school, he's the lowest of the low. But here—here, he's the gatekeeper.

"She's not with me," Avalon corrects him with an arched brow. The bouncer frowns at her before glancing at me. "Rylie?" She looks at me expectantly and I realize what she's doing. She's giving me an opportunity here to assert myself.

My insides riot against it. I don't want to. But one look at the bouncer's annoyed expression makes my irritation flare to life. I step up until I'm right in front of him and when he moves back, I just do it again until he realizes that I'm not going anywhere.

"I don't need to be with anyone," I tell him slowly, "to be allowed in this club."

He blinks. "But—"

Avalon laughs, cutting him off. "There," she says. "You heard her. Let the goth princess in or you can suffer my wrath and then Abel's."

The guy's eyes widen impossibly large and he practically catapults himself away from me, slamming into the brick wall at his back as I step past him and into the club. I don't turn my head and glance back to see if he's okay, or to see if anyone's watching. I know they are. And though it still makes me uncomfortable—the thought of being anyone's center of attention curdling anxiety in my gut—I keep my head up and keep walking.

Avalon leads the way and I follow behind, content to just be for now. In fact, that little run in at the front door has my body buzzing with adrenaline. I glance to the dance floor with longing. I need something to release it all.

"You coming?" Avalon's words have me jerking my head back as I realize she's already ascended the stairs all the way to the top of the VIP area and I'm still standing at the bottom, looking back the way we came.

"Yeah." I take the first step. "I'm coming."

The VIP area has far fewer people than the last time I was here. Last time there were still several of the football players from Eastpoint milling about, plus the Sick Boys, and a few women I hadn't recognized. Now, despite the crowded first floor, the VIP lounge is empty save for the three men sitting around a grouping of lounge furniture with drinks in hand.

Though I haven't been gone for long, it feels like eons ago that I had been summoned up here. My head lifts and my gaze meets a pair of striking blue eyes across the room. Abel doesn't bother waiting for me to come to him. As Dean sits back and opens up his arms for Avalon to slide into his lap, Abel does the exact opposite.

My feet fix themselves to the floor as I watch him stand and make his way towards me. His arms come around my body,

341

pulling me into a solid chest as he leans down and takes my mouth. His kiss is wicked. Sinful. Like an out of control fire that cannot be stopped. I can't help but give into it—and him. My mouth opens for him and I wrap my own arms around his neck as I accept his kiss, letting him feed me his tongue as I stroke it with mine. My chest pumps up and down as I try to draw breath. Every time I think he's going to pull back, he turns his head and dives in for more.

It isn't until someone behind him coughs meaningfully that Abel finally releases me from the confines of whatever spell he wove over me. With a huff, he turns and glares at whoever it was behind me. Then he leads me over to everyone else and we sit.

And suddenly, it becomes simple. Sitting here, talking with Abel's friends, talking with Avalon. As if they're normal people and not the ones who've controlled my life for the last year and a half. I realize it's because they are normal people. To each other, they are everything everyone else is. They're college students. Kids in love. Kids in hate. People on the verge of life that haven't yet discovered the breadth of what they can truly do.

I never saw it before because I was always on the outside looking in. Not through any fault of theirs or mine, but because that was how it had to be. If only temporarily.

For the longest time, I sit there, lounging against Abel as he talks to the guys. When they offer me alcohol, I shake my head and accept soda water instead. After what feels like an hour or so, the need to get up and move can't be denied any longer. I eye Avalon, willing her to meet my gaze. It's time to put those freak of nature observation skills of hers to use.

She glances my way and raises her brows. I nod to the exit and she grins. "Well, guys," she announces, pressing her palms down against Dean's legs as she pushes herself up to standing, "I'm gonna go for a dance. Rylie?"

I'm up and out of my seat before she's done saying my name and making my way towards the exit. "We'll be back soon," Ava calls behind us. I doubt they'll let us stay gone for long, but for now, maybe she's right—maybe it's time to just dance and forget the stress and danger we're all facing.

One night. That's all I want. One night to feel normal. One night to just be a regular teenage girl. Who knows? Maybe Abel will come down and remind me. After all, he's the only one that's ever made me feel normal.

40

RYLIE

THE MUSIC IS a thumping bass that echoes up the walls of Urban's open industrial sized interior. I feel it speed through my bones, thrumming in my marrow as I move in time to the beat. Avalon has her hands up in the air as she dances alongside me.

Anywhere else, she would probably suffer from guys trying to grope her. She's that fucking beautiful. I'm as straight as can be, but even I can recognize that. Her face lifts to the ceiling and a smile spreads her lips. I glance and follow her gaze to where all three guys stand against the VIP balcony's railing, watching us.

I sway back and forth, slowing my movements as my gaze attaches itself to Abel and his to mine. Lights flicker over the support beams above his head, reflecting back down on the dance floor. Red. Blue. Purple. Green. Yellow. Lasers shoot across the room, spreading out into a million different directions. So many at once that I can't even imagine where they all end up.

Abel watches me with the corners of his mouth tilted down. *Is he upset?* I wonder. *Why?*

My heartbeat scrambles inside my chest when he suddenly pushes away from the railing, turns, and disappears. Across from me, Avalon chuckles.

"What?" I ask her.

Light flashes over my eyes, blinding me momentarily as my swaying picks up with the next song.

She shakes her head in a non-answer, but I watch as her eyes glance back up anyway. Once again, I follow them to see that Abel's not the only one that's disappeared.

Ahhh. I see now.

My own lips curve upward, and it's only a matter of time before I catch sight of a familiar blond head working its way through a crowd that parts easily enough. Where others are struggling to find and maintain their space on the dance floor— with people crowding and drinking and laughing and acting up —Abel doesn't have a problem moving through the throng of people until he finds me.

And I don't hesitate to lift my arms to him when he approaches. His palms find my hips and I'm pulled into his body. I go without resistance, closing my eyes to the feel of him against me as he grinds into my stomach.

"Do you like playing with me like this, Riot Girl?" he asks. "Did you know how hot I'd find your little dance? Did you want to tease me?"

No. It hadn't been about that at all, but am I sorry? Again, the answer is not at all.

Chuckling to myself, I arch my arms around his neck and tip my head back. The tips of my hair scrape against the small of my back where my shirt has lifted just enough for a scant couple inches of skin to be revealed. Abel wastes no time sliding his fingers right beneath the fabric, the warmth of his palms making me shiver in both surprise and anticipation. My flesh feels cold against his. So much that it feels like he's on fire and he's burning me from the inside out.

"You're fucking with me, Rylie," Abel confesses on a growl that only serves to make me smile even more.

I'm really not, but I like that he thinks so. It means that his thoughts are in line with mine.

"Do you want to do something about it?" I challenge.

My answer comes in the form of action more than words. Abel lifts me up off the floor, his hands shooting under my thighs as he urges me to wrap my legs around his waist. My cheeks burn with embarrassment and I'm really starting to wish I'd worn pants instead of a black and purple plaid skirt. It's long enough that it still falls over my ass to cover everything, but if he drops me, I'll flash far more than I want to.

He doesn't say a word as he pivots and starts off. I lift my head, gazing back over his shoulder as I see Avalon and Dean dancing on their own with her back to his chest as she reaches back with one hand clasped around the back of his neck. She's got her eyes closed and her body molded right to his. Before, I would've been jealous. I would've wondered how the hell could someone look so content with another person touching them— like all was right with the world when she was with him?

Now, I know.

Abel carries me off the dance floor and as soon as the others are out of sight, I burrow into the place where his neck meets his shoulder—unwilling to look at anyone else we pass. His fingers dig into the skin of my thighs, more heat flashing through me.

It isn't until the music grows startlingly quieter—only an echo through walls and doors—that I finally lift up and take a look around. "Where are we?" I ask. It looks like a long hallway. Perhaps an employees' entrance? The walls are painted black and at the end of the corridor is an illuminated neon red sign reading *exit*.

Abel doesn't answer me. Instead, he whirls around and presses me against the side of the hallway—my back to the wall.

A gasp leaves my lips as his head dips down and he takes my lips with a savage intensity. Want. Desire. Longing. It all piles up inside of me and only releases when he puts his mouth on mine.

A groan bubbles up his throat as his hands work their way beneath my skirt. "You naughty girl," he whispers, pulling back slightly. "I told you that underwear only gets in the way."

I close my eyes and inhale sharply. He should be calling me naughty for another reason, I think as I reach down and touch his hand. Though I didn't expect we'd be doing it here, I knew he would be at Urban and I know how easy it is for me to get carried away when I'm around him. I guide his hand up the sides of my legs until he touches the strings of my panties.

Abel freezes when he feels the little ribbon on the side and with an arched brow, he stares down at me as he tugs and it loosens. A brilliant smile overtakes his face. "I take that back," he whispers, ripping the rest of the ribbon free before doing the same to the other side. "Good girls that come prepared should get rewarded." My underwear flutters to the floor between us as he forces my legs open, making me release him from my grasp, and my feet drop to the floor.

My breath catches in my chest as he gives me an entirely too devious look and slowly—ever so fucking slowly—goes to his knees before me. I never in a million years thought this would be something I'd ever see. Abel Frazier ... on his knees in front of me with a reverent look on his face as he leans forward and presses an open-mouthed kiss to my thigh.

His fingers lift the hem of my skirt and he disappears underneath it. A split second later, his hot mouth finds my core. A cry is ripped from my throat. I couldn't stop it even if I had wanted to. The pleasure that zings through me lights me up inside. It's heavy and almost terrifying, the things he makes me feel.

Fingers grip one of my legs and direct it over his shoulder, giving him more room. I'm standing there in the back hallway of Urban with my legs spread and a Sick Boy sucking at my clit. This could not be further from the future I predicted for myself, and yet, I couldn't give a fuck less. I'd willingly walk the same path I always have—scars and nightmares and all—so long as that route will always lead back to him.

One of my hands snakes its way down until I'm touching the back of his head, feeling the silky strands of his hair against my palm. God, he knows how to move his tongue. Back and forth, he sinks it into my pussy before pulling it out and moving back up to circle my clit and suck it into his mouth. Dangerous, wicked men and their mouths are the most deadly of creatures.

My back arches against the wall as one of Abel's hands comes into the mix. Two fingers spear me deep and I go up on my tiptoes as the pressure becomes too much. Against my will, my hips begin to rock.

I don't want it to end yet, I think. *I'm not ready. I want it to last.*

I want to stay here in this fantasy world with him for a little bit longer.

"Rylie..." Abel's voice is harsh, a rasp on the stale air. "Come for me, sweetheart." I squeeze my inner muscles as he continues thrusting his fingers in and out of my pussy and blows a slow breath across my clit. That little puff of air does horrible things to the fragments of my mind that he'd already shattered into a million little pieces. "Come all over my mouth and fingers, Riot Girl," he orders. "And when you're done, I'm gonna make you taste yourself on my tongue."

Fuck. That does it. That last sentence sends me screaming over the edge. My hand locks against his head as Abel leans forward and seals his lips against my clit and sucks. Fuck him, but I never knew dirty talk could be so good. It's not just good with him though; it's catastrophic.

I'm thankful that no one appears to use this hallway when

people are working. I'm thankful that the walls are thick and that the music is loud enough on the other side of the door at the end that hopefully no one can hear me. Because as a white light bursts behind my closed eyelids, my lips part and I release a scream so loud it could wake the dead.

Body shaking. Limbs numb. Pussy throbbing. I come. I come hard and fast—like being hit by a freight train.

That's it as well, I realize. That's exactly what it feels like to fall in love with Abel Frazier. Surprise over my own internalized thought fills me. I realize what I just admitted—if only to myself. I ... love him. I love Abel Frazier. Holy fuck.

When I come back to my senses, he drops my leg and stands up in a quick rush, gripping my face and tilting my head up—mouth open. Just as he always does, he invades—taking no prisoners and destroying everything in his path. My sanity is not spared.

He kisses me openly, our tongues moving against one another and there's no room for me to pull back. Not that I would, but even the feel of his fingers gripping my jaw—keeping me in place—as he lets me taste myself on his lips, is having an effect. I can't think. I can't breathe. I can't fucking spare a millisecond of time to even do anything else but bask in this moment. In him.

When he finally deigns to release me from his grasp, I'm panting and soaked between my legs. I can feel the wetness there, against my inner thighs. The smile he gives me is just as breath-stealing as his kiss.

He strokes my cheek. "Let's go home, Riot Girl."

My chest rises and falls as I try to squeeze as much oxygen into my lungs as possible. Somehow, I manage a reply. "What about the others?"

Abel shakes his head. "We'll take my car," he says, reaching into his pocket and holding up his keys—they're not the Mustang keys, though. My internal slut—which I didn't even know I had—is a little disappointed by that. I want to fuck him again in the Mustang, specifically in his front seat or maybe even on the hood. I've never truly wanted to fuck someone, but Abel, I'm realizing, is the exception to all of my rules.

I reach down, letting my fingers intertwine with his, and I grin back at him. "Let's go then."

Together, we head down the hallway, towards the red exit sign. Abel moves forward first, pushing against the latch bar handle and dragging me out after him. He half stumbles over a brick laying in the alleyway and I laugh as he catches himself.

It could've been a scene from a cheesy romantic movie. The boy who was damaged finding his girl. The girl who didn't know her own worth finding her guy.

But unfortunately, our story was never supposed to be some sweet, loving film.

A minute later, as the two of us head towards the open mouth leading into the parking lot, reality comes crashing back down.

A lone figure steps out, backlit by one of the street lamps. My heart stops and restarts, this time racing faster than it has before. "Abel!" I gasp, reaching up and latching onto his arm as I try to stop him. My feet stumble and I turn back. We have to run. We have to go back inside. We have to call the cops. Something!

But it's too late. For him and for me. Because the man at the edge of the alley isn't the monster I fear. That monster is far closer than I thought.

Another shadow passes over the pavement under my feet and I glance up just in time to watch as a baseball bat comes down hard—crashing against the back of Abel's skull. Blood splatters across my face—over my cheek and nose as Daniel lifts it again and Abel crumples to the ground.

My face tilts back, and I know there will be no running for me. Even if I could get away, I wouldn't leave Abel here like this. I can't. Tears fill my eyes and spill down my cheeks as Daniel looks down at me—his dark eyes gleaming in the darkness.

"Hello, little Rylie," he says. "Did you miss me?" A moment later, the baseball bat cracks across my face, and I, too, fall into a pit of oblivion. There's no more room to fear what we don't know is coming because it's already here.

41

RYLIE

Drip.

Drip.

Drip.

There's an ache behind my eyes, at the back of my head. A pounding in my temples and a dryness in my mouth. Everything hurts. The pain in my head doesn't explain the pain in my back and arms though. The skull agony is obviously from taking a baseball bat to the cranium. My back and arm pain, however, is because I've been tied to a metal bed frame in an uncomfortable position.

I know I shouldn't move. I shouldn't do a damn thing except take deep breaths and try to keep up the facade that I'm still unconscious.

Drip.

Drip.

Drip.

Ugh. There's that annoying sound again—the repetitive tinking of water slowly dripping against a basin—probably a sink.

Come on, Rylie, just do it, I order myself. *Open your eyes.* I need to check the room. I need information. I need answers. Where am I? Is anyone else in the room? And most importantly, where is Abel?

That last question is the one that encourages me to finally do it. My eyelids crack open into little slivers the second it passes my mind and when I find the room empty save for myself, I open them all the way, craning my neck as I take in the rest of the dingy little room.

Shockingly, it looks like Daniel has made plans for me. The room itself isn't exactly equipped, but it is prepped for a longer stay. There's a toilet in the corner next to the source of the infernal dripping—not a sink, but an open shower with a drain in the concrete beneath it. The whole room is made of it—like a concrete prison.

There isn't a single window and no clock in my line of sight. With mounting panic, I realize I don't know how long I've been out for. I don't know where I am. I don't know what time of day it is. My chest squeezes tight and another horrible reminder comes to me as I shift my legs against the lower half of the striped mattress beneath me. My underwear is missing.

My head thumps back against the mattress. Fuck. Abel and I had been so absorbed in what we were doing, we'd let our guard down. We're lucky Daniel didn't catch us in that hallway. If he'd seen what Abel was doing to me—and how I was reacting to it—there's no telling what he would've done. How he would've reacted.

The door across the room clicks, signaling the entrance of an intruder. My head jerks up, but a moment later, my brows lower in confusion when a rather skinny, greasy-looking man enters, his hands shaking as he holds up a tray and shuffles across the room. He doesn't even look at me as he leaves the door open and moves to the table beside the bed, setting it down. It's no use anyway, but I still try to see what's on the tray. It's just there in my peripheral vision. I can catch glimpses of white and shapes, but nothing definitive that tells me what it is.

The not knowing is worse than anything else.

I always wondered if Daniel knew that. If he understood that even on the nights he didn't visit me, I would lay in my bed with eyes wide open and locked on the bedroom door—waiting. I wondered if he got off on the fear and the fact that I was always thinking of him, when he would come back. Maybe that's why he was convinced I was in love with him, because I was always watching him—trying to gauge his interest or attention or mood, ready to adapt if he seemed angry or something else. Or maybe he never even noticed. Maybe my fear never even occurred to him. He's self-absorbed and delusional after all.

I shake my head. Now is really not the fucking time to reminisce. I need to find out where Abel's being held. "Who are you?" My question comes out on a dry croak and I wince when my throat tightens in resistance to the words.

The man pauses and finally looks at me. That's when I realize his eyes are dilated—his pupils blown. His face is haggard and dirty, his beard laced with a white dust. I blink. Oh fuck. An addict?

"Get out!" I jump at the sound as a deep, reverberating voice sounds throughout the room.

The man starts and his hand smacks the tray on the table. Something I can't see clatters to the floor. My eyes jerk to Daniel as he strides into the open doorway and without a second of hesitation, he backhands the older man across the face. A moment of pity hits me as the man goes flying into the wall.

"Get your disgusting self away from her," Daniel growls. "Go fucking sleep off your damn high, you piece of shit."

"I-I was just doing w-what you asked." When the man speaks, it's with a whimpering stutter.

"Does it look like I give a shit?" Daniel snaps. "If you saw she was awake, you should've come to get me." He reaches down, hooking his paw-like hand into the back of the man's shirt collar, and lifts him up as if he weighs nothing. Daniel tosses him towards the door and when the man lands, he scrambles up to his hands and knees and hurries from the room —slamming the door on his way out and leaving me alone with the very creature who started this all.

Fine trembles start in my limbs, working their way across my body. Daniel's head turns towards me. It's one thing to see his looks in a photograph on a computer screen. It's a completely different thing to see it in person after so many years.

Vomit threatens to rip up my throat and by sheer force of will, I manage to keep it down, even as Daniel moves closer, grabbing a chair and dragging it to my bedside as he reaches out and runs a finger down my face.

"It's been a long time, Rylie girl," he says.

I hadn't been given a chance to really reconcile myself with it but his voice hasn't changed once in all the years we'd been separated. By the time I met Daniel, the croaky and cracking voice of puberty had already passed. His voice is just as deep now as it was then. It's the voice of a man, but I'm not the same scared little girl.

Resolving myself to getting my answers, I lick my lips and open my mouth. "Here," he says, stopping me before I can speak. He reaches for the bedside table and lifts a glass of water.

I narrow my eyes on the offering as he pushes it against my lips. "Don't worry," he says, "it's not drugged."

"How can I trust you?" I say.

"I don't want you asleep yet," he says simply. "We have so much to catch up on."

He gives me a smile. Hesitantly, I part my lips and take a

sip of water. The cool liquid is like manna on my tongue. I gulp back more. He shushes me as his free hand touches my hair, smoothing it back from my face as I drink down half the glass. I want to throw him off me. I want to—for the first time in my life —be brave. I want to fucking stab the hands that think they can touch me without my permission.

Yet, here I am ... powerless.

"There's a good girl," Daniel praises me as he takes the glass back and puts it back on the table.

I lick my lips again. "Where's the man I was with?" I finally demand

He stiffens in his seat, half facing away. "Why?" he asks, cutting a hard look at me as he turns back to me. "Is he important?"

He has no fucking idea how important Abel Frazier is. Not just to me, but to the people who love him.

"Is he dead?" I ask.

Daniel leans back in his chair. "Maybe he is," he hedges. "That would be a deserving punishment for you, I think."

I grit my teeth, the back of my skull pounding. I shouldn't provoke him. I know it's wrong, but the words are spilling from my lips before I can stop them. "You better hope he's not dead, Daniel," I hear myself say. "Or you're in so much fucking trouble."

Daniel's eyes harden. Silence descends between. It's the kind of quiet that happens in horror movies right before someone's about to die. It sinks in my ears, burrows in my mind, and sets my fear on fire. I shove it back. I don't have the luxury of giving in to my fear, no matter how much I want to. Maybe before I would have, but I have more than myself to think about now. I'm not the only one who can be hurt by Daniel's actions and obsession. That, more than anything else, is what now drives me.

"It doesn't have to be like this," I say. "Let me go, Daniel. If you just let me go, I promise you'll walk away from this." *Tonight,* I mentally amend. *You'll walk away tonight.* After that, though ... Abel and the guys will be after him and there won't be a corner on this Earth that he can run to or hide in.

Daniel is quiet for a moment and then he leans forward, the shaggy brown hair around his face shifting over his features as he sets his elbows on his knees and laces his fingers together beneath his chin.

The strangest thing about seeing my childhood nightmare brought to life before me again is that I'm noticing things differently. There's no denying that Daniel Dickerson is a big guy. He's easily six feet tall if not bigger, but when I was a small six-year-old girl, he'd seemed like a giant. In my nightmares, he'd had razor sharp teeth and jagged bones under his skin. Beady eyes and veins that stuck out. Reality is far different. Reality proves that he's just ... a man. An average man.

He's neither handsome nor particularly ugly. Not like villains in movies or novels. If anything, he's kind of plain. With the right clothes and dressing, he'd be just another face on the street. And no one would know the obsessive stalker lurking beneath. It's almost funny. Perhaps it would be, if I wasn't so piss-my-pants scared right now over what he's done to Abel.

"Now," he begins, disrupting my thoughts. "Why would I let you go, Rylie?" he asks. "When I've spent so long searching for you."

I open my mouth to tell him—to warn him, but he beats me there.

"You have no idea how long I've waited for our reunion, do you?" he asks. "Thirteen years away from you." He shakes his head, sitting up straight as he pushes back his hair to reveal his full face as he stares at me. "I was angry at you, you know," he says almost conversationally.

I swallow reflexively, waiting for those words to turn into actions, but he doesn't move. He doesn't get up. He doesn't start yelling. That was something he definitely would have done thirteen years ago. Instead, he remains seated as he watches me.

"I was angry that you told everyone about our secret time. I knew they wouldn't understand it. I warned you it was a bad idea." His exact words, as I recall them, had been *you wouldn't want everyone to know what a little whore you are for me, would you?* And I'd believed him.

"But you know, all that time in prison really helped me. They give you a lot of things in there—but the best thing they give you is time. You know what I did with that time, sweetheart?" I want to punch his stupid fucking face at that nickname. I used to hate it when people called me that, but every once in a while, the word will slip from Abel's lips into my ear and it makes me feel things I thought I'd buried. Things I thought weren't meant for me anymore. To hear him call me that feels like an insult. Instead of saying so, however, I just grit my teeth and wait for him to finish.

"I learned," he says. In a burst of movement, he's up and out of his chair. My eyes widen as he leans over me, hand on my throat. "I learned the necessary skills to find you again and bring us back together."

He squeezes until I feel heat in my face not from embarrassment or self-imposed humiliation but from lack of oxygen. His grip is too tight, and I can't breathe.

"I know what you've been doing, Rylie girl," Daniel says. "You think you're the only one with technology skills?" Shock rockets through me. He knows? He grins as if to say 'yeah, that's right.' "Did you know prisoners can get access to college courses even in jail?" he asks, though it's clear by the way his hand remains on my throat, keeping me from responding, that he doesn't expect an answer. "They felt so sorry for me, you know. A lot of people didn't believe that a sixteen-year-old would fall in love with a little girl. The other prisoners didn't really give a shit. After they moved me to my more permanent home, they ignored me. And all I did after I turned eighteen was work out, learn, and wait."

His fingers press down on the sides of my throat; the space between his thumb and forefinger crushes against my trachea. "Workout," he says again. "Learn. Wait. And. Repeat."

Black spots dance in front of my vision and no amount of working my jaw loosens his grip enough for me to squeeze in even an inch of breath.

"I was on my best behavior for you," he tells me, growing ever closer until his face is hovering right above mine. Just like one of my nightmares, only this time, it's for real. "They didn't even notice when I started experimenting with the coding I was learning in my classes. All they thought was—wow, this kid is so smart. How sad that his life was ruined by a little girl who lied. They didn't know that it was all for you. All so I could track you down when I got out, so I could find you. And all that coding? I was building websites, hacking into security cameras —did you really think adding more on campus would be safe?" He laughs at that and it finally clicks.

He had probably hacked the security footage to find out where I was and as soon as he saw an opportunity where I was vulnerable, he struck. He had planned all of this. Had he started the day he went away?

"You tried to run and for a while, it was hard to follow you, but then imagine my luck," he continues. "You pop back up at your university—your face all over the cameras as you walk towards class like it's no big deal—a week later. I was so happy to see you."

Those extra security measures Abel and the others had put in had backfired so fucking hard.

"But." I cough as his arm jerks down and the back of my head is pressed even harder into the mattress—making the dull ache from the baseball bat flare up once more. "What I wasn't happy to see was that little parasite, hanging all over what was mine." My chest tightens. "Watching him touch you and kiss you on campus all week was its own personal brand of torment," he confesses. "I was wondering if you were punishing me for not coming soon enough."

I try to shake my head, to tell him no. I can't think clearly. The black dots have gotten wider and I feel like I'm going to pass out. Then, just as abruptly as he grabbed me, he releases me. I cough, the sound wet and dry in the same instance. It's a hacking cough and I turn my cheek to the side and spittle flies out. Oxygen—blessed, fresh oxygen—enters my lungs and the black dots grow fainter and fainter until they're almost completely erased. The aftereffects, however, remain in place. My throat still feels like it's been ravaged.

"Even if you were trying to torture me, Rylie girl," Daniel says, "I've decided the best thing to do was just ... kill him."

"No!" The word is breathless, barely there. My voice gone, ripped from me by his own hands. Tears burn in my eyes. "No!" I try again, but it's the same result.

"Don't worry," Daniel says, cupping my cheek. "I wanted to wait until you woke up. You wait right here. I'll be back. I'll punish him for you, sweetheart. And once he's dead..." His hand drifts down my chest, over my stomach, and lingers above the apex of my thighs. "We can start all over again."

42

ABEL

THERE'S dust in my eyes when I slowly rise to the waking world. I feel the grimy, gritty particles clinging to my lashes and my skin. I'm dirty and sore all over. That's what I get for being taken out by a fucking baseball bat of all things. I groan quietly and the sound echoes around the empty room I'm in. When I shift and bump into something, I realize I'm kneeling in a fetal position with my hands tied at the small of my back. From the feel of the hard plastic digging into my wrists—it's zip ties. That, thankfully, is in my favor. This would be easier to pull off if my hands had been tied in front of me, but I just have to work with what I've got.

I adjust and move again, bumping into something cold and metal on the opposite side. Blinking my eyes open, I see long bars, several in a row and a few across. My head jerks up and I curse as it bangs into the ceiling of the container I'm in.

No. Not a container. A fucking dog kennel. I'm locked in a dog kennel with my hands zip tied at my back. If I'd had my hands free, this would've been a cakewalk, but no. Rylie's fucking stalker wasn't as dumb as I'd pegged him. Now it's time for me to admit the truth.

I fucked up.

Not just a little bit, either. I royally fucked up. And in this case, it's unacceptable. Because this isn't just my life we're talking about. It's Rylie's.

Dean and Braxton and I had spent all fucking week prepping for something like this. It was the whole reason we'd been alright with coming out tonight when Avalon had asked. We thought we were good. We thought we were safe, at least for the time being.

We'd been dead fucking wrong.

I'm on my knees, bent over—my head screaming at me as blood dries on my scalp and temples.

The second I'm free, I'm going to rip through this place and find my girl. Once I know she's safe, then and only then will I make that fucker pay.

Ignoring the pain in my wrists, back, neck, and head, I move down the black sheet-like bottom of the kennel and squirm my fingers back and forth. I'm gonna risk breaking my own arms or popping them out of place, but if that's the price I pay for freedom, so be it.

I tug at the bands as much as I can, tightening them until I can hardly feel the tips of my fingers. With a deep breath, I lower my head to the bottom of the kennel and lift my arms up and stretch them as far up as I can. Before I can bring them down hard and fast, effectively snapping the zip ties, the door to the room I'm being held in kicks open, and the man who thrust me in here earlier steps into view.

His eyes are cold as he glares down at me. "Time to serve your fucking purpose, dog."

Oh yeah, I think. *I'm gonna fucking kill you. And I can't fucking wait.*

The man walks over to me and opens the kennel door, reaching in and locking his hands on the back of my head. Using my hair as a hold, the fucker drags my ass out of the kennel; my numb legs make it hard for me to get to my feet once I don't have something keeping me in the fetal position. I grit my teeth against the pain and ignore the anger pounding through me. With any luck, he's taking me to Rylie and that's exactly where I need to be.

I need to see her. I need to establish that she's okay.

Thankfully, it seems that's exactly what the dead motherfucker is doing. Tugging at my hair and yanking me along a dim hallway and down a set of stairs that looks like a half-finished basement with some of the walls ripped up and soundproof insulation only partially installed. He drags me across the space before he throws me into a room at the end of the basement and when my eyes hit the bed, I spot her.

My chest squeezes in relief and in renewed anger. There's blood on the side of her face as well, fear in her eyes, and her hands are above her head tied to the metal headboard of a bare twin sized mattress.

My knees hit the floor, but that doesn't stop me from moving. I jerk up and I'm already launching myself towards her —despite not being able to do shit with my own hands—before I'm even in the room for a minute.

"Whoa there, buddy." The big, burly man behind me says in clear amusement as he catches my ass and turns, slamming me down against a chair. I clamp my jaw shut when he reaches back, grabbing my impossibly tightly bound wrists, and yanks them up and over the back of the chair to keep me stable— damn near breaking my arms in the process. "There we go," the fucker says. "Nice and stable." He turns to Rylie. "Now. Let's get started. Shall we."

The punch comes flying out of nowhere, his big ass knuckles slam into the side of my face and up to my eye socket. "Fuck!" The word shoots out of my mouth as the room spins and the skin above my brow splits.

The blows don't stop there. No, they keep coming. He must

have been wanting to do this for a while because the next thing I know, they're raining down like goddamn confetti and all I see are his fists. He doesn't just go for the face either, he peppers them all over. In my gut. My shoulder. My temples. He hits me wherever he can reach me, and when I'm gasping for air after having the air knocked out of my lungs, he grips my hair once more and yanks my head up.

He jerks it towards the bed and through blurry, tear streaked eyes, and red—fuck, is there blood in my eyes?—I see Rylie laying there, kicking and screaming, as she fights against her bonds.

"Shut the fuck up, Rylie!" the man screams. "You know I have to do this. I'm teaching him a lesson. He's going to learn what it costs to put his hands on what's mine. After this is all over and we bury his body together, I'll make sure you never have to see something like this again, but Rylie girl ... look at me."

She's sobbing, her pale cheeks layered with black makeup as she grits her teeth and glares at him. That's my girl, even scared out of her mind she's still got some fight in her. I suck in a breath and pray the guys are already on their way. Never in my fucking life have I been more grateful for our emergency security measures, and even if Rylie's stalker got the drop on me once, my shoes are still on and I know there are microchips embedded in the bottom. The guys will know I haven't made it home. They'll know when I don't answer the phone—not even for our emergency line—that I'm in trouble.

It's only a matter of time, but this fucker has already signed his death warrant.

Then what he says hits me.

"The fuck did you just say?" The words snap out of my mouth and I turn my cheek, spitting blood onto the concrete floor. "Did you just say she's yours?"

He turns back and glares at me, releasing my head as he

arches a brow. "That's right," he states. "The girl you've been fucking with is mine." He points to Rylie. "And she's the reason you're going to die tonight."

I laugh, the sound loud as it echoes up the hard walls. "I knew you were ugly, man," I tell him honestly, shaking my head even as the room spins. It hurts to breathe, so I must have a few fractured ribs. Possibly even broken ones. I can't think of them right now, though. There's too much at stake to give a shit about a few broken bones. "But I, at least, gave you the benefit of being not completely fucking stupid."

With a roar, the man attacks me. His punches hit—but they no longer feel as concise and planned. He screams in anger, spittle flying in my face, and he hits me so hard that the chair I'm in falls over and my whole body slides up and I'm free of the back support.

Turning my cheek, I spit out a wad of blood and grin up at the behemoth standing over me. "Wow, is that really the best you got, man?" I taunt. "Does it make you feel better to fuck me up, knowing she doesn't want you? That she never fucking wanted you and you were just a sick perv who took advantage of a little girl?"

"Shut! Up!" He then rears back and slams the toe of his boot right into my gut. It takes everything I have not to vomit right then and there. If my ribs weren't shattered before, they certainly didn't make it through that unscathed. He bends down, his voice rising in pitch. What a little fucking bitch he is. A petulant child, mad because the toy he wants to play with is no longer his. Was never his to begin with. "She loves me!"

"She fucking hates you!" I scream back, even as my sides cave in on themselves and dizziness assails me. Fucking hell, I can't pass out here.

His fat fingers latch onto my shirt, gripping tight as he lifts me from the floor and slams his knuckles into my face once more. "Yeah, you keep fucking hitting me," I slur. "It won't change the fact that you're a child molester and a rapist."

He roars, drops my ass against the floor, and my skull cracks against the cement. Fuck. Me. Breathing becomes a chore. I can hear my breath wheezing in and out and, just as I planned, I sag into the floor—pretending to pass out.

"Abel!" Rylie's horrified scream reaches my ears and sinks into my chest.

She doesn't know what I'm planning and it's better this way, it really is, but I hate knowing how scared she is and I hate that I can't tell her it's all going to be okay. Because I won't accept another outcome. No matter what happens, she will live through tonight and that fucker won't have her. Never again.

I can hear his panting above me and I half expect him to keep kicking me even though it should be obvious that I'm not conscious—at least I'm pretty sure I've perfected the weightlessness I'm currently forcing as I keep my eyes shut to convince him. A moment later when I hear his feet shift across the floor and the creaking springs of the mattress, I know I've done my job.

Several minutes go by and I'm just waiting to make sure he's not looking my way before I start to move. Rylie's breath hiccups in her chest as she hisses out something I can't hear.

"Rylie girl." I want to rip his fucking tongue from his throat when he calls her that. "You know it had to be this way."

Slowly. I urge myself not to rush as I shift on the floor, bringing my arms up further and further—hoping he's completely distracted by her. I just need one opportunity to break free and then it's all over. My back arches and I pull my wrists as far away from my spine as possible.

Three.

Rylie's voice filters over the side of bed. I don't hear what she says, but I hear the man, especially when his hand connects with her flesh as he slaps her.

Two.

I'm going to rip those hands off and beat him to death with them. Rylie doesn't stop talking, but I can't tell what she's saying. There's a ringing in my ears that's too loud for me to distinguish complex sounds. Fuck this. I'm done waiting.

The last number to my countdown sounds in my head.

One.

Time to break these damned bonds and wreak some havoc.

43

RYLIE

A scream rips out of my broken throat. Snot clogs my nose. Tears track down my cheeks. Abel's poor face is an absolutely fucking shredded mess. Blood drips from a cut above his eye. My throat closes in on itself when he disappears from my view as the chair he's strapped to falls over. The monster from my past is angry—his face beet red as he kicks and kicks and doesn't stop until he's panting and breathing like a wrathful dragon. I've never seen him like this—so fucking out of it. Eyes wild and glittering, pupils like pinpoints when they should be blown to all fucking hell.

For the longest time, I've been terrified of that face of his. I've seen it in my nightmares, ran from it, screamed when it came too close. He broke me so long ago, all I am is a bag of shattered pieces walking around in a bodysuit.

I'm not Avalon.

I'm not strong. I'm not a warrior. I'm just ... me. A survivor. And I don't know if I'll survive more of this. I don't think I can be any more broken.

Even as my mind rolls through all of this Abel is getting beaten to a bloody pulp and there's nothing I can do. Acid sits on the back of my tongue and I bite back my sobs even when all I want to do is rip off my own arms so I can crawl to him.

Finally, Daniel steps back and I hear nothing from the floor. *Is Abel unconscious?* I wonder. A sinister thought snakes its way into my mind and coils around my brain, shutting off all logical thought, as Daniel wipes the sweat from his upper lip with his thumb and moves over to the bed I'm lying on. Is *Abel dead?*

Fingers touch my thigh. They slide upward under the hem of my skirt. "Rylie girl," he says. "You knew it had to be this way." He brushes away some of my tears.

I turn my head and stare at the man now crawling over my body. It's taken me nineteen years to realize it, but ... there are so many ways to kill a woman without actually stopping her heart. And Daniel has been killing me for years.

He killed my childhood.

He killed my dreams.

He killed my innocence.

He killed every good thing I ever felt about myself because the second he touched me, the second he claimed me as his, I ceased to exist as anything else. And for the last thirteen years of my life, I've been living as a runaway object. I've been his *for years.* Against my will, I've let him dictate my actions.

I close my eyes as his hand trails higher. My mind recedes back into the furthest reaches and I don't feel it anymore. Not his skin against mine. Not his hard cock pressing against my thigh on the inside of his jeans. Not his breath as he leans down and kisses my neck. Not even the words he breathes against my throat.

This is what it was like thirteen years ago, too, I remember. On the nights I couldn't fight back. On the nights where I was just too tired, I would lay back and I would go away to another place. I would pretend I was sleeping and it was a horrible nightmare and in the morning when I woke up, everything would go back to normal.

I thought I'd changed in the last thirteen years, but it's clear now that I haven't. I'm no stronger than I was as a child. In fact, I'm weaker. If I really think about it—if I'm honest with myself —I'm not skinny because I want to be. I'm not flat chested completely because of genetics.

I eat like shit. I sleep like shit. I don't take care of my body. And it's all because it has never made sense for me to care. Why would I give a fuck about a body that has never once been my own?

It's his and it's always been his.

And for once, for once in my life, when I was with someone ... there was no disgust. No revolting in my skin. No self-loathing that made the acid in my stomach curdle and churn. When someone touched me, I didn't feel gross. I felt ... like I was giving them permission.

"Rylie girl." Daniel's hand finds my chin and his fingers bite into my cheeks as my eyes open and I stare up at him.

"Why me?" I ask.

Daniel lifts up and looks down at me. "Because you were so pretty," he whispers. "When I first saw you, I knew you'd be the one." He rolls his hips against my body as he groans and his fingers press against my bare pussy.

"I was six." The words are barely a whisper, but he hears them.

"And you were perfect," he says. "So innocent and so broken. Mama told me that you didn't have any parents and that no one wanted you, and I decided then that I wanted you. I would keep you. I could have you and fix you—"

"I wasn't fucking broken," I snap. I was sad. I was scared sometimes. But I wasn't broken before him. Daniel doesn't hear me, though as a moan lifts out of his mouth and his hips press even more insistently against me.

"Do you like that?" he asks. "You want more?"

"No."

He freezes. "What?"

"You're sick," I say blandly.

Daniel's head cranes back and his eyes widen as he stares down at me. His fingers dig ever harder into my flesh until it feels like he's going to rip my cheeks. "What did you say?" he demands.

I suck in a breath and feel saliva pool in the back of my throat. I rear my head back and spit at him. "You. Are. Disgusting." The words are yanked from my throat. The real truth I've always wanted to say. "Abel was right," I tell him. "I don't want you now and I didn't want you then. I hated it when you touched me. It made me sick."

His hand releases my face only to come down hard as he slaps me across the face. I clench my teeth to keep from crying out, cutting the inside of my mouth in the process. Then his hand is on my throat and his face is in front of mine.

"You're a liar!"

I laugh. It's just too fucking funny. "You just can't accept that everything he said about you is right," I say. "You're a pervert, a pedophile, and you deserve to either live the rest of your life in prison or rot in the ground."

"You ungrateful little bitch," he hisses, spittle flying out and landing against my forehead. "You want him? Is that what you're saying? You want that little pussy bitch? No!" The flesh of his face is molting—turning from red to purple. "I was good to you, Rylie! I treated you like a princess!"

"You treated me like your fucking plaything," I snap, squeezing the words out, as hoarse as they are. "You were a sick little boy who wanted to dress me up and play out his sick fantasies with me like I was some toy."

"You're mine!" he yells.

I shake my head. *No,* I think as his hand clamps down

harder, refusing to let the word out of my own mouth. *I was never yours. You just made me think I was.*

The world grows blurry as the black dots from earlier return, wider and fuzzier as they attack my vision. He's using both hands now as his face grows red above me. He's crying—sobbing like a pathetic little baby.

Maybe he'd survived in jail because no one had really thought a sixteen-year-old could do this. But he never grew up. He's still just a needy child with a twisted obsession.

There's a roar from somewhere else in the room—it hits my ears slightly off key and then Daniel's hands are gone as a white blur flashes in front of my field of vision. Abel launches himself at Daniel and they smack into my legs before going over the side of the bed.

The sound of flesh hitting flesh. The curses that spill from both Daniel and Abel's lips reach my ears. And more ... there's another sound ... footsteps out in the hallway—running. Deep voices that I recognize.

My head turns to the side and with a warped vision, I watch as Abel locks his hands around Daniel's throat and lifts him up, slamming the back of his skull against the concrete once, twice, three times before Daniel's body sags.

The two men in the doorway have stopped and then one jumps into action, hurrying across the room. I flinch when a hand moves towards my face. Too fast. Too close.

"Rylie." I recognize that voice. "It's okay. I'm just going to untie you."

I blink, my eyesight clearing a little bit. Dean's face is drawn. There are lines around the corners of his mouth as he frowns at the bonds tying me to the bed, but it doesn't take him long to figure out the intricate knotwork and even when he only gets it half undone, he finally just curses and pulls out a knife—slicing the rest of the way through the bindings until my hands and arms fall back to the mattress.

Feeling returns to my limbs and I roll onto my side, gasping for air as I reach down and shove my skirt between my legs to cover myself and try to hold back the puke.

"Is he..." I try to ask, but it's too hard to get the words out. "Is he ... dead?"

Dean looks back over his shoulder for a moment and I hear the scraping of metal and Abel's grunting. "No," Dean finally says, answering my question. Dean gets off the bed and moves across the room.

I'm shaking so hard it's difficult to even sit up, but somehow, I manage to slide my legs to the edge of the mattress and over the side. Using my death grip on the corner of the bed, I force myself to straighten and when the room spins again, I lower my head until my nose is right above my thighs. I suck in a breath and another and another until I feel the nausea abate.

"Rylie."

My head lifts at the sound of my name being called and Abel moves towards me. He looks so fucking wrecked. More so than me. There are cuts all over his face. Blood on his lip, his temple, his neck. Hell, there's more blood than skin at this point. I reach up and cup his cheek.

"I love you," I rasp.

He grips my hand in his. "Dean's gonna take you to Avalon," he tells me, his voice low. Quiet. As if talking too loud will be detrimental to me. I almost laugh at that. I'm not so broken ... or am I? Do I seem that way to him? I don't feel broken anymore. "She's going to take you to the hospital and I'll meet you there. Everything's going to be okay."

I look to the side where Braxton is slowly cutting Daniel's clothes from his body and Dean is helping to tie him down. Braxton's mouth is curved into a brilliant smile, and though he's fucking gorgeous when he smiles—it's disconcerting to see such an expression as he hurries from the room and comes back a moment later with a tool box. I don't even want to know what he's got in there.

Slowly, I return my focus to Abel. He hasn't moved or shifted from his position at all despite the fact that he's got to be in pain. I know I am, and I didn't take the beating he did. His breaths are shallow and choppy.

"You need to go to the hospital," I tell him.

"I will," he agrees with a nod. "When I'm done here."

"Are you going to kill him?" I ask. It's the most important question.

Abel looks at me, and even past the blood and the bruising and vicious expression on his face, his clear, blue eyes soften. "Yes." That's it. No excuse. No explanation. And I don't need one.

I lean forward until my lips are a hair's breadth away from his. His eyes don't close. They remain on me. "Make it hurt," I say.

I feel where his mouth curves upward and when he replies, they brush against me. "I'll make him regret ever touching you, Riot Girl," he promises. "And no one will ever be able to find his body."

I kiss him hard, biting into his lower lip and then giving him my tongue as I delve into his mouth. I taste blood and I don't even care. Those are the sexiest words he's ever said to me.

A man I don't know steps into the doorway of the room and I jerk back, but Abel's there to soothe me. "It's okay," he assures me. "That's just Viks. He's a friend."

Viks' gaze trails across the room; he spots me and gives me a gentle smile, and then he's shoved out of the way by Avalon.

"I thought I told you to stay in the car." Dean's harsh words almost have me chuckling despite myself.

She flips him off and moves towards me. "We found a body on the second floor—old guy. Looked homeless. Hasn't been dead more than twenty minutes, according to Viks," she says.

I remember the man who'd come in here when I'd first woken up. "I think he was working for Daniel," I croak as she approaches.

She winces at the sound of my voice. "You sound like shit." She deadpans.

"Gee," I muster up as much sardonic amusement as I can. "Thanks."

"Well, come on then. Let's go." She reaches for me.

"Avalon." Dean's voice stops her.

She groans and glares over her shoulder at him. "To the hospital," she says as if she needs to remind him.

He glares at her and I sigh, thumping my head forward against Abel's shoulder. "I'm so tired," I confess.

"It'll all be over soon," he promises. I turn my face into his neck and press another kiss to his pulse point. He'll never know how fucking happy I am that he's still alive. How relieved I am that my past monsters didn't kill him.

I lift my head and stare across the room at Daniel's bleeding, slackened face. The sight of him makes me want to turn away, but I force myself not to. Maybe I'm not stronger than my past. Maybe six-year-old me hadn't been stronger than him. But present me? Present me has new monsters.

My new monsters are far more terrifying than he ever could've been. My present monster loves me and I love him. I *can* love him because I'm stronger than a six-year-old girl that everyone wanted to ignore.

Abel is alive.

I'm alive.

And as long as I have both of those—life and Abel. I win.

44

ABEL

"You okay?" Dean asks as Avalon and Viks take Rylie away. She keeps looking back over her shoulder, her eyes bouncing between me and the guys and the man strapped to the same chair I'd been in not but a half hour ago.

I answer him honestly. There's no reason to lie at this point. "No." I'm far from fucking okay. I am wrath. I am anger. I am vengeance.

"She was right," Dean tries to tell me. "You do need to go to the hospital. You sound terrible, and you might have some internal bleeding."

I won't go, not until I've taken care of business. I turn and push past him back into the room as Braxton finishes filling up a bucket with water using the sink in the corner next to the shower and toilet. I stand with my arms crossed over my chest as he strides back over and that bucket goes flying into our victim's face.

Daniel Roy Dickerson.

Rylie's stalker. The source of her fear. The source of her nightmares. The reason she ran from me. I'm sorry she can't be here to watch me end his miserable excuse of an existence, but her health is more important.

He comes sputtering back to life as the ice-cold water drenches his naked body. I don't even wait for Braxton and Abel to start pulling out the instruments that I plan to use on him in the next hour. I lift my foot and bring it down, crushing his dick under my heel.

A garbled scream escapes his throat.

Dean's gaze bores into the back of my head. He knows me—he knows that this isn't what I usually do—but this time is different.

I've seen their skeletons. Burned and buried them alongside them without remorse. This is the first time that I've ever truly wanted to take a life. Where it isn't something that's predestined and I've just resigned myself to fate. This is a necessity. This is a desire. So fierce inside my gut that it flames to life with passion more in tune with Brax's own sick, twisted desires.

Is this what he likes? I wonder absently as I turn my foot, pressing down harder. When the chair wobbles, I shoot Dean a look, and with a sigh, he walks around the back and holds it steady so that I can crush the fucker's puny cock and balls without hesitation.

More screams, and they'll litter this room by the end because I don't plan on stopping. Not until my body forces me to.

I don't look up from the man in front of me as my nostrils flare with the scent of blood in the room. I hold out my hand. "Give me the Burdizzo," I say. I'm going to start with how I mean to finish.

With extreme prejudice and hatred.

Braxton doesn't waste a single second. He hands me the device—something that farmers use on cattle, but it'll work for this. After all ... it's primarily used for this exact purpose.

Castration.

Seconds turn into minutes that turn into an hour. I work the man over good. Sweat slips down my temples. My limbs are shaking and he's half out of his mind with agony by the time Dean finally puts a stop to me.

His hand lands on my arm and I drop the pliers I'd used to rip off every single one of his fingernails. There's blood and puke and shit and piss everywhere. "That's enough," he says. "It's time to end it."

Yeah, I think. He's right.

I hold out my hand once more and this time, he places a gun in my palm.

I wish I could've made it last longer. Years. As long as she suffered, I wanted him to. But this will have to do. This will have to be enough.

I inhale and let the scent of my own violence spread through my pain filled chest. Fuck. I may have overdone it. My breath creaks through my lungs. Each second is another filled with the throbbing pain that's getting sharper and sharper. My hand shakes as I lift the gun. I'm not afraid of it—of death. Giving or receiving. But my body is shutting down. Exhaustion and pain is making the world harder to perceive.

Dean's hand lands against mine and helps me hold the Glock more steadily. Braxton's comes down on my shoulder. "You got this," he says, where Dean just helps me adjust my finger against the trigger.

My friends. My brothers. Always having my back. Even in this.

As I pull the trigger, I can't help but smile.

Some people just don't deserve to keep living.

45

RYLIE

6 days later...

A HOSPITAL IS a lot like a morgue. The only difference is ... the people are still breathing. It's a technicality I don't care for because after nearly a week in the hospital, I'm ready to turn it into a real one. Avalon makes no qualms about taunting me either. I have a feeling she does it just to get on my nerves and distract me from the reality—Abel killed someone and I asked him to do it.

Maybe she thinks that'll break me. I'm not as strong as her after all, but honestly, ever since he returned—covered in blood and swaying on his feet as he refused treatment until he saw me —I've slept like a baby.

I'm not ... afraid anymore. The nightmares are practically gone. Abel offered to take me to see Daniel's body—offered to have it put on ice like he was offering to run and grab me a cup of coffee. I turned him down because I trust him. I trust that he killed Daniel and that the man who has plagued me for thirteen years is long gone.

My issue now is getting out of this damn prison cell.

The door opens and Avalon breezes inside with a backpack and an energy drink. "Here ya go," she says, slapping the Monster down on the side table next to my bed. "Drink up."

I don't even question her good deed. I snatch the damn thing up, pop the tab, and down the first half. Caffeine hits my system like a drug and I can feel my mind clearing already. With a sigh, I take another long swallow and set it down.

"What's in the bag?" I ask.

"Clothes," she says, plopping it down on the edge of my bed.

I sit up straighter. "Am I getting out?"

She grins as she turns and props her ass next to it, the mattress dipping with her weight. "Yup," she answers, "and then you've got plans."

I narrow my eyes on her. "What does that mean?" I demand.

She chuckles and shakes her head. "You've got a date," she tells me. "Abel is going to finish up his physical therapy out of the hospital for the next week and you"—she points at me—"have one last meeting with the doctor this afternoon. As long as he clears you, you're good to go."

"Thank God." I sigh and reach for my Monster once more. "I thought I'd die in this place."

Avalon tips her head back. "Yeah, I thought the same thing when I ended up here two months ago."

"I recall," I say dryly.

Her lips quirk and for a moment she remains silent, staring at the ceiling as the sounds outside of the room filter in beneath the closed door. Needing something to keep me occupied and yet also viscerally aware that I'm slowly running out of something to fidget with, I continue drinking my Monster until there's not a single drop left.

With a saddened sigh, I set the now empty can back on the bedside table. The clinking sound of the aluminum can hitting the surface seems to draw Avalon out of whatever thoughts were circling around in her crazy-pants brain. She jerks and glances my way, noting the can in my hand as I finish setting it down.

"You done?" She doesn't wait for me to answer as she lifts it up and then tosses it across the room, hitting the corner and then smiling in pleasure as it bounces off and dunks into the small trash can set there.

"Thanks," I say awkwardly, reaching up to scratch at one of the bandages on my arm. I look to the side and try to think of something else to say. More silence descends between us. Until finally, I suppose, she can't take it anymore either.

"Do you remember when the original Havers burned down?" she asks, surprising me. The question feels random and I stare at her a moment before answering.

"Of course I remember."

Her hands move across the sheets covering my legs as she picks at invisible strands. "Do you remember when I woke up and you were here?"

My lips pinch down and I follow the movement of her fingers as I reply. "Yes."

I remember it well, though we've never brought it up until now. I remember sitting in this very hospital room, ironically, waiting for her to wake up as Braxton and Abel were hurrying to figure out a way to save their brother's life. Dean had nearly died that night. And as I look at Avalon now—recalling how she'd been then—I know that if he had ... she would've followed him into the grave.

I've never seen two people more right for each other. It almost makes me laugh to think of how I'd warned her to stay away when I'd first met her. Back then, I thought I'd been helping her. I didn't know just how strong she could be. How much of a Queen she was because, for the life of me, I couldn't understand how someone like us could rise from the ashes of our past and be more than just the broken little girls society had made us.

"I never cried to my mom," she admits, lifting her gaze to meet mine. "Not after I realized what kind of person she really was." I don't say anything. After all, what *can* I say to that? Is she saying she regrets crying to me? That she's embarrassed by it. I want to tell her she shouldn't be but there's a massive difference in words and feelings. Even if I tell her there's no shame in her tears, that doesn't mean she'll automatically stop feeling it.

"Not everyone deserves to be a mother," I finally settle on saying.

She snorts. "Yeah, you got that right," she agrees readily enough. "Though I don't think you'd be too bad."

I smile, thinking maybe that's the end of that, but then she surprises the shit out of me by moving forward and folding her arms around me. "Thanks," she whispers as I freeze, my hands moving up automatically because that's just what you're supposed to do when someone hugs you, but this is Avalon. She doesn't hug.

"Uh ... you're ... welcome?" My words come out tinged with confusion. After a moment, she releases me and sits back. "Did you put a 'kick me' sticker on my back?" I ask.

Avalon's long black hair falls back as her head does and she releases a loud laugh. "Jesus, Rylie," she says. "No."

"Uh huh." I reach back and feel anyway and she shakes her head.

"Okay, enough with the emotional shit, I guess," she says, swinging her legs off the bed as she hops up and whirls around. "Get dressed," she orders. "Doctor's gonna come around."

"When do I get to see Abel again?" I ask even as I'm reaching for the backpack. "Is he still talking to the physical therapist?"

"He's coming back in time for your last talk with the doctor before you'll be discharged," she tells me, striding towards the door. "Chop chop, Ry-Ry. Make it fast. We've got a flight to catch."

I don't have a chance to ask what the hell that means because, in the next instant, she's out the door—letting it swing shut behind her. I release a groan as I throw back the covers and shift my legs over the side. My poorly-used muscles protest the sudden movement, but I don't give a shit. I'm so ready to get the hell out of here, I hurry through changing out of the thin hospital gown I've been trapped in for the last week.

By the time I've changed into a pair of shorts and a black Hollywood Undead t-shirt from the backpack, run a comb through my tangled hair, and scrubbed my teeth clean—I feel somewhat human again and Avalon is back. With company.

As soon as I step out of the bathroom, Abel makes a beeline for me. I don't even hesitate anymore to lift my arms and let him pick me up. Avalon strides over, right behind him, and snatches the clipboard attached to the end of the bed, using it to smack him in the shoulder.

"No!" she yells. "Stop. Put her down. You're fucking healing, dipshit."

Realization hits me and I squirm. "She's right," I say. I can't believe I forgot.

Abel groans, but acquiesces and lets me down even as he shoots Ava a death glare. She holds the clipboard up. "Don't mess with me, Frontman," she threatens.

"Alright, that's enough of that." Dean plucks the board from her hand and returns it to its original placement. "Let's just hurry up and get this over with so we can get to the airport."

"Where are we going?" I ask curiously. Abel takes my hand and leads me over to the bed.

As a unit, the group drifts around the room, each of us finding our place—Abel and I on the edge of the bed, Dean and

Ava on the love seat across from it, and Braxton stands against the wall with his arms over his chest.

Dean opens his mouth, but is halted a moment later as Avalon slaps a hand over his lips. "You'll find out soon," she tells me.

I frown at her, the corners of my mouth pulling down. Before I can say anything, the door opens and the same doctor that I've seen nearly every day this past week walks in. He pauses and takes a look around the room. I can see the trepidation in his eyes—it's not unnatural in a room full of the Sick Boys plus Avalon, especially when their attention all turns to you. I almost pity him.

"I see we've got a crowd in here tonight," he says with a forced smile.

I return it as he moves towards the end of the bed with the papers in his hands. He lifts the clipboard and sets the papers on top, snapping them into place as he tugs his glasses from his pocket and slips them up his nose.

"You ready to get out of here, Miss Moore?" he asks.

"Beyond ready," I say.

He nods and peruses the files in front of him. "Well, that shouldn't be a problem. As per Mr. Frazier's request, we kept you for observation." I shoot a quick glare to Abel before returning my attention to the doctor. "Other than some internal bruising, that concussion, and your throat, you're doing well. Mr. Frazier is being discharged today as well." The doctor lifts his gaze from the papers and looks at us over the rim of his glasses. "Which I just want to remind you is against my recommendation. However, if you keep insisting—"

"I do," Abel cuts in without remorse. "If Rylie's getting out today, so the fuck am I."

"Yup," Ava pipes up. "Plus we have plans."

The doctor sighs at that. "I don't recommend any hard

physical activity for the next several weeks, Mr. Frazier," he says meaningfully. "Your ribs need time to heal."

"And here I thought I'd be the one off the field this year," Dean says with a quiet smirk.

Abel flips him the bird. "You were only just cleared, asshole."

Dean grins anyway. "Maybe we should see about getting you a cheer uniform," he replies.

"Go fuck—"

"As for you, Miss Moore," the doctor cuts in, returning his attention to me. "I've taken the liberty of calling in some medications you'll need to start taking as soon as possible. We'll have you check back in with us in a few weeks, but the vitamins I've got recommended on your chart should help you start feeling better. Unfortunately, in light of your condition, we can't give you anything stronger than acetaminophen for pain, but—"

"Wait," I hold up a hand, stopping him as my brows draw down low over my eyes. "What do you mean *my condition?*" Abel's hand tightens on mine. "What's wrong with me?"

The doctor frowns and glances from the chart and back to me. "Uh ... well, I ... the nurses haven't spoken with you?"

I shake my head.

He blows out a breath and lowers the clipboard to his side. "Okay, um, well, Miss Moore. We took another blood test this morning, just to make sure that everything was alright," he begins.

"And it wasn't?" I ask.

"No!" His eyes widen. "No, you're perfectly fine. Well, you should certainly be more careful over the next few months. No more joy riding or getting into bar fights." I wince at the lie the guys had come up with to cover the wounds we'd received. Pathetic, at best, really, but with the Eastpoint PD in their back pocket and this hospital owned by Braxton's family—I know the doctor didn't look too far into it.

"So, what's her condition?" Abel snaps.

"You're pregnant." And then as if it's an afterthought, he offers an awkward, "Congratulations."

Silence.

Bone numbing, ear drilling ... silence echoes throughout the room.

"I'm sorry..." I shake my head, sure I heard incorrectly. "What?"

Avalon snorts. "That's so ironic."

I ignore her and her comment and focus on the doctor. "Can you repeat that?" At my side, Abel has gone completely still. I can't even hear him breathe. I'm almost terrified to look at him. The doctor must be mistaken.

"It's very early on," the doctor continues to explain. "You must only be a few weeks along. It's why we didn't catch it when you were first admitted. We can usually only pick up a pregnancy in blood tests six or more days after conception—"

"You're serious?"

Shock hits my system, along with a barrage of other emotions. Panic. Horror. Confusion. And most of all ... an odd quietness. That doesn't make sense at all.

"Yes, I'm quite sure," the doctor says. "While at home pregnancy tests are often late to pick up the pregnancy hormone, the blood doesn't lie."

He keeps saying that word. Pregnant. Pregnancy. I'm ... pregnant. I release Abel's hand and touch my stomach. There's ... something inside of me.

"But I thought it'd be hard for me," I say absently. "My periods are irregular and I don't have one every month. And my size..." I gesture down numbly.

"Irregular periods do make it harder but not impossible," the doctor explains. "And you may have some issues with labor—we can talk more about it when the time comes, we can offer a cesarean birth. Your hips are quite narrow. It can depend on the size of the baby as well."

And we'd never used condoms. Not once. Why am I so shocked now? Because I'd stupidly thought that it was impossible. Brilliant hacker; zero. Baby making Abel Frazier sperm; one.

"Can she still get on a plane?" I dimly hear Avalon say. The question is so ridiculous, it makes me laugh.

I shake my head. "I'm pregnant, Ava," I snap. "Not an invalid."

"Yes," the doctor confirms. "She's perfectly safe to get on a plane. Once she hits thirty-six weeks, though, we don't recommend it."

I'm almost afraid to look at the man sitting by my side, but a sense forces me to do it anyway. He hasn't said a damn word since the bomb was dropped. Hesitantly, I lift my gaze and meet his—shocked to find his eyes watery. The second our eyes meet, his hands arch up, grasping my face as his mouth comes down on mine.

More emotions pour into me. Want. Need. Desire. Hope.

When his kiss is over, he pulls back and stares at me for what feels like the longest time. "A-Abel?" I stutter over his name. "Are you okay?"

He throws his head back and laughs, and to my complete and utter shock, he releases my face and slips off the bed to go to his knees in front of me. He presses his face against my stomach and wraps his arms around my waist.

"Yes," he says, rubbing his cheeks back and forth over the black fabric of the t-shirt covering my belly. "I'm okay. I'm so fucking okay right now, you have no idea." Reverently, he kisses my stomach. "So fucking okay."

"Maybe now would be a really good time to tell you the

truth, I guess," Avalon pipes up. "I wanted to keep it a secret, but with your new bun in the oven, maybe that's too much."

"Ava..." I can hear Dean's exasperation.

My lips twitch as she continues. "We're going to Vegas so you two can get hitched," Avalon says.

I run my hands through Abel's hair. "Was that your plan?" I clarify.

He lifts up and tips his face back, and even with the bruising and cuts, he's still the most beautiful man I've ever laid eyes on. The asshole. When he smiles, it lights up his whole face. "Yeah," he admits. "I was hoping you wouldn't notice until we were already walking down the aisle and you had a ring on your finger."

"It was my idea," Ava says. "We're doing a two-fer. Your bun won't come out without a daddy and I don't have to worry about wearing a dress and doing the big fancy shit. Congrats."

Against the wall, Braxton shakes his head.

"Well, um ... I can see that we're all done here," the doctor says. "I'll go ahead and be signing off on your discharge, Miss Moore."

"I'll see you out," Brax offers, reaching across the wall, gripping the handle, and letting the door swing open with a flourish. "We'll be leaving momentarily."

I look up just in time to see the doctor scurry out with a bob of his head. He takes off like the hounds of hell are behind him and not a group of fucked up kids. I shake my own head in disbelief.

"I was actually planning on doing this a while back," Abel confesses in a whisper, drawing my attention back to him.

I frown, tilting my head to the side, trying to remember when he had the opportunity. "You were?"

He nods. "Do you remember that bet we made on our first night?" A rush of heat steals across my face, but I find myself nodding anyway. His lips tip into a grin. "I never told you what I wanted."

"It was this?"

Abel's hands grip my thighs and his hot breath reaches through the fabric of my shirt as he presses a kiss to the edge of them. "It was always you, Rylie," he says. "I just wanted you. Forever."

I try not to. I really do, but my own laughter can't be held back. I shake my head as I bend over, hugging Abel's face to my body. Corny. Stupid. So fucking cheesy, my gut hurts. My kid —our kid, Abel's and mine—is gonna have such a weird life, I think, but ... at least I know they'll be well cared for. They'll be loved. And no one will ever be able to hurt them.

EPILOGUE
BRAXTON

4 weeks later...

I STARE at the front of the house—or rather the shit hole trailer on stilts—watching for the girl I've come for. The rental I picked up at the airport runs smoothly, no sound, no backfiring, and no otherwise obvious noise that might attract the attention of any neighbors. I don't like using rentals for this type of business, but when I got the notification that my lead had come through, there hadn't been much choice. It would've taken the better part of thirteen hours to drive here, and I couldn't risk the chance of losing this opportunity. So here I am, sitting behind a dumpster and a wad of overgrown bushes across the street from the barren Florida trailer park. Waiting.

I've been tracking that bastard Ace for months now. Each time I get close, he disappears—like a ghost on the wind. I've always hated ghost stories. If I can't make the damn thing bleed or cry then it's of no use to me. Thankfully, my current target is very much alive, and no doubt, she'll be crying by the end of the night.

I sit up straighter in my seat and lean towards the tinted windows as a light flickers on in the front room. It's a wonder the house is still standing. There are cracks in the peeling, mud gray stilts holding the damn thing up in the middle of this swamp hell and I'd bet money the rat trap has termites and other insects crawling all over it.

My head jerks up and over as the shriek of metal on metal pierces through the thick glass of the truck I'm in and reaches my ears. My hand twitches, palm down on the gun in the passenger side seat. It's just a fucking cat—a big, fat orange one with eyes that go in either direction. It lifts its mangy head and pivots until it's staring straight at me. Weird ass feline.

I return my attention to the front of the house, but my hand remains on the gun. With my free arm, I reach across and into the glove box, popping the thing open and retrieving the file I shoved in there when I picked this vehicle out. I set it in front of me and flip it open.

My nose twitches and I flip the air conditioning on. It's hotter than a fucking witch's tit in June down here. Humid too. Even through the glass and metal, I can feel the moisture in the air. It's thick and steamy. I lick my thumb and peel the first page away—it's full of nothing but basics anyway. What I'm after is the nitty gritty details.

One Clover La Roux.

There's a photo of the chick, but it looks a few years old at this point. Taken in high school. Picture day. Wide woodsy green eyes, a face full of freckles over pale skin, and red hair. Smooth, stick straight red hair, pulled tightly away from her face to outline her cheekbones and jawline.

In the image, she's skinny. Too skinny. Probably malnourished and uncared for. Not necessarily a foster kid, but she might as well be one considering the information outlining this chick's crappy life.

From age four to eleven, in and out of hospitals for what many doctors and nurses suspected as abuse in the home. Then from twelve to fifteen, in and out of juvie for petty shit—stealing, fighting, drinking, smoking pot. The stupid shit they throw kids away for nowadays. I shake my head. If only they knew that the elite do far worse and they don't see anything but the insides of their lavish, expensive bedrooms full of Wi-Fi signal, on-call hookers, and premium grade food delivery as a punishment.

The poor get shit on and the rich get luxury house arrest. All for the same crimes. Even I have to admit this world is garbage.

Fortunately—or rather unfortunately as will soon be the case for this girl—after fifteen, all of her little problems seem to have vanished. Her list of previous addresses are all over the place, ranging from shoebox, roach-infested apartments to homeless shelters to addresses that technically don't exist. She was smart, this one—no doubt ran off on her own before whatever home she was in could kill her or make her wish for death.

I won't be letting her get away though.

I snap the folder closed and slide it back into the glove box as the light in the front room goes out. 2 a.m. On the dot. A regular night owl finally turning in for some shut eye. I lean forward and slip the barrel of my gun under my black t-shirt and into the waistband of my jeans. Once it's secured, I pull on the black leather gloves and reach for the ski mask I prepped for this event.

Ace Volkov—Avalon's torturer—can run and that mother fucker can hide, but now that I've found his weakness there's no fucking way I'm not going to take this little opportunity. Who knows? Maybe I'll take a little revenge on Ava's behalf. Maybe I'll enjoy fucking this girl wide open and then drop her back on Ace's doorstep in a few months—drugged out of her mind and addicted to pain.

For now, I'll just have to wait and see what happens when he finds out his precious girlfriend is missing. See if the fucker shows up when it's not him who will pay for his crimes.

But *her*.